W9-AHZ-121

The Fifth Woman
A RICK MORGAN MYSTERY

G. William Parker

authorHOUSE®

AuthorHouse™
1663 Liberty Drive
Bloomington, IN 47403
www.authorhouse.com
Phone: 1-800-839-8640

© *2011 G. William Parker. All rights reserved.*

No part of this book may be reproduced, stored in a retrieval system, or transmitted by any means without the written permission of the author.

First published by AuthorHouse   05/17/2011

ISBN: 978-1-4567-5435-8 (sc)
ISBN: 978-1-4567-5434-1 (hc)
ISBN: 978-1-4567-5436-5 (e)

Library of Congress Control Number: 2011904879

Printed in the United States of America

Any people depicted in stock imagery provided by Thinkstock are models, and such images are being used for illustrative purposes only. Certain stock imagery © Thinkstock.

This book is printed on acid-free paper.

Because of the dynamic nature of the Internet, any web addresses or links contained in this book may have changed since publication and may no longer be valid. The views expressed in this work are solely those of the author and do not necessarily reflect the views of the publisher, and the publisher hereby disclaims any responsibility for them.

ACKNOWLEDGEMENTS

Many thanks to five terrific women who helped make this book possible.

Meg, for her encouragement to start writing again
Denise, for all the editing
Divina, for the countless lunches discussing characters
Jan, for your excellent eye
and
Janet, for understanding why I locked myself in my office for days at a time.

CHAPTER 1

With Cindy it was always special. Just like the first time. But that night was going to be something extra special.

My meeting in Los Angeles ended sooner than expected, so I took an earlier flight home to Seattle to surprise my love on our 10th wedding anniversary. Ten years with this flawless goddess. How did I get so lucky in love? I stopped along the way and bought eleven long-stem red roses—one for every year of our marriage, plus one for the wonderful year to come.

I found the house still, with soft music faintly drifting down from the bedroom. Before a special night out, Cindy liked to spend hours getting ready. I pictured her in a sea of bubbles, with scented candles enhancing the mood as she primped for an out-late dinner and dancing. With roses in hand, I crept upstairs. As I quietly opened the bedroom door, a slight mist wafted from the bathroom across the way. Instead of the bath I envisioned, I could hear the shower running full bore.

It seemed wrong somehow.

My eyes darted around the room, taking a quick inventory. A pair of high heels was tossed on their sides in the middle of the floor. A black bra and panties rested next to them as though dropped carelessly. With blankets and spread crumpled at its foot, the bed was in total disarray. The sheets were wrinkled and mussed as though recently used, and a pair of men's pants draped loosely on its corner. A box of condoms sat on the nightstand.

My mind was racing, thinking, "Where ... the hell ... is Cindy ... and who has been screwing in our bed? And who was showering in my bathroom?"

I quietly moved closer to the door. I could hear murmuring voices under the pounding shower. With each step the voices became more distinct. The first, a familiar sensual giggle and the other, a deep husky moan from a man obviously short of breath.

My heart began to pump hard. It was Cindy in the shower, and she was not alone.

I pushed the door back slightly and squinted through the steam. My jaw dropped and my legs buckled under me. Behind the foggy glass of the shower door, my Cindy was on her knees. A man was moving toward her making it very clear what he was demanding. Though his outline was not recognizable, his voice now was. It was the college kid from next door, home for spring break.

Knowing what she was about to do, my heart began thumping harder. Each beat increased an unbearable pressure in my chest. Between my heart's thundering and my stomach's churning, I tried to scream, "No, don't! Please, Cindy, don't!" But no words came out. As my mouth formed the words in silence, Cindy's mouth moved toward her target under the pounding shower. The young man's hands gripped the sides of her face as his pelvis squirmed. His head tilted up and back and he began to groan as Cindy's lips pumped more and more vigorously.

I begged my wobbly legs to run, but they wouldn't. Frozen, I was forced to watch each thrust of her head. And with each, my hand clenched the anniversary roses tighter. The thorns tore my flesh, but the pain meant nothing compared to the pain of my heart being ripped from my chest.

Cindy pulled him from her mouth momentarily. She cooed something in a sultry voice and then, suddenly and swiftly, her lips moved the entire length of his shaft and it disappeared inside her mouth.

I fell backwards into the bedroom as if I'd been sucker punched. For a few minutes I stayed that way, on my back. Every ounce of strength was gone. I wanted to die.

They probably would have found me lying there like that if it wasn't for a horrible stomach spasm that compelled me to flip over onto my hands and knees. I started vomiting and dry-heaving, still clutching the roses like my life depended on it. I tried to catch my breath between each violent contraction, and as my eyes rolled up and down, they caught the brass handle of my nightstand. Instinctively, I knew I needed to get there. Letting loose my death-grip on the roses, I managed to crawl across the room, leaving a dotted trail of blood from my torn-up hand. The pain was unbearable, yet inconsequential. I had to get to my nightstand.

On my knees, I pulled open the drawer. There it was, something

2

that could make this wrong very right—a Glock with a fifteen-shot clip. I paused to contemplate the next step, but hearing the neighbor's grunts and moans shut down the debate which was beginning in my head. The blood from my cuts made the cold steel slippery, and grasping the grip harder added fuel to the burning pain. Blood was dripping to the floor. It didn't matter. Nothing mattered. The pain sparked anger in me. Like a spark becomes a wildfire, an all-consuming rage took control of both my body and mind. Feeling the clip lock into place, consequences meant nothing. I racked the slide, loading a round into the chamber. It was time to go hunting.

Feeling the power of the gun, strength returned to my legs. I stood up and moved quickly to the bathroom. I pushed the door wide open and stood on the threshold, pointing the Glock directly at the punk kid. His head was still tilted back, his hips aggressively moving, with Cindy's lips wrapped around his manhood. So intent on giving pleasure, Cindy didn't notice me standing in the fog. But I wanted her to see me. I wanted her to see the hurt on my face, feel the gut-wrenching pain I was feeling. I wanted her to see my blood dripping to the floor as it dawned on her she was about to watch that son of a bitch's blood swirl as it went down the drain. With a fifteen shot clip, the first wouldn't be fatal, nor the second or third. Time was on my side.

I moved forward and pulled open the shower door, startling both of them. Now she saw me. And she saw the gun pointed directly at her lover.

Cindy, still on her knees, pulled back and screamed, "Rick, don't! For God's sake, don't! Don't!"

My ears were deaf to her plea. Gripping the gun with both hands, it was only a matter of seconds before that bastard realized he was a dead man. Ah, there it was ... his contented moaning became a whimper. He cowered in fear as his eyes flicked back and forth, desperately seeking a place to run. But he couldn't run. He was a trapped animal. I was vaguely aware of Cindy still screaming "DON'T SHOOT," but my focus was on this young man who made a fool of me—on his ashen face, his shaking body, his terrified eyes moving frantically back and forth from my eyes to the gun, the gun to my eyes. He must have understood the "don't give a damn" look in them as he realized he was about to die.

Tearfully, with a cracking voice, he pleaded, "Please, no! Please, Mr. Morgan, I'm sorry! Please, don't shoot!"

He slumped to the floor and curled into a fetal position, covering his face with his hands. The shower spray was still pounding full strength as he trembled and muttered repeatedly, "Please, don't shoot. I'm sorry. I'm sorry."

Cindy's voice had now turned from a high-pitch scream to something calmer.

"Rick, listen to me. Put the gun down." To emphasize her words, she illustrated the "down" movement with her hand.

"Rick, this doesn't mean anything. Just ... put ... the gun ... down."

Cindy had managed to find a certain calm in the storm. No one needed to tell her death for both of them was only a squeeze away. I was enraged, irrational, and ready. But, fortunately for both, my voice never returned. And the silence gave me space to think. Numb to everything except the physical distress of my bleeding hand and my knotted stomach, I began to come to my senses. Slowly, with each beat of my racing heart, I lowered the weapon, inch by inch, until it hung by my side.

Looking into Cindy's eyes, I saw something I'd never seen (or noticed?) before. Though relieved she was still alive, she had the eyes of a stranger, someone I never knew. They were hard somehow. They were almost defiant. Before we were married, Cindy had been a player, sure. But I thought our love had changed that. Was my love so blind? Ten years? Had she ... been cheating the whole time? Turning, I slowly left the room. I walked out and never looked back.

Cindy never called. And I never shed a tear through the whole divorce process. It wasn't until a few months later, alone in a Las Vegas hotel room, I broke down sobbing. Ten years of life together, and I *thought* we were happy. Ten years of deceit, and not so much as an "I'm sorry" from Cindy's lips. Cold, I shivered as I gazed out at The Strip from the 20th floor. The cry felt good and the dazzling lights of The Strip lightened my mood. I began to chuckle. I realized Cindy's lover and I had something in common. We both got screwed by Cindy.

The divorce was final about 5 years ago. Four years, eleven months, and three days, to be precise. I'm a numbers guy. I calculate that sort of thing.

I have slowly reclaimed my mojo from pre-married years. As far back as I can remember I've loved females and they've loved me. Even before steaming up the windows in the backseat of my mother's '64 Buick, girls had always been a big part of my life. Playing street games with the neighbor boys, I wanted to include the girls. If the boys teased or berated them, they learned the wrath of Rick Morgan. In high school, while the jocks were trying out for football—and for some strange reason enjoying the thrill of bashing and rubbing their bodies into each other—I found females to be softer and far more delightful. Being with a woman was like dying and going to heaven. By the time I hit college, unlike most the guys in my dorm who would always take a bird in the hand, I was generally talking sweet to that bird. But still, I was willing to risk everything for something or someone new. Not that I was a dog (or a bird dog). It's just to me they were all beautiful. And I did long for "the one." So I had to keep seeking, sorting through all that loveliness, one woman at a time. Until the day I laid eyes on Cindy. From first glance, I was in love. Walking through a café door with poise and confidence, every step in perfect rhythm, Cindy knew how to capture attention. And capture mine she did.

But no more. I play my cards a little closer to my chest these days. But I still yearn for perfect harmony with some "one," someday. Would I find her in San Francisco? Was it Caroline here in Seattle?

I was sitting with my back to the desk, staring out my 16th floor office window, psychologically preparing myself for what was going to be a very long, busy and stressful day. There had been thunder showers through the night with torrential downpours. The wind pushed the rain sideways across the window, blurring my view of the Space Needle. Between the hammering noise of the rain and my thoughts roaming the shady back streets of my memories, I failed to hear my office door open and the 98 pounds in 2-inch pumps moving across the carpet.

"Rick?"

A voice broke my concentration just as a hand softly touched my shoulder. I nearly jumped out of my seat.

"Damn, Emily, you scared the hell out of me!"

Emily is my administrative assistant who has been with me about two years. Fresh from UW, I hired her after only a two-minute interview. She is one of the most intelligent young ladies I've ever met. Small-framed, about 5' 1", short dark hair and a smile that could charm any man—including me—out of anything. Emily is always punctual and can read me like a book. And she keeps my computer running better than the idiots in IT.

"Unusual weather for Seattle," she began.

"Hmm," was my only response.

"So, Rick, where are our thoughts this morning?" she quizzed. "Caroline, Las Vegas or San Francisco?"

"Now, Emily, what makes you think it's one of those?"

"Well, let me think," she said with a coy little smile. "To start with, you spend every waking minute in or out of the office with Caroline Edwards."

"No, I don't," I fired back.

"Rick, the only time you and Caroline aren't joined at the hip or other places is when you're off getting an adrenaline fix in Vegas, or sneaking off to San Francisco to see your mystery woman."

"What woman?"

"The one you keep a deep, dark secret."

"I don't keep her a secret."

"Oh really! Does Caroline know anything about her?"

"Now, Emily ..."

"And," Emily continued, "you won't even tell me her name. And I'm the one who makes your reservations every time you go. But don't worry, your secret's safe with me."

"Emily, thank you for all your hard work, but would it make a difference if you knew her name?"

"No, not really, but one of these days you're not coming back."

"Now are we talking about Vegas or San Francisco?" I asked.

"San Francisco."

"Emily, she and I are just friends."

"I know," she continued, with that smug female look I could never figure out. "I can tell by the look on your face when she's mentioned. But I'm telling you, Rick Morgan, your feelings for her run deeper than you think, and one of these days ..."

"Well, Emily, if I don't come back," I said gravely as I jutted my chin toward the front of the office, "then all this is yours." Then changing the subject, I added, "So, anything up this morning?"

"Yes, there are a ton of messages in your in-box, and Mr. Briscoe's office just called. He wants to see you at 9:00."

I glanced at my watch. It was only 8:30.

"Buzz me at 8:55."

"Right," she said, turning back toward her office.

"And close the door on your way out," I added.

Swinging my chair back around to the window, I watched the sheets of rain still moving sideways across the glass. Smiling, I thought about

Emily's question, "Caroline, Vegas or San Francisco?" Lightning flashed in the distance. I tilted my chair back and counted one, two, three. Then a rolling boom of thunder shook my office. My smile continued as I murmured under my breath, "One of these days ..."

CHAPTER 2

As the elevator door opened, I glanced at my watch. Ten seconds before my meeting. No problem.

The 20th floor contained the offices of the senior management team and there was nothing cheap about the setup. With luxurious carpets, rich paneling, elegant furniture, and million-dollar views from every office, the stockholders would have coronaries if they knew how the corporate men-in-black spent their money.

Don Briscoe's office was no exception. As the Vice President of Finance, he worked on the right side of the tracks. A mahogany double-door entry led to the reception area with four leather couches, ten wingback chairs, mahogany end tables, Tiffany lamps—all professionally coordinated, of course—a portrait of Ronald Reagan, and enough floor space for a football game.

Their administrative assistants were all attractive, of course. Most were older and more experienced so there was an air of sophistication about them you didn't find in the rest of the company. Their efficiency, like their attractiveness, was exceptional. Don's administrative assistant, Debbie, was slightly different. While possessing the same refined qualities as her counterparts, she also had a wild streak that came alive from time to time.

"Debbie, my favorite," I greeted her in my usual way.

Normally flirtatious, Debbie was solemn that morning.

"You're late," she scolded.

"Wait a minute ... No, don't tell me. Someone lost a dog," I countered with my usual sarcasm.

"Rick, be serious for a minute. Phil Carter and Caroline Edwards are in with Don."

With that information, my demeanor changed to match Debbie's. Phil Carter was the company's CEO and Caroline Edwards the company's HR director. Yes, *the* Caroline. Someone who, I might add, has violated company policy with me many times, usually between the sheets. Since this meeting convened with the four of us, there had to be a connection and maybe a problem.

"I'll buzz you," Debbie continued.

"Mr. Briscoe, Mr. Morgan is here."

"Yes, sir."

Taking me to the door of the inner sanctuary, Debbie knocked and then whispered, "What did you and Caroline do now?"

Bewildered, "Nothing," I muttered before she opened the door.

Turning to me, she mouthed, "Right," and rolled her eyes with a look that said, "You've got to be kidding."

Don's desk was big enough to land a 747 on. He glanced up from a pile of papers in front of him and gestured for me to enter.

"Come in, Morgan," he muttered quietly. When the V.P. of Finance speaks quietly, it means he is deep in thought. "Have a seat," he continued.

Glancing at Caroline, we both nodded. Her eyes told me this meeting was not about us. I sent a silent prayer up to heaven. "Thank You!"

Philip Carter was just the opposite of Don Briscoe. Where Don was physically small, Phil was big. Where Don had health issues, Phil was a perfect specimen for his age. Where Don was a financial genius, Phil was a natural salesman. Separately they were as different as night and day, but together they were dynamite. Neither was afraid of tackling new ideas, a combination that created financial growth for the company, making everyone—especially the stockholders—very happy.

Sitting in a wingback chair facing both, I felt like a death row inmate sitting in the electric chair waiting for the warden to throw the switch. Phil started the conversation.

"Rick, there's a problem in the San Francisco branch."

Noting his serious tone and the bleached-out look of his face, I knew he was definitely worried. And if Phil Carter was worried, there had to be a good reason.

"What's the problem?" I asked gravely.

He didn't answer but instead glanced over to Caroline to give the details.

"Everything's sketchy," she began. "All we know for sure is one of the employees has been arrested, another is in the hospital, and a third is involved somehow."

"Where's the office manager through all of this?" I asked.

"At the moment," Phil interjected, "his wife is in labor with my grandchild. You are aware, Rick, the manager is my son?"

"Yes, sir, I am. But I need to ask one question. As the Chief Audit Executive I must, so forgive me, but is there any reason to believe there's a problem with the books?"

Shaking his head, Don answered, "We don't think so. But you need to look anyway."

Leaning across his desk, Don's tone became as serious as Phil's. "Rick, your position gives you the authority, by the board, to go where you feel necessary. Your responsibility is not to us but to them and to the stockholders. Take this investigation as far as you deem necessary. If anyone's toes get stepped on, including anyone in this room, too damn bad."

"Understood," I replied.

"Look," Phil continued. "My son's not the brightest one in the family—takes after his mother—but still he's my son. I can't get involved with this directly based on conflict of interest. But you already know that. I want you and Caroline to head down there tomorrow morning and find out just what the hell is happening. Then report back to me."

I peeked sideways at Don. He was quietly nodding as Phil spoke. I looked back at Phil and said bluntly, "I gather your involvement is off the record?"

This put a grin on Phil's face. He turned to Don and said, "You're right! This is definitely the man for the job."

Then turning his attention back to me, Phil spoke somberly again.

"Rick, as Don said, do your job no matter what. Just keep me apprised of what you find. And there's one more problem. As you know, we've been hitting the airwaves with advertisements telling the public and our policy-holders we are a family-friendly company. Having an employee arrested isn't good for business."

And with a half-smile on his lips, he continued, "Of course, neither are members of our management team playing house together." He turned to Caroline. "You're not aware of that happening are you?"

Watching as horror spread slowly across her face, I interjected, "Phil, I promise you, we'll keep this whole San Francisco problem hush-hush."

"Yes, Morgan, I have every confidence you will. Now I have another meeting to get to. Caroline will fill you in with all the details. As soon as you know something, call me."

On the elevator ride back to the 16th floor, Caroline was very quiet. "So," I began, "what do you think?"

"I think Phil and Don know I've been sleeping at your house."

I smiled. "Woo! Exciting, isn't it?"

With a slap to my arm, she said, "Why do I put up with you?"

"Because I have a big ..."

"Rick!" she exclaimed, blushing. "That might be true but ..."

"I was going to say because I have a big ego."

"Well, I guess you could call it that," she chuckled.

As the door opened on my floor, we were both laughing. By the time we reached my office, the laughter had consumed us. I could only motion for Emily to follow, and she couldn't help laughing, too. It was contagious.

"Why ... are we laughing?" Emily asked.

"Because Rick has a big ol' ego that always needs attention!" Caroline chimed.

"Funny, very funny, Caroline," I managed between chuckles.

Pulling myself together, I attempted to explain and move on. "It was a little tense in the meeting for awhile, Emily, but everything's going to be just fine. Down to business, I need you to book two tickets to San Francisco early tomorrow for Caroline and me. And two rooms at the airport Hyatt."

Caroline gave me "a look," but before I could say anything, Emily spoke.

"That's two adjoining rooms at the Hyatt. Check."

She and Caroline just smiled at each other. I said nothing.

"Car?" Emily continued.

I asked Caroline, "Any input from the peanut gallery?"

"No," she answered in little girl fashion. "I'm happy."

"We'll take a cab," I said to Emily.

"Anything else?"

"Yes, ask Chris to step in for a minute."

As Emily left, I directed my attention back to Caroline.

"So you're happy?"

"Hmm, I think so," she said. "I was a little worried, but I'm happy now."

Taking her hand, I seized the opportunity to ask, "Then how about making me happy tonight?"

Pulling her hand back quickly, Caroline said, "Now, Mr. Morgan, you just heard Mr. Carter talk about how that violates company policy."

"Ah, too bad," I said. "I was thinking of things we hadn't done in awhile."

Her demeanor changed. "Oh-h," she cooed. "What did you have in mind?"

"Well, it doesn't matter, I guess. We shouldn't violate company policy."

"Hmm, well, maybe tonight—just this once—we could?" Leaning into me so her breasts just barely brushed against me as she kissed my cheek, "See you at 5:00," she said.

Caroline turned slowly and deliberately, holding my gaze as she moved. Watching her leave my office was breathtaking. The 2-inch pumps gave a curve and firmness to her legs which is best described as perfect. Disappearing under the tight skirt, I could see the outline of the back of each thigh as she swayed. It was a most erotic sight. I couldn't help but think of how many ways I was going to violate company policy after dinner.

Chris was the number two guy in my department. About 40, tall, slender, orange hair (don't ask), and single (again, don't ask). Called me "Chief" and everyone else "Dude," including Emily. He was my "go-to guy" whenever I needed something done quietly.

He popped his head through the door and asked, "You need me, Chief?"

"Chris, come in and close the door."

"Right, Chief."

"Have a seat. I have something special I want you to work on."

Noting my use of the word "special," Chris asked, "Off the record, Chief?"

Nodding my head, Chris got the drift.

"I want you to pull all the payables and expense reports for the San Francisco office going back six months."

"What am I looking for?" he asked with some excitement.

"Anything out of the ordinary. Unusual patterns with credit memos to a specific agent, expense reports—you know the drill. Also, check the petty cash account."

"Anyone in particular?"

"Not sure. I'm heading down tomorrow morning. If so, I'll let you know."

"OK, Chief, I'll get right on it."

As he opened the door, I added, "Chris, one more thing. All communications will be with me personally, and use the cell phones."

"Right, Chief."

At exactly 5:00 P.M. I strolled into Caroline's office. She was fussing with her bag, a big black thing with the letters "CJ" on the side. I believe it stood for Caroline Jean. Her office was much more orderly than mine. I had files everywhere, but her workspace was always well-maintained and neat. Though the furnishings were very warm, the personal items were sparse—only one five-by-seven picture of a young family: a father, mother, and three very young girls. It was probably taken somewhere around 1975. Two of the girls appeared to be twins, about three years old. Both had blond hair and matching outfits, and each held by a parent. The other little girl was quite the opposite. Maybe about five, she had long, dark hair falling across her shoulders and the sultriest look for a child that age. The picture was taken in front of what appeared to be the family home. It was Spanish architecture, with a red tile roof and a red walkway leading to the front door. It looked to me like a home from California's San Fernando Valley. I asked Caroline about the photo once, but her response was dismissive. "Just family," was her only reply. I never pressed further.

With no one else in the office, I slipped behind Caroline's desk and wrapped my arms around her small waist.

"Are you ready?" I whispered.

"Oh, Rick, it's been such a stressful day," she said as she responded to my hug with a squeeze of her own.

"Hey, I'm here now. Let me take you away from all of this."

"That sounds wonderful," she said as we moved toward the door. "But then there's tomorrow and the next day."

I turned off the light and locked her door.

"Yeah, I know. But I'll be there too."

Chapter 3

The San Francisco office is located in the heart of the financial district. Arriving by cab about 10:00 A.M., Caroline and I found the office in total disarray. Of course, it didn't help matters that the manager's wife had her baby and he was gone. The office staff consisted of ten: three who belonged to accounting—handling all the billing and local collections—and seven in sales and marketing. I didn't know the other seven well, but knew the accounting people could be a handful. To say the least, they were a tad different.

I called them Peter, Paul and Mary—you know, like the old peace-and-love singing group. All three were retreads from the Haight-Ashbury thing of the '60's. Though too young to be actual participants (no doubt their parents had been) they were flower children all the same, always talking down the establishment (with severe disapproval of large corporations, meaning their own employers), wanting to legalize drugs, believing in universal peace and love of mankind, etc. To me, all three were nuts ... but proficient at their jobs, so they made very good salaries even by San Francisco standards. (I never heard them complain about their own corporate money, by the way.)

It came as no surprise to me when it turned out these three were the culprits in the office chaos. Caroline began to piece together the events.

The day before yesterday, Peter and Mary decided to go to lunch and not invite Paul, a questionable choice on their part because the three typically lunched together. While at lunch, the two smoked a few joints to relieve the stress of the morning. Another questionable choice, but this is known as being "420 friendly." And they were extremely 420 friendly. This too, came as no surprise. But as far as I was concerned, what they

15

did on their own time was their own business. Their gender, race, religion, sexual orientation, political views, and whatever were no concern of mine. As long as it didn't interfere with company duties, who cares? But that day things were different.

Maybe the grass was a little stronger or the moon was in the seventh house, who knows? But after a few extra puffs on the "Magic Dragon," Peter and Mary decided to come back to the office and—in their challenged state—thought it would be entertaining to have sex in the copier room, making photocopies of intimate body parts and sundry behaviors. If they weren't in a mystical land, they might have realized a webcam would have been a lot safer. (Practice safe photo/video sex, people!) When Mary sat on the machine to photocopy her other smiling face, the glass broke, and she fell in. Hearing a loud scream, Paul came running in (along with a majority of the office personnel) and caught them both with their pants down, quite literally. Paul put two and two together (he was an accountant after all) and became insanely jealous. Who knew Paul was secretly in love with Mary! Paul grabbed a chair and proceeded to pummel Peter with it. How many times is still in debate, but Paul was very thorough, striking the head, the vital organs, the kneecaps, etc. So much for loving your fellow man. And so much for the free love thing. Turns out love isn't free, it's expensive. Their roller-coaster of love landed Paul in jail for assault and battery and Peter in the hospital with a concussion and miscellaneous abrasions. Mary also went to the ER to treat a small laceration on her derrière, but she was released the same day. Oh, and while she was there she discovered she was pregnant. It's not clear who the father is because she was apparently laughing (and crying) too hard for the nurse to get much information out of her.

The co-workers who were not involved were all talking at the same time, but it was clear opinions were strong and varied. The words misconduct, termination (and fire their crazy asses), discrimination, prejudice, and destruction of company property were intermingled with claims of mere youthful exuberance, pleas for mercy, leniency, and "oh-what-a-horrible-shame-but-they-only-hurt-themselves."

Only in San Francisco.

After the day we had, it was like heaven arriving at our rooms that night. Caroline and I went in our separate doors. As I was throwing my bag on the bed, I heard a knock on the adjoining door.

"Who's there?" I queried.

"Me," she intoned with the implied question, "who else would it be, stupid?"

"Me who?"

"Will you open the door?"

It was a command, not a question. So I cracked the door a tad, saying "Sorry, I gave at the office."

"Well, I guess you'll never know what you missed," she countered, in a lighter tone. Ah, there it was, the playful mood I was looking for. A mood that meant we would definitely violate company policy that night ... a couple of times. We agreed to dinner at 7:00 giving us both a chance to wind down and prepare for our quiet meal at the main dining room downstairs.

Caroline, as always, was a fantastic dinner companion, impeccable in every respect. With our romantic interactions, the laughter, teasing, and touching, all who observed would have concluded we were a couple in love. And, for that night, maybe we were. Or maybe the moon was still in the seventh house.

Though a breath of fresh air in my somewhat stagnant daily life, there were times I had a nagging feeling, something deep in my gut, that Caroline was not who she appeared to be. What she did with her hair, the gestures of her hands as she spoke, her words and the tone behind them, her stroking the swizzle stick in her martini, all spoke one message: this beautiful woman was indeed attracted to me. But more than the subtle messages of her body, there was the message of her eyes. Dilated, they were as big and deep as any I'd ever seen. Yet, there seemed to be something different behind those gorgeous eyes. Something I could feel rather than see. It was as though there was another person looking at me, a reflection of another set of eyes hiding a secret. I wasn't sure if it was just my imagination or something else. Was it paranoia from being burned so badly by Cindy, whose eyes I thought I knew but didn't?

No matter. Pushing all concern aside, I focused on the fact Caroline caused my heart to pound hard and deep. We weren't married, so how could she hurt me anyway?

Leaving the dining room for the ninth floor lounge, Caroline slipped her arm in mine. It was a habit she had that I loved. I must admit pride filled my heart, as it always did, knowing everyone could see this beautiful woman was with me.

The elevator to the lounge was an express with floor-to-ceiling mirrors, so no matter which direction I gazed there was a fabulous view of Caroline.

It was exhilarating to look at her from so many angles! Each glimpse audaciously boasted a special part of her succulent body, from her 3-inch heels that framed her lovely ankles to the snug blouse that imprisoned her firm breasts. Every view stimulated my imagination and anticipation of the night that waited.

The observation lounge was pretty low-key, with only a few patrons indulging. On the weekends, with the onset of conventioneers and locals, it throbbed with excitement. But during the week the locals are home and most businessmen were too tired from a hectic day to partake of the wonderful amenities offered. For us, the setting was ideal: a small, quaint table-for-two hosting a spectacular view of the airport. The twinkling lights of the East Bay gently stretched their reflections across the calm water. The soft, easy sound of a piano tinkled in the background. A small candle cast its gentle glow, reflecting the silhouette of a very beautiful woman.

After ordering our drinks, I moved my chair next to Caroline. Putting my hand on hers, "Do you remember the first time we met?" I asked.

"Oh-h-h, it was nice," she murmured. Taking her hand back, she slipped her arm through mine and snuggled into my shoulder.

"Did I make you nervous?" I pressed.

"No. Remember I had already seen you once? We met officially in my office, but remember, it was in the parking garage before when our eyes first met. You definitely caught my attention, and I deliberately walked slowly so you could catch up. Then when you didn't, I figured you were married or something."

"I was just admiring the view."

"Oh, Mr. Morgan, you have such a dirty mind!"

"And you have a great pair of legs."

"Why, thank you. Anything else you like?"

With a small smile she couldn't see, "There are a couple other admirable things," I replied.

Positioning herself upright in her chair, she turned to me. Her mouth said nothing, but her eyes and lips said "kiss me." Moving slowly to take that kiss, my pants began to vibrate.

Startled, "What's that?" Caroline exclaimed, jumping back slightly.

"My cell phone … I think. But maybe I'm just glad to see you."

I looked at the caller ID.

"It's Chris."

"Chris? Now? You're kidding!"

"If he's calling this late, he must have found something."

"Hey, Chris," I answered. "Find anything?"

"Nothing? OK, that's good."

"What?"

"Tell me that again."

"Twenty million?"

Hearing "twenty million," Caroline's ears perked up.

"Really?"

"What's the connection?"

"Jack Webber? The marketing manager?"

"He was?"

"He did?"

"Interesting! Good work. Go home now and get a good night's sleep."

"Oh, you are? OK, double check your facts and be in my office after lunch tomorrow."

"Right. Bye."

"What was that all about?" Caroline asked.

"Chris said the books were fine."

"What was the twenty million thing?" she asked with a curiosity I'd never heard from her before.

"Ten years ago the company paid a twenty million dollar life claim on a key man policy."

"Is that a lot?" she asked innocently.

Turning to her, "It's a hell of a lot!" I blurted.

"Well, Rick, people *do* die."

"Yeah, I know. But ..."

"And what was that about Jack?" Again with the newfound inquisitiveness.

"Did you know he was the office manager here in San Francisco eleven years ago?"

"Uh, no. I didn't."

"Caroline, Jack's the biggest kiss-ass skirt-chaser in the company. How the hell could he land a twenty million dollar policy? Those take time to cultivate. He's not bright enough to do it."

"Rick, maybe he has some qualities you're not aware of."

"Maybe. But I wonder ..."

Putting her hand on my face, she quietly said, "Wonder about this."

And for the next few moments I was lost in the softness of her lips.

Pulling back with a very satisfied look on her face, "Still wondering?" she purred.

"About what?" I smiled.

This response seemed to make her happy as she settled her head back on my shoulder. I shifted my head slightly and gently kissed her forehead with a few butterfly kisses. Caroline repositioned herself, melting further into me. Feeling her soothing warmth, I touched her cheek only to feel the dampness of a tear slowly trickling down. For some reason, Caroline had begun a soft cry.

I moved back to look at her face.

"Hey, what's wrong?"

Answering between the sniffles, she managed, "I ... (sniff) ... I just ... (sniff)"

After a few seconds of continued sniffling, I asked, "You just what?"

"I just wish things were different, that's all," she said, trying to maintain her composure, but failing miserably.

Looking deep into her misty eyes, I smiled.

"What could be different?"

"Oh, Rick, where were you ten years ago?"

"Ten? Why ten?"

"Things could have been different. That's all," she said.

"How?" I pressed.

"Just different, that's all."

"Do you need a handkerchief?" I continued, with a slight grin.

"Yes," she said, with a sniffle and a smile.

"Do you have one?"

"No," she answered sweetly.

I've never known a woman to have a hankie when she needs one. Reaching into my coat pocket, I said, "Here, take mine. It's clean."

"Well ... (sniff) I'm glad to hear that!" she said, laughing weakly.

As she began to wipe her face and eyes, I asked, "Tell me ... What about ten years ago?"

"Oh, Rick, it's over and done with. It's not important now."

I was thinking, "important enough to make you cry," but what do I know about women's tears? So instead of speaking I just wrapped my arms around her. My hug told her everything was alright. With Caroline safe in my embrace (and sniffling), we pretended to watch the activities of the San Francisco International Airport.

As we arrived at Caroline's door—the one next to mine—I posed the question, "Do women like making love better in their own beds?"

"Well, since I'm always in yours, let's find out," she suggested as she unlocked the door and took me by the hand.

We went in together, bolting the door for the night. As we moved toward the bed, I stopped. Turning to each other, I took both her hands in mine. I moved my hands to her face, cradling her soft, warm cheeks as I leaned down to kiss her delicately. Her lips were smoldering as she moved closer for a deeper kiss. Dropping her purse, she encircled my waist, pulling me ever tighter, opening her mouth slightly to surrender her sweetness.

The first few kisses were soft and tender, our tongues briefly touching then darting in retreat. But the gentleness soon gave way to an aggressive hunger. Tongues were no longer retreating, but probing deeper with a passionate appetite. Drifting from her fiery lips, I glided down her neck. She tilted her head, begging without words for each kiss to touch more of her smooth and silky flesh. Delicately grazing with the tip of my tongue, I felt her stiffen, clutching my shirt and flesh. With each touch sending new waves of excitement through her already-quivering body, she was yielding to blazing desires deep within. She wanted to be taken.

Catching my breath, I moved my hands back to her face. Her eyes reflected the mystic twilight that filled the unlit room. Even in that faint glow, I could see and feel incredible passion radiating from her. Her eyes were the windows to her passionate soul.

I began slowly rubbing her back, massaging gently with my palms then moving beneath her soft hair. From her neck, I traced down her spine with my fingers, touching every vertebra. Caroline purred. I found her bra and traced it, too, slowly tracking the fabric around to the front and ultimately resting my hands on the sides of her full breasts. Feeling my hungry touch, she knew what I needed.

Looking quietly down at her breasts, she smiled demurely and asked, "Are you ready for your girls?"

Being caught up in the moment, I could only nod.

Caroline took my hand and led me over to the bed, motioning for me to sit down on its corner. Moving one step back she paused, commanding with her eyes that I give her my complete attention. Slowly, starting at the top, she began to unbutton her blouse. With each button undone, she hesitated briefly while revealing a fresh morsel of the precious commodity underneath. She wanted me to savor each bite as she rationed this food for my all-consuming hunger. By the second button I was addicted, already needing another fix.

Gradually and purposefully, button by button, she made her way to the bottom. She never looked at what she was doing. Her eyes were locked on mine. In a room filled with more shadows than light, watching Caroline's silhouette performance was erotic beyond words. It was exhilarating.

With her blouse draped open, but not yet pulled back, Caroline stood patiently, teasing my famished eyes with a glimpse of the wonders behind the magic curtain. Slowly and seductively, she pulled back her blouse to unveil the most beautiful set of breasts snuggled in a soft, black, lacy bra. With their fullness held only by shallow cups, each seemed to reach toward me, pressing ardently and pleading to be released from its tormented confinement.

Leaning down with wanting lips and desire in her eyes, Caroline kissed me. Not the hot, passionate, tongue-twisting kiss of some minutes ago. This one was pure and true and loving. It was a kiss that said, "I love you."

"Take a shower with me?" Caroline's eyes were riveting when she asked me that question. They were not filled with lust … not whimsy, either. It was like the kiss. Her eyes said love. This was new for us.

"Yes, baby," I said. "Yours or mine?"

"Mine," she answered with a smile.

While Caroline was preparing our shower, I slipped into my room and out of my clothes. Hearing the water running, I took it as my cue to make an entrance. As I pulled back the shower curtain, the sight of this beautiful woman standing bare before me literally took my breath away. From the top of her head to the bottom of her feet, she was perfect. Her eyes went down my body and stopped at the place she desired the most—her toy. It was hard, thick and very ready. Her eyes were getting bigger by the second as her tongue ever-so-slightly licked her lips. She wanted it, and now.

The morning sun shone through the arboretum outside the room, lighting it with an interesting shadow. Caroline lay naked next to me, covered only with a sheet, exhausted from the night of passion. She had been, as always, a fantastic lover … more than once. As I was leaning over, kissing her bare shoulder, she stirred. Facing me and wiping the sleep from her eyes, she smiled and whispered, "I love you." Kissing the end of her nose, I whispered the same. Gliding on top of me, she opened herself and again we made love. Soon we would have to catch our flight back to Seattle.

Two thoughts consumed my mind that morning: Caroline (of course!) … and twenty million dollars.

And, yes, we were in *her* bed.

CHAPTER 4

It was a little after lunch when I arrived back at the office. The sight of my exhausted and battered body dragging through the outer office sparked lovely words of greeting from Emily.

"Well, well, look what the cat dragged in," she said, looking up from her desk. Her sarcastic observation was right on the money.

"Emily, don't I hear your mother calling you?" I said as I inched myself toward my office.

Ignoring my mutually respectful remark, she continued, "It looks like someone had an interesting night."

"And let's not forget the morning," I added.

Smiling, she just shook her head. "Chris is in your office waiting for you."

I was still moving slowly toward my door. "If anyone wants me, take a message. And please get me some aspirin."

Finally making it into my office, I closed the door behind me. As I was falling into my chair, Chris began, "You OK, Chief?"

"Chris, were you ever with a woman and ..." I ventured, but then, noting the blank look on his face, retreated shaking my head. "Never mind. What do you have for me?"

"Well, Chief, eleven years ago we insured a business partner with a key man policy."

"Twenty million?" I asked.

"Right, Chief. A year later, the insured died from a heart attack."

"So tell me, what's the problem?" I quizzed.

"Well, you asked me to look for something out of the ordinary."

"And?"

"Here's the problem, Chief. You have a man who was in perfect health a year before. Probably didn't smoke, drink, or do drugs. Not overweight. Our doctors checked him inside out and upside down. He's in perfect shape. If he wasn't, we wouldn't have insured him for that much. Then he dies of heart failure a year later? Doesn't make sense."

"Chris, how did you find this? I only asked you to go back six months."

"Right, Chief, and I did what you told me and found nothing. Then after dinner last night I got to thinking about death benefits. So I took it upon myself to start checking the archives. When I found a claim for twenty million, I thought you might be interested."

Chris was always the one in the department to go above and beyond with everything. And now he had my curiosity percolating.

"You were home last night when you found the information?"

"Well, yeah, Chief," he said quietly.

"May I ask, Chris, how you obtained this information?"

"Well, Chief, I ... well, you see ..."

"Chris, you penetrated the firewall, didn't you?"

With his somber look turning to a grin, he bubbled, "It was easy. All I did was ..."

I put up my hand in a "stop" motion and closed my eyes. "Chris, don't tell me. I don't want to know. And besides, I wouldn't understand. But after this meeting, go tell IT how you did it."

"OK, Chief." Then, with his grin fading, he added, "Am I in trouble, Chief?"

"No, Chris. Everything's fine."

I was trying to be serious and not laugh my head off. I just love it when someone as simple as Chris can get around the geniuses in IT.

"Now, Chris, you mentioned Jack was the agent?"

"Right, Chief. Jack was the manager of the San Francisco office at the time. He was also the agent. That sale got him promoted to HQ."

"How did you find out Jack was the agent?" I asked curiously.

"I went back to the company's monthly magazine for that month. It had an article about Jack. He was agent of the month for the company."

Shaking my head in disbelief, "Jack got a twenty million dollar policy," I puzzled.

"Actually, Chief, he sold two for twenty million."

"Of course, there was a partner ... Do you have their names?"

"Check, Chief. The insured was Johnson. The other I have to look up."

I swiveled my chair to the window and began to think. Was this worth checking out? In about five seconds I would have my answer.

I turned back to Chris. "Get me the underwriting files for both. Let's just have a look."

"It's all archived in the computer, Chief."

"No, I want the hard files. I want to see the applications, medicals, the physician's notes, everything."

"They'll be in storage. It might take awhile to find it."

"That's fine," I agreed.

"Will do, Chief," he said as he rose from his chair to leave.

"Chris? Good work. But work on this solo." (Meaning keep your mouth shut.)

"Right, Chief."

As Chris walked out, Caroline walked in. She had gotten my aspirin from Emily.

"What's up with Chris?" she asked.

"Nothing, really," I replied. But she could tell my thoughts were a million miles away—or twenty million.

"Still chewing on that death benefit we talked about last night, aren't you?"

"Yeah, I just told Chris to pull the underwriting files. I want to see the notes. I'm just curious about a couple of things, but mainly how Jack pulled it off."

Turning my full attention back to Caroline, I continued, "So what's up with you?"

"Oh, nothing. Here's your aspirin," she replied while handing me the two little white pills. "But why Jack?" She had a puzzled look on her face.

"That's a good question," I responded. "There's something that makes me wonder how anyone so focused on breasts and legs could find the time, desire, or energy to go after a big fish like that. It's not in his character."

"Hmm," she replied as though looking for something to say. "It's true, he does like the women." She continued with a coy smile, "And this woman was just thinking about last night."

"And this morning, too?" I interrupted, grinning broadly.

Then abruptly, with a total change of countenance as though

remembering something that needed to be done, she said, "I need to go. See you tonight?"

"Dinner and a repeat?" I asked.

"That all depends," she said, with her tongue gently licking her lips. "Are you up to it?"

Looking down below my belt, "I am, but I'm not sure your toy is," I responded playfully.

"I can re-inflate it if need be," she said with a devilish smile.

"I'll bet you can," I mumbled, watching her sway as she turned and walked out the door.

I tilted my chair back and popped the aspirin in my mouth. My thoughts returned to Jack.

"How the *hell* did he do it?"

Lifting my handset, I dialed Phil Carter's office.

"Hi, it's Rick. Is your boss in?"

"Phil, Rick Morgan."

"Fine, thanks."

"Yes, everything's fine. No, your son has no problems, though Caroline had to fire the three accounting people."

"Oh, you heard. Good."

"There is another matter I'm following up with regarding Jack Webber."

"I'm not sure yet."

"Well, I don't care much for him either."

"I'll keep you apprised."

"Right. Goodbye."

About 4:00 P.M., Chris returned to my office.

"Chief, got a problem."

Looking up from my desk, I knew by the look on Chris's face it would be something that wouldn't make my day.

"Well, Chris, what is it?"

"The files are missing."

"What do you mean 'missing?'"

"Records said they've been misplaced."

"How can that be?"

"I don't know, Chief."

"Then get the computer files. We'll start there."

"I can't. The files are not on the system."

"Not on the system?" I repeated back in disbelief. "How can they be gone?"

"IT's not sure."

A rock settled into my stomach.

"The backup?"

Again the look on his face gave me the answer.

"IT said the file is corrupt and can't be retrieved."

"How the hell did that happen? What did IT say about that?"

"This backup of the archive files was made about five years ago before they installed the new system. No one knows how it went south. They said it shouldn't have happened."

"So the underwriting file could have been erased anytime over the last five years?"

"Or maybe before the new system was installed," Chris added.

"Did anyone know what you were up to?"

"No, Chief. I swear I told no one."

I paused.

"Thank you, Chris, that will be all for now."

"Right, Chief."

Walking out the door, Chris stopped and turned to me with a very serious look on his face. "You believe me, don't you, Chief? I swear I didn't tell anyone."

Nodding my head, "Yes, Chris, I believe you," I said gravely.

He had a look of relief. "Thanks, Chief."

"Chris, one more thing. The file you looked at last night was the claim file, right?"

"Right, Chief."

"Be in my office tomorrow morning at 9:00."

With one last usual, "Right, Chief," he left my office.

If Chris said he told no one, I believed him. Chris might be the biggest nerd in the company, but he was loyal to me. If he said up was down, it was.

Turning to the window, I watched the rain bounce off the panes of glass. I could see Emily's reflection as she came into my office.

"Is everything alright, Rick?" she asked.

"Emily, you're a computer person. How hard would it be to lose a file in the system without anyone knowing?"

"You mean erase a file?"

Nodding my head, "Yeah."

"Not hard at all if you knew what you were doing and had a password."

"Who has those passwords?"

"Only IT. But if you're really good, it wouldn't be hard to get around it."

"Could Chris do it?"

Emily stood thinking for a moment. "Hmm, probably. But he would have to know precisely where to look."

"How about corrupting data on a backup so it's unreadable?"

"Piece of cake. Why?"

"Oh, nothing. Just thinking."

"Anything else?"

"No. Why don't you knock off for the day?"

"Sounds good to me. Thanks."

"Just leave my door open."

"Good night, Rick."

"Good night, Emily."

Once again I turned to the window, deep in thought. It was a few minutes after five when Caroline walked into my office. Seeing me in think mode she asked, "Rick, are you still thinking about that loss from some years ago?"

Rotating my chair around, "Yeah, there's just something about this that troubles me."

Slipping around my chair she leaned against my desk, slid her right hand behind my head and slowly played with my hair.

"Tell me, dear, what's the problem?"

"The underwriting files are gone."

"You mean they've been misfiled."

"No, I mean gone. I can understand the hard copy being misplaced for one insured but not both. And especially when they're related."

"Well, things do get lost," she added. "It's been a lot of years."

"I know, but the computer file is also missing."

"That's impossible!" Caroline exclaimed.

"That's exactly what IT said."

"Aren't all the files backed up?"

"Yes, they are. But it seems the location on the drive that backed up this particular file is now corrupt and can't be read."

Still stroking my hair but with a slight change in touch, Caroline asked, "So what are you going to do?"

"Right now, nothing. But in about three hours I'm going to ravish your body."

"Oh, Mr. Morgan, are you going to give me instructions on what you want like last night?"

"No, it's your turn to tell me."

"Well, in that case," she said, taking my hand and pulling me from my chair, "come on. It's time to go home. And no more discussion about that twenty million dollar death benefit. All the benefits are for me tonight."

"But, you know, it's strange that …"

"Rick," she reprimanded sternly. "Hush. Now, your place or mine?"

Smiling, I never answered her question. But … I believe men, like women, do enjoy sex better in their own beds. I know I did that night.

CHAPTER 5

Arriving at the office at 8:00 A.M. with coffee in hand, I went directly into think mode. This meant staring out my window. I instructed Emily I was not to be disturbed until Chris arrived at 9:00. Though my body was numb from a night of passion and other enjoyable activities with Caroline, my mind was clear and alert, pondering questions which had no obvious answers.

What started off as simple curiosity as to how Jack could have sold a twenty million dollar policy (or two) had now blossomed into something more. Over and over, like a skipping record, I had a nagging feeling deep in my gut there was far more to this story than Jack's extraordinary and surprising sales abilities. My thoughts kept coming back to those missing files. As someone who has spent his fair share of time in Vegas, I am very familiar with playing the odds. The odds that two separate underwriting files are missing are negligible at best. But when connected by the common thread of a partnership, the odds begin to increase. Add the missing files on the computer, those same odds begin to compound. Then having that one in a million file on the backup corrupted and unreadable, the odds become astronomical. And when the odds on a bet become astronomical, the game is usually rigged. And that bothered me.

At 9:00 A.M., punctual as usual, Chris arrived.

With my door closed and Chris sitting in a wingback chair I began. "So, Chris, what do you think about these missing underwriting files?"

"Well, Chief, that's something I've been thinking about since yesterday. How can both hard copies of the files be missing? I mean, what are the chances they both would be gone?"

"Chris," I said in agreement, "that's the twenty million dollar question."

Tilting my chair back and looking at the ceiling with my hands behind my head, I continued. "What do you think we should do?"

"Well, Chief, I've been thinking about that, too. I think I should go back to Records and pull the claim file for Johnson. Then go to the computer and print off all the information I saw the other night."

"Why print it off?" I asked. But I already knew the answer.

"Just in case that file becomes corrupted, too," Chris said.

"Good thinking, Chris," I smiled. He might be a nerd, but he's smart.

"Now, Chris," I continued, "when you were in Records yesterday, did anyone seem concerned about the files you wanted?"

Squinting his eyes in thought, he answered, "Uh, no, Chief. They seemed as surprised as I was that the files were missing."

With my chair still tilted back, I nodded my head as I continued. "When you went to IT about the missing file on the computer, what was their reaction?"

"They told me it was impossible."

"It figures they would say something brilliant like that. And ..."

"And then they said the file must have somehow got deleted."

"Did they seem concerned?"

"No, not really. You know how IT thinks. It was a low priority."

"What about the backup?" I continued.

"Oh, then I asked if they could find it on a backup."

I was nodding my head again as he continued.

"They said they didn't have time and I needed to fill out a request. Then it would take about a week."

"A week?" I interjected, a little irritated.

"Yeah. I told them you wouldn't be happy with their answer."

"And?"

"And then the lady—you know, the tall redheaded one—phoned the IT manager. You know, Chief, I don't think she likes you."

Smiling at Chris's observation and knowing everyone in IT hates my guts, I quipped, "Chris, I could give a rat's ass if she does or doesn't. Then what happened?"

"Well, the IT manager told her to pull the backup and restore the file ASAP, then to call me when it was finished. So she called about 3:45 and told me the file was corrupted and the info was lost. Uh, you know the rest, Chief, from my report yesterday."

I swung my chair upright and leaned forward across my desk. Focusing my eyes directly into Chris's, I asked a point-blank question. "Chris, what's your feeling about this whole thing?"

Chris has always been a very somber type of guy. Always taking his job seriously and never expressing much of a sense of humor. Leaning forward with his elbows resting on his thighs right above the knees, he began to speak quietly, as though he didn't want anyone to hear.

"Chief, I think someone *really* doesn't want these files to be examined."

His observation was most excellent, and I agreed totally. I had arrived at that very conclusion about eight hours prior while lying beside lovely Caroline as she slept soundly next to me.

Still leaning across my desk, I laid out some very specific instructions. "Chris, this conversation doesn't leave this room. You are to talk to no one about it, including Emily. Talk to no one in the department. If anyone and I mean anyone—even Mr. Carter—wants information, you know nothing and you direct them to me. Understand?"

"Understand, Chief."

"Now, this is what I want you to do. Go back to Records and pull the claim file on Johnson. That is if *it's* not missing *too*! Make two photocopies of the entire file, then return the file back to Records. Print everything you can off the computer. Then photocopy that as well. I want duplicates of everything. Call me on my cell if there's any problem."

"Right, Chief," Chris said as he got up and headed toward the door.

With his hand lightly touching the doorknob, he paused, turned back and asked, "What do you think we'll find, Chief?"

I looked up from my desk slowly, giving the question some thought before answering.

"Something I hope I'm dead wrong about."

Nodding his head, Chris understood.

Of course I wasn't sure what we would find, if anything. But one thing seemed sure, Pandora's Box was about to be opened. The very thought of it sent a shiver down my spine.

It was a little after lunch when Chris returned with a box in his hand. I motioned for him to put everything on my small oval conference table.

"Chris," I asked anxiously, "what do we have?"

"Well, Chief," he began, "I did everything you asked. Had Records pull the claim file."

"It was there?"

"Yeah, Chief, I was surprised."

Actually, I was, too.

"While they looked for it, I printed everything off the computer twice like you wanted. When I returned for the claim file I saw it was sealed. I didn't want to break it. I thought you would probably want to see it and break it yourself."

"Well, let's look at the computer stuff first."

There were only two pages giving the usual data: insured's name, date of birth, benefit amount, date and place of death, beneficiary. Just the highlights. It was interesting to note the death benefit was paid in care of a big Los Angeles law firm whose name I recognized as one which represents only high-profile individuals. The details would be in the folder. What I really wanted to see was the death certificate and medical examiner's report.

I picked up the folder. It was heavy and bursting at its seams. The corners were tightly wrapped in tape and the company's corporate seal was stamped across the flap, which was also covered with clear tape which had begun to yellow and peel on the sides.

Chris asked, "Have you ever seen a file sealed this way, Chief?"

"No, Chris, I haven't," I replied with some curiosity.

"What do you think it means, Chief?"

I didn't answer his question, but instead began examining the folder more closely. After inspecting every square inch, I could only arrive at one conclusion.

"Chris, see how this folder is bound tight with tape?"

"Uh, yeah, Chief."

"And see how the corporate seal was stamped across the flap in such a way that if anyone opened it, it would be noticeable?"

"Right, Chief."

"All this was designed with one purpose in mind."

"What's that, Chief?"

I couldn't believe what I was about to say.

"Chris, somebody went to a lot of trouble to make sure the secrets within this folder were well-guarded. In short, it was designed to scare off anyone from opening it."

The scare tactic seemed to be working on Chris, whose eyes had gotten big. He stepped back a little and said, "Wow, Chief, what are you going to do?"

"Chris, I'm glad you asked that. We're going to open this puppy up."

He slid his hand across the folder to stop me.

"Chief, we're not going to get in trouble for doing this, are we?"

Turning to him with an open expression, I said, "Chris, whoever wrapped this file was banking on the fear you just had, hoping you would walk away. No, *we* won't get into trouble, but if I find out who wrapped this, *they* will."

I pulled a small knife from my pocket, and Chris took back his hand. I began to cut the tape, breaking the sacred corporate seal. Pulling back the flap, I took hold of the contents, pulled it from the folder, and laid it out on the table. My eyes grew wide. Chris's eyes grew wider. Both of us were in shock.

Chris was the first to speak.

"What does this mean, Chief?"

I didn't know. It was too bizarre. I spread the papers loosely across the table to make sure I wasn't missing anything. As I visually digested what I saw before me, the rock that had settled in my stomach the day before was joined by its bigger, harder brother.

Looking blankly at the stuffing on the table, I slowly began to speak.

"Chris ... it is ... obvious ... someone wants to play a game."

"Play a game, Chief?"

"Yeah, Chris, a game."

The folder contained nothing more than newspaper. The first section of the Los Angeles Times dated July 6, 1976.

"So, Chief, what do we do now?"

With a half-muffled voice and my mind running in circles, I agreed, "What now indeed, Chris. What now indeed."

I tried to collect my thoughts. Though I had attempted lightheartedness with Chris moments ago, the questions I had that morning just became more confusing. And now add to the puzzle the newspaper, dated so many years back—too many years. Was this really nothing more than someone pulling a prank or something more devious?

I turned my attention back to Chris. I decided it was time to join the game.

"This is what we're going to do," I said.

Walking over to my recycle bin, I pulled my morning copy of the Seattle Times. After removing just the first section, I stuffed the rest of it into the folder, replacing the newspaper we had found there. Then I resealed it … with lots of tape.

Handing it back to Chris, I said, "Take this back to Records and have them refile it."

Then I picked up the computer printout and looked it over.

"It appears our Mr. Johnson died in Clark County, Nevada. That would be Las Vegas. Contact Vital Records down there. I want a copy of the death certificate ASAP. If they give you any crap, tell them as the insurance carrier which paid a claim, we have every legal right to a copy."

"Gee, Chief, I didn't know we did."

Smiling back at Chris, I replied, "I don't know if we do! But it sounds good, and they probably don't know, either! But, Chris, I want it ASAP!"

"Will do, Chief."

As Chris was leaving, he turned again as he had done earlier that day—with a question.

"Chief?"

"Yes, Chris?"

With his voice quivering slightly, he asked, "Do you think someone is going to be mad at what we're doing?"

Hearing the slight crack in his voice, I looked up to his face. He was afraid and needed reassurance. I didn't blame him.

"Chris, if you don't want to work on this, I understand."

"No, Chief, I'll work on it. But honestly, it scares me."

Smiling I said, "Chris, everything will be alright. I promise."

"Thanks, Chief."

As my door closed, I pondered that promise. Could I deliver? *Was* everything going to be alright? We both had a right to be scared. It appeared someone had put a lot of work into hiding the facts. And with twenty million dollars on the line, how far might that someone go?

That night, at dinner with Caroline, my thoughts weren't with my lovely companion. A little perturbed by my distance, Caroline quizzed me.

"Darling, you're quiet tonight. Something wrong or just tired from the last three nights?"

I didn't notice her smile when she asked her question.

"What, dear?" I asked back, like a deer-in-the-headlights since I hadn't been paying attention.

"Rick, what are you thinking?"

Before I could answer, "No, wait, let me guess," she continued with a trace of sarcasm. "You're still thinking of the twenty million and Jack. Right?"

"No, actually," I responded. "I'm thinking of going to L.A. this weekend to see my friend Steve."

"Isn't he the musician?" she asked.

"Yeah, I haven't seen him for awhile and I just need to get away for a few days."

"Is that the only reason, Rick Morgan?" she asked with a directness I've rarely seen.

"What other reason could there be?" I fired back.

"I'm not sure, but somehow I have a feeling you're up to something else. I know you, Mr. Morgan, and your eyes tell me there's something processing in that mind of yours."

I didn't confess to Caroline that in fact there were additional things on my mind about a California trip. The first was the Los Angeles newspaper from years past. After Chris left my office, I had thoroughly scoured through it. I wasn't sure what I was looking for, and I found nothing that caught my attention. But that paper was put there for a reason. The claim file was ten years old. The newspaper was twenty years older than the claims file. That date had significance. But what? Maybe I could poke around for some answers in L.A. But the other reason I was California dreaming was that I wanted an excuse to stop and see my friend in San Francisco. When overwhelmed and needing an escape, a quiet dinner with her in San Francisco always cleared my head.

The next morning was Friday. I called Emily into my office and advised her I would be gone for a few days.

"So, Rick, heading out to see your mystery woman again?" she asked.

"Just because I'm heading south for a few days doesn't mean I'm sneaking off to San Francisco," I said. "In fact, I'm actually heading to L.A. to see Steve."

Shaking her head like a mom whose child is lying through his teeth, "Oh, so San Francisco is not on your itinerary?"

"Well, maybe a stopover for dinner Sunday."

"Mr. Morgan, I've worked for you for over two years now and still believe there's a whole lot more to you than meets the eye. So, will I see you Monday morning?" she asked.

"About 10:30," I said.

Turning to walk out of my office, she paused at the door. "One of these days, Mr. Morgan, you won't be coming back."

I only smiled in return.

As the door closed, I sat in my chair and turned to my window. A soft mist was falling in Seattle that day. The Space Needle stood like a ghost in the distance. My thoughts drifted to San Francisco in the wake of Emily's breezy words.

Thinking out loud, "Emily, you never know," I whispered.

CHAPTER 6

True to my word, I arrived back at the madhouse Monday morning at 10:30. The office was always crazy on Mondays. Booting up my computer, I had over a hundred messages. Everyone had a problem. And everything, including my computer, was a problem. But the worst part was my coffee was cold.

"Emily!" I shouted to the outer office. "This damn computer won't work again."

With patience, intestinal fortitude, and love, Emily sat at my desk and did whatever she does. Then like magic, it was running again. The damn thing is haunted and the ghosts prefer her touch. Either that or she's simply better than the idiots in IT.

Now comfortable in my chair, Emily began a new topic. "What do you want to do about Valentine's Day, Rick?"

Sitting in a wingback chair (it was either that or the floor), I thought teasing Emily might make me feel better about being here instead of anywhere else (like San Francisco), so I gave it a try.

"When is Valentine's Day?" trying to sound oblivious.

"Rick! It's tomorrow!" she exclaimed with the annoyed tone I was going for.

"Well, then I guess I need to send all the girls a red rose."

"You mean the women," she corrected sternly. "And what about the men?"

"The men? They're guys. Guys don't do flowers."

"Rick, you have to do something for them too."

"Why?" I asked in a bewildered tone.

"It's discrimination if you don't," she explained flatly.

"Discrimination?" I said, shaking my head. "What the hell is discriminating about it?"

At this point, by the look on Emily's face, I knew I'd better wrap up this conversation and move on. Waving my hands, and with more than a hint of sarcasm in my voice, I said, "Fine, get the men whatever you think. Buy posies or perfume or jock straps! Put all of it on my Visa—the one with the air miles."

"Thank you, Mr. Morgan," she responded, gloating slightly. "Now, what about Ms. Edwards?"

"Caroline?"

"Rick, you can't forget her."

"I was planning to take her to dinner."

"And?"

"And what?" I asked.

"Rick, in case you haven't figured it out, she likes you a lot."

"Well, gee, Emily," I said mockingly, "I like her, too. *Just maybe* that's why I'm taking her to dinner?"

"Rick, you two are always going to dinner. Maybe she would like something a little special … more romantic."

"How do you know?"

"Rick, in case you haven't noticed, I'm a woman. I know these things."

"Fine. I'll get a waterbed and take her on a cruise."

"Rick Morgan, that's the most sexist thing I've ever heard you say! You should be ashamed of yourself!"

"Emily, I was just kidding. But really, you don't know the whole story between Caroline and me."

"Oh, you mean like how you two started alternating whose bed you're sleeping in every night?"

"How did you know that?"

"It doesn't matter. And by the way, I'm the only one who *does* know that."

Thinking back to Phil Carter's comment, "You're not the only one," I said under my breath.

"Listen, Rick. The only reason she's sleeping with you every night is she likes you. And right now Caroline Edwards is in conflict."

"Conflict?"

Noting the bewildered look on my face, she commented, "You really don't have a clue, do you?"

"Of what?"

"Rick. Get a grip. She's in love with you."

"In love? How do you know?"

"Remember?" she asked, pointing to her chest. "Me woman."

Slumping down into the uncomfortable chair, I wasn't sure how to address Emily's observation. Emily could see by my befuddlement the conversation was hopeless, so she started back to her office.

Stopping at the door, she turned and said, "Rick, the question here is, are you in love with her? Or is your heart in San Francisco?"

With that, Emily walked out and closed the door. I sat in the wingback chair for a few minutes desperately trying to digest everything Emily said. She sure turned the tables on that exchange! It was frustrating. Two things were for sure. When it came to Caroline Edwards I didn't know what the relationship was. And as for San Francisco, I didn't know what that was, either.

At about 11:00 A.M. on Valentine's Day, Caroline walked into my office with a smile on her face like I've never seen before—beaming from ear to ear.

I was looking up from my desk as she began, "Mr. Morgan, a messenger just delivered a dozen of the most beautiful red long-stem roses. But I'm puzzled. It was signed 'From a friend.' Do you have any idea who that might be?"

"Aw-w, you have a secret admirer?" I suggested, playing stupid and trying to keep a straight face.

"Well, hmm, I guess I do. Too bad you don't know who it is. I would like to thank him personally."

My eyebrows rose. "Personally?"

"Personally," she said with a devilish smile.

She turned to walk out and hesitated at the door. Turning back she said, "Oh, by the way, if by some odd coincidence you find out who my friend is, tell him to look in the middle drawer of his desk."

After hearing her footsteps clear the outer office, I opened my middle drawer. A neatly folded note lay in plain sight. I unfolded it carefully and read its message.

What a wonderful surprise! The flowers are absolutely beautiful. Maybe you will let me thank you personally for the gift?

Since I'd been in my office all morning, her note must have been planted yesterday. I didn't have to wonder for long how she knew I would give her flowers before the fact. There was only one suspect, the person who knew everything about everything. I picked up my phone.

"Emily, would you come in here, please?"

Leaning back in my chair, I turned toward the window. Caroline was one of the most beautiful women I'd ever met. I loved so many things about her, but was I in love with her?

Emily walked through the door with a sheepish look.

"Emily, how did Caroline know I was giving her flowers?"

Raising her hands and shaking her head, she stammered, "Uh-h ... I don't know ...?"

"Hmm. Must be that damn flower fairy again," I said solemnly.

"Yes, I believe you're right," she said in a very agreeable tone.

"Thank you, Emily. I don't know what I would do without you."

"That's why you have me," she said, nearly skipping out of my office. Emily's frown had turned upside down into the smile of a little girl.

"Damn flower fairy," I chuckled to myself, shaking my head as I went back to work. But it wasn't long before I noticed my stomach was knifing my throat from hunger. I glanced at my watch and was surprised to see it was nearly noon. I guess there's some truth to the old saying "time flies when you're having fun."

I thought of Caroline and dialed her extension. "Hey, it's me. How about lunch? I'll buy if you'll be my Valentine."

My invitation was met with an, "I would love to, but I can't."

Of course I had to ask why. And after hearing the reason, I said, "I'll be up in a few minutes."

"Emily?" I shouted to the outer office.

She stuck her head through the door.

"You know Jack Webber in Marketing?"

As she was nodding yes, I continued, "Get his file, the special one, and then meet me in Caroline's office ASAP."

With Emily off on her task, I made one quick call to the 20th floor before heading to HR.

As I walked through the HR door, Holly's eyes met mine directly.

"Hey, Rick." Her voice was solemn.

"Holly, your boss is expecting me."

"I know. Go right in."

The atmosphere in Caroline's office was tense. A very frail girl, one of our roaming temps, was sitting in a wingback chair sobbing uncontrollably. About five feet tall, she looked like she should have been in high school. Small, attractive, and with an air of innocence, she was the type of young lady which certain older gentlemen—and I use the term loosely—love to prey on.

Someone in personnel, not Caroline, had dispatched her to the marketing department on temporary assignment that morning. It seems her boss for the day, Jack Webber, got a little carried away (as he has a habit of doing), sharing a few sexual innuendos and an inappropriate hug. When the temp got upset and protested, he began to bully her. She was smart enough to leave and report the incident to Caroline personally.

Hearing the whole story, I pulled Caroline aside and asked (well, more like begged, actually), "Would you mind terribly if I got involved with this?"

Looking at me curiously, Caroline responded, "That depends, Rick. This is really an HR problem. What do you have in mind?"

"What if I could get Jack to resign … today?" I asked cautiously, but with a grin.

Caroline raised an eyebrow. "You're not going to threaten him, are you?"

"Well, yeah, kind of."

"Kind of?" she said with some apprehension.

"Let's just say it won't be physical."

With her interest piqued, she asked, "Mr. Morgan, what does that devious little mind of yours have cooking?"

"Devious?" I repeated, smiling. "Actually, I prefer contentious … but, whatever!"

I shrugged my shoulders and gave her another grin.

"Why do I have the feeling I'm going to regret this?" Caroline continued.

"Do you trust me?"

"In or out of bed?"

"Well, yeah. But seriously, do you trust me to do the right thing?"

After thinking briefly before she answered, "Well, yes."

"Good. Just trust me now. If I fail, go ahead and bring him up on harassment charges. Fair?"

With hesitation, Caroline agreed. I leaned back to whisper in her ear, "Besides, if I fail, it will give you an excuse to punish me tonight."

"Hmm," she mumbled with a sexy smile. "Maybe I should hope you fail?"

As much as I loved to be at Caroline's mercy, the truth was if what I planned backfired, Caroline and I would be spanked by corporate. And probably out of our jobs.

Jack arrived promptly at HR when he was summoned, wearing his usual smug expression. I wanted so badly to slap it off his face. I took a deep breath in preparation to do just that. Figuratively, of course.

From her swivel chair, Caroline began outlining the charges. Of course Jack denied everything. It was the newbie's word against his. As she sat quietly sobbing in the corner, he demanded she be fired.

That's when I stepped in.

"Jack, are you sure you want to bring charges against this young lady?"

"You're damn right I do," he went off. "She came on to me, and I can't have that kind of behavior in my department."

Talk about BS here in HR!

I looked at the teary temp, then back to Jack before asking, "You're sure, Jack? This pretty young lady came on to you, the much older man?"

"Yes, she did. The little tramp," he countered defiantly. "Probably a gold-digger."

At this, the temp gasped and began blubbering again. Caroline shot me a stern look that said "get on with it!" as she crossed the room to comfort the girl.

"Then you're sticking to your story?"

"Definitely."

"Jack, I am so glad you said that," I exclaimed, smiling.

"You ... are?" he asked suspiciously.

"Yes, Jack, delighted! Now let me tell you what's going to happen."

"What do you mean?" he asked slowly while repositioning himself in his seat.

"I mean you are going to resign today. You're going to write a letter of resignation right here and now, give it personally to Caroline, then go down and clean out your office and be gone within one hour."

"Like hell I am," he snorted.

"Oh, did I mention you're also going to apologize to this young lady?"

"What?" Jack shouted as he jumped out of his chair.

I placed my hand firmly on his shoulder and said, "Sit down, Jack. We're not done."

Reluctantly, he sank back into the chair.

"If you don't do exactly what I just said," glancing at my watch, "in now 59 minutes, Phil Carter is going to learn how you intentionally misused company funds for personal gain."

"What? You're crazy!" he blurted.

Seeing the broad smile his words brought to my face seemed to distress Jack.

"Jack, I believe it's called misappropriation of company funds."

Again he began to rise. Again, with my gentle hand on his shoulder, he sat back down.

"Caroline, would you ask Emily to come in, please?"

Opening the door to the outer office, she beckoned Emily. Emily entered carrying a thick manila folder with the name Jack Webber across the top.

Directing my attention to Emily, I said, "I see you have Mr. Webber's file. Good."

I took the file from her and added, "Thank you, dear." The "dear" was for Jack's benefit.

Seeing a file with his name in bold letters across the top, Jack demanded, "Hey, what the hell is going on?"

"In due time, Jack. In due time." I was enjoying this.

Moving in front of Jack, I opened the file and began to peruse its contents. Throwing out an occasional "Hmm" or "Oh!" added a little to the dramatics.

Focusing on the file I began, "Now, Jack, it seems some of your lunches in L.A. and Vegas were with women."

"So, big deal. I talk to a lot of women."

Looking him straight in the eye, "So you do," I agreed. "However, I did a little investigating on an establishment in Vegas: 'Debbie's Dining at the Y.' At first I thought you were frequenting the Young Woman's Christian Association, but apparently this 'Y' stands for something else. Each bill is around $500. Interesting! They must have a hell of a lunch. Then there's 'Sunshine Delicious' in Los Angeles. Again, another very expensive dining experience, I see. And there are others. A *lot* of others. Do I need to go any further?"

"Where the hell did you get that?" he yelled. "I'm the marketing manager and my expense account is private."

That's when my patience began to wear thin. Just a little, mind you. I dropped my face in front of his—much like my drill sergeant did in the Marine Corps. I set him straight.

"Look, stupid, I'm the CAE, remember? I can go anywhere in this company I damn well please and look at anything I want. My authority comes from the board. Don, Phil, or you, it doesn't matter. I've got the power. Capisce?"

Turning his attention to Caroline, Jack blurted something that caught me off guard.

"CJ, we go back a long way. Are you going to let him do this to me?"

Turning to Caroline for her response, I saw something I'd seen before. Behind those beautiful eyes was someone else. Someone I didn't know. But apparently someone Jack did.

Shrugging her shoulders, "You did it to yourself, Jack. I'm sorry," she said blankly.

Jack's face had turned ash-white. I believe he'd finally "capisced." He knew I had him cold and he had no allies in that room.

"What do you plan to do with that file?" he asked as small beads of perspiration began to trickle down his forehead.

"Jack, I'm so glad you asked. Now you're talking sensibly. My answer depends on what you do in the next," glancing again at my watch, "57 minutes."

"If I resign, what happens to the file?"

I grinned, "What file?"

"You'll destroy it?"

"Trust me, Jack."

Holding out my hand to Emily, she passed me a pad and pen.

"Now write. You only have 56 minutes."

It took Jack about five minutes to write his resignation. Upon finishing the letter, he rose from his chair and handed it to Caroline. For a moment they just stared at each other. Though no words were exchanged, they were communicating about something. What? I sure didn't know.

Turning to me, he advised—quite eloquently—that I was the offspring of an unwed female dog. When finished, he turned to leave. As he approached the door, I called, "Webber?"

He turned.

"Didn't you forget something?" I said as I nodded toward the sniffling young lady.

Moving back toward her with great reluctance, Jack emotionlessly smiled and said, "Forgive me?"

The young lady responded with a twisted expression that was most likely an attempt to smile.

Turning again to leave, he stopped directly in front of me. His eyes pierced mine. If ever I saw rage in a man's eyes, it was then. Somehow I knew all this with Jack was not over. But for today, it was. I understand he was out of the building ten minutes after he left that room.

I turned to Caroline. I think she had been holding her breath the whole time.

"Okay?" I asked.

Caroline only nodded. Emily, the young temp, and Holly—who had been standing by the door since Emily came in—were all in shock. No one believed what had just happened. Me, neither.

"Rick, this meeting never took place," Caroline started.

"What meeting?" I turned to Emily and Holly. "Did we have a meeting?"

Both shook their heads no.

Moving to the young woman, I bent on one knee in front of her. Grabbing a clean handkerchief, I wiped the tears from her cheeks. As she began to smile I asked, "Are you okay now?" With a sniffle and a nod of her head, she indicated she'd be alright. Before rising to my feet, I asked her, "Did we have a meeting?"

Smiling broadly, she—like Emily and Holly—agreed silently there had been no meeting.

I rose and turned my attention to Emily.

"Take this file upstairs and give it personally to Mr. Carter. He's expecting it."

"But, Rick!" Emily said, surprised. "You said you'd destroy it."

"I know," I said, grinning like the Cheshire Cat. "I lied."

Chapter 7

Dinner that night was quiet for Caroline and me. Usually talkative about our respective days, we would pepper our conversation with teasing about intimate activities that lay ahead. But tonight both our minds were somewhere else.

I was bothered by Jack's comment to Caroline, referring to some sort of history between them. It was a surprising revelation. He called her "CJ." Her name is Caroline Jean and, of course, she has those initials on her handbag, but I had never heard anyone at the office call her CJ until that day. But what troubled me the most was the look in her eyes when Jack handed her his resignation. For a fraction of a second—only a heartbeat—I saw in Caroline's eyes a shadow I'd seen once before. That silent moment spoke of a secret they shared, something I judged went back many years.

I speculated Jack could be an ex-lover. But my gut told me no, this secret was not personal … it was business. That was my hunch, but anything more would be blind guessing. So, as a gambler, it was time to put my chips on the table and roll the dice. With Caroline, that roll would be in the form of a question.

"Caroline," I began calmly, "your association with Jack, will you tell me about it?"

Her eyes got big. I could tell the question rattled her, yet I sensed it wasn't unexpected.

"What do you mean?" she asked, trying to sound innocent, but failing. She was as phony as a three dollar bill.

I continued, "Well, to start with, I've never heard anyone call you CJ until today."

Caroline hesitated, obviously fishing for an answer. "Oh, that," she said, trying her best to brush it off. "He saw the initials on my purse ... so then called me that a couple of times."

"Makes sense," I said, nodding my head slightly like I was satisfied with her answer. My words and gestures were designed to put her at ease. It was a ploy on my part.

Quiet prevailed for several minutes before I picked up the dice and threw them again.

"Dear, what did Jack mean when he said you and he went back a long way?"

This blunt inquiry triggered an extreme reaction in Caroline. Caught off guard, I again glimpsed that "other" woman who I did not know, the one who shared some dark secret with Jack.

"Well, Mr. Morgan—if you must know everything about my life— I've known Jack for a lot of years. He used to date a roommate of mine in college. Now are you happy?"

I wasn't happy ... because it was obvious to me this confession only measured a portion of the truth. But I couldn't prove it, and I couldn't force her to tell me more. I had to let it go ... for now.

That night in bed, alone, I played the events of the day over in my mind. I focused mainly on two areas: Jack and Caroline's silent message and Caroline's defensive posture when I questioned her. There was far more to that relationship than met the eye. And it was about to have a profound effect on my relationship with Caroline.

One that would drive me closer to my friend in San Francisco.

It was a little before lunch when I heard a knock on my office door. It was Emily, asking if Chris could see me. I peered over the stack of files with great anticipation as I motioned to let him in. I knew what Chris had for me—a death certificate.

"So, Chris," I chimed while rising from my chair, "what do we have?"

"Well, Chief, I have a death certificate for Mr. Johnson."

"Excellent!" I said, taking it from his hand and motioning for him to have a seat. "Let's see what we have here."

Unfolding the three parts, I began to read.

"It looks like our Mr. Johnson did indeed die in Las Vegas. Cause of death, 'congestive heart failure.' Do you have any clue what 'congestive heart failure' is?"

"Not a clue, Chief," Chris responded, just as bewildered as I was.

Looking toward my door, "Emily!" I shouted. As she peered in, I asked, "Emily, do you know what 'congestive heart failure' is?"

"I'm only guessing, but I assume it's a heart attack," she answered.

"Hmm, thanks, Emily." Why couldn't we figure that out?

"What do you think, Chief?"

"I think I want you to find out who the company investigator was for this claim. I want to have a chat with him."

"Right, Chief. But since the file is missing, how will I find out?"

Chris posed a good question.

"Chris," I began with a slight smile, "let's really begin to shake up this game a little."

"Yeah, Chief?"

"Call Claims and let them tell you."

"But they'll have to go to the file, won't they?"

"Yes, Chris, they will. Let's see what happens."

Chris's perplexed look turned into a grin as he figured out exactly what I was up to.

It was about 3:00 P.M. when Chris returned to my office. Judging from the astonished look on his face, he had good news.

"So, Chris, what did you find?"

"Well, Chief, I went to Claims like you told me, and I asked the supervisor who the investigator would have been. She didn't know, so we went together down to Records to pull the file."

At that point I was dying to know her response when opening the file and finding only newspaper!

"Records said the file was missing."

My jaw dropped. I couldn't believe my ears.

"Chris, we just put it back a few days ago. How can it be missing?"

"I don't know, Chief, but Records show I turned it back in, and no one checked it out since then."

It was apparent someone had been one step ahead of us the whole time. And based on the limited information I had (and my gut feeling) the only person it could be was Jack. He probably grabbed the file before he left the building. But why? As the agent who sold the policy, why would he care about the death claim?

"But, Chief," Chris continued, "I did find out who the investigator was."

Chris's golden words brightened this otherwise cloudy day.

"Chris!" I exclaimed. "You're fantastic! Who is it?"

"Robert Nielsen out of Los Angeles," Chris responded with a big grin. "But, Chief, don't get too excited. He died about three years ago."

"Died? Shit." Falling back into my chair, my sunshine just got blocked by cloud cover again.

With my elbows on my desk and chin resting in my hands I moaned, "OK, Chris, give me the story from the top."

"Well, Chief, finding the box was missing, I asked Claims what office would have handled a Las Vegas investigation. They said Los Angeles. So I called L.A. and had them check their investigation files and found Robert Nielsen was the investigator."

"And how did you find out he's dead?"

"When I asked for his phone number the lady advised me he died a few years back."

I looked at Chris with admiration and said, "That was good work."

Chris seemed delighted to hear my words of praise. So before dismissing him, I repeated the compliment and reminded him again to keep everything he found to himself. He agreed.

Turning my chair to the window, I began commiserating with the Space Needle, my ghostly friend in the distance. We had a long talk about how this whole thing kept getting weirder by the minute. My curiosity was growing. What did Jack, missing files, a dead investigator, a twenty million dollar claim, and maybe Caroline have in common?

I was reluctant to suspect Caroline because of my personal feelings for her, but I had to keep her in the dark about what I was doing. So I decided it was time for some off-the-record digging. I picked up my phone and asked Emily to come into my office. As she walked through the door, I asked her to close it and directed her to sit.

I began, "Emily, your dad's a cop, isn't he?"

With a look of surprise to such a strange question, she answered, "Well, yes, Rick, he is. Why?"

"I need an investigator, someone not connected with the company. I want someone, maybe a retired detective, to do some work for me. Someone very street-smart and knows his way around, someone local."

"Sounds like you need my Uncle Vince," she said with a smile.

"Your Uncle Vince?"

"Yes, Uncle Vince. He retired from the Seattle PD a few years ago after thirty years, twenty of which as a homicide detective."

Hearing the word "homicide," my ears perked up.

"Does he have an investigator's license?" I asked.

"Yes, he does," she said proudly. "He does a lot of freelance work helping other departments solve cold cases."

Hearing "cold cases" was the clincher. I knew I wanted to talk with him.

I continued with Emily. "Could you contact your uncle and ask him to come and see me within the next few days?"

"Actually, the whole family's meeting for dinner tonight. I'll talk to him then."

"Good, but just one more thing, Emily. No one's to know about this. Not Chris, Mr. Carter, anyone. Understand?"

"No problem, Rick." With that, she was out the door.

Realizing I hadn't spoken to Caroline at all that day, and the clock was pushing 5:00 P.M., I gave her a call. I knew she was mad at me and I was a little concerned about her silence. Her phone was answered by Holly.

"Holly, Rick. Where's your boss?"

"Oh, hi, Rick. Didn't you know? She took a few days off."

"Oh, hmm ... No, I didn't know. Where did she go?"

"She didn't say, only that she would be gone a few days."

Bewildered she simply packed up and left without saying a word, I mumbled, "Just tell her I called, Holly, and to call me when she gets back."

This was the first time Caroline had taken time off and not told me. Turning toward the window and gazing out at the Space Needle, I started speaking softly to my ghostly friend again.

"Old buddy, I think Pandora's Box has just been opened."

At nine o'clock the following morning, I had a visitor. He was in his mid 50's, 5'10", stocky build, with sandy brown hair combed straight back and dressed in a two-piece brown business suit. As we shook hands, I noticed his were rough and square. From the scars on his face to the look in his eyes, there was every indication this was a man who'd been around the block a few times, a man who could handle himself very well in a dark alley. A man named Vince Guarino.

After the usual small talk, I came to the matter at hand.

"Vince, I have a small problem I want you to look into for me. Emily says you're good with cold cases. I have a death," pausing only long enough to hand him the death certificate, "that occurred about ten years ago in

Vegas. Our insured died of a heart attack. The problem is that a year before we had insured him for twenty million on the assumption he was in good health. In doing some in-house investigation to verify that supposition, we found our underwriting files missing. That concerns me. Further, upon examination of the claim file, the contents had been replaced by a copy of section A of the Los Angeles Times dated July 6, 1976."

Vince sat quietly until he heard what was in the claim file.

"That's a message if I've ever heard one!" he exclaimed. "Does that date mean anything?"

Shaking my head, I responded, "That, Vince, is the question. I'm sure it does. But what or to whom, I have no idea."

"Rick, you do know, based on what you're telling me, there's a strong possibility of fraud here."

Moving forward leaning on my desk, I responded seriously, "I know. The thought has crossed my mind more than once. And that's what you're going to help me find out. But for now, my copy of the Medical Examiner's report is missing. I want you to obtain a duplicate from the ME's office in Clark County, Nevada."

"Oh, Vegas," he said thoughtfully. "Just to let you know, the ME's office and the Sheriff's Department there don't take kindly to strangers poking around in their old files."

"Understood," I replied. "Just do the best you can for now. Also, a former investigator of ours who died a few years back, a Robert Nielsen from Los Angeles, was the original investigator on this claim. I want you to find his family. Like any good cop, he probably kept his own file. I want to know if there's anything about my insured in it."

With a slight grin, Vince knew what I was referring to—his little black notebook.

"Now, there's just one more thing. Recently we fired a man by the name of Jack Webber. Or, hmm, I should say officially he resigned. But it was forced. Jack was the agent who originally sold the policy some ten years ago. Somehow I think he has an involvement in this. How, I'm not sure. See if his name crosses the path."

"Sounds good. Give me a few days, and let's see what we find."

"Great, I'll send you an email confirming our agreement."

Rising from our seats, we shook hands. "I'll call you in a couple of days."

Stopping at the door, Vince turned back to me and said, "Rick, is there a reason why you just don't do all this yourself and save the expense of me doing it?"

I hesitated with my answer. But he already knew.

"There's someone here you don't trust, do you?"

He hit the nail square on the head.

"Let's just say for now I am your only contact in this company. And, don't be offended, that includes Emily."

Glancing back toward her door, he nodded, "Understood. Call you in a few days."

"Vince?"

"Yes."

"One more thing. Contact me on my cell."

Nodding his head, he opened the door and left.

I sat down, leaned back in my chair and swung my feet up onto my desk. Vince was right. There was someone I didn't trust, the same someone who I also wanted to protect, keeping her name out of it. Was it love, trust, the intimacy we shared that kept me wanting to believe Caroline wasn't anything more than an innocent bystander? I didn't know. The question was ... did I want to know?

CHAPTER 8

No news is good news? What a load of crap. Whoever came up with that phrase hadn't waited five days to hear from a "vacationing" Caroline. I hadn't heard from Vince since he headed for Vegas either, and I was getting nervous. This lack of news might be bad news on both fronts.

It was about 7:00 A.M. and I was fighting traffic on the floating bridge when my cell phone rang.

"Rick Morgan," I answered. "Hey, Vince! I was beginning to worry. Thought maybe you hit it big at blackjack and decided not to come home."

"Oh really?"

"Locked tight, huh?"

"Well, you did say they don't like anyone playing in their sandbox."

"No. Not the office. There's a coffee place right across the street."

"Yeah, that's the one. An hour? I'm in traffic, so if you get there first, order me a black coffee, will ya?"

"Right, see you soon."

An hour later, I walked into the coffee place. Vince was already seated at a small table in the back. He slid a black coffee to me as I sat down.

"Thanks," I said warmly before jumping straight into our conversation. "So I gather the ME's office in Vegas wasn't too thrilled with your request?"

"I'm lucky I wasn't taken out and planted in the desert," he said grimly. I don't think he was kidding.

"So, tell me. What happened?"

"Rick, let me tell you straight off. Someone with a lot of juice doesn't want me, you or anyone else asking questions regarding this case."

Hearing this initial report, my countenance sobered as well. Dropping my voice to a near-whisper, I urged, "Vince, tell me what happened."

"I went to Vegas the day after we talked, arriving about 10:00 P.M. Checked myself into the hotel on the strip where your Mr. Johnson died, per your email. The next morning I headed to the ME's office. Along the way, I stopped at the Sheriff's Department and introduced myself, explaining I was an ex-homicide detective from Seattle looking into an old case for an insurance company. You know, just a courtesy call. They were friendly enough and thanked me for stopping by. Then I went over to the ME's office. I gathered they were expecting me. Again, we made a little small talk and everything seemed cozy. I explained I was working for an insurance company and needed a copy of the ME's report for an old case. No problem until I mentioned the name. All of a sudden everyone clams up, and I learn that all the records for Mr. Johnson had been sealed by the court. Then they politely thanked me for stopping by—and don't let the door hit me on the way out."

Trying to collect my thoughts, that were chaotic after hearing that little story, I sputtered, "What the hell is going on here, Vince? My records are gone. I have a date that means nothing. And now I learn the court sealed the records!"

"Rick," Vince continued, "there's more. I decided to stay over a few days and just poke around the hotel on my own. You know, ask a few questions here and there. Came up with nothing except a shadow."

"Someone was following you?" I choked.

"Yeah, from the moment I checked in."

"It appears he was waiting for you."

"Exactly. Did you tell anyone about my trip down there?"

"No, Vince. I didn't."

"Well, somebody knows something."

"Yeah, and that concerns me," I replied quietly. "Did you get a good look at him? Could you describe him?"

"An older man, Caucasian, about 60, 5' 11", maybe 210 pounds."

"Would you remember him if you saw him again?"

"Better than that. I got a picture of him with my cell phone."

"You're kidding!"

"Nope. I'll email it to you."

"Any idea who he is?"

"No. But two things are for sure. He wasn't any good at tailing people, and he's an ex-con."

"An ex-con? How do you know?"

"If you were a cop as long as I was, you'd know. He had a tattoo on his upper right arm, a clock without hands. It symbolizes doing time. This guy has definitely spent time inside."

Having heard Vince's full report, I leaned back in my chair, rubbing the side of my face. My mind was racing. We said nothing for a few minutes. Sipping on my now-cooling coffee, I knew I needed to make a decision. So far, someone had gone to great lengths to conceal the facts of this claim, and no one had been hurt (that I knew of, anyway). But as Vince so eloquently stated, "someone with a lot of juice" was pulling the strings. How far would that "someone" go to protect their twenty million dollar secret? Men have been killed for far less. Added to all that, it seems our "someone" was one step ahead of me the whole time. So the question was: wrap it up and forget about it, or roll the dice and pray we don't crap out six feet under the Nevada desert?

Moving forward in my chair and leaning across the table, I began cautiously, "Vince, are you willing to move forward on this?"

Nodding slightly, "Yeah, I'm curious, and I don't like people following me," he responded without hesitation.

"It means another trip to Vegas," I added.

"I know the risks of being in the lion's den. I've been there before," Vince said.

"Yeah, but this time you won't be alone."

One of his eyebrows rose.

I was formulating a plan that required the very special talent and expertise of a man who knew everyone in Vegas, a man who knew how to open doors that were locked tight, a man who had a lot of favors owed to him, much like the one he owed me (don't ask). As Chief of Security for a major Strip hotel, this man was tough, and the word no wasn't in his vocabulary. He was an ex-LAPD cop who happened to be my friend. A man named Frank.

I pulled the cell phone from my pocket, scrolled down to "Frank" and pushed the button.

Three rings later, there was an out-of-breath "Hello" at the other end.

"Frank, it's Rick Morgan."

"Yeah, I know it's early, but I need a favor."

"No, I'm not in town and, no, it's not that kind of favor. Are you going to be in your office today?"

"After 11:00? Fine."

"No, an investigator named Vince Guarino who's doing some work for me needs a few doors in Vegas kicked opened."

"No, I'll have him call you. You guys can talk directly."

"No, he's an ex-Seattle homicide detective."

"Yes, you should have a lot in common. Frank, this whole thing is on the QT. It may involve a high roller."

"Right. I'll have him call you after lunch."

"Yes, go back to whatever you were doing. Or, *whoever* you were doing."

"Who?"

"Tell her I say hello. Sorry to interrupt your dictation."

"Yeah, you too. Later."

As I was shoving my phone back into my pocket, Vince asked curiously, "Dictation?"

Shaking my head, "Don't ask," I chuckled.

Chuckling as well, "Fine, I won't," Vince replied. "But knowing how deep this may go ... can this friend of yours be trusted?"

"I trust him," was my reply.

Vince nodded then added, "Just remember, we're not going up against some john trying to hide his indiscretions from his wife. Whoever this is has influence that goes to the courts or maybe higher. That makes them dangerous, maybe *very* dangerous, and so far they've known my every move."

Sitting back again, nodding in agreement, I quietly muttered, "I know, Vince. I know."

Before our meeting concluded, Vince had another serious question for me. It sent a shiver down my spine.

"Rick, are you licensed to carry?"

Squirming, "In Washington, Oregon and California," I responded.

"What do you have?"

"A Glock 23."

"Good weapon. Since you've decided to move forward on this," he continued, "you may want to keep it close-by. You may also want a pocket gun as a back up."

Understanding his street-wise advice, I nodded in agreement then changed the subject.

"Any leads on Nielsen?" I asked.

Shaking his head no, "I thought the ME report might take priority," he replied.

Nodding back, I agreed.

I gave Vince all the pertinent information about Frank and asked him to let me know what happens. Shaking hands, we agreed Vince would call as soon as he and Frank had something worth reporting.

Arriving at the office, there was a message from Caroline asking me to call. She was back.

I went to her office instead. Finding Holly away from her desk and Caroline's door ajar, I went in. She was sitting at her desk behind a mound of files. She glanced up with a smile, but no twinkle in her eye like I usually see when she greets me.

I started the conversation, trying to be upbeat.

"Hey, I missed you! Where have you been?"

"Oh, hi Rick," she said without enthusiasm. "I just needed a few days to myself, that's all."

"I was surprised you didn't tell me you were leaving," I pressed.

"I know. I'm sorry. But this whole thing with Jack upset me so. Then when you gave me the third degree, it just pushed me over the edge. I just needed to get away ... to think and to explore some other options."

Her reference to Jack brought to mind a thousand questions, but I sensed this was neither the time nor place to mention them.

"Think about what?" I asked cautiously.

With only a half-smile and some hesitation, "About us," she replied.

Sinking down into a wingback chair, her "us" answer triggered a bit of surprise. Though we had been, as Emily put it, joined at the hip on a daily basis for quite awhile, we never really talked about "us." I guess the conversation was long overdue, but not necessarily one I wanted to engage in now. I was still smarting from the mystery of Caroline and Jack.

"So tell me, dear," tip-toeing delicately with my question, "where have you been this last week?" I wondered if her answer would include the aforementioned asshole, Jack.

"Atlanta," she responded quietly.

"Atlanta? Didn't you go to school in Atlanta?" I fired back.

Caroline nodded her head as I continued.

"Right. Georgia Tech. So-o-o, did you stop and see the old alma mater?"

"Well, as a matter of fact, I did."

I could tell by the look on her face there was a long story to tell, but her voice restrained the eagerness to tell it. It was complicated, but I knew the topic of "us" was in the story somewhere.

"Caroline," I urged softly, "something's on your mind. What?"

She sat back in her chair and formulated her words carefully.

"Rick ... I've ... been offered a job with Georgia Tech."

My mind went blank. Talk about left field! All sorts of responses were whirling inside my head, but all I could do was sit there with a deer-in-the-headlights look.

"Rick, I need to know where you and I are. You told me so many times you loved me, yet I was never quite sure if you meant it. Sometimes you seem to be preoccupied with something or someone else. Is there someone else, Rick?"

Now there was a question I didn't want to answer! Yes, there was someone else. My friend in San Francisco. We'd never been physically intimate, so it was a different type of relationship. Something I didn't quite understand, yet was drawn to. But honestly, up until that connection I witnessed between Caroline and Jack, I never preferred one over the other. But now I felt estranged from Caroline. Burning questions left unanswered seemed to char my feelings for her. I was unsure, so I had to play the hand I was dealt, and play it very close to my chest.

"Caroline, at the moment there's no other woman in my life." My answer was a half- truth, but one she accepted readily for the moment.

"Rick," she began again, "I accepted the position. I was thinking, would you move to Atlanta with me?"

As I was looking into Caroline's eyes, the twinkle was beginning to return to them.

Leaning across her desk, I took her hand. She gave it willingly. As always, it was warm and soft. Looking deep into her blue eyes, I wondered if all those questions I had about her had merit or were just my imagination running wild. Reality? I did love Caroline very much. But even though she was beautiful, fantastic in bed, and a wonderful companion, somewhere deep inside me I questioned who it was I might be running away with. Would it be her or that "other" woman hiding in the shadow of her eyes?

For now I just needed to think.

"I gave Phil my resignation this morning," she said. "I'll be leaving at the end of the month."

"That's six days from now," I gulped.

"Yes, Rick, it is. I'm taking the redeye back to Atlanta Friday night, and will be back Monday morning. Tuesday will be my last day. You need to give me an answer by then."

Moving behind her desk, I pulled her from her chair. Slipping my arms around her small waist, "Honey, you're putting me in a tough position. I have a great job, a home, friends, connections—a West Coast life. How can I just hang it all up in a week, pack up and go to Atlanta?"

Moving out from my grip, Caroline said matter-of-factly, "Rick, you need to make a decision. Do you want to spend the rest of your life with me or not? It's your decision."

Her words were final.

It was Friday afternoon about 5:00. I had just wished Caroline a safe trip, promising her an answer upon her return, when my cell phone rang. The caller ID said "Vince." I swiveled my chair to the window.

"Vince, give me some good news."

I slumped in my chair hearing his answer.

"Still sealed?"

"Interesting. Frank had no clout?"

"Really?"

"Is Frank with you now?"

"Good. Put this on speaker phone."

"Rick, it's Frank."

"Hey, Frank, I hear we're batting zero."

"Man, I've never seen the ME's office so tight-lipped."

"Did anyone there seem to take a personal interest in your request?" I asked.

Vince answered, "No, not really. It seemed they took the sealing of the records very seriously. No one would say a word."

"OK, what do you guys think the next step should be?"

"Well," Vince continued, "Frank and I discussed that on the way back to his office. Frank is familiar with that ME. He's retired now. Frank thinks we should have a little talk with him. ME's are like cops. They tend to keep private records."

"And I would love to see them!" I added enthusiastically. "Frank, do you think he will talk with us?"

Hearing them both laugh I asked, "OK, will you let me in on the joke?"

Frank continued. "Rick, the guy's an old degenerate gambler who has three major vices, besides cards and dice: blond, brunette and redhead."

"And you're thinking with maybe a small gift—a token of our appreciation—he might give us everything we need?"

"I think a gift would make him very talkative," Frank said.

"Do you have someone in mind?" I asked.

With a small chuckle, the response was, "As a matter of fact, I do. She's great at taking dictation."

"Oh-h, I think I know who you mean," I said. "Do you think you can find him?"

"Given time," Vince interjected, "we'll find him."

"OK, you convinced me. Let me know when you do. I want to talk with him personally."

"You got it."

Hanging up the phone, I fell back in my chair and began rubbing my face vigorously. Caroline, the problems in Vegas ... I was a bit overwhelmed. I needed time to think. I grabbed my cell and pushed a speed-dial number. Moments later, a friendly voice was on the other end.

"Hey, it's me. Dinner in Carmel tomorrow?"

"Wonderful. Pick you up at noon?"

"Great. See you then."

I buzzed Emily.

"Would you please book me a flight to San Francisco tonight?"

CHAPTER 9

Early Sunday evening, I made my way through the suburban maze to that little patch of grass resting high on a ridge above Seattle's city lights, that place I call home. The trip left me exhausted, but my San Franciscan had been charming and our time together in Carmel exhilarating. Although I still couldn't put my finger on the reasons why, my weekend away did help me push aside the erratic questions whirling through my head long enough to answer one question. Clearly, my desire for Caroline was not strong enough to include Atlanta.

Pulling into my driveway, I clicked the remote to open the double garage door. The fatigue I was feeling got a shot of adrenaline when I saw a familiar red Corvette parked in its usual spot. I had a visitor. Wondering how long it had been there, I touched the hood. It was cold.

I quietly opened the door from the garage. The living room had a faint glow that fell somewhere between twilight and shadow. The view of the city through the large picture window was lovely. When nights are cold and crisp, the city lights twinkle.

As I was walking to the center of the room, I tripped over a pair of high heels. I picked them up. Just beyond was a dress, then nylons, still farther a bra and panties. On the end-table beside the couch was a cold pepperoni pizza in an open box. Two pieces were missing. A warm, slightly-dented can of Dr. Pepper sat next to it. Approaching from behind, I leaned over the couch to find a body wrapped loosely in a comforter, sound asleep. It was Caroline. The reflection of the glittering city lights danced across her face and figure, accentuating her charms. She was one of the most beautiful women I've ever seen. I couldn't help but smile.

I sat down on the couch's edge, and Caroline began to stir. I leaned and kissed her softly on the forehead, pulling the comforter up snugly to her neck. Opening her eyes, she smiled.

"Hi-i-i," she mumbled while slightly stretching.

"Hey, babe, how long have you been here?"

"Oh. I don't know. I guess I got here about 5:00. My flight got in early this afternoon. I went home and thought about you and decided to surprise you with some dinner. But you weren't home. I guess I fell asleep waiting."

I held up her heels and did a sideways look toward the scattered clothing.

She smiled. "You know I can't sleep with my clothes on." Then, glancing across the room she asked, "What time is it?"

"About 8:00," I replied.

"8:00?" she asked, surprised. "Where have you been?"

"Since you decided to go out of town, I flew down to San Francisco. I just got home."

Her smile faded quickly when she heard "San Francisco."

"Oh," she began quietly. "Did you have a good trip?"

Nodding my head, "Yeah, it was fine. I just needed to get out of town and think about your question."

"You mean about us?"

"Yes, dear, about us."

"And what did you come up with?"

"That's a loaded question, babe."

"Rick, I'm going to ask you a question, and I want the truth."

"Ok."

"Do you love me?"

Looking directly into her beautiful eyes, "Yes, Caroline, I do. I love you very much," I answered sincerely.

"Then what's been holding you back?"

The answer to that one was complicated. Finding Cindy in the shower with another man after ten years of trusting her had taken its toll on my willingness to give myself completely to another woman ... any woman. But my relationship with Caroline was different. We spent every waking minute together. Was it fair to keep caution signs up with her when she was clearly not Cindy? But as much as I wanted to give her my heart, there was still a nagging suspicion she wasn't the person I thought she was. Was this just my old wound getting in the way, or was my uneasiness grounded in something real? I kept thinking about the look she had given Jack.

"Holding me back?" I asked.

"Yes, Rick. Holding you back. Why do you run away to San Francisco every few weeks? And if you love me, why haven't you ever asked me to go along?"

"We did go to San Francisco a few weeks ago. Remember?" I countered.

"Yes, I remember. But that was business. Rick, is there someone down there I should know about?"

I didn't answer her question, but apparently the look on my face did. Caroline pried deeper.

"Who is she?"

Searching carefully for the right words, I took too long to speak, so Caroline asked again. This time vigorously.

"Who IS she, Rick?"

"Just someone I met after my divorce that helped me out of my depression."

"And?"

"And what?"

"Is she married, single?"

"Single, but with a significant other."

"Woman?"

"No, it's a guy," I answered quietly.

"What's her name?"

Dodging her question, I offered, "Caroline, she's just a friend. That's all."

"Then tell me her name."

"Why? It doesn't matter."

"Yes, Rick, it does. It matters to me."

"Yeah, well, what about Jack Webber?" I countered defensively. "You know, he said you two go back a long way. I heard him call you CJ, something nobody I know has ever called you. You told me he used to date your girlfriend. Fine, I can live with that. But the look you two exchanged when he handed over his resignation went far deeper than him being just your girlfriend's lover. What is it, Caroline? What secret is it that you and he share? And, if there were nothing between you two, why so damn defensive when I brought it up last week? And why now are you suddenly running back to Atlanta?"

Pouncing on Caroline the way I did made her cry.

"Oh, Rick," she began. "It's just so complicated. You wouldn't understand."

"Understand what?"

Burying her head deeper into the couch, she began sobbing loudly. Though I wanted to push her farther for answers, it seems I had already pushed her over the brink. More questioning would be futile. But before there could ever be an "us," I would need to know what the secret was or had been between her and Jack.

Pulling her to me, I held her until the tears began to subside.

Moving her head into my chest she asked in a very small voice, as though she was afraid to know the answer, "Rick, are you and your friend lovers?"

I leaned her back slightly so I could see her. I brushed the hair from her eyes.

"No, dear, we're not. We've never slept together or even come close. We just talk."

"Nothing else?"

"No, nothing else. Now it's my turn," I said. "Were you and Jack lovers?"

Shaking her head, "Oh, Rick, no. He's never touched me."

"Then what, Caroline? What is it with Jack?"

Burying her head in my chest, she never answered. Beginning to cry softly again, she sniffed, "Rick, I do love you. Why can't it be different?"

I tipped my head down, with my lips near her ear and whispered, "I guess ... because ... it is what it is."

Pulling me tighter, she whispered back, "Take me upstairs and love me, Rick. Love me like never before. Like something in a romance novel."

Instinctively, I swooped her up in my arms. We kissed passionately as I carried her to the bedroom. My hands marveled at the touch of her silky skin as the comforter partially covering her naked body slipped off and dragged on the floor. Our embrace continued as we flung ourselves on the bed, both tugging insistently at my shirt, my belt, my pants.

For the next four hours, we loved each other as though it was our last time. I think we both knew it was.

When we heard twelve dongs from the grandfather clock in the foyer, we were lying quietly in the dark. The wee hours of the morning were upon us, and there was still so much to say.

"Rick," Caroline began quietly. "You're not going to Atlanta with me, are you?"

"No, dear, I'm not."

"Tell me, is the reason me, your friend in San Francisco, or something else?"

"Something else," I muttered.

"Is it Jack? Is he your reason for not going?"

"Partially," I said.

"Rick, honestly, Jack means nothing to me."

I shifted to my side so I was facing her.

"Caroline, I can't be second fiddle with anyone. You said he's never touched you. I believe it. But there's something about you and Jack that bothers me. Something I can't put my finger on. You two hold a secret. What? I can't begin to imagine. But it's a bond that's far more powerful than your love for me. And you know it."

Turning away, "I need to go," she said in a shaky voice.

"Why? What is it that you would leave me for? To keep a secret?"

Caroline turned back and put her hand on my cheek. "Rick, I wish ... I pray every night I could ..."

"Then tell me now, Caroline, why you have to run off to Atlanta?"

Her eyes became moist, her voice broken.

"Because if I don't, I'll ..."

She never finished. With a kiss to my cheek, she wrapped the comforter around her smooth naked body and went back to the living room. I followed. Sniffling, she gathered her clothes silently and got dressed quickly. She walked to the door and gripped the knob. Hesitating, she turned to me.

"Rick, I ..."

"What, Caroline?" I asked, desperate to know something before she left.

"Rick, be careful," she warned me. "Not everything is what it appears to be."

"Even you?" I asked.

Her weary eyes answered before her lips did.

"Yes, Rick, even me."

As I watched the door close behind her, my heart dropped to my stomach. I moved to the front window, my eyes following the Corvette until the taillights were out of sight. Hurt and dejected, I flopped down on the couch and stared out at the city lights. Somehow they had lost their twinkle. I touched my cheek. I could still feel her last kiss. I smiled a hollow smile, reached absent-mindedly for a piece of pizza and took a bite. It was cold and stiff ... like cardboard ... like me. I threw it back into its box.

It was late, and I needed to sleep. I didn't have the heart to go back to my bed alone, so I stretched out on the couch and pulled the comforter over me. I brought it up close to my face so I could inhale the sweet scent of Caroline that lingered. Silently, in a room with a glow somewhere between twilight and shadow, I closed my eyes just as my drifting thoughts were pondering Caroline's final words ... "Yes, Rick, even me."

CHAPTER 10

Many people believe executives have enormous amounts of free time for playing golf at the country club, sailing yachts and leisurely dining at the most extravagant restaurants. It was a Monday, and this executive had files on his desk ten deep. Caroline had been gone a week. I was busy and lonely and irritated. And my only wish was to finish my crummy lunch, a dry turkey on rye from the local food cart, before the next phone call. But somehow my recent wishes were not coming true. I got a call. Of course.

Hearing that all-too-familiar buzz, I pushed the speaker button of my phone. With my mouth full of dry rye, I still managed to blurt, "What?"

It was Emily. "Rick, Kathy Gibson's on the line. She needs to speak with you."

"Kathy who?" I knew the name but couldn't place it.

"Kathy Gibson. She's the office manager for the Santa Barbara satellite."

"Is it important?"

"She said it is."

With a sigh I said, "Put her through."

"Would you like me to wait so you can swallow first?"

"Smartass," I replied.

Emily laughed. I picked up my phone.

"Rick Morgan," I managed while forcing down the last swallow.

"Hi, Mr. Morgan, my name is Kathy Gibson. I'm the office manager here in Santa Barbara, California."

What a pleasant voice! My ears perked up. There was something there … something in her tone. The sound of innocence and sweetness mingled with the sexual resonance of late-night FM.

"Hey, maybe this day isn't so bad after all," I thought.

"Kathy, how are you today?"

"Well, Mr. Morgan …"

I interrupted, "Please, call me Rick."

"Well, thank you, Rick. I will," she continued. "Things are moving smoothly here in the office, but I'm not sure if we are totally complying with company policy."

"I understand completely," I lied. Actually, I did not understand. I've never known a manager who gave a damn if their office was within company guidelines or not. But if this lady with the sexy voice had concerns, who was I to argue?

"Kathy, do you have the latest manager's manual?"

"No, I'm fairly new here, and if I do have one, I have no idea where it would be."

"Well, we can fix that easy enough. I'll just email you one right now."

"Wonderful," she said.

Since she was new, I welcomed her to the company and offered to tell her my version of its history. She explained to me, sweetly I might add, although she was new to management in Santa Barbara, she was not new to the company. She had been in the L.A. Claims Department prior to Santa Barbara.

Being the CAE of a major insurance company puts me on a pedestal for everyone to look at and scrutinize. Not that I gave a damn about it when Caroline was around, but the idea is that I must always be professional and above reproach in everything I say and do. Now, taking all that into consideration, I thought, "What the hell, let's gamble!" and tried a little wit and charm on this lady with the lovely voice. Doing so produced a positive response accompanied by a delightful giggle. And I just love giggles! We chatted briefly about claims—big ones, little ones, and I somehow even mentioned really big claims such as Jack Webber's. It was odd I even mentioned him, but I guess he was on my mind more than I cared to admit. She said she knew the man, but not well.

After milking the chit-chat for all it was worth, our conversation had gone about as far as it could on a professional level. But I wanted to talk to this woman again, so I took a shot in the dark.

"Kathy, let me give you my cell number. If you have any questions, please feel free to call me personally."

"Why, thank you, Rick. That's so very nice of you."

With a grin from ear to ear I replied, "That's quite alright."

At this point, something extraordinary happened. Sensing our conversation was drawing to a close, Kathy started a flirtation shtick that was quite obvious. My gamble paid off!

"Well, Mr. Morgan ... Rick," she said with a playful giggle, "there may be more to you than that charming voice. Perhaps I *will* have questions of a personal nature that will warrant a call to your cell phone."

"Indeed? I look forward to talking with you again, then," I replied.

"We'll see," she returned in a distinctly sultry tone.

After saying goodbye, I snatched the last morsel of sandwich and turned toward the window. The sky was gray, and it was drizzling. Another normal Seattle day. I addressed my friend the Space Needle, "What do you think, old buddy?"

As usual, he said nothing. But his silence, as I finished chewing my lunch, allowed me time and space to think. (That's why he's my "Space" Needle.) I decided I would surely hear from Kathy Gibson again. And if not, at least she got my blood flowing. Food for thought. And some naughty thoughts at that ...

As I watched the rain trickle down the window, I was suddenly overtaken by curiosity. I walked to the outer office.

"Emily, I'm heading down to Personnel."

"Rick, you haven't been there for a week. Old habits die hard?"

Responding with a sarcastic, "Smartass," I was out the door.

"Holly, my favorite!" I announced, walking into Personnel.

"Hey, Rick," she returned with a smile.

"How's the new boss?"

Glancing toward her door, "She's not Caroline," Holly answered gloomily.

Moving behind her desk, I touched her shoulder lightly, "Yeah, I know. You miss her, don't you?"

Wiping some mist from her eyes, "What can I do for you?" she asked.

"Do you have a picture of Kathy Gibson in Santa Barbara?"

"Did you look on the computer?"

"No, I didn't know you could."

"All managers have their picture in the database. But she's only been there a short while, so maybe not. Let me see."

After several minutes of frustration and keyboard pounding, "This darn thing is locked up again," she huffed.

75

"Time to call the brain trusts," I said jokingly, referring to the idiots in IT.

"If Caroline was here, she would fix it," Holly whined.

What did Holly just say?

"Holly, what was that you just said?"

She looked up at me and repeated, "If Caroline was here, she would fix it."

I was puzzled. "Caroline knew about computers?"

"Yes, didn't you know? She has a degree in computer something."

"From Georgia Tech?" I asked.

"That's right. And a masters from someplace, I don't remember where, but something to do with computers."

"You're kidding?" I sputtered. "Caroline never told me about her abilities!"

"Well, Caroline was always one to protect her past. Oh, it looks like my computer is up and running again! I guess banging on the keyboard really does work!"

She chuckled at the absurdity of it all.

"Now, that was Kathy Gibson in Santa Barbara, right?"

My thoughts were now on Caroline, so I just nodded in answer to Holly's question.

"No, nothing on her," she said after scanning the screen. "Let me check another file ... Sorry, Rick. No photo."

"Well, it was just a thought. Thanks for checking."

Walking to the door, I turned to Holly with one more question.

"Holly, where did she come from?"

"Kathy or Caroline?"

"Kathy."

"I believe she worked in the Claims Department in Los Angeles. Before that, San Francisco."

"San Francisco?" I muttered. "Was she there the same time Jack Webber was?"

"Hold on. Let me see ... yes, she transferred to L.A. the same week he came here to corporate."

"Doing what?"

"Claims."

"Hmm. Interesting."

"Does it mean something, Rick?"

"Probably not."

Back at my office, I closed the door and swung my chair to the window. I was now thoroughly confused. It wasn't long into my conversation with Kathy that I felt there was an agenda on her part. An office manager contacting *me* regarding compliance is automatically suspect. But if my suspicion was correct, what was her agenda? And it turns out she worked with Jack in San Francisco and didn't mention it when I brought him up. In fact, she said she didn't know him very well. I can't imagine any woman working for Jack and not knowing everything about him. He would make sure she did. And San Francisco is such a small office. Intimate, even. Case in point was the Peter, Paul, and Mary incident! And why transfer to claims in L.A. when Jack came to HQ? Was I being paranoid or was I being an amazingly adept auditor-detective?

And then there was Caroline the computer wiz. After everything we'd been through she never told me *that*. Why?

But what bothered me most was that common ingredient that kept popping up in both my business and personal affairs. Jack. That jackass, Jack. No wonder I talked about him even when chatting up a woman on the phone. He was everywhere! But how did he fit in? Was there a link to Kathy now, too? After all, they did work for the same company, in the same office, at the same time. But there was something so alluring about Kathy. How could I resist pursuing her if she gave me a chance? Still, my gut twinged "danger." Why?

They say good news and deaths always come in threes. It was mid-afternoon that same day when my cell phone rang. It was Vince.

"Vince, give me some good news."

"You found him? Great. When can I see him?"

"Back when?"

"You're kidding? A month?"

"Fine, keep your man on it, and let me know when he's back."

"Right."

Apparently my retired Medical Examiner, a Dr. Jack Takahashi, was on some sort of trip and wouldn't be back for a month. I would have to wait. Could I be that patient?

Even though I replayed Kathy Gibson's sweet, sensual voice in my head many times over, I didn't actually hear from her again for about a week.

Emily's page echoed from my phone, "Rick, line one."

Picking up the phone, I responded with my usual cheery disposition.

"Hello, this is Rick Morgan. How may I help you?"

"Hi, Rick, this is Kathy in Santa Barbara."

"Kathy, my favorite, how are you today?" I asked warmly. The sound of her voice made my heart skip a beat.

"Well, your favorite is getting back to you regarding this manual you sent me. I've just read the whole thing and honestly don't understand half of it. This will take some time."

"Hey, I can help if you need it," I said, oozing charm. Then I couldn't resist adding a wisecrack. "But they're designed with simplicity because they're for managers."

"Oh, a little sarcastic today, aren't we?" she continued in a most playful tone.

"I prefer contentious, but sarcastic will work fine," I explained with serious mock-patience.

We both laughed out loud, pleased with our round of verbal sparring. But behind my laughs, I had a different line of questioning in mind and had promised myself I would not get too distracted by her silky voice if I heard from her again. So I changed the subject and the tone slightly.

I *had* to ask, "Kathy, I understand you worked in the San Francisco office about eleven years ago."

There was silence on the other end.

"Kathy, are you still there?"

"Uh, yes, Rick." My question caught her off guard. She was nervous.

"How well did you know Jack Webber, the manager?"

Again there was a pause before she answered.

"I really didn't know him all that well," she replied. "He was just my boss."

"Do you remember a double key-man insurance policy he wrote at twenty million each?"

"Uh, well … uh, no, I really don't. When you and I spoke last week you mentioned Jack and some big policy, but I didn't really remember it. That was a long time ago. Why?"

"Oh, it doesn't matter. Just a bit of information I ran across the other day."

I found it odd she didn't remember, or claimed she didn't. Twenty million dollar policy, twice, is a number no one in the industry easily forgets. It's memorable. And besides that, Jack's ego would be huge!

But I moved away from my questions regarding Jack, trying to re-engage her in banter. She began to open back up and did so for the next hour. As our conversation began to wind down (we both had to get back to work) my curiosity was winding up, wondering what she looked like. Was she as sexy as her voice? I thought of asking her to send a picture, but that seemed professionally unethical or at least it would be if she found the request offensive. Not that I hadn't tiptoed oh-so-slightly around it already. But somehow I didn't think Kathy was worried about either of us crossing a line. So I took a shot.

I happened to know all of the California offices had celebrated Mardi Gras with office parties this year. One of the California managers is originally from Louisiana and came up with the idea. I heard many employees "masked" like they do in New Orleans.

"So tell me, Kathy, what were you for Mardi Gras? Did you wear a costume?"

"I was a madam," she said plainly.

"A what?" I asked, knowing full well what a madam was, of course.

"A madam," she repeated.

"You mean the kind that tells you to leave the money under the pink kitty?"

"Woo!" she chirped with enthusiasm. "You've been here before!"

"Yeah, and you were too expensive," I fired back.

"Expensive, maybe, but I'll bet you got your money's worth."

"And I'll bet you got a piece of the action."

"In more ways than one," she said with that sensuous giggle.

We both laughed heartily.

"You don't believe me, do you?" she poked.

"I believe you." At least I thought I did.

"I'll just send you a picture to prove it."

Wow! Bingo! Yahoo! Jackpot! I was going to see what Kathy looked like ... and in a very sexy prostitute get-up, no doubt! Of course, my response was a little more subdued.

"Yeah, I'll believe it when I see it," I said stubbornly. "But one thing, make sure you don't violate any obscenity laws sending it over the internet."

"Well, I guess the picture I had in mind just won't work then. I don't want to break any laws," she said demurely.

I knew she was teasing about the picture. At least I thought she was. But now she had my imagination going wild. Something she intended to do, I'm sure.

"But," she continued, "there's one stipulation."

"Great," I said. "There's always a stipulation."

"You send me one of you."

"Hey, I didn't do Mardi Gras."

"No, silly, just a regular picture."

She knew exactly what I looked like long before she made that first call. My picture and biography are in the company database. But playing her game was fun, refreshing after the loss of Caroline. I had a great picture of me next to my Mustang in front of my house. I sent it to her as soon as we hung up. I received an email shortly after.

"Well, Rick, the women in the brothel say you're cute. They want to know if you'll take them for a ride ... in your car, that is."

Kathy was great at keeping a joke going. Plus, she was an artist when it came to flirting and sparring. She was witty, had a comeback for everything, and thought fast on her feet ... a woman after my own heart.

The photo attached to her email took me by surprise. It was a stunning woman lying on a snowy white rug, with her elbows on the floor and her chin propped up on her hands. She was gazing into the camera with the most beautiful face. Her long, dark hair fell across her shoulders just barely touching the rug, as were her breasts that showed just enough cleavage to see they were full. Her eyes were incredibly blue with a piercing look that, even in a picture, seemed to be burrowing right through me. Her smile was incredible, as though inviting me to come and join her. This woman was drop-dead gorgeous and surpassed my wildest imaginings of what she looked like.

As stimulating as the picture was, it didn't show any part of her body except for the top side of her nice breasts. From what I did see, I could make the assumption that she was more than physically fit, and her body was probably spectacular. But ... since this was *not* the photo promised, I emailed right back.

"Hey, I thought you were doing the madam thing?"

Within moments I had a response.

"Sorry, wrong picture."

"Yeah, I bet," I said aloud. Kathy was beginning to remind me of my ex-wife, especially in the slyness department. They aren't called foxes for nothing.

Attached to her response was another picture. In this one Kathy was dressed like a madam out of the 1800's. With her long, dark hair flowing down across a very nice set of shoulders, wearing an extremely low-cut dress with her bosom pushing out the top, obviously confirming my first thoughts about her breasts. And with a most sultry look on her face Kathy definitely looked the part. I bet she was the hit of the party, and if she wasn't, the men there were blind and stupid. I saved that photo to my hard drive. And I do mean hard.

The next morning, I called Kathy. I had a plan.

"Kathy, how's my favorite?"

"I don't know. I haven't talked to her today. But as soon as I do, I'll let you know."

"Smartass," I retaliated. This was met with a bubbly giggle. "Interesting news ... I'm heading to L.A. this weekend ..."

"Are you going to come and see me?" she interrupted before I could even finish.

"How about dinner Saturday night in Santa Barbara?" I asked.

"I would love to!" she exclaimed without hesitation.

"Great!" I said. "Email me your address, and I'll call you later."

Wonderful! I had a date with a beautiful woman, 1126 miles from home, on Saturday night. After hanging up the phone, I sat basking in the thought of dinner with Kathy. There was an excitement in me about this rendezvous ... and a fear of equal proportion.

I looked at my reflection in the office window. No doubt a lot had changed in me over the years and I wasn't the athletic young man I used to be, but I liked to think I was still attractive. Would Kathy? Putting ego aside (both fragile and inflated, depending on the moment), I had a hunch she would.

And I also had another hunch. I asked Emily to have Chris come see me.

Sticking his head through the door, Chris asked, "You wanted me, Chief?"

I motioned with my hand for him to come in and have a seat.

"Chris, I'm going to be gone a few days, and there's something I want you to do while I'm away."

"Sure, Chief, anything."

"I want to know who handled the Johnson case in Claims. And keep it on the QT."

"Right, Chief."

On my desk is an oversized calendar pad that I scrawl all my appointments on. I've always been the type of guy who needs to see the whole picture before me, whether it's daily operations or planning a trip.

- Friday evening, fly into Burbank. Rent a car and stay with my old friend Steve (that is, if he's sober enough to remember I'm coming)
- Saturday afternoon head north to Santa Barbara — and hopefully to a nice, quiet, romantic dinner with Kathy
- Since dinner will probably run late, a hotel in the area might be a wise investment
- Sunday, my friend in San Francisco
- Monday morning, fly home from SFO

I thought it couldn't be better. I was wrong.

CHAPTER 11

"The best laid plans of mice and men often go awry." This was the theme of the day.

It was early Friday afternoon and I still hadn't found a room in Santa Barbara for Saturday night. The town was booked solid ... story of my life.

With every option exhausted, I called Kathy and told her what was going on. I was expecting her to say, "That's OK. We can do it another time," or "I'm sorry it didn't work out." But no, to my surprise, she made a completely unexpected suggestion.

"Did you try Kathy's Hotel?"

I'm very seldom at a loss for words, but this rendered me speechless. After a moment of silence and still at a loss for any kind of rational or interesting comeback I blurted, "No, I didn't. Do they only take cash?"

To my continuing surprise, there was laughter on the other end.

"Cash is fine as long as you place it under the pink kitty. But I was actually thinking of another kind of payment."

"Another kind?" I asked, starting to get my balance back. "Well now, what do you have in mind?"

"We'll see," she said, sweet and sexy. Kathy enjoyed being a tease.

"We'll see? Does that mean I might need a shot of Vitamin B?"

"Woo, Rick, from what I hear, you don't need any help."

"Oh, really? Now, who have you been talking to?"

My question caused her to stumble.

After a few seconds of silence, I said, "Kathy? Are you still there?"

"Oh, yes, sorry. I just got interrupted."

Before I could quiz her further, Kathy said she was needed. She'd talk to me later. Saying goodbye, my mind launched into full-tilt racing mode. What just happened? This woman I've never met in person invited me to spend the night at her house, suggesting slyly there may be more on the menu than just dinner. I wasn't used to women being that bold, at least not this quickly and from a phone flirtation. So I have to admit I found myself a bit leery of this dark road, not knowing who else may have traveled it and with what frequency. Maybe even Jack? But another concern was Kathy's comment about my sexual abilities. Was she just guessing … playing? But if that was the case, why did my question make her lose her steam? Who would she have spoken to that knew anything of my sexual prowess (or not)? Caroline? She was the only person I could think of that Kathy could have encountered since my divorce, unless she knew people in Las Vegas! The puzzle just seemed to be getting bigger. But, speaking of Vegas, I already knew I would take the bet and roll the dice on Kathy. I pushed my concerns to the back burner … for now. The big question was will this be an easy pass or a crap?

"Rick," Emily chirped coming through the door. "I have your ticket and itinerary. You'll be back Monday morning?"

"Emily, how could I ever leave you? You know you're my favorite," I replied, smiling.

"No, Rick, your friend in San Francisco is."

Chuckling, I picked up my bag and headed for the door.

"I'll see you Monday, Emily."

As I opened the door, Emily called out, "Rick?"

Turning to face her, she continued, "One of these days you won't be coming back."

"Then, my love," I countered, jutting my chin toward the office, "all this will be yours."

Pulling into Santa Barbara Saturday evening, I was running an hour late. It was nearing twilight, and the sun was glowing red on the horizon. I had called Kathy earlier for advice on any shortcuts since I was late. She seemed amused. But her directions were perfect, and I found her condo easily after winding through the hilly backstreets.

Kathy lived in a standard condo project of about eight units, all separated with little yards and white picket fences. They were all two-story units with single-car garages. I guessed from the outside they probably had three bedrooms and not much square footage. Parking was easy.

I went to her door wondering what I was doing. With my ears feeling the deep pounding of my heart, and the sands of the Sahara Desert sitting in my throat, I knocked on her door and nervously waited. Hearing footsteps approaching from inside and then a "thunk" of the deadbolt, the door slowly opened.

There stood a woman even more beautiful than her pictures revealed. Kathy was about 5' even, 110 pounds, with long, beautiful dark hair falling across straight, soft shoulders. She was wearing a cream-colored blouse that fit snugly across her breasts, outlining their above-average size and mouthwatering shape. With the top two buttons undone, just enough cleavage peeked out to stimulate my mind and body with indecent fantasies. Her matching pants clung to her lower abdomen and thighs with a snugness that had only one purpose, the enhancement of a very nice set of hips. With 3-inch open-toed heels, very little was left to my imagination.

Without a word we both let our eyes drop, absorbing the crucial parts of the other's body, then back up reconnecting with direct eye contact. Hers beamed with pleasure. I guess I met her approval. With a big, welcoming smile, Kathy gave me a life-sized hug. She appeared at ease wrapping her arms snugly around me, forcing her breasts to push tightly against my lower chest. I hugged her back with equal enthusiasm, causing my manhood to press firmly against her tight abdomen. Gently and without permission, I kissed the top of her head. Her hair was soft on my lips and filled my lungs with the sweet scent of wildflowers. Her arms gripped my back just a little tighter, as though she was trying to absorb me. For that moment, it was like I'd known this woman all my life and our bodies were familiar with physical intimacy. It was a very strange and wonderful feeling indeed.

Kathy was the first to speak, pretending to be annoyed at my tardiness.

"Well, Rick, I'm glad you finally decided to show up."

"Traffic was awful," I said with a scowl. "I was in a traffic jam from Ventura to Santa Barbara."

"On the phone you said Oxnard," she corrected with more teasing.

"You say potato, I say Ventura ... but I'm finally here!"

"And I'm so glad," she said with a twinkle in her eye.

And after meeting this sweet little package face-to-face, the feeling was mutual.

"Come on in," she invited.

By the tone of her voice and her body language, I felt a little like the fly being invited by the spider, but I decided quickly that I was a willing fly … especially when I noticed, as I was following her into the living room another body part caught my attention, one that snugly filled her pants. Wow!

Forcing my thoughts to retreat from fantasyland, I managed to speak.

"So, what's on the agenda tonight for dinner?"

"It's a surprise," she said.

"Will I like it?"

"Maybe," she said coyly.

"You're not going to do sushi on me are you?"

"Heavens no, I hate sushi!"

"Let me guess, then." I put the back of my hand against my forehead, with my head tilted and eyes closed. "I'll bet we're going to do … let me see now … it's coming … Mexican!"

"How did you know?" she asked, with her eyes squinting, and a frown on her face. "You cheated, didn't you?"

"I just got here. How could I cheat?"

"I'm not sure, but somehow I know you cheated," she scolded me playfully.

Moving back to the entryway, I picked up a note I had noticed. Something about dinner reservations at 7:30 at some Mexican restaurant whose name I couldn't pronounce. In doing so, my eyes briefly caught another note: "Only four months to go. Yippee!" It was signed AJ. It was the initials that caught my eye.

I put the restaurant note in front of Kathy's face and confessed, "Just so you don't think I'm psycho, this is how I knew. And, yes, I like Mexican food."

"The word is psychic," she replied, rolling her eyes.

"That's what you think," I said darkly, trying to look psycho.

"You are a very observant fellow, Rick. Observe anything else you like?" she asked as she turned to grab her jacket.

"I see a few things," I mumbled.

"What?" she said. "Speak up, don't be shy!"

"I should ask the same question," I responded.

Turning, with her jacket in hand, her eyes again gave me the once-over. This time I noticed something different, a slight tongue action moving across her lips. They say a picture is worth a thousand words. The picture of her response was just one word … yes.

The setting for dinner was a small, quaint Mexican restaurant within walking distance of Kathy's home. It looked to be a family-owned business with only a few tables and booths, all situated for privacy and intimacy. It gave me a clue as to Kathy's intentions. You don't pick this kind of restaurant unless you have romance in mind.

After ordering our drinks, a margarita for each of us, we began to talk. It was stimulating. She seemed hungry to know as much about me as possible. She projected a familiarity I usually find only in lifelong friends.

"I feel like we've known each other for years," she confessed. "With you, there's no pretending, no anxiety, no wondering if I should or shouldn't do something. I can just be myself and don't have to play stupid games. You know how long it's been since ..."

The look in my eyes seemed to cut her off suddenly. I already knew what she was going to say, but needed to ask anyway, "How long has it been?"

Looking down at the table, then back to me, she puzzled, "I really can't remember! Does that make any sense?"

It seems for just a moment the real Kathy came out. She showed vulnerability she never intended to show. Then, realizing her exposure, she quickly retreated and changed the subject.

Picking up a menu, she said, "So, Rick, what shall we have tonight?"

"Let's share the combo," I suggested.

Squinting her face up, "Ew, that's nasty!" she groaned.

"How can a combo be nasty?"

"It has beans on it."

"This is a *Mexican* restaurant, remember? There's bound to be beans. I can eat the beans."

"Yeah, but then ... you know ... all night."

"I'll leave the window open."

"Then I'll get cold!" she said.

"Oh, does that mean you're sleeping in the guest room with me?"

Looking down at the table, then back up again at me, Kathy only smiled. Before she could answer or I could press any further, the waitress arrived.

"We'll take the combo," I said.

We resumed our conversation, but at this point I was having trouble focusing on Kathy's words or even her beautiful face. My eyes kept being summoned to her breasts. Kathy's blouse was designed to be provocative. It was tight across the bust-line and displayed in detail the outline of her breasts, accenting their shape and curves. With those wonders of nature thrusting against her top, the buttons were being pushed to the limit. They looked like they might give way any minute. With each sneaked peek, they taunted me, begging to be unbuttoned. The breasts moaned for me to release them from their captivity, and then chided me because I couldn't. I found this to be very distracting. Kathy quickly picked up on the problem I was having.

Looking directly at me, then down at her chest, "Do you like what you see?" she asked seductively.

She knew I did. My face grew red. I was embarrassed being busted like that. (Hmm, I guess I was "busted" both literally and figuratively!)

"Well ... I ... um ..."

"I'm sorry," she apologized. "I didn't mean to embarrass you."

"Well ... I ... umm ... well, that is ..."

"Rick, it's OK. In fact, I'm glad you're embarrassed."

"You are?" I responded with some surprise.

"Yes, it means you like me for me and not just my boobs."

Looking down at the table, I said tentatively, "I do like you, Kathy. I like you a lot."

"I know, and I like you a lot, too. Come sit next to me," she said as she slid over in the booth.

Sliding in next to Kathy one thing became evident. She was not shy about sharing her personal space. With the arrival of the meal the waitress brought everything on one plate and, as requested, a second empty plate. Kathy took the initiative right away and began divvying it up ... giving me all the beans, of course. Besides being very beautiful, this was a woman who knew how to take charge and get things done. Something I truly admire.

While juggling two plates and trying to separate our dinner in our small booth, Kathy found a way to brush her C-cups against my arm, grazing my skin through the thin material. Whether deliberate or not, feeling the ladies was stimulating and confirmed my impression of their size, shape and firmness.

Dinner was beyond enjoyable as we spent the next hour laughing, teasing, and conversing about everything except work. I learned about her divorce and her son, who was an only child. I learned she made a new rule not to date co-workers after the last relationship she had been in turned ugly. In return, I shared a little about Cindy, shying away from the gory details. I wanted to bring up Jack again. I wanted to see the look on her face and to observe her body language when trying to answer my questions. But I didn't want things to go sour, especially since I needed a place to stay the night. I thought it best to save specific Jack questions for another time. So I proceeded down a slightly different path.

"Kathy, I know you worked in San Francisco for awhile," (I deliberately did not mention Jack), "and then Los Angeles. But how do you like Santa Barbara?"

Realizing this was a safe question, "I love Santa Barbara!" she said with enthusiasm. "Los Angeles was always so dirty and crowded. But here, everything's always clean and the people are wonderful. I just love the ocean."

"Where did you live in Los Angeles?"

"Out in the Valley."

"So did I," I said with some excitement. "Where?"

"I had an apartment in Van Nuys. So where did you live?"

"Actually, I was born and raised in the Valley. Canoga Park High and Cal State Northridge."

"Really?"

"Lived on Strathern across from the park for about fifteen years. Moved to Seattle about ten years ago when I went to work for the company."

"So, Rick, any female friends in Seattle?"

Bingo. Her question opened the door I wanted to go through.

"Only one. You may know her. Caroline Edwards. Up until two weeks ago she was the company HR Director."

Nodding her head slightly, "I remember her. She's very pretty. Were you two …?"

"Now, Kathy, you know it's against company policy for members of the management team to fraternize after hours."

"Oh, you mean like we're doing now?"

"Heavens, no! This is a business dinner."

"Oh, is that what this is?" she said with a laugh.

"So tell me, Kathy, I understand you didn't know Jack well," (I wanted to throw that in to catch her off guard). "How about Caroline?"

The question made her a tad uneasy.

"I didn't know her well. Met her a couple times at company functions. That's about all."

Her eyes lost their dilation, and she shifted her weight while answering. She told me what I needed to know. She was lying.

Even though the night was still young, I was exhausted, and Kathy could see it. Using this to change the subject, she said, "You're so tired— look at you! I think it's time to take you home and put you to bed."

She was right about one thing. I was tired. The only thing that kept me alive for the last few hours was an adrenaline rush caused by Kathy and my pre-occupation with her lovely ladies. But fatigue was now winning the battle, and—no offense to the girls—sleep was the main thing on my mind. But still … putting me to bed did have a playful ring to it.

And after spending some time with her, certain pieces of the Kathy puzzle were coming together. I had a morsel of insight about her now. The invitation to spend the night, the hug at the door, the accepted kiss on her head, the intimate discussion, having me sit next to her, her breasts touching me—all individual actions—but when I pieced them together, they formed a picture. The image was that Kathy liked me very much and was true to her word about her comfort level, or another motivation was stewing in the pot to make her behave this way toward me. What? Something to do with Jack, and maybe Caroline, too? But the biggest question looming at the moment was how far would Kathy go … with me … tonight? Every indication was "damn the torpedoes, full speed ahead!"

Yet Caroline's warning came to mind, "Not everything is what it appears to be."

Chapter 12

With my bag in hand, Kathy led me up the dimly-lit stairs to her absent son's room. Pausing at the door, her face shimmered from the reflection of a streetlight coming through the window at the end of the hall. The soft rays highlighted her lovely features ... she was indeed a very beautiful woman.

I dropped my bag on the hallway floor, deciding right there to see how far Kathy would go. Whatever her reasons for courting me as she had been since that first call, I was too intrigued by her to care. Impulsively I settled my hands on her cheeks, leaned down to her gorgeous face tilted up at me and pressed my lips to hers. I was delightfully surprised by Kathy's most willing, eager and immediate response as one kiss led to two, and two led to more.

With each kiss, I felt her heart beating faster, her breath getting shorter. Her hands were unrestrained, and I could literally feel the blood in her veins growing hotter. With hungry passion, the heat of her hands radiated through my shirt's fabric as they explored my chest, my back, my ribcage, touching each bone, dwelling on every muscle. With our tongues wildly intertwined, her exploration moved to my pants. She fondled the bulge there, exploring like Columbus visiting new worlds. Her intensity and enthusiasm suggested it had been a long time since she'd been with a man. Either that or she had the world's quickest ignition from zero to fiery hot.

Not surprisingly, I didn't feel so tired now! A new surge of adrenaline flowed into me as each beat of my heart replaced weariness with strength, injecting particular vigor into the area Kathy was so desperately exploring, a place starved for more of the tender attention she was giving it.

Kathy's body too, was being researched by my hands. Fair is fair and a gentleman must reciprocate. With each impassioned kiss, my touch to her special place produced lovely quivers. The fires of desire were consuming her, carrying her dangerously closer to the threshold of complete surrender.

So we paused. We tried to catch our breath. Both at a loss for words, we were overwhelmed by this intense passion which moved from a spark to a wildfire so quickly. Our eyes met, questioning the wisdom of continuing.

"Are you alright?" I breathed.

Wrapping her arms tightly around me, she puffed, "Oh, Rick, you just do something to me."

"Now's a good time to stop," I suggested tentatively.

"I know. I just …"

"Just what?"

"Oh, Rick," was her only reply as she pulled me tighter while boring her head deeper into my chest.

Just as Kathy pushed a button in me, I also did in her. Her fire, her grip, the way she tenderly nuzzled my chest. These all spoke of a yearning, a consuming desire that had nothing to do with rational thinking. This woman wanted … no, needed to be picked up and carried into the bedroom. To be laid on the bed and slowly undressed, savoring the moments with each button undone. With each layer of clothing removed, more of her would be exposed, stripping off all restraints. She longed to have her neglected sexual needs satisfied with a man's touch, kissing and exploring of each private place, discovering new heights of passion. She needed to be taken and taken hard.

But as for me, between the adrenaline stimulating my body and the fatigue from the last 24 hours each demanding exact opposite responses, I felt like a drunk filled with coffee. Still drunk, but wide awake.

Pulling back from her embrace, she spoke softly, "Baby, you're tired. You need some sleep. But first I have something I know you'll like."

Hearing those words, a felt the strange tug of déjà vu. With her eyes penetrating mine, Kathy backed away a few steps down the hallway. The streetlight through the window created a halo effect behind her. Her long hair fell softly around her face and shoulders. Her breasts pushed against her blouse. I knew exactly what she was about to do. The look in her eyes told me. I'd seen that look before.

Seductively, she began unbuttoning her blouse. She worked her way down, emphasizing each button one at a time. With each button undone, she paused, allowing me the pleasure of savoring the moment. Her tease was designed to build anticipation, and it was working. But as much as I enjoyed the show, I couldn't help thinking how well she knew what I liked. Maybe too well? Or was this simply a sexy show that plenty of women do?

When the final button was undone, she stood posed like a lingerie model, total eye-candy and the candy made me salivate. Her eyes were fixed on mine and she could tell I was pleased. So she took the next step and unsnapped the front of her bra. The lacy cups fell to the side, and her naked breasts bounced slightly at their release. They were magnificent, perfect.

"Do you still like what you see?" she asked, like a woman free from all sexual boundaries.

My answer was obviously yes, but my tongue wouldn't work, so nodding my head would have to suffice.

"Cat's got your tongue, I see," she continued with a playful giggle.

But when I grabbed her by the waist and pulled her toward me, she immediately abandoned her playful kitten demeanor and turned into a wildcat. We kissed deeply and lustfully. Feeling her firm, naked mounds pressing against my clothing, I was overcome with the desire to have them touching my skin. I tore at my shirt to bare my chest and press her against me. My hands shot between her skin and her blouse, baring her shoulders and pulling the fabric roughly from them. Her blouse fell to the floor along with her lacy bra. This fanned the flames of passion in Kathy beyond a wildfire. She seized my neck with both hands for support as she jumped up and straddled my waist, linking her legs behind me. My hands instinctively cupped that delicious derrière and squeezed. She threw her head back like a bronco rider, and I began hungrily feasting on the smooth skin of her exposed neck. Kathy tilted her head first to one side and then the other, silently directing me to take more, to taste further. Purposefully, I glided the tip of my tongue across her flesh. She trembled. The more I kissed or flicked my tongue, the more her body shook as the waves of pleasure crashed across her beach. A consuming passion was only moments away, a passion that would take two strangers to a place where rational thinking didn't exist. A place ruled by raw animal passion. A place that was very dangerous for both of us.

She pulled back suddenly from our embrace, breathing heavily. We gazed into each other's eyes. Nothing was said. Nothing needed to be. She unlinked her legs and hopped down to the floor. We knew we had to stop. It was too soon and too complicated.

Still trying to recover her breath, Kathy gave a slight brush below my belt, saying tentatively, "I'm ... sorry ... I can finish if you'd like ...?"

As tempting as the idea was and as much as my body was screaming yes, there was something in me that said no.

"Not like this," I said.

"You are so sweet," she returned.

I took her face in my hands, leaned over, and kissed her on the forehead. With that, nothing more happened. Kathy picked up her clothes, turned, and disappeared into her room.

Taking a deep breath and picking up my bag, I turned and stepped into my room. I didn't notice until later that two buttons on my shirt were missing.

The room was empty except for the bed, a dresser, and a poster of a thin woman with stringy blond hair dusting over small bare breasts. She was standing next to a motorcycle. The blond was nothing to write home about. The motorcycle ... ah, now that was a different story.

Fatigue had finally won the battle that raged through my body most of the evening. Everything in me was beginning to shut down quickly, especially Kathy's new-found friend. As my body collapsed onto the bed my only thought was a nice long trip with Mr. Sandman. But even though total exhaustion consumed every working part of my body ... and some parts that had died hours ago ... sleep eluded me. With all the traveling, the lack of sleep the night before (from listening to Steve and his girlfriend flying the midnight mattress until dawn) and the heavy make-out session with Kathy, my mind was going nowhere. And it was going there *fast*.

Trying to access any logical thought from my dead brain was nearly impossible. But still, lying in bed, I was determined to reason out exactly what had happened in the hall. I wanted to make sense of the mystical and delightful connection I had with Kathy ... if that's what it truly was. For us accountant types, everything must always be in order. Two and two must always equal four. But with Kathy, nothing added up right. It was... weird. And it was about to get weirder.

It was around midnight, and a full moon beamed over the neighboring mountains, filling the bedroom with a soft light. Half asleep, I thought I heard my name.

"Rick. Rick, are you still awake?"

"What?" I grumbled.

Was someone calling me? I raised my groggy head from the pillow and looked around the room. Except for the thin blond in the poster, I was alone. I dropped my head back onto the pillow. I must have been dreaming.

Again, some disembodied voice asked, "Rick, are you awake?"

This time I was sure I heard my name.

"What?" I asked, trying to shake the sleep from my brain. I thought of Kathy. Still mostly asleep, I jumped out of bed, envisioning her in trouble.

"I'm here! I'm here!" I stammered.

"May I come in for a moment?" Kathy asked sweetly.

"Uh," I responded, not quite sure what I heard or even if I heard it. Before I could collect my thoughts or answer, Kathy appeared in the doorway wearing only a thong and an unbuttoned white blouse. Her beautiful long hair, slightly mussed, fell softly over her shoulders. The tiny thong was cut low. Everything I knew or imagined about her body was there before my bleary eyes.

Gently she said, "I don't want to be alone."

Her words generated no question, but her eyes asked volumes. They inquired about tenderness and affection and attention. By stopping the stimulation so abruptly like we had, there was a void left in her, a deep chasm echoing "fill me, fill me with passion."

Silently and still mentally incoherent, I held out my hand as an invitation. With a smile and no hesitation, she accepted my offer by placing her small, soft hand in mine. Together we walked back to the bed and slipped under the covers. The moonlight's iridescence filled the room and our eyes were intently fixed on the other. Each of us was very aware that the line in the sand had nearly been compromised earlier. We'd been mere moments from being washed away with the rising tide of passion.

But now, lying side by side, it didn't matter. We didn't care about being co-workers or even adversaries, if my suspicions turned out to have any merit at all. We were two hungry individuals silently sharing a growing, unrestrained emotion. It couldn't be explained. Nor could it be contained.

Taking the cue from her eyes, I gently rolled Kathy onto her back. Still on my side, I reached across her body and effortlessly pulled her to me. The feel of her flesh on mine was immediately intoxicating. Fatigue was once again pushed aside by a new rush of adrenaline. Vigor and vitality were returning to my mind and body, and the evidence of it was firmly pressing against her thigh. It was a firmness she wanted. I had to oblige. I was a man possessed.

Pushing aside her unbuttoned blouse, I paused in awe. Two firm, magnificent mounds majestically towered over a smooth, hard stomach. Ready for the graze of my tongue and the touch of my lips, I moved toward them with soft kisses. First on her lips, her chin, down her neck, and then into the deep canyon between the breasts where I would surely die happy if allowed to be smothered there. Cupping one in her own hand, Kathy guided my lips to a sensitive place. She moaned. As my mouth tenderly suckled, my hand groped toward her moist thong. I began gently massaging the thin fabric and a shiver from deep within shook Kathy's body. With her eyes closed, her head tilted back, and her shallow breathing, I knew what she needed ... a long, hard, sweet trip to Never Never Land, where fantasy becomes reality and where time stands still. And that night, until the moon moved across the sky taking its shadow with it, time stood still for her.

Morning came early, and I was alone in bed. Exhausted beyond belief, I awoke trying to pull together the events that led up to the mini-marathon of the wee hours.

What could I expect from Kathy that morning? I keenly listened for any stirring in the house, but all was quiet. Seizing the opportunity, I silently left my bed and headed toward Kathy's bedroom. The door was ajar slightly, allowing me a view. Lying across the bed with a sheet partly covering her naked body, Kathy was even more beautiful in the morning light. Her long hair was mussed across her bare back, and her exposed thighs were slightly spread, illuminating a peek-a-boo look at her secret place. I was enticed to cross the threshold into this heavenly chamber.

Entering slowly, attempting to be quiet with each step, I noticed the thong and blouse on the floor next to the bed, confirming my suspicion that Kathy sleeps in the nude. She began to stir. Freezing in my tracks, I wasn't sure what to do. Run or stay still. She rolled over onto her side, with the sheet cocooning her body. Wiping sleep from her eyes, she had no problem with me in her room. If anything, she appeared pleased.

"Good morning, sunshine," she said with a warm smile.

"Good morning, moonlight," I returned.

Pulling the sheet back, "Come join me," she suggested, giving no thought to revealing her naked body. As I joined her in bed, she wasted no time snuggling close, abandoning the sheet. With a sigh, she pressed her warm body to mine. The feel of her was exhilarating, causing a subtle but very positive reaction in my groin. Putting my arm around her brought back vivid memories of the romance we shared, but it also triggered a question.

"Hey, what happened to you last night? I woke up and you were gone."

"I know. I woke up and couldn't go back to sleep."

"Was I snoring?"

"Oh, no, not that. You were sleeping so soundly and I just ..."

She paused.

"Just what?" I asked.

Kathy didn't answer my question but instead repositioned her snuggle next to me.

"Just what?" I reiterated.

"I just wanted to touch you again," she replied sheepishly.

Moving my hand to her breast, "You can touch me now if you like," I offered.

Taking a firm grip on my manhood, she smiled. "Hmm, very nice, Rick. I knew you were big last night, but never realized how big. Do you like me to touch you?"

"I think Kathy has a new friend!" I replied.

"Hmm, I think so too," she agreed.

Kicking the sheet completely off the bed, but with her grip still firm, she offered, "Let me thank you for last night."

And for the next half hour, it was my turn to have time stand still.

"Do you feel like breakfast?" she whispered in my ear.

"Are you kidding? I can't even move."

"Ah, does baby need his nourishment to keep up his strength?" she asked with a little giggle.

She began to rub her hand over my chest, showing the same enthusiasm as she did a few moments before.

"Yes, baby does need some nourishment, but what about a shower first?"

"Woo, more fun!" she chirped. "Give me a couple of minutes to get ready."

And with a peck on the lips, her very beautiful naked body disappeared into her bathroom.

We spent quite a bit of time in the shower that morning. It was amazing. But I'm not sure if I should tell you about it.

It was private.

Breakfast was at a little coffee shop around the corner from her condo. The meal was huge and, same as the night before, we split it. When you split a meal with a woman, it helps create an atmosphere of intimacy, opening doors in conversation that would normally never open. Following the same pattern as dinner, we talked. This time, however, the conversation was far more intimate and explicit, reminiscing in detail about the events, the touches, the desires from the night before ... and from this morning in the shower, of course. Sprinkled throughout the conversation, Kathy dropped little sexual innuendos just to see my reaction. Stroking the spoon in her coffee cup, for example, she asked, "Remind you of anything?"

Kathy wanted me to stay another day, but after the insanity of the last twelve hours, I knew both of us needed to cool off and think very carefully about where we had gone and, more importantly, where we now wanted to go. Besides, I had a dinner engagement in San Francisco I was not going to miss.

Back at her house, while gathering my things to leave, I popped into Kathy's room to make sure I hadn't left behind some dirty underwear or maybe some testosterone or something.

A small picture tucked into the frame of her dresser mirror caught my eye. When I took a closer look, a shiver ran down my spine. The photo was Kathy and *Jack* with their arms around each other. They were at the beach, both in very revealing bathing suits, and obviously happy.

What the hell?

Why had Kathy hidden her relationship with Jack? And why the quick invitation to spend the night? Was the hot sex planned? And the show with the blouse? It was as though she and Caroline mimicked each other button for button. Does she know Caroline well, too? Yes, we clicked in bed, but was it because she liked me or was it an act? Or was she a little spitfire who was hot for *all* the boys? Was I being setup? And if so, for what?

I never planned for the events to roll out the way they did. Could someone else have planned them? Could I be that predictable and easily manipulated? I was plagued with questions and hungry for answers. But one thing was sure. It all happened too easily.

Saying goodbye to Kathy was extremely difficult, since she was crying (fake?), asking me again to stay and I was holding my tongue until I had time to think things through. I didn't want her to know (yet?) I saw the photo and caught her red-handed in a lie. With tears trickling down her cheeks, Kathy reached out for a hug. I tried not to be cold, but I'm sure she detected a change in my demeanor.

"Call me tonight?" she asked.

"If it's not too late," I replied. "Take care of yourself, Kathy."

I managed to kiss her on the forehead before bolting out the front door. I slid into my rental car. Heading out, I could see her in my rearview mirror. She had followed me outside. She watched until I turned the corner.

Pulling onto the freeway, my mind was running faster than the cars around me. I needed to think … clearly. And for the next five and a half hours I would try. The signpost up ahead read, "San Francisco 335 miles."

Chapter 13

It was Monday just after lunch, when I arrived back at the office. As I passed through the reception area, Emily looked up from her desk. She looked like Armageddon was upon us.

"Rick, I'm so glad you're back," she began. "Chris has been calling every five minutes for the last couple of hours. He says he needs to see you ASAP."

Without stopping or even glancing at Emily, I said, "Yeah, he left a couple messages on my cell phone, too. Call Chris back and tell him to be in my office in two minutes."

I closed the door behind me. Two minutes later there was a knock. It was Chris.

"Come on in, Chris," I offered while gesturing for him to take a seat.

He was wearing a full-face grin, so I knew he had something good for me. I was impatient to hear it.

"OK, Chris. Out with it!"

"Well, Chief, it was Kathy Gibson who handled the claim for Johnson. She's now the branch manager for Santa Barbara."

"I knew it," I mumbled under my breath as my smile spread immediately from ear to ear.

Upon hearing that bit of trivia, I leaned back in my chair, hoisted my feet onto the desk and slid my hands behind my head. From the moment Holly told me Kathy transferred to Claims in L.A. when Jack came to HQ, I had a gut feeling there was something more about her I needed to know. I couldn't put my finger on it at the time, probably because her sultry voice got me thinking with the wrong head right away. But now I had another piece of a bizarre puzzle. I had two solid verifications that Kathy hadn't been completely honest with me.

In fact, she downright lied.

First was her claim that she didn't know Jack all that well. For a liar, she's not very skilled at the finer points of deception. She should have thought to hide that day-at-the-beach photo the minute she invited me to "Kathy's Motel." The other lie was her nonchalant dismissal of questions about the twenty million dollar policy. Since she handled the claim, she damn well knew everything about it. But why contact me in the first place? If she's trying to hide something (which is the usual reason somebody lies), why this elaborate charade? And what is it she's hiding? It smells of fraud because of all the odd circumstances, but how can a natural death be insurance fraud? Then again, maybe it wasn't a natural death.

I thanked Chris for the information. As he walked out the door, Emily walked in.

Settling herself in the same wingback chair which Chris had just warmed up, "I hope you've got things worked out with Chris so he'll stop calling and stressing me out," she began.

It was both a statement and a question, but one that needed no answer. She continued, "So tell me, Rick, how was the trip?"

She was dying for a tidbit of gossip.

Still kicked back, I answered, "Very enlightening, Emily. Very enlightening."

Pressing further, she asked, "Was Kathy Gibson everything you thought she would be?"

It was a question that warranted a little thought before answering.

"Hmm, let's just say, Emily, she was … everything … plus … a little more," I replied with a coy smile.

With a grin and a raised eyebrow, "Rick Morgan, you two did it, didn't you?" she exclaimed.

Dropping my feet to the floor and bringing my chair upright, "Did what?" I asked with a straight face.

"You know what I'm talking about, Rick."

"Emily, please. It was all business."

Emily continued, "And I suppose you still went and had dinner with your mystery woman?"

"That was the best part of the trip," I teased.

"You know, Rick, one of these days you're …"

Before she could finish, my cell phone rang.

"Hold on a minute, Emily," I said as I eyed the caller ID.

It read "Vince," so I answered it and motioned Emily with my hand that it was private. She closed the door on her way out.

"Vince, give me some good news," I said hopefully.

"OK, how about the coffee place in ten minutes?"

"The bar next door?"

"Right."

I commandeered a small table in the back of the bar. My drink arrived at the same time Vince did. He sat down and ordered one for himself. He had a solemn look on his face as we shook hands. I started the conversation.

"Vince, why do I have this feeling your news isn't good?"

Taking out his small black notebook, he began, "Well, as you requested, I did a background check on Robert Nielsen. Died three years ago of cancer at the age of sixty. At age twenty joined the LAPD. Was a patrolman for seven years then moved to detective. Appeared to be a pretty savvy guy. Stayed with LAPD until he was forty-eight. Took an early retirement. I couldn't find out why. Went to work as an independent insurance investigator and worked for a number of insurance companies, yours being one. Wife Cathy died three years before him. Had only one child, daughter whose name and whereabouts are unknown at this time."

"Sounds to me like we ran into a dead end," I said.

Tilting his head with a curious look, Vince responded, "Maybe not."

He turned a page in his book and continued, "A couple years after Nielsen moved to detective he investigated a DUI accident in the San Fernando Valley. From what my sources told me, he took the investigation personally. Though the information is somewhat sketchy, it seems a drunk crossed over a double line and hit this family head on, killing three adults. The drunk was uninjured. There were three children in the backseat who survived."

"Vince, as tragic as all that was, what does it have to do with my death claim?" I puzzled.

Putting his hand up, he said, "I'm getting to that. It seems the drunk was well-connected in Los Angeles and used his muscle to squash the investigation. Drove Nielsen crazy."

Being from Los Angeles, I thought I might recognize a name, so I asked, "Who was the high roller?"

"I don't know," Vince replied. "But whoever it was had a lot of muscle. It seems every record from the initial accident investigation to the Grand Jury has been sealed or, like your files, gone missing. Nielsen became obsessed with the case. Worked on his own time as I understand it, but could never get an indictment. Everywhere he went he was stone-walled."

"If everything was sealed, how did you get this information?"

"Don't ask," was his answer.

"Sealed, missing, or stone-walled! I don't get it. Why does everything about this case end with a roadblock?"

"Rick, it gets even better."

"Better?"

By the look on Vince's face, I wasn't sure I wanted to know.

"Although the information on the accident is sealed, I did manage to find out something of a coincidence."

Thinking about Kathy, I said sarcastically, "Vince, I just got back from Southern California. Nothing about this case is a coincidence."

"Exactly," said Vince. "Nothing is."

The sober look on Vince's face told me there was more.

"OK, Vince. I'll bite. What are you hinting at?"

"The date of the accident," he said quietly.

"The date of the accident? What does that have to do with anything?"

"Maybe more than you think."

"OK, let me guess."

I put the back of my hand to my forehead, and mocked, "The date of the accident is …"

I stopped in mid-sentence as our eyes met. My gut screamed, "Rick, just walk away." I was about to suggest a date that would crack open Pandora's Box. Vince's face confirmed my suspicions.

Taking my hand from my forehead, I gripped my glass and quietly said, "July 6, 1976?"

As Vince nodded his head, that familiar rock settled in my stomach. I was speechless for a few moments.

"Are you sure?" I managed, stumbling on each word.

"Yes, Rick. Dead sure," Vince said gravely.

With a deep sigh, I mumbled, "The same date as the newspaper."

"YEAH, the very same," Vince replied while leaning across the table. "The same date as the Los Angeles Times that you pulled from the claim file. Somebody was indeed sending a message."

Looking down, with my hand still gripping the glass, I asked directly,

"Vince, what does a thirty year old accident in L.A. have in common with my insured's death in Las Vegas?"

Staring at his drink while swirling the last sip around the bottom of the glass, Vince replied, "I don't know, Rick. I really don't know. But something."

Again, there was silence as we both nursed our drinks and absorbed the magnitude of this revelation. It was Vince who broke the silence.

"Rick, you do realize the rules of the game just changed."

As I nodded in agreement, the cocktail waitress appeared and asked if we wanted another round. Yes. And we both made them doubles.

We said nothing for quite awhile. When fresh drinks arrived, we still didn't speak. What could we say? There were now a million questions. Or maybe, better put, twenty million. Vince was right. The rules of the game had definitely changed. The question now was whether to move forward or to walk away?

I had to make a decision.

After taking a gulp of my drink, I began, "Vince, this is what I want you to do." I was thinking as I went, thinking out loud. "I want you to go back to L.A., take as many investigators as you need, and find out everything there is to find about that accident. I especially want to know who the high roller was."

"That may be hard or impossible, Rick. It was over thirty years ago."

"I know," I agreed. "But Nielsen had partners on the force. I want you to find and talk to them. Find out where he lived and talk with old neighbors. Go to the newspapers. Check the back issues for that date. Check newspapers that have gone out of business. Any article that even remotely seems related, get a copy. Track down old reporters. Talk to everyone who will talk to you."

"Should I bring in Frank? He used to be LAPD."

"That's a great idea," I confirmed. "He can help open doors. Somewhere there's someone who knows something. Find him ... or her ... or them. I want to know what they know."

"Then," I continued, "since we seem to be jumping into this with both feet, send someone to Vegas."

"You don't want me to go personally?"

"No, Vince, they know you down there. At this point, outside of Frank we have no clue who's friendly or not. Send someone inconspicuous."

"Good thinking."

"I want the Vegas papers checked around the date Johnson died. I want reporters talked to. And the hotel staff. Have your people talk with anyone who will talk to them. And have them steer away from anyone official."

"I have two operatives who are husband and wife. They'll blend in as tourists."

"Good."

"We can do this. But I do have one question."

"What's that?"

"What are you hoping to find?"

It was an interesting question. I hadn't given it much thought.

"Vince, I have a manager who sold a twenty million dollar policy even though he didn't have the skill to do so. The woman who handled the claim said she barely knew him and she only vaguely remembered the twenty million dollar policy. She lied ... twice. I have missing underwriting files and a corrupted computer backup. The claims file had a newspaper in it dated July 6, 1976, and nothing else. I've just learned the police detective who handled an accident in L.A. on the same date as the newspaper was also the same guy who investigated the insured's death for the company. The odds that all of this is a coincidence are astronomical. No, my friend, someone is covering something up. I want to know who, what and why."

"Is that all, Rick?"

"What do you mean?"

"I mean, when we first met, I wondered if you were protecting someone. Are you?"

Thinking of Caroline, I had to pause before answering.

"No, Vince. Not really. I just remembered her last words to me. She said, 'things are not always what they appear to be.'"

"Did she die?"

"No, they were her last words before moving away recently."

"Then you think she was talking about this case?"

"I don't know. But one thing is for sure. Everything and everyone connected to this investigation seems to have something to hide."

"Even her?"

Nodding my head, "Yes, Vince, even her," I said, smiling ironically at his choice of words.

"Rick, we may open something better left closed."

Still thinking of Caroline, I gripped my glass hard as I splashed down the last swallow.

"I know. Before we're through, I might wish I'd moved away with her."

CHAPTER 14

Silence is golden?
    Maybe sometimes, but not when you're sitting on pins and needles waiting for specific information. It had been about two weeks since I met with Vince. I was growing impatient.

It was Tuesday morning at 8:15. The rain was beating hard against the window as a northern wind blew down from Canada. The sky was black and nasty, and so was my coffee. I had just gotten off the phone with Kathy, which had become a daily occurrence, when my cell phone rang again. Since we had literally just hung up, I thought it was Kathy calling back with something she'd forgotten.

"Did you miss me, baby?"

"Oh, oops! Sorry, Vince, I thought you were somebody else!"

"Ha, ha … yeah … funny. So give me some good news."

"Meet where?"

"Coffee place it is."

"OK, see you in ten."

As I walked through the outer office, Emily asked where I was off to.

"For a good cup of coffee," I replied.

Vince already had a table in the back when I got to the coffee shop. His head was down. He was either tired or deep in thought. He looked up, and I could see it was both. I pulled up a chair. He had taken the liberty of ordering me a black coffee. I thanked him for it as I picked up the hot cup.

Emotionless except for a slight twinkle in his eyes as I thanked him, he pulled his little black book from his inside jacket pocket and began his report.

"Rick, my operatives worked Vegas for a week."

"What did they find?" I asked hopefully.

"More than I expected," he said as the twinkle morphed into a small smile.

"To start with, the hotel has had a complete change of personnel over the last ten years."

"To be expected," I said while nodding in agreement.

"My people did find one employee, an older Hispanic housekeeper who remembered the death. Fortunately, my female operative is fluent in Spanish and was able to interview her off the premises. They took this lady and her husband out for a nice dinner. It's amazing what people can remember when they're relaxed."

"Good thinking. And ...?" I asked excitedly.

"And they found out who the housekeeper was who actually found the body."

"Beautiful!" I exclaimed with increasing enthusiasm.

"Were you able to track her down?"

"Better than that. I already interviewed her."

"Vince, you're the man!"

Nodding his head with a touch of arrogance, he continued, "Her name is Maria Anita Guadalupe Gonzales. About 32 years old, married, has five kids, lives—guess where. The San Fernando Valley!"

"The Valley? You're kidding?"

Shaking his head from side to side, "No, I'm not," he replied. "She and her husband, Manuel, own a Mexican restaurant in Burbank. I interviewed her yesterday. As best she could remember, she and another housekeeper were working the suites that morning. She couldn't remember the name of the other housekeeper. They found the body around 9:00 in the morning. Someone left the card on the door asking that the room be made up."

"Someone wanted the body found ASAP," I added.

"Right, Rick. Someone did. When the housekeepers walked in, they found Mr. Johnson lying on his back in bed, naked and not moving. She then called her supervisor who called Security. The hotel doctor was called in and pronounced him dead. About fifteen minutes later, the cops arrived."

"What else?"

"Both housekeepers were interviewed at the scene then released."

"Did she remember anything else? Anything unusual?"

"Funny you should ask that, Rick. Yes, the smell of perfume."

"Perfume?"

"Yeah, perfume."

I sat back for a moment, then added, "Our Mr. Johnson was not alone."

"Well, that explains why he was naked," Vince alleged.

Visualizing a stiff Mr. Johnson naked was not a pretty thought, but one that stirred up my imagination nonetheless. What happened in that hotel room? Leaning forward, resting my elbows on the table, I slowly began.

"Vince, follow me for a minute. Johnson's a high roller who checks himself into a suite. Gets a little horny and wants some companionship. Meets up with a woman ..."

"Or hooker," Vince interjected.

"Right! Brings her back to the room. They have sex. The guy's on his back. She's on top going full bore when BAM! Remember the death certificate said he died of 'congestive heart failure'?"

"A heart attack?"

"Right."

"But, Rick, what you're suggesting isn't a crime."

"No, Vince, it's not. And if it's not a crime, why the sealed records?"

"That's a good question. Wish I knew the answer," Vince mumbled. Then added, "Was Johnson married?"

"Not according to my records."

"Then the idea of scandal doesn't hold much water."

"Not at the moment, but you never know," I speculated.

"So then, who's the woman?"

"A million dollar question, Vince. Who knows?"

I continued, "Did our housekeeper remember anything else?"

"Only, before they removed the body, a very nice-looking, young, dark haired woman talked with her."

"Cop?"

"She wasn't sure, but by the description of her dress and ID, I would bet she was an Assistant District Attorney," Vince said.

"DA? What would a DA be doing at an apparent heart attack?" I asked, puzzled.

"Well, if she was, it would be another million dollar question. Mrs.

Gonzales did remember telling her about the perfume. This woman, whoever she was, thought it wasn't important."

"Now, Vince, I'm not a cop. But I would think if I had a dead body in a hotel room, and the scent of perfume in the air, I would want to know where that perfume came from."

"Exactly. Both a cop and a DA would want to know who that person was right off. And then find her."

"Vince, I have another question. How does a minimum wage housekeeper end up owning a Mexican restaurant in Burbank?"

"I was wondering if you would catch that."

He turned the page in his notebook.

"It seems a few months after your Mr. Johnson died, our housekeeper received an inheritance from a relative she didn't know she had."

"Nice!" I said. "But somehow I have the feeling there's more."

"Guess who the law firm was that handled her inheritance?"

After thinking about it for a moment, I shrugged my shoulders. I had no clue.

"Greenbrier, Morris & Perry," Vince said. "They're a big-deal L.A. firm that only handles high-profile cases."

"Vince, I know that name. That's the same firm that handled the estate for Johnson! We sent them a check for twenty million dollars!"

Surprised, Vince repeated slowly, "You're telling me ... the same law firm that represented the beneficiary of your twenty million dollar death benefit ... is the same firm that handled our housekeeper's inheritance?"

I nodded my head in disbelief.

Resting back in his chair, "Interesting ... very interesting," Vince said, obviously deep in thought.

"Find anything in the papers to back up what the housekeeper told you?" I asked.

"No, nothing in the Vegas papers at all about your Mr. Johnson. From talking with some old reporters, I believe the papers knew nothing about the incident. But we did find something curious ... a small article about a former United States Congressman who was missing."

"And?"

"And I was curious. So I pulled one of my guys working the accident to do a little research. It seems the same day the insured is found dead in Vegas, an article came out in the Los Angeles Times about a former United States Congressman's boat that had been found adrift in the Catalina Channel ... abandoned."

"So, what's the connection to Vegas?"

"Well, maybe nothing. It was the name of the Congressman that caught my eye—Peter Cole."

"Peter Cole?" I repeated as my eyebrows raised. "I know that name from someplace, but where?"

"Well, besides being a United States Congressman, he was also on the board of a large insurance company … your company."

"Of course, I remember now. About ten years ago, right around the time I came aboard. He disappeared without a trace. Big to-do within the company. He was hired to work with lobbyists. Had more connections in Washington than anyone. Knew everyone and, from what I heard, knew their dirty little secrets, too."

"Well, that explains a few things," Vince said.

"A few things about what?" I asked.

"Let me finish first. His body was never recovered. According to the newspaper article, Mr. Cole kissed Mrs. Cole goodbye in the morning and headed to Marina Del Ray where he moored a boat. Witnesses saw him arrive, get on the boat, and head out. He was going fishing. When he didn't return that night his wife called the cops, who in turn checked with the Harbor Master and found the boat didn't return. The Coast Guard was notified and a search commenced. The following morning, that's the same morning they find your insured, his boat was found adrift about a mile off Avalon. It was out of gas, but the ignition was still on. When they boarded, they found fishing gear and a few empty bottles of tequila. It was assumed he had been drinking, fell overboard, and drowned. They searched for the body, but it was never recovered. The FBI was called in and also found no evidence of foul play. The case was closed."

"The FBI?"

"Yeah, Rick, the FBI. If what you said is true, there could be some people out there who don't want his disappearance investigated. As long as he's gone, so are those dirty little secrets."

Vince's words worried me a little. What started as a simple query on how a jackass of a salesman sold a twenty million dollar policy turned into an investigation involving a missing United States Congressman who had dirty little secrets.

"Nothing ever comes easy," I thought, and then said quietly, "So, Vince, you think there's a connection between Peter Cole and Johnson?"

Vince chewed on the question for a moment before answering.

"I really don't know. There are just too many coincidences about this case. It bothers me your board member goes missing the same day your insured dies, that the woman who finds Johnson's body miraculously inherits enough money to buy a restaurant only a few months later and the law firm who handled the inherence is the same one that handled the Johnson estate. Too many coincidences, Rick. Just too damn many."

As I was finishing my coffee and listening to Vince, I decided to give him more instructions. God only knows why.

"Vince, continue to research the accident in '76. But also get background on Eric Johnson. I would like to know more about him. Do a full profile. See if his and Peter Cole's paths ever crossed. While you're at it, let's get some more detail on Cole."

"Rick, you do realize Cole was a former Congressman and the FBI already investigated the case? They're not going to be happy with me, you, or even God for asking questions."

"I know. But maybe we won't have to poke where it's sensitive. Peter Cole was a politician. Politicians always have aides and rivals from the other side of the aisle, people like that. Find out his and talk to them. Ex-politicians and aides have one thing in common. They love to talk off the record."

"Good thinking. But, you know doing this will stir the pot more than we already have."

"I know. That's what I'm hoping for."

"Are you sure you know what you're getting into?"

Taking my cell from my pocket I said, "Vince, I don't have a clue. But I need to find out."

As I pushed a speed-dial button, I looked back at Vince and said, "Let's start stirring."

There was an answer on the second ring.

"Mr. Morgan!" came a sweet and sexy voice. "Two times in an hour? Woo-oo, I'm impressed! Do you have something you want me to do for you?" Kathy asked coyly.

"Well, a thought just crossed my mind ... But the reason I called is, I'm thinking of driving my Mustang down this weekend and was wondering if Sunday you'd like to go to the Rock Store."

"There's a store for rocks?"

CHAPTER 15

Tucked away on Old Mulholland Highway in Southern California, the Rock Store has a long history including many film shoots for movies, TV shows and commercials. Built in 1910 entirely out of rock, it served for a time as a stagecoach stop and watering hole. In recent years, the watering hole aspect has been revived as a pit-stop for motorcyclists. They are drawn to the winding canyon roads of the picturesque Malibu Mountains to test out their riding skills. On any given weekend, you will find a wide range of motorcyclists and machines from your suburban "wannabe" bikers to the speed freaks, from the old-school choppers to the modern slide-rule crotch rockets. All will congregate at the Rock Store.

It was Sunday about lunchtime when the Mustang arrived. Sunny and 82 degrees, a far cry from the drizzle of Seattle. The parking lot was a sea of motorcycles and enthusiasts, gathered for only one purpose ... to check out and drool over the other man's machine.

Kathy, much like the boys and their toys, enjoyed generating a wet chin. The wetter, the better. Showing off, like flirting, was just part of her nature. From her first step out of the Mustang with those 3-inch open-toed heels, tight Levi's, and long dark hair flowing across a tiny low-cut top, Kathy caught every man's eye. And from the look of things, a couple of women's as well.

We spotted a small table toward the back of the patio and moved in that direction. While splitting a burger and fries, we laughed and talked and enjoyed our meal. Kathy and I had been there for about a half hour when the rumble of four Harleys echoed across the parking lot. The sound of a Harley always catches my attention. Right off there was something different about these four riders. From a distance, I wasn't quite sure why, but there was a twitch in my gut. Maybe it was just the onions from my burger. Maybe not.

From the moment they parked their bikes, they seemed fixated on Kathy and me. I know Kathy's one hot woman and can easily attract a man's eyes, but I grew concerned when the four deliberately headed across the patio toward us, passing a number of free tables closer to the action. Maybe it was the way they walked or the look on their faces, but I had this distinct feeling they were on a mission. And their target was us … or me.

As they passed us, doing their best to be intimidating, I noticed a couple of things that put my mind and gut at ease. Even though these morons had long hair, tattoos and were dressed like the modern-day outlaw biker, a blind man could see they were phonies. First of all, they were missing the scars of the profession on their faces, scars from many battles over just as many years. Plus, their faces were too smooth. A real biker has a weathered face from years of riding through all kinds of climates. But the biggest give-away was they had no women. A true outlaw biker will have his old lady with him. No, these were middle-aged idiots who thought they were tough and wanted to relive the glory bad-boy days of their youth. Nothing more than stupid exiles from middle-class white suburbia.

They sat behind us and immediately turned up the volume of their intimidation attempt with pathetic catcalls to Kathy. I watched her closely as signs of fear began to emerge. I decided not to intervene. With all the extraordinary coincidences associated with Kathy and considering her history of lies, I wasn't sure if the fear was real or just an act. So I waited.

It wasn't long before Kathy quietly pleaded, "Rick, can we go?"

As much as I agreed with Kathy's request, I needed to push her just a little further to settle my debate about her part in this.

"What's the matter?" I asked calmly.

She looked down at her food then back at me and whispered, "I'm afraid."

"Of what?"

She glanced at their table.

"Kathy, they're idiots. Don't worry about them," I said casually.

But looking into Kathy's eyes, I was beginning to think her fear was genuine.

This cast a whole new light on the situation. What could be going on here? Was this random or orchestrated? In sizing these guys up, it was painfully obvious which one was the leader. He was about my height, had about thirty pounds on me (probably beer) and was definitely not a fighter. He had a full set of pearly-white teeth. Fighters don't. I knew right off I could take care of this bozo, but the other three posed a problem. I needed an equalizer. Luckily, having heeded Vince's advice, I had a 22-caliber automatic (small but effective) shoved between my belt and pants. Covered by my shirt, nobody noticed.

I told Vince I wanted to stir the pot, and I felt strongly this little scene was part of the stew. But to find out with certainty, it was time to turn up the heat.

Focusing on Kathy, I announced loudly, "Honey, I think it's time to go."

If they were going to make a move, they would do it now.

Kathy smiled with relief as we rose from our table. As I figured, this forced the leader to act. Directing his attention at me, he said gruffly, "Hey, you can go, but leave the broad."

The other three laughed.

Like I said, it was time to stir the pot, turn up the heat and see what was cooking. So I suggested he go sexually penetrate himself. I confess he wasn't as stupid as I thought. He got the drift. And the others stopped laughing.

My provocation seemed to work. The four came over and surrounded Kathy and me.

"What a joke," I thought. "My dead grandmother could be more frightening."

But when the leader suggested we all sit down, I played along and acted scared. As Kathy and I sat, we were flanked on each side. From her facial expression, her eyes and her quivering hands, I had no doubt now that her fear was genuine. If Kathy's scared, she must have had no idea they were coming. If that's true, then who sent them? Vince and I felt there was someone looming in the dark behind all this. Maybe these fools could shed some light.

One of them started to paw Kathy while the leader sat down next to me. It was now my turn to be in charge. Sliding the gun from under my shirt, I shoved the barrel deep into the leader's fat belly. It took him only a second to realize what that cold piece of steel was.

Whispering into his ear, I badgered, "That's right, stupid. That's exactly what you think it is pressed against your gut. Now let's make it more interesting."

I pushed the gun down to his manhood.

"Now, stupid, if you don't want to be somebody's bitch for the rest of your life, tell these three assholes to back off, especially the one touching the woman."

Pushing the gun barrel harder against him, I commanded, "Now speak!"

With a cracking voice, he told the cretins to back off. They were bewildered. It was time to emphasize a few points.

Directing my attention to them, I said quietly, "Gentlemen, I have a small caliber gun resting on top of your leader's pecker. If one of you so much as blinks wrong, I'm going to blow it off."

Looking back at their leader, I asked, "You think they understand?"

With a cold sweat trickling off his forehead, he said shakily, "Do what he says! Just do what he says!"

At this point, there was no doubt I was in charge.

"Fine," I began again. "Now, not to cause any suspicion or problems from our fellow bikers, I want everyone's hands on the table, palms down. NOW!"

Slowly, each hand did as I commanded. Every fingernail was manicured! Now I had no doubts at all. These boneheads were definitely not what they appeared to be.

Kathy sat in awe. She couldn't believe what was happening. She was stiff with fear. I diverted my attention back to her.

"Babe, go to the car. Get in, and lock the door."

Rising quickly from the table, Kathy did exactly what I said.

Once I knew she was safe, I addressed the smallest moron, "You, dummy ..."

Pointing his finger to his own chest, he sputtered, "Who me?"

Referring back to the leader, shaking my head I asked, "Are the other two that stupid?"

He didn't answer.

"Yeah, dummy, you," I instructed. "Go over to your bikes and pull all the spark plug wires. Then place them on the ground next to the passenger door of my car. Then come back and sit. Any problems and your fearless leader here will sing soprano for the rest of his life."

Pushing the gun harder against him, "Right, stupid?" I chided.

He responded with a quivering, "Just do it! And hurry!"

"Good thought," I added.

It took about five minutes. With the wires sitting next to the Mustang door and dummy back safely in our circle, I began again.

"OK, gentlemen, I want some answers. Who sent you?"

"What do you mean?" the leader asked.

Pushing the gun harder against him, I thought he would cry.

"Please, mister, please don't shoot. I've got a wife and two kids."

"I won't if you tell me."

"I don't know. Honest."

"Don't know?"

"Yeah, really. We were on a run yesterday when this old guy approached us and asked if we wanted to make a few bucks. That's all."

"Who was this old guy?"

"Honest to God, we don't know. He just said he wanted to scare his girlfriend a little and the guy she was with. Told us you'd be here today and gave us each two bills."

"Describe him," I demanded.

"Like I said, an older guy ... white ... early 60's ... 5'11" maybe ... 210 pounds."

By that description, it could be one of fifty guys there that day.

"Did the woman know anything about this?"

"No, I don't think so. I think he just wanted to scare you both."

"How?"

"He wanted us to get you into his van then he was going to take you someplace."

"Take us where?"

"I don't know. All we were supposed to do was get you to the van."

"Do you see him here now?"

"Yeah ... uh ... no. He was over in the corner," nodding with his head, "when we first got here, but he's gone now."

"Gone?"

"He must of left when you stuck the gun into me."

I couldn't remember seeing anyone over in the corner. Glancing quickly to the parking lot, I saw only one van, a green minivan.

"What kind of van was it?"

"A white Chevy utility van."

"Out of curiosity, what do you do for a living, besides trying to scare little girls?" I asked.

The leader started with his voice still cracking, "We all work for a studio."

"Doing what?"

"I'm an accountant and Mike there," referring to the guy who got the spark plug wires, "is an electrician."

"The other two?" I pressed.

"They work in wardrobe and makeup."

"You're kidding!" I crowed in disbelief. "Then on weekends you idiots dress up and pretend to be bad? How pathetic. OK, fearless, this is what we're going to do. You and I are going to rise slowly from this table. Your three girlfriends will sit here and just look pitiful until I tell them to move."

Standing, I slid the gun inconspicuously from his groin to his back. We moved slowly to the Mustang. With the gun still pressed hard in stupid's back, I told Kathy to open her door and grab the spark plug wires. Still scared, she did exactly as I instructed.

Turning my attention back to their fearless leader, I told him to walk back to his buddies and sit at the table. He must have been extremely scared. As he walked away, I noticed his butt and upper thighs were wet. Somewhere through it all, he had an accident. I wonder what he told his wife. You just have to love tough guys.

Pulling away from the Rock Store, we headed toward the beach. I kept an eye on the rearview mirror. My gut told me this wasn't over. I didn't let on to Kathy, but we did have company ... a white Chevy utility van.

It was apparent someone was now playing for keeps. Obviously, Vince and I dug just a little too deep, and someone was getting very nervous. I still didn't know what or why. But a kidnap attempt was serious business. How did Kathy play into this? My plan was to spend time with her this weekend to see what other clues I might uncover, but I wasn't figuring on this. And apparently neither was she, even though she must have let someone know we'd be at the Rock Store. Kathy was scared, and she had a right to be. Once in that van, God only knows what would have happened. We were lucky.

The description the bikers gave me generally fit Vince's tail in Vegas. A professional would have used real bikers. This guy didn't. Amateur hour? I wasn't quite sure. But whatever it meant, someone was indeed getting very, very nervous.

Opening the console, I pulled out heavier artillery ... my Glock. Kathy's eyes got big. Using my knee to steer, I loaded the clip but didn't slide the rack. I placed it back in the console. I prayed I wouldn't need to use it. In shock, Kathy said nothing.

Reaching Pacific Coast Highway, there was a little diner stop with a few custom cars in the parking lot. I had noticed it on the way up the mountain. It was a perfect place for cover and possibly protection. After all, car guys do stick together. So I pulled into the parking lot, and we were immediately surrounded by car enthusiasts. They were all in heat, panting over my awesome set of wheels.

"Rick …" Kathy said nervously.

"Don't worry, baby. You're as safe as in your mama's arms here."

To prove the point, when Kathy got out, not one head turned. It's all about cars.

Within minutes, the white van passed us on the highway going south. Shortly, Kathy and I would head north. I couldn't get a look at the driver, but had a hunch I'd have another shot at seeing his face soon enough.

Traveling back to Santa Barbara, I could not only feel but see a difference in Kathy … a big difference. The normally talkative and flirty Kathy was as quiet as a church mouse. For an hour, she leaned into me with her hand on my thigh and her arm tucked through mine, as though trying to pull herself into me. Normally, such a pose from a woman would be full of teasing and a little sexual foreplay, but Kathy was somber, literally holding me for dear life.

"Hey, are you hungry?" I asked.

"A little."

"Want me to buy you dinner?"

Trying her best to contain a sniffle, she managed, "OK."

"Any place special?"

"No, you pick."

A few miles south of Santa Barbara there was a small steakhouse just off the highway that looked inviting. I decided to take a chance. As customary when driving my Mustang, I pulled into the outskirts of the parking lot, hoping to keep a good distance from the boneheads who like to play bumper car with their doors. A parking lot light is also mandatory. But there was also a method to my madness that particular evening. I wanted a clear, well-lit field when returning to the Mustang. I wanted to make sure there was no way someone could be hiding behind another car.

As I opened Kathy's door, she wasted no time getting out and wrapping her arms around me tightly.

"Hold me," she said desperately.

I pulled her firmly against me as she buried her head in my chest. I kissed the top of her head.

"Are you OK?" I asked.

With tears in her eyes and a quivery voice, "No," she responded.

"Kathy, no one's going to hurt you. I promise. But you need to level with me about what's going on."

Repositioning her hold on me, she sighed, "I know, I know."

I could still feel Kathy quivering as she clung to my arm while we walked to the restaurant. We picked a booth in the back, and her moist eyes said, "Come sit next to me." We faced the door. Kathy began to calm down as she nursed a double vodka martini.

"Kathy," I began. "Tell me what's going on."

"What do you mean, Rick?"

"Kathy, no more lies. I know you and Jack Webber have been close and know you handled Johnson's twenty million dollar claim. I also know that every step of the way, someone has been one step ahead of me."

"You don't understand."

"Well, tell me so I'll understand! Do you realize how close you and I came to being kidnapped today?"

"Kidnapped? What do you mean?"

"I mean those bikers had orders to get you and me into a white van. Listen to me, Kathy. Someone's out there playing for keeps, and with twenty million on the line, they're going to play rough."

Taking my arm again, Kathy begged, "Oh, Rick, just walk away from this. It's not what you think."

"Tell me then, Kathy. Tell me what it really is."

"I can't."

"Can't or won't?"

"Can't."

"Kathy, why did you call me that first time?"

"Rick, please, just let it go."

"So, your invitation to stay the night and the lovemaking was all an act?"

Her voice became soft and her eyes warm, "No, Rick, the love I gave to you was never an act."

For some reason, I believed her.

Before we could continue our conversation, my cell rang. It was Vince.

"Hey."

"You found someone?"

"Yeah, Santa Barbara."

"Where?"

"How about 8:00 A.M.?"

"Great, see you there."

"Who was that?" Kathy asked as I hung up.

"I need to go into L.A. tomorrow."

"For what?"

"Just company business, dear. But I'll be back early afternoon. And we can finish this conversation."

Slipping her arm back through mine, she laid her head on my shoulder and said nothing.

Arriving back at Kathy's, I put the Mustang in her garage and made sure the condo was locked. Kathy invited me to share her bed for the night, but I felt it best to sleep downstairs. With Kathy tucked in safely upstairs, I stretched out on the couch and pulled my special comforter over me. For some reason, I always take it with me on my road trips. It still had the faint scent of Caroline. I grabbed my Glock, racked the slide, and took off the safety. I set it on the floor close by. Then I slid the 22 under my pillow.

Tomorrow would come early. For the moment, I just wanted to make sure it came.

CHAPTER 16

It was Monday morning, 6:00 sharp. Key to ignition, I sparked the Mustang's 300 plus ponies to life. If only it was that easy to start me up! Squinting at the clock, it now read 6:01. Twenty minutes before sunrise, and I would need every hour of daylight. First stop, the San Fernando Valley. Then backtrack to Santa Barbara. And let's not forget my late dinner in San Francisco.

Traveling down 101 gave me time to think. Over and over, I played the facts of this inquiry. What was making someone so very nervous? The thought of fraud, for a twenty million dollar payout, had crossed my mind of course. But as I reminded Vince, a heart attack from sex is not fraud. And if there's no fraud, there's no crime. And if there's no crime, then what the hell was going on? Kathy pretty much admitted she knew. "It's not what you think, Rick," she told me. But that's all she'd tell me. Why? Jack had to have something to do with it … but what? And Caroline? All I had were questions and more questions. But the events of the previous day sent a shiver down my spine.

It was a little after 8:00 when I pulled into the coffee shop parking lot in the Valley. Vince was already there leaning against the hood of his rental car. I pulled up next to him and he jumped into my car with a smile.

"Nice set of wheels, Rick. Very nice," he commented, looking briefly around the interior.

Grinning from ear to ear, "Thanks," I said proudly.

Before we got started on the business at hand, I gave Vince a rundown on what happened yesterday with Kathy and the bikers. My emphasis was on the man responsible for the setup, the older guy who might have also been Vince's tail in Vegas, his white van and his attempt to kidnap us.

After listening to my report, I saw something in Vince's eyes I never expected. Fear. It took a minute before he spoke.

"Rick, we've opened a door someone wants to keep closed. Somehow, somewhere, everything we've touched from your initial inquiry about your agent to the incident yesterday ... all of it's related."

Vince paused then began again.

"Listen to me, and listen good. From this moment forward, trust no one. Not the people you work with, friends, family, no one. Take everything you are told with a grain of salt. Be on guard like never before. Understand this. Maybe tomorrow or maybe next week, there will be another attempt against you. Watch your back very carefully. Like your lady friend said, 'not everything is what it appears to be.'"

"Vince, you sound like you're trying to scare me," I said with a half-chuckle.

With piercing eyes, he said, "I am. But if it's any consolation, I'm scared as well."

"I have to move forward on this no matter where it leads."

"I know you do. But after you hear what this person has to say this morning, you may want to change your mind."

"Understood," I said. "So, where are we going to meet this mystery person?"

"We're here," Vince said.

"Here?"

"Yeah, inside saving us a table."

"Who is he?" I asked curiously.

"It's a she."

"She?" I questioned him with some surprise.

"Yeah, an ex-aide who worked for Cole. Her name is Harriett Miller."

"How the hell did you ever find her?"

"Simple. I was reading some old newspaper articles about him. One mentioned a statement from his aide and gave her name. I googled her, and the rest is history."

Following Vince into the coffee shop, I saw an older lady sitting by herself in a booth in the back corner. She appeared to be in her late fifties. By her profile and appearance, I would bet ten years ago she turned a lot of heads.

When we arrived at the booth, Vince began with an introduction.

"Ms. Miller, this is Rick Morgan, the man I spoke of yesterday."

Shaking hands, we exchanged greetings as Vince and I sat down. The look on her face said she was a woman with a story to tell.

"Ms. Miller," Vince began, "please tell Rick what you told me."

Taking a sip of coffee first, she began, "Well, Mr. Morgan, you must first understand that Peter Cole was a very ambitious and cold man. He would do anything to advance his political career and did. He kept a detailed record of indiscretions on everyone he perceived to be an enemy, on either side of the aisle. He was never afraid to use dirt for leverage."

Vince interrupted, "Tell Rick about that Tuesday night in 1976."

Hearing 1976, my ears perked up as I glanced at Vince. Nodding his head slightly, he was telling me to pay special attention.

"It was about 11:00 P.M. on July 6, 1976, when Peter, uh, Mr. Cole, was driving home from a fundraiser and drifted over the line. He hit another car head-on, killing three people. He had been drinking."

I looked at Vince incredulously. I couldn't believe what I just heard! I was speechless.

"Please go on, Ms. Miller," Vince said quietly, reassuring her everything was alright.

"Well, as I said, his car drifted over the line and hit this other car head-on. It was a family coming home from somewhere (I really don't remember), but the mother and father were killed, leaving three very young orphaned daughters. I think there was another adult in the car, but I can't remember who."

At this point, her voice cracked and tears had already begun to trickle down her cheeks. Lightly cupping my hand over hers, I did my best to assure her that neither Vince nor I were blaming her and to keep going with the story as best she could.

Wiping her eyes with a hankie and a sniffle, she continued, "Peter was so drunk he didn't know what had happened. After the accident, he used his position to hamper the investigation and avoid prosecution."

"Do you remember a police detective named Nielsen?" I asked.

Nodding her head, she said, "He went after Peter with a vengeance. But Peter was just too powerful for him. Peter had dirt on the DA and half the cops in L.A., including some very high in the department. He fished with judges and newspaper editors."

"Do you remember names?" Vince asked.

Shaking her head glumly, she said, "That's a secret I must keep. But with Peter's connections, he was able to block Mr. Nielsen at every turn. Then he would laugh about it."

"Ms. Miller," I began again, "do you remember anything about the family? Their name? Anything?"

"No, only that three very young daughters survived. Peter made sure all three were *not* adopted by the same family. Didn't want anything to come back and haunt him later. He was very thorough."

"Do you remember who adopted the girls? Or who handled the adoptions?"

"No, I don't. It was kept very quiet. Peter used his influence with a judge to make sure everything was sealed. I do know the two youngest were adopted by someone here in L.A. The older one, I can't remember."

"Why are you telling this now?" I asked.

Still tearful she replied, "For years I was in love with Peter Cole. Even though he was married we had a secret life together. But now he's dead and time has a way of changing memories."

"Mr. Cole ended up on the board of the insurance company I work for. Do you know anything about the events leading up to that?"

"After the accident, the party chairman stepped in and told him not to run again, that he should quietly bow out of politics. They said he was too much of a liability. Peter fought them, even threatened the chairman with blackmail from his infamous black book of indiscretions. But shortly afterward, three men came to the office. They had a long and loud conversation with Peter, and things changed after that."

"Do you remember anything specific from the argument?"

"Only that if Peter proceeded with the election, he …"

She stopped in mid-sentence. The tears again began to trickle down her cheeks.

"He what, Ms. Miller?"

"He wouldn't live to see election night."

Vince and I just stared blankly at each other.

"Do you remember who the men were?"

"Peter once told me when he was drunk."

"And?"

"He said they were FBI."

"FBI?" I blurted out.

"They scared Peter more than anyone ever had. After their visit, Peter announced he would not seek re-election."

Again, Vince and I just stared at each other. Her story was unbelievable.

"Ms. Miller, how did Cole end up with my company?" I asked again.

"All I know is someone with lobbyist connections in Washington, D.C. arranged it. With his little black book, he became very effective in getting the legislation the industry needed."

"What do you think happened to his black book after his death?" Vince asked.

Shaking her head, she replied, "I really have no idea. And I don't want to know."

Vince continued, "What do you know about Cole's death?"

I was a little surprised with Vince's boldness in asking the question. But I was even more surprised at Ms. Miller's lack of emotion in answering it.

Shaking her head with a calm voice, "Nothing," she replied. "Only what I read in the papers."

Her response emboldened me to ask another rough question.

"I know this may be hard, but ... did he have ... any other friends besides you?"

"You mean mistresses, don't you?" she asked.

Nodding my head I said, "I'm sorry. I tried not to be so obvious, but yes."

"Besides being a drunk, Peter Cole couldn't keep it in his pants."

"Then why did you stay with him all those years?" I asked quietly.

Looking down at her empty coffee cup, her answer was just as quiet as my question.

"I guess you could say I have self-esteem issues."

Our meeting with Ms. Miller lasted less than an hour. After thanking her for her time and honesty, Vince and I retired to the bar across the street. Normally, 9:00 A.M. is a little early for a vodka martini, but after hearing what we did, one was needed.

Seated in the back corner, Vince began, "Well, Rick, at least we know the significance of that date now."

Nodding my head, I took another sip of my drink.

"But, Vince, I have one question. What does that accident have to do with Johnson?"

"I have a man working on that now," Vince said. "Somewhere there's a connection between the two. It may take some time, but I'll find it."

"Dig as deep as you can with both. And keep digging with Nielsen. I'm still curious how he fits into all of this, besides just being a cop and investigator."

"Here's a thought, Rick. Did Nielsen take work with your company just to stay close to Cole?"

Shaking my head, I said, "Another good question that doesn't have an answer ... yet."

The stop and go traffic back to Santa Barbara made the trip longer than normal, but gave me time to think. Not only about what Ms. Miller said, but also about what questions to pose to Kathy. I was deep in thought when my cell rang.

It was Kathy. Her voice sounded troubled. She wanted to meet in an hour in the parking lot of the restaurant where we dined the night before. I agreed to the meeting.

As I was pulling into the parking lot, I saw Kathy's car next to the same light pole from last night. She wasn't alone. In the driver's seat was someone I knew I'd see again before this was done. It was my old friend, Jack Webber. I parked my car next to hers and we both got out. Kathy seemed very upset. Jack never moved.

"Rick," Kathy started, "I resigned from the company this morning, effective immediately. I'm going to live with Jack and my son."

"Well, Kathy, I figured you knew Jack better than you were letting on. I guess I was right."

"I'm sorry, Rick. I never wanted to lie to you."

"Kathy, I need some answers."

"I know you do. Maybe someday I can tell you."

"Someday? Tell me what? All I have is ..."

Putting a finger to my lips, Kathy quietly said, "Sh-sh-sh. Listen to me. Stop digging. Let it go."

"Not without answers, Kathy," I fired back.

Shaking her head she said, "You won't like the answers."

"First Caroline and now you. What are you two trying to tell me?"

"We're just trying to protect you, Rick."

"From what?"

"Oh, Rick," Kathy said softly so Jack wouldn't hear. "I really wish things could have been different. But now I need to go."

She reached up and gave me a kiss on the cheek then quickly turned. Gripping the door handle she paused and turned again to me. Looking up into my eyes she said in a near whisper, "Be careful."

I knew pushing her would be futile. I just nodded. As she climbed into the car, her door wasn't even shut before Jack sped off. As they pulled away, I noticed Kathy looking back in the side mirror. It was only a quick glimpse, but even at a distance I saw in her eyes the same serious concern as in her words … "be careful." I watched the car until it cleared the parking lot and turned the corner.

After sliding behind the steering wheel of my Mustang, I sat collecting my thoughts. Jack never said a word. I wondered why. A small part of me wished things could have been different with Kathy too. Maybe that's why.

Slipping the key into the ignition, something caught the corner of my right eye. Across the parking lot sat a white utility van, alone. By the faint, dull, grey smoke coming from the tailpipe, it was apparent the motor was running. My gut told me it was the same one from yesterday. Opening the console, I inserted the clip and racked the slide on the Glock and then did the same with the twenty-two. After putting the Glock back in the console and the twenty-two under my jacket on the passenger's seat, I fastened my seat belt. With a quick glance back at the van, I put my car in gear and headed for the freeway. The on-ramp read "101 North—San Francisco."

CHAPTER 17

Traveling up 101 North, I kept my eye on the rearview mirror. Laid back about half mile, the white van had been following me for the last 120 miles. Like a faithful puppy, it was always there. Vince had warned me that another attempt would be made against me.

I was concerned.

As long as I was driving, there wouldn't be a problem. But on the outskirts of Atascadero, California, my fuel gauge was sitting on top of the big E. My baby needed more go-go juice and very soon. A pit stop was unavoidable.

A sign said, "Gas Next Exit." I had no choice. Would the white van follow?

As I arrived at the pumps, a young mom in an older minivan pulled in behind me. She had a daughter, about a year old, sound asleep in a car seat. A pink top gave the baby's gender away. The woman was about 25, average in looks, with shoulder-length blond hair that was showing its roots. She was about 5' 3", 130 pounds, with fair complexion. Under her long, frumpy sweatshirt was a fantastic bustline and a matching set of hips. I decided she'd be a knockout with different clothes, hairstyle, and make up. She was having trouble with her credit card. She kept putting it in the pump then, with much frustration, taking it out and trying again as if some magic would transform the card between tries.

My eyes were diverted as the white van pulled up to the pump across from me. The driver was an older man fitting the description the biker gave. The picture Vince took of his shadow in Vegas wasn't terribly clear, but this could be the same guy. He was wearing a dirty white polo shirt, and his sandy brown hair was in desperate need of a cut, or at least a comb.

His face had scars that blended awkwardly with his deep wrinkles. He got out of his van, paused for a moment and our eyes met. His were cold and heartless. This was a man who had lived a hard and violent life. A shiver went down my back. I took comfort in the thought of my weapons, loaded and ready.

His cold eyes quickly found the young woman with the credit card problems who was now leaning against the pump beginning to cry. He seemed momentarily preoccupied by the helpless appearance of the young mother. The look on his face screamed "predator." I suddenly became more concerned for her safety than mine. I needed to intervene.

Walking a few steps to the minivan, "May I be of assistance?" I asked cautiously.

"Oh, this thing won't work," she said, referring to the credit card in her hand while wiping the tears from her cheeks.

From the code on the pump, I knew immediately what the problem was. Her credit card was over its limit. Her vehicle was full of personal items, so I figured she was on her way someplace and ran out of money. I suggested she go in the store and have the clerk punch the numbers manually, just to make sure. Taking my advice, she went inside, keeping an eye on the minivan with her sleeping baby. The white-van-man followed her in. I could see her talking to the clerk, and his head was shaking no. Then the van guy approached her, but I couldn't make out the conversation. The woman began vigorously shaking her head no, and she ran outside in tears. She threw open her van door and fell across the seat, crying hard.

I walked back over to her and asked, "Are you alright?"

I was keeping one eyeball on the white-van-man who was now back at his pump. From his scowl, it was apparent he didn't like my intervention.

The woman sobbed, "I don't know what to do."

Tears were streaming down her face. I took a shot in the dark and asked her, "You're out of money, aren't you?"

With her head down, I heard a muffled yes.

"Where are you going?"

"Seattle."

"Do you have family or friends there?"

"My mom."

"And the baby's father?"

The question startled her. No doubt she was wondering who this strange man was, asking such a personal question. Seeing the despair on her face, I asked the question again, softly. Not as a stranger, but as a friend.

"Where is the baby's father?"

Fighting back her tears, "He left me a few days ago after clearing out our checking account. He wanted me to choose between him and our daughter," she sputtered, gazing lovingly at the child with a wet smile. "She's my life."

Tears filled her eyes again. With passionate frustration, she blurted, "I just need to get home!"

She was one scared young lady with no one to help her. I could only imagine what the white-van-guy had said to her in her fragile condition. I felt partially responsible for adding him to her troubles. His van hadn't moved, and he loomed in the background. I was scared for her. I couldn't just leave her and her baby in his crosshairs as I drove away. I decided to intercede, if she would let me.

"What's your name?" I asked.

"Alicia," she replied with a slight smile.

"Alicia, I'm Rick. This is what we're going to do. I'm going to fill your tank with gas, then … see the McDonald's over there?" It was right next to the gas station.

"Yes."

"After I fill your tank, I want you to follow me over there. OK?"

With tears still trickling down her cheeks, she nodded her head.

"Now get back in your van, and let me fill your tank."

Although she could have simply driven away with her full tank, Alicia followed my instructions. We both pulled away from the pumps and met in the adjacent McDonald's lot. The white van was still at its pump, and I knew our guy was watching us.

I began before she could say thank you.

"Alicia, if I ran a background check on you would it come back clean? No drugs, arrests, felonies or anything?"

She looked puzzled. She had no clue where I was going with my line of questioning. But she nodded her head.

"Do you want a job in Seattle?"

Her face pleaded yes as she answered with anticipation, "I was hoping to get one."

I took out my cell phone and pushed a button. After two rings, it was picked up.

"Emily, Rick."

"No, I'm in California."

"Yes, I'm coming back. I want you to do something. I want you to interview someone Thursday and see if she's a fit for anything in our department."

"No, I won't be back until Friday."

"Yes, I'll clear it with personnel when I get back. Her name is Alicia. Is 3:00 open?"

As I asked that question, I was also asking Alicia. She looked dazed, but she nodded.

"Great. I'll leave her in your capable hands."

"What?"

"Yes, I promise I'll be back."

Handing Alicia my card, I explained, "Congratulations. You're about to be exposed to the exciting world of insurance. And if you ever believe it to be exciting, you're a sick puppy."

Alicia had an odd expression on her face. It was a combination of excitement and anxiety. She was probably still wondering who this strange man was—helping her, but with what secret motive?

Pointing to the card, I instructed, "Go to this address Thursday at 3:00, and ask for Emily in my office. Wear something conservative and clean. Now, no guarantees, but let's give it a shot. OK?"

"Are you serious?" she asked, with a slight smile spreading.

"Very. Now, I know your credit card's maxed. I assume you have no money on you?"

"About two dollars," she answered quietly.

Taking my wallet out, I handed her seven twenties and a ten.

"This will get you home. You can pay it back later."

She paused, not sure if she should take the cash.

"Here, take it. It's alright. Just don't let me down."

Taking the money, she broke down in tears again and buried her head in my chest mumbling, "Thank you ... thank you ..."

Her tears touched me. This woman had been seriously let down by men. It was hard for her to trust. I was glad to reintroduce the word to her ... trust ... and I was hoping she now believed in me enough to answer one more question.

"Alicia, when you were talking with the guy in the store, what did he say to you?"

I could tell she was embarrassed and hesitant to answer. She didn't have to. I already knew. I searched carefully for the right words to use.

"Did he … proposition you?"

With her head down, she nodded yes. I needed to know as much as possible about this man, so I pressed further.

"What did he ask?"

"He said he'd give me money if I …" She couldn't finish her thought.

"Alicia, get in your van and lock the doors. Head for home. Stop someplace this evening and get a good night's sleep. See Emily Thursday, and everything will be alright soon. You'll see."

Burying her head in my chest again, with a hopeful tone she said, "Thank you. Thank you very much."

As Alicia's old minivan took off, I turned back to the Mustang. By now the white van had pulled away from the pumps and was parked on the side of the building. Leaning against a fender, the man was staring at me intently. Our eyes met again, this time holding contact longer. Each was sizing up the other. Even at a distance, his eyes gleamed with trouble. The eyes invited me, dared me, to come meet him face to face. A tiny voice of reason inside my head told me, "Walk away, Rick. Just get in the Mustang and go."

Yes, I should have listened. But in case you haven't noticed, I'm a tenacious guy when I have questions. And I had a lot of questions I was sure he could answer. So instead of driving away, I pulled up next to his van. I noticed his rear license plate was the old California black and yellow style that hasn't been issued since 1969. The van couldn't have been more than a few years old. And the plate had bugs on it, meaning it had once been on the front of a vehicle. Conclusion: stolen plates on a stolen vehicle.

With the Mustang between him and me, I got out. He looked unarmed. I left the Glock in the console. We just stared at each other. Him, still leaning on the fender. Me, with my car door open, leaning and looking across the roof. He started the conversation.

"I had plans and you fucked them up. Again."

"Life's tough," I responded.

He didn't like my answer, and I really didn't care. But then something caught my eye on his upper right arm: a tattoo of a clock face with no hands. Now I had no doubt. This was certainly the same man who tailed Vince in Vegas. The dynamics of the game just changed. I began to press for some answers.

"Look, you followed my friend in Vegas. You tried to kidnap me yesterday. Now you're here. Who are you working for?"

Smiling, he began slowly, "Someone … who wants you to back off."

"Why?" I asked.

"Why ain't important. But if you know what's good for ya, ya'll back off."

"And if I don't?"

"Then I'll fuck ya up a little," he grinned.

Again—going back to the eyes—there was something there that told me to run. Run away. Run fast. That chill I felt earlier just got colder.

Trying desperately not to show fear, I responded sarcastically, "Yeah, whatever."

With that, I ducked into the Mustang and crouched behind the steering wheel, grabbing for the keys in the ignition. Simultaneously, he pulled a gun from under his shirt, and pointed it directly at me through the passenger's window—a blue steel 38 Special with a 4" barrel. Using the gun, he indicated for me to roll down the window. I did. It briefly crossed my mind to grab my 22 from under the jacket lying on the passenger seat, but considering the facts, that I was outgunned and he was most likely a murderer, I decided against it.

"OK, fucker, got your attention now?" he asked as he pulled back the hammer of the double action revolver.

With my eyes glued to the weapon's barrel—about four feet from my head—yes, he had my attention … my complete attention. I said nothing. I couldn't. Instantly my throat was dry, bowels were moving, and I'm almost certain both my breathing and my heart had stopped.

I prayed I was wrong, but looking at that deeply-cratered, angry face I figured this was someone who had seen and done it all, someone with no fear and nothing to lose. But what worried me most was not what came from his lips or eyes, but rather his hands. They were shaky. Guns in shaky hands have a way of going off. And at four feet, I had a big problem. Keeping both my hands on the steering wheel, my instinct as an ex-marine told me two things: move slowly and play it cool. Very cool.

Though I managed to take a deep breath, my heart still wasn't beating as I started talking.

"So tell me," I began, trying to keep my voice from cracking. "How long have you been out?"

"What d' ya mean?" he spit angrily.

"Folsom? Quentin?"

"What's it to you, asshole?"

"Nothing, really. But there are security cameras everywhere."

I had no idea if there were or not. But if I could bluff my way out of this, I was sure going to try. He glanced around the area.

"I don't see none, man."

"Of course you don't. They're always hidden. But next time smile, because they see you. In fact, the cops are probably on their way right now."

"Stop messin' with me, man, or I swear to God I'll blow you away."

I believe he meant it. His tone told me this psycho wasn't kidding.

"Look, you're an ex-con with a gun. That means parole violation. That means a one-way ticket back to the joint. I'm guessing, but I'll bet the van is stolen. Right?"

He said nothing. But the gun was quivering.

"It's probably already on the hot sheet. Every CHP officer on 101," I continued, jutting my chin toward the freeway, "has the license and description. They'll pick you up before sundown. Now think for a minute. You have a choice. Put the gun down, wipe your prints from the van, and walk away."

"Or what?" he asked, his hands still shaking.

"They never come with their sirens on."

I meant when you least expect it. I could tell by his eyes this got him thinking. But I couldn't tell what he was thinking.

"So tell me, friend," I started again. "Who are you working for?"

I needed the answer desperately. Enough to ask this second time with a shaky 38 aimed at my head.

"I told you it don't matter."

"How did you know where I'd be yesterday or today? And how did you know my man was in Vegas?"

His hands were a little calmer, but still somewhat jittery as he answered, "I got a phone call."

"A phone call?" I asked, surprised.

"Yeah, a call. I was told to stop ya any way I could."

And if it meant killing me, I think he would have.

"What was it about the girl in the minivan today or the woman yesterday?"

"Oh, man," he said. "I wasn't gonna hurt da bitches. I just wanted me some ass."

"So Kathy never knew anything of you?"

"Who's Kathy?" he said blankly, not caring about an answer.

137

As he was speaking, he glanced over the roof of my car. He saw something that definitely distracted him.

"Shit," he cursed.

Looking directly at me, he commanded, "Get the fuck outta here."

He waved the gun as though I should go in a certain direction. I felt my heart start again. I was surprised by his sudden change, but I still played it cool, starting the Mustang up without making any quick moves. But before I could put it in gear, three CHP cruisers silently converged with precise execution. Each cruiser's nose pointed directly at us. The officers moved quickly to crouching positions behind their doors with guns drawn. The ex-con looked confused, but he'd never give up. He wasn't going back.

An officer shouted for him to drop his weapon. Instinctively, I crouched low in my seat. A single shot rang out. It was instantly followed by seven or eight more from multiple weapons. Then silence. Slowly, I rose from my seat. The officers came out from behind their cruisers with guns still trained cautiously. The white smoke of gunfire lingered in the air as did the smell of sulfur. A figure in a dirty white polo shirt lay on the ground in a pool of blood next to my Mustang.

I never did find out who hired him.

For five hours the CHP questioned me, mostly wanting to know my relationship with this man. Remembering Vince's words from earlier that day, I said very little, trusting no one. But I wanted to ask the cops some questions myself. I was plagued with curiosity. How did the cops know he was there? Their assault seemed too well-orchestrated for a simple operation, like if someone at the gas station had called 911. Had they been watching him as he watched me? I tried to find these things out without showing my hand, but their responses—like mine—were not informative. Their reason: official business. After the marathon interrogation, the CHP finally let me go. I'm sure the call to my attorney helped persuade them I'd had enough.

Sitting at the bar very late that night in San Francisco, I thought of the cold, blue steel, 38 caliber barrel pointed directly at my head. I had a vodka martini. Thinking of the shaky hand that held it, I had another. It didn't help. But her warm hand on my thigh did.

CHAPTER 18

It was 6:30 A.M., and I was at the dining room table waiting for breakfast. There was a ringing in my ears. I wasn't sure if it was my cell phone or the byproduct of too many martinis from the night before. It was my cell. Vince was calling me.

"Hey, Vince," I said, trying to focus both eyes and brain.

"No, I'm awake ... sort of," I muttered somewhat incoherently.

"What?"

"No, it's not too early."

"You did? Great."

"Where?"

"Tonight? What time?"

Pausing to collect my thoughts and negotiate the cobwebs in my head, I said, "OK. Yeah, have Frank get me a room, and I'll call you as soon as I book a flight. And Vince, one more thing, let's stop by the mortuary and have a talk with them while I'm down there."

"You did? What kind of problem?"

"Oh, well, let's talk about it tonight."

"Right."

"See you tonight."

Walking out of the kitchen wearing a white full-length terrycloth robe, she looked gorgeous. She sat down next to me and began with a half-smile, "Are you leaving me?"

"Yeah, but hold that thought," I said, smiling back.

Pushing a speed-dial on my cell, a voice answered on the second ring.

"Emily, it's me."

"Alive? I think so. Are you at your computer?"

"Great. Find me a flight from SFO to Vegas tonight around 6:00."

"I'll wait."

Directing my attention back to my friend, "I need to be in Vegas tonight," I whispered.

"Vegas?" she asked, wondering.

"It's business."

"Ah-ha," she said with a raised eyebrow and a teasing tone. "Business with dice?"

"No ... well ... maybe a couple passes."

"Anyway," she continued, "what shall I make you for breakfast?"

Before I could answer, Emily was back.

"Hold on," I mouthed.

"Yeah, Emily."

"What time?"

"Great. Book it for me, and I'll pick up the ticket at the airport."

"Right. Bye."

My plans for the day were beginning to formulate. I had a slightly different idea for breakfast.

I put my hand on hers and asked, "How about taking the day off and we'll have brunch in Carmel."

"Oh-h, Mr. Morgan," she cooed with a big grin. "That sounds wonderful."

"But there's a cost," I added.

"Cost?" she asked, gazing back at her bedroom door.

"Maybe someday," I said with a smile. "But for now, let's take your car, and you can drop me at the airport on the way back. Then pick me up tomorrow?"

"And I suppose you want to keep your Mustang in my garage again tonight?"

"Well, yeah."

Hitting me on the arm, she ribbed, "Mr. Morgan, I think you love that car more than me."

It was dusk when the plane landed at McCarran. A black Lincoln Town Car was waiting to take me to the hotel. Vince and Frank were in the backseat, both anxious about our meeting tonight.

"So, guys, I guess our missing ME has returned?" I started.

"Yeah," Vince began, "our stakeout team advised me that he returned yesterday afternoon. He's a creature of habit, so all indications are that he will be at his favorite strip club about ten o'clock tonight."

"Does he know we're coming?"

"No, he doesn't."

"The question is will he talk to us?"

"Frank's sending a special gift to help his memory," Vince offered. "I understand she's great at taking dictation."

Frank laughed.

"Oh-h," I replied with a chuckle. "Must be Heather."

My chuckle turned to a sigh. "I hear she's great at everything."

Frank's only response was, "Amen."

Turning back to Vince I asked, "So tell me what you found out with the mortuary?"

"Nothing."

"What do you mean 'nothing?'"

"They won't talk based on the privacy policy."

"Privacy policy? You have to be kidding."

That's when Frank spoke up.

"Rick, give me some time. I'll find you someone who'll answer your every question."

"Frank," I countered with some caution, "what do you have in mind?"

"Just remember everyone has a secret, including upstanding funeral directors."

"So we're talking blackmail?"

"Rick," Frank said shaking his head, "that's such an ugly term. I prefer the term 'enhanced persuasion.'"

I hadn't yet told Vince or Frank about the events of the day before, but figured this was as good a time as any.

"Guys, I need to tell you what happened yesterday."

By the tone of my voice, they both knew it was serious. For the next ten minutes, both sat in rapt attention as I recited the events that took place after Vince and I left the bar. When finished, their expressions were grim. These two ex-cops sat quietly, deep in thought.

Vince began, "You were right about one thing. The precision in the CHP response was not from a simple call about a man with a gun. Three cruisers that quickly? No, they were waiting for him to make a stop then converge. Those officers were sent to take him, alive or dead. And the fact they were so tight-lipped about their tip tells me there is someone else out there still pulling strings."

"Vince, if our theory is correct, we're making someone nervous, and if that someone's a high roller, the question's the same as before: why send an amateur?"

"Because," Frank interjected, "he was expendable."

We sat quietly pondering this. They sure did "expend" the guy.

"Rick," Frank began again, "any idea who sent him?"

Shaking my head, "None. But one thing I do know. He didn't want to kill me."

"How do you know?" Vince asked.

"When he saw the cops coming, he could have plugged me right then and there. But he didn't. He told me to leave. No, the kidnapping at the Rock Store was nothing more than him wanting some ass. He was trying to get some as a bonus while he did the job. Just like with the girl at the gas station. He was sent to scare me, then after his mission was accomplished, to be disposed of before he could talk."

"Possibly," Vince said while rubbing his chin.

"It would make sense," Frank added.

Directing my attention to both, I said, "But that makes whoever's pulling the strings cold and dangerous. Right?"

"Cold and *very* dangerous," Frank emphasized.

Vince nodded his head in agreement. "Just keep watching your back, Rick. This whole thing isn't over yet."

It was about 10:00 P.M. when Vince, Frank and I arrived at a strip club on the north side of Vegas. It was one of the seedier establishments in town that catered to degenerate locals rather than tourists. Passing the bouncer at the door, the smell of cigarettes, cheap liquor and body sweat (sex) was overpowering. A twenty dollar bill could buy you any sexual favor from a woman too strung out on drugs or alcohol to be halfway coherent.

Across the dimly-lit room was a stage with a scantily-dressed, middle-aged woman dancing with some difficultly around a pole to a monotonous sound someone had interpreted as music. Sadly, even at a distance, I could tell she had hit rock bottom. No doubt this joint was the end of a road that began years ago as a classier place such as "Debbie's Dining at the Y."

At a wobbly table center-stage sat our Jack Takahashi. He was a small grey-haired man of about 60. Once a most revered and respected Clark County coroner, he was now a man wearing tattered clothes who couldn't pass up a bottle of cheap wine, a dice game in a back alley, or a street hooker. Rumor had it he was deep in debt with some local sharks, so Frank already had the dope on who and how much Takahashi was into. Thought we could use that to our advantage if our gift of lovely Heather didn't loosen his tongue.

Vince, Frank and I sat at his table uninvited. His attention stayed on the stage.

"Dr. Takahashi?"

"Who wants to know?" he asked, glancing at me suspiciously.

Handing him my card, "My name is Rick Morgan," I replied.

"Should I care?" he responded, brushing off my card.

"Dr. Takahashi, how about we go into the parking lot and talk for a few minutes?" I suggested.

"I like it here just fine," he replied, turning his attention back to the dancer.

"Doc, I'll make it worth your while."

This caught his ear.

"How?" he questioned cautiously.

"Trust me. If you don't like what I offer, you're free to come back in."

"Yeah, how do I know I can trust you?"

That's when Frank spoke up. Making direct eye contact with Takahashi, he said, "Doc, Lou sends his regards."

I gathered Lou was the bookie the good doctor owed some money to. Hearing the name generated some anxiety. We now had his attention.

"Hey, guys," he began, "Lou said I could have until next week to pay."

Frank continued, "No, Doc, we're not collectors. But if you don't come with us, I can make a quick call to Lou and have a couple guys here in ten minutes."

Knowing he had no choice, Dr. Takahashi accompanied us to the parking lot.

Once outside, I began again.

"Doc, I'm interested in an autopsy you did about ten years ago," I said while handing him the death certificate.

"Ten years? I can't remember what I had for breakfast," he grumbled, handing it back without looking.

"Doc," I began again, "it's been my experience that accountants can remember every tax return they ever did. I'm betting you remember every autopsy you've ever done as well. But if not, I know you have your own records someplace."

With a cocky tone, he huffed, "Why should I tell you anything?"

"Do you like presents, Doc?"

"Presents? What do you mean?"

Looking over at a black Lincoln Town Car, Frank raised his hand. Immediately, its lights came on and moved in our direction, pulling alongside the four of us. The back window came down. A smiling and sexy young lady appeared.

Gesturing my hand toward her, "Doc, this is Heather," I announced.

The doctor's cocky look turned into a broad smile.

"Heather, say hello to Doc."

"What's *up*, Doc?" she cooed.

"Thanks, Heather," I said, signaling that she was done for now.

With an alluring smile, she blew a kiss and rolled up her window.

With a tap on the hood from Frank, the Town Car moved back to its parking spot.

"Doc, Heather will take you back to Frank's hotel where she will fulfill your heart's desires until tomorrow morning. In exchange, I want to know everything about that autopsy."

"Until tomorrow morning?" he grinned as his tongue moved across his lips.

The bait was working.

"Did I mention, Doc, that Heather loves to explore?"

"Explore? Hmm … Let me see that death certificate again."

Snatching it from my hand, he studied it briefly, rubbing his chin.

"Yeah, I believe I do remember this one."

"Don't you need your records, Doc?"

"Hell, no. Like you said, I remember every one of them pretty damn well."

"OK, tell me about this one."

"Yeah, about ten years ago. It was around 10:00 in the morning when I arrived at a suite on The Strip."

Vince and I nodded to each other. We knew the Doc was remembering the right case.

"The deceased was in bed, lying naked on his back. No visual signs of a struggle or foul play."

"How long had he been dead when you arrived?" I asked.

"About ten hours."

"So he died around midnight?"

"Give or take a half hour either way," he said, shrugging his shoulders.

"So, what then, Doc?"

"That's the interesting part. I was asked to hold off on transporting the body back to the office until an assistant DA arrived on the scene."

"Why?" Vince asked.

"I don't know."

"Do you remember the name?" I continued.

"Only 'AJ.' That's what everyone called her."

"Describe her, Doc."

"Oh, that's easy. Brunette, about 5'5", 125 pounds, maybe early twenties. Best pair of legs I've ever seen."

"That young, huh?"

"Yeah, I remember now. She came straight from school. Been there about a year. But *damn*, she was hot."

"Doc, I've heard there may have been a woman with Johnson when he died."

"Who told you that?"

"Doesn't matter. But is it true?"

"Yeah, I remember, the faint smell of perfume and the condom lying on his pecker."

Hearing that, Vince and I nodded to each other again.

"So what did you think, Doc?" I pushed.

"Simple. He wasn't alone in that room."

"I'm assuming you did a full autopsy?" Frank asked.

"Didn't have to. Died of congestive heart failure."

"Doc, put it in English," I said.

"Your deceased died of a heart attack. Plain and simple."

"This brings up an interesting question. My insurance company's doctor examined him about a year before and found him to be in perfect health. What's your opinion on how a perfectly healthy man has a heart attack?"

"Who said he was healthy? Your insured had, in plain English, a heart that should have given out years before. Gentleman, I won't go into all the details, but your insured had a weak and expanded heart from too much drinking, smoking and red meat through the years. And he was on a number of medications for blood pressure and a few other things, if I remember correctly. Hell, the meds were probably the only thing that kept him alive. So I would suggest maybe your records are a little confused or your examining physician was a quack."

Vince, Frank and I all looked at each other not knowing what to think.

"Doc, if a woman had been in the room, and if they were having sex with her on top, could he have ..."

Holding up his hand to stop me, he said, "That's exactly what happened. I'll still keep it in plain English for you. Your man was screwed to death."

"Is that your professional opinion?"

"Off the record, yes."

"Off the record? It's not in your official report?" Vince asked.

"No, it's not."

"Why?"

"Because a very pretty assistant DA asked me to omit it."

"Why?" I asked again.

"To save the family from some embarrassment, I would assume."

"Did someone from the family ever identify the deceased?"

"Yeah, a daughter."

"Do you remember her name?"

"No, I really don't."

"How about what she looked like?"

"How could I forget? About 5' 5", 125 pounds, blond hair, very pretty."

"That sounds like a blond version of the DA you just described."

"Yeah, about the same age and build, but definitely not the same woman."

"A question, Doc," Vince pressed. "How did you officially have the body identified?"

"Driver's license and the daughter's ID. Nothing more," he replied.

"Never verified finger prints?"

"You sound like a cop, mister."

"Retired Seattle PD, Homicide."

Shaking his head, he continued, "No, the DA's office wanted to close the case ASAP so we never bothered to send them out. There seemed to be no need to. As a cop, you know the drill."

"One last question, Doc. I see from the death certificate who picked up the body. Do you recall anything special about that?" I asked.

"Yeah, usually after an autopsy we try to put the deceased back together as much as possible. You know, to show some respect. The daughter didn't want us to take the time to do it. Wanted the body picked up and cremated ASAP."

"Do you remember why?"

Shaking his head, he said, "No. They were in more of a hurry than any family I'd ever dealt with. It was strange."

Thanking the good doctor for his time, Frank signaled the Town Car. As Doc was getting in, he stopped.

"It's my turn to ask a question," he said.

"Why so much interest in a ten-year-old case?"

Vince answered before I could.

"Just routine, Doc. You know the drill."

Nodding his head and smiling, he replied, "Sounds like a good cop answer."

He got the drift.

The three of us got back to Frank's hotel about midnight. I was exhausted. Frank offered Vince and me a little something to help us sleep—business associates of Heather's. Vince took Frank up on the offer. I didn't. Instead, I kept thinking about the incoherent older woman on the stage that night and of Heather. I wondered if that would be her in another thirty years. The visualization was disturbing.

Chapter 19

It was early Friday morning and I was back in the office struggling to find the top of my desk beneath a mountain of accumulated paperwork. Before I could even figure out where to start, Emily barged in without knocking.

"Mr. Morgan," she began. (The "Mr." told me either she was mad, or I was in trouble. Probably both.) "What's going on with you and my Uncle Vince?"

Her tone was a mixture of concern and defiance. But I was extremely tired from my hectic week and in no mood to play twenty questions.

Looking up from my desk, "What the hell are you talking about, Emily?" I fired back.

"I talked with Uncle Vince last night. He was in Los Angeles and, Rick, he's scared."

Her answer pushed me back a bit, so I softened, asking, "What did he say?"

I was concerned something happened that I wasn't aware of.

"Nothing."

"*Nothing?*" I repeated, with more than the usual irritation in my voice.

"That's the problem. When he gets scared, he shuts up—to me and everyone else in the family."

I motioned Emily to sit in the wingback chair. I came around and sat on the corner of my desk.

Emily continued, "Rick, since you and Caroline went to San Francisco awhile back, things have been different. That thing with Jack on Valentine's Day. Then Caroline all of a sudden quits—which makes no sense since she's in love with you. You hire Uncle Vince when the company has investigators coming out its ears. You have me interview Alicia yesterday, out of the blue. You're never in the office anymore. Then when you're here, you're like Uncle Vince—quiet. You gave Holly the third degree about Kathy Gibson, and now she's quit."

"Holly quit?" I exclaimed.

"No, Rick, I'm talking about Kathy Gibson."

Noting the look on my face, Emily continued, somewhat puzzled, "But … you … already knew, didn't you?"

I answered her question with a slight nod.

"Rick, what's going on?"

Before I could answer Emily's inquiry, my cell rang. Saved by the bell. And, speak of the devil. It was her Uncle Vince.

Motioning to Emily that the call was private only enhanced her irritation and curiosity. On her way out, she closed my door a little more vigorously than usual.

"So, Vince, what's cooking?"

"You found Nielsen's old partner?"

"Encino? I can be there tomorrow."

"Yeah, Burbank Airport."

"Great, I'll email you when I have my flight info, and you can pick me up."

"Talk to you soon."

Telling Emily I needed a ticket to Burbank for tomorrow morning only exasperated her more. So did the fact that I never answered her question. But I was too exhausted to worry about her right now and too energized by Vince's news to think about anything else. Since I first started this investigation, Nielsen's report on Johnson was key. It was the most important of all the pertinent information that had been replaced in the claim file with the 1976 Los Angeles Times. And after learning so much since then, it has become pivotal for any hope of connecting the Johnson death claim with Peter Cole. With Nielsen dead too, the only alternative is to speak to Nielsen's partner. This was the break we needed.

I like arriving at airports a little early. That Saturday morning was no different. There is generally a lounge across from my gate, and I can sit and relax before the flight. It's a nice preparation because I always seem to be seated next to some annoying moron.

That morning the lounge was quite full and I took the last table. It wasn't long before my eyes fixed on a very attractive lady looking for a seat. Peeking over the top of my Wall Street Journal, I could see that she was about 5'7" and maybe 35 years old. She had long, dark hair, a well-developed bust line, and a killer body squeezed into blue jeans. But it was her eyes that first caught my glance. Deep and dark, they were the kind of eyes that could murder a man and make him happy in the process.

"Nice," I thought. "Very, very nice."

Suddenly, I didn't feel wrung out from the week I'd had. I felt the old Rick stirring. I decided to take a shot.

Standing, I began, "Excuse me, may I offer you a seat?"

I gestured toward my table. She was still looking around and showing signs of despair.

"Well, thank you, but no."

The old Rick, the refreshed Rick, would never retreat on the first no!

"Please," I insisted, gesturing with my hand again. "The lounge is full. It would be my pleasure, and I really don't bite. Well, at least not 'til I get to know you," I teased warmly.

With just the slightest smile, she responded, "Well, thank you. I'm not imposing, am I?"

She was looking at my open paper as she began to sit.

"No, not at all. I just pretend to read the Journal to give the impression I know how to read."

With that, her smile became a touch brighter. A little levity can go a long way.

Meeting her smile with one of my own, I offered, "I'm Rick."

"Hi, Rick. I'm Crystal."

She and I made small talk for the next half hour. During this brief interlude, two things became "Crystal" clear: this woman knew how to handle men and she and I would be on the same flight.

Hearing the first boarding call, Crystal gathered her things, thanked me for sharing my table and, like the throngs, proceeded to the gate. Watching her walk away in those tight jeans reminded me of my friend in San Francisco. The snugness around the hips and thighs left little to the imagination. With each step, her hips gently swayed to the right and then the left, sending a coded message to every man watching: "I've got it, and you can't have it."

It was a common practice of mine to board the plane after everyone else. As usual, almost all the passengers were seated by the time I stepped on. I looked down the aisle to judge where my seat should be, and my eyes locked on Crystal's. Walking up to my seat, I re-checked the number on my ticket then re-checked the number on the bulkhead. As fate would have it, Crystal was sitting in my seat.

"Well, hello again," she said graciously.

"Well, hello back. I guess you and I will be sharing a seat this flight."

She gave me an innocent look, the kind that says, "Oh. Is there something wrong?"

Hovering over the seat, I explained, "It appears you and I have the same seat number."

Pulling out her ticket she asked politely, "Isn't this 14B?"

"No, it's actually 9B," I corrected.

"Oh … that's too bad. I was intrigued by the idea of sharing a seat with you," she said, laughing.

"Might have been fun!" I agreed.

That's when the older woman in 9A piped up, "It appears you two would like to sit together. I could move to the other seat. I don't mind."

Looking at Crystal, I asked, "Sound good?"

She said, "OK," and then turned to the stranger and thanked her. I'm not sure, but I think the woman winked at Crystal.

So Crystal and I were now sitting together. She moved to the window, and I took the aisle. It was really quite cozy. During the first part of our two-hour and twenty minute flight, we laughed, teased, and made small talk as we had in the lounge. Each of us was trying to get to know the other better, but without being too conspicuous. But sometime mid-flight, without any warning, Crystal's attitude and facial expressions began to change from carefree to serious.

"Rick, is there anyone special in your life?"

Talk about a bold question from out of left field!

"No, not at the moment," I said after a moment's pause. "She … Well, it just didn't work out."

Though her question triggered thoughts of both Caroline and my friend in San Francisco, my answer referred to Caroline.

"Can I ask you a personal question?" she continued.

"If the question is, 'will you take me to Vegas,' the answer is yes."

"No, seriously," she said, then paused, searching for the right words. "Did you love her?"

An odd question considering we just met. And I was thinking of two women. But before a reply could be formulated, Crystal squinted at me and declared, "You did. I can see it in your eyes."

I never gave her an answer beyond what she saw in my eyes, and she didn't press any further. But I wondered about her intentions with that line of questioning. Again, it was odd.

Crystal then began to tell me personal things about herself: where she lived in Seattle, where she worked, family, everything. I was a little off on her age. She was forty, but in great shape for four decades. The more intimate in detail she went, the softer and quieter her voice became, as though it was a secret for my ears only. I gathered her husband was quite a bit older, by about twenty five years, and extremely domineering. After asking a number of times how they met, she finally replied, "I was stupid."

For some reason "I was stupid" caught my attention more than anything else she shared. The question "How did you meet your husband?" is an ordinary one, and is not typically met with an evasive answer. I had a gut feeling she was guarding some deep, dark secret. There was probably more to this sexy woman than met the eye. Each time her husband was mentioned, her demeanor changed. And it looked like fear to me.

"Ladies and gentleman, we will be landing in five minutes. Please make sure your seat backs and tray tables are in an upright and locked position. Prepare for landing."

By now, I felt I wanted to see this woman again. The prime opportunity was to act now, before we landed.

Taking a deep breath, I began, "I know this is very forward, but I'll be in town just through the weekend. Would you have dinner with me?"

With a look of surprise, she hesitated then softly answered, "I can't," in an apologetic tone.

"Is it because you're married?"

"No, it's … well, you see … yes, it's that I'm married."

"That's not the reason," I ventured, looking straight into her beautiful eyes.

"Are you sure you want to spend time with me? You don't know what kind of … you don't know me," she said with just the slightest quiver in her voice. "We just met and …"

"And what?" I pressed.

Crystal gazed at me. She was thinking and thinking hard. But I knew what the answer was. I could sense it. There was a connection here. Something unique and intriguing, and no matter what she said or how she said it, she wanted to say yes. It seemed like an eternity waiting, but Crystal finally broke through with a smile, giving me that magic answer.

"Yes, I think I would like that," she stated firmly, nodding her head in agreement.

She rummaged through her purse and produced a business card on which she wrote a local phone number where she would be staying. I gave her my card and cell number.

"May I call you later today and set up a date?" I asked.

"Yes, that would be nice."

"Ladies and gentleman, this is your pilot. We will be on the ground in three minutes. Please make sure your bags are secured and your seatbelts fastened. Thank you."

I slipped the business card into my pocket as we both turned toward the window, watching the ground approach. A few moments before touchdown something unexpected happened. Without thinking, Crystal reached out and took my hand. The squeeze indicated she was nervous, needing some type of reassurance. But for what, I wasn't sure. Crystal was an avid traveler. Landings were obviously not a problem for her. There was something else.

Exiting the plane, Crystal and I walked together until we arrived at the main entrance. She was meeting someone and Vince was standing on the curb leaning against the hood of a Lincoln Town Car.

"I'll call you later," I said brightly.

This was met with a smile, the kind that doesn't lie.

"Yes, I'm looking forward to it."

Watching her walk away, again swaying those beautiful hips, she turned and caught me gazing at her. She did not give me the look of disgust that women give gawking men. Instead, I got an "I'm glad you're looking" glance ... accompanied by another smile. Before I could respond, she raised her hand slightly, and in a little girl fashion, faintly waved—like it was a secret between the two of us. She turned and continued on her way as I was returning the gesture.

Still leaning against the fender, Vince was watching the whole thing.

With a big smile he asked, "Who the hell was that?"

"Someone I met on the plane," I returned.

"Ni-i-i-ce," he commented as we both watched those perfect hips sway.

Randal Pierce had been Nielsen's partner up until the time Nielsen retired. Now retired as well, Pierce and his wife lived on a quiet tree-lined street in Encino. It was mid-afternoon and warm when Vince and I arrived. He answered his door. I introduced Vince and myself and I asked if we could have a moment of his time. Taking my card, he appeared delighted to have visitors.

Settled in the small living room I began, "Mr. Pierce ..."

"Please, call me Randy," he interrupted with a smile.

"Randy," I began again, "I'm interested in any information you might have about an investigation your partner Robert Nielsen handled about thirty years ago."

"You mean the Peter Cole case?"

"Well, yes, but how did you know?"

"I knew one day someone would reopen that case."

"Why?"

"Why?" he said with a slight chuckle. "A United States Congressman kills three people while driving drunk, then uses his power and connections to stifle the investigation. Isn't that reason enough?"

Nodding my head, I continued, "Please tell us everything you can remember."

Before starting, he looked at Vince and asked, "You're a cop, aren't you?"

"Retired, Randy," Vince said while nodding his head.

"LAPD?"

"No, Seattle. Thirty years. Homicide. Sergeant."

"Hmm," Randy said. "Thirty-two years watch commander, Devonshire Division, LAPD."

Noting the connection, I decided it best for Vince to take the lead. After all, they were buddies now.

For the next twenty minutes, Randy told us just about everything we already knew from our interview with Ms. Miller, but with additional tidbits interjected here and there which emphasized points of corruption on the part of police personnel and a few judges. During this time, Mrs. Pierce offered Vince and me some coffee which we gladly accepted.

Once Randy appeared to be finished with his overall story, Vince did the cop thing—asked questions.

"Randy, did the name Eric Johnson ever come up in the investigation?"

Shaking his head, "No, I don't believe the name rings a bell. But that doesn't mean Cole didn't know him."

"I know three adults were killed that night and the three children survived. Do you remember anything about that family? Names? Where they lived? Anything?"

Sitting back in his chair, Randy began again.

"Their name was Rose. Harry and Caroline Rose. The wife's sister was also with them. Her name, I think, was Cohen. But that was a long time ago," he said, shaking his head.

"Do you remember anything about the children?"

"No, honestly I don't. I know they were adopted out very quickly. It seemed Cole used his influence with some judge to expedite their adoption."

"Didn't anyone try to track down some family?"

"No, Cole wanted to break up the family. I guess he didn't want any loose ends down the road. Anyway, after the adoption, all the records were sealed, like everything else in the investigation."

"Randy, I heard the two youngest girls were adopted by someone here in the Valley. And the oldest one possibly San Francisco?"

Shaking his head a little, "Maybe. I really don't know," he replied.

"Why did Nielsen retire early?"

"I don't know that either," he said, shaking his head again. "I know the case took a lot out of him. He took it very personally."

"Anything else?" Vince asked.

"Just before he retired, he told me he had a visit from a couple of Feds asking him to drop the investigation. Said it had something to do with national security."

"Do you believe that?"

Shaking his head he replied, "No. I think what everyone was afraid of was Cole's little black book. More like self-preservation than national security. I heard he had the dirt on everyone. Rumor had it, all the way up to Pennsylvania Avenue. His black book was actually not so little."

Vince and I looked at each other not sure what to say or believe. The White House?

Randy continued, "Soon after the Feds visited, Nielsen took a job with some insurance company. Cleaned out his locker and was gone. Never heard from him again. His daughter called me a few years back and told me he died."

"Do you know what happened to his personal records?" Vince asked.

"I can only assume his daughter has them."

"Do you remember her name?" I interjected.

"Yeah, Kathy. Named after her mother."

"Do you know her last name?"

He thought briefly and said, "Sure, Gibson. Kathy Gibson."

"Kathy Gibson?" I blurted, louder than I meant to.

Surprised, Mr. Pierce commented, "Sounds like you know her, Mr. Morgan."

"Yeah," I said quietly. I was rattled. "She used to work for my company."

After spending an hour with Mr. Pierce, Vince and I thanked him for his time and said goodbye. Vince drove, and I stared out the window, deep in thought.

"Rick," Vince said, "I didn't say anything in front of Mr. Pierce, but wasn't Gibson the name of the woman in Santa Barbara?"

"Yeah, it was. I was just thinking. Her boyfriend, Jack Webber, sells the policy to Johnson, who dies a year later, and she handles the claim ... her father investigated the death ..."

"And let's not forget Cole and that accident in '76," Vince added.

"That's the problem, Vince. I can justify everything except the Cole incident. If that newspaper hadn't been in the claims file, I would have walked away long ago."

"Do you think we're into something over our heads?" Vince asked.

"FBI? Pennsylvania Avenue? You're the cop. You tell me."

"The thought has crossed my mind," Vince answered.

Looking back out the side window, "I never dreamed Kathy could be Nielsen's daughter," I complained.

"Do you want me to find her?" he asked.

"Find her?" I thought.

Turning to Vince, "No, let her go," I said and then turned again to concentrate on the storefronts whizzing by.

We rode in silence for a couple miles.

Eventually, in a concerned tone, Vince asked, "Did you know her well, Rick?"

Vince's question caught me off-guard. I flashed on Caroline's last statement to me before she walked out the door.

I groaned, "I guess she was not what she appeared to be."

CHAPTER 20

I dialed the number. On the third ring my guts churned and palms sweated. On the fifth, I was questioning what the hell I was doing. By the seventh, I decided maybe this wasn't a good idea. I was just about to hang up when a raspy voice answered, "Hello?"

Wondering if I dialed the right number I said, "Hello, I'm trying to reach Crystal."

"Hang on, and I'll get her ..." The gruff voice then turned to a half-laugh and asked, "Is this Rick?"

"Uh ... why, yes it is," I answered, muffling my surprise.

"You're the one from the plane. I heard all about you."

In the background I heard, "Sh-sh, give me the phone! Hello?"

"Hi."

"Hi, I'm sorry about that. It's not what it sounds like."

"Well, gee, I'm sorry it's not. I'm calling regarding dinner. So, how about it?"

"Tonight?"

"If you're not busy," I sputtered. From our conversation on the plane, I already knew she wasn't.

"Do you have someplace special in mind?" Crystal asked.

"Actually, I do. There's a delicatessen on the boulevard ..."

"I know the place!" she bubbled. "Would you like me to meet you there?"

"Actually, I was thinking I could pick you up at 6:00, if you don't mind."

"That would be fabulous," she responded.

She gave me the address where she was staying and a dinner date had been made. I had a pretty good idea where the address was located. Being raised in the Valley, I knew my way around.

Crystal was staying in an older neighborhood in Burbank. The street was lined with mature trees standing guard over the individual stucco homes, each tucked back on a narrow lot. By the age of the trees, I would guess this was a pre-World War II neighborhood. The house was no different than the cookie-cutters on either side except for the obvious lack of maintenance. A long, cracked driveway paralleled the house, ending at a detached garage in the backyard. Broken Spanish tile covered the roof, and its red color had long faded in the hot California sun. The grass—or what little there was of it—was brown and most of the yard consisted of weeds. It didn't take a keen eye to see the house was in total disrepair. Looking at it, I got a feeling of déjà vu.

I checked the address again to make sure I was at the right place. Could it be that Crystal mixes up addresses as well as airplane seats?

The walkway shared the same ill fate as the driveway. I could feel the wide, deep cracks under my feet with every step I took. In Southern California, most of the older homes with Spanish architecture have red painted walkways. The red paint of the sidewalk must have been as old as the house. Where people walked most, I could see the gray of the concrete underneath from the years of wear.

It was 6:00 P.M. as I rang the bell.

An older lady answered the door. She looked about sixty, overweight, with bottled blond hair. She had a tired, wrinkled face with a cigarette dangling from her lips and a beer bottle in her hand. She wore an unflattering tank top over her very large, drooping breasts that obviously needed a little more support from a bra. I was somewhat surprised as her eyes moved up and down my body in a way that made me feel ... violated.

"You must be Rick," she said with the same raspy voice I'd heard on the phone. I assume the voice was from a lifetime of smoking.

"Yes, I am."

"I'm Candy," she offered, holding out her fat hand to shake.

"You've got to be kidding," I thought.

She shouted over her shoulder, "Crys, your date's here."

Back to me she continued, "I've heard a lot about you. Come on in."

"Good things, I hope."

The house was dark and had that closed-up smell. The furniture was dark green and dated. I believe they called it Spanish Mediterranean. Over the mantle was an 8 x 10 group photo with a much younger Candy along with two men and another woman. They seemed to be family. And judging by the hairstyles, it was probably 1970. Looking from the picture back to Candy, it was obvious the thirty-five plus years had not been good to her.

Before I could say another word, Crystal came into the room.

"Hi. I see you met my aunt."

"Yes, we had an interesting conversation."

"I can only imagine," she smiled, as she rolled her eyes. "Ready?"

"Let's go," I said.

I was surprised by how Crystal was dressed. On the plane she was wearing Levi's. I guess that planted a seed about how I thought she would dress tonight. But instead she wore a short denim skirt with a dark blue pullover top—that showed more than a little cleavage—and boots with 2-inch heels. She looked hotter than any woman I'd seen in a long time. Or, at least since the last time I saw my friend in San Francisco.

Driving down Ventura Boulevard, Crystal watched the shops as we passed by. Deep inside, I felt a gentle pull to this beautiful woman—an attraction much like the one I had felt with Caroline a few years back. There was something in her quiet stillness that intrigued me, yet something else that caused uneasiness ... as though I was looking at someone in a mirror, seeing only the reflection.

At dinner, for the better part of an hour we laughed and teased, poking fun at each other whenever we could. I found her easy to talk to. She commented more than once how easy it was to talk to me, just as Kathy had told me at our first dinner together.

I wanted to know more about Crystal and the mysteries behind those beautiful eyes. They say be careful what you wish for, because you may get it.

"So tell me a little about your job, Crystal. Weight loss consultant, right?"

"About ten years now," she answered with some pride.

"Well, that explains why you're so fit and trim."

"You're so sweet," she said, touching my hand.

Without thinking, I put my hand on top of hers, and for a few moments we sat gazing into each other's eyes, searching—or better, waiting—for something to happen.

Finally breaking the silence I began, "Crystal, you asked me some personal questions on the plane, and I gave you straight answers."

Nodding her head, she replied, "I remember."

"Tell me about your husband."

"I did tell you about him."

"No, I mean what he's like and ... how he treats you."

She pulled her hand back very quickly. The question made her noticeably nervous and fidgety. Her eyes began to scan the room as though making sure no one overheard the question. Her whole countenance changed. I saw fear in her. A fear so deep it reached the very foundation of her soul.

Witnessing such an immense transformation I began to wonder what strange hold her husband had over her. Was it physical abuse? She didn't have any of the telltale marks or bruises that I could see. Maybe it was emotional. Mental anxiety can sometimes be worse than physical pain. But something told me it was neither. Answers, like relationships, are not always simple.

As Crystal sat thinking, I waited respectfully before I spoke again.

"Crystal?"

She picked up her coffee and, holding it tightly, began to speak in a very soft and fearful voice. She began with her head down, staring at the cup.

"My husband is a very wealthy, cold man."

She paused, and I could see she was again trying to formulate her words.

"And?" I encouraged her, gently.

Her face was still looking down.

"He ..."

"He what?"

"Nothing."

"I gather you don't love each other?" I asked, still trying to pry open something—anything—that would give me a glimmer of an answer.

Shaking her head in response, I took it as a no.

"How long have you been married?"

"We're ... well, umm, ten years."

"Crystal, look at me," I softly commanded. Using my index finger, I lifted her head slightly. I wrapped my hands around her hands—that were still clutching the coffee cup.

"If things are so bad, why don't you divorce him?"

With a helpless look, "I can't," she answered.

"Why?"

"He won't let me go. I know ..."

"Know what?"

"Rick, you just don't understand. I can't."

"Then tell me why."

"You wouldn't understand. I'm not the girl you think I am."

I had been hearing this kind of thing a lot in both my personal and professional lives lately. At this point, I assumed *everybody* was hiding *something.*

"Crystal, I don't care about your past. I just care about you now."

I was surprised those words came out of my mouth, but they came straight from my heart.

"I know," she replied, showing a little smile. "I can tell. That's what makes you so special."

"I like being special," I said with a little tease.

Crystal was on the verge of losing it emotionally. I needed to change course with my questioning.

"Do you like cheesecake?" I asked brightly, lightening the mood.

I took her slight nod as a yes.

"Would you share a piece with me for dessert?"

Finally raising her lowered head, she smiled. I took it as another yes.

The cheesecake seemed to please Crystal, and the two of us began nibbling at it from our opposite sides of the table. Within a few minutes, I could see her returning to her normal state of mind. But our intense conversation was not over. She turned the table on me.

Snatching the last bite of dessert from our plate, she stated plainly, "Rick, now it's my turn to ask questions."

"I don't think I want to play this game anymore."

"Well, you're just going to have to," she said. "You told me you were involved with someone that didn't work out."

As I was nodding my head in agreement, Crystal continued.

"Who broke it off, you or her?"

I paused to think.

"You did, didn't you?" Crystal said.

I never answered.

"You were in love with her. I saw it in your eyes on the plane. Was she in love with you?"

"What woman wouldn't be?" I responded wryly, trying to bring back levity—and to end this line of questioning.

In her eyes, I could see the flames of curiosity were consuming her thoughts. She had more questions, but was debating whether or not to push the envelope. It didn't take long for the female inquisitiveness to take control, and she was back to her interrogation.

"Were you lovers?" she asked, hesitating slightly.

"Well ..." I wasn't really sure how or if I should answer such a direct question. "Yes, I guess you could say we were."

"What was her name?"

"Caroline."

"Was there someone else?"

I didn't answer again. But Crystal's female intuition told her my answer.

"Rick, who was this other woman?"

"Who said there was?"

"Your eyes did, Rick. Your eyes say there's someone else. Who is she?"

"Oh, just a friend."

"No-o-o, she's more than just a friend." Prying deeper, she asked, "Did you ever feel guilty having a 'friend' while being with Caroline?"

After considering the question, "Honestly, no," I replied.

"Hmm. Did Caroline ever suspect anything?"

Before I could answer, she quizzed me again.

"Did you ever feel guilty you didn't run off with her?"

"What makes you think I was going to run off with her?" I sputtered, surprised.

"Oh, I guess I just assumed ..."

I thought, "If all of this is from female intuition, damn, this woman is good."

The mutual interrogation eventually stopped though, and the evening flew by, just as our time had on the plane. For every big, heavy, serious matter we discussed, we shared five laughs and even more teases. The chemistry between us was exhilarating, and it wasn't only me who noticed.

Since the sidewalk was empty as we were leaving the restaurant, I asked Crystal if she was up for a walk. She silently linked her arm through mine. We sauntered to the west, feeling the coolness of the evening breeze against our faces. Not much was said during our slow-paced stroll. We enjoyed the closeness, the touch of a warm body, the emotional connection to another human being. I felt she craved this and desperately needed it. Our stopping every few stores to look at the displays was nothing more than an excuse to prolong our wandering.

After a bit of this, Crystal commented that she was chilly, and she held my arm a little tighter. In doing so, her breast ever-so-gently pressed against my arm. I was a little surprised at her action (because ... it wasn't that cold out!), but in no way rejected it. I enjoyed what I felt. The farther we walked, the closer Crystal drew her body to mine, her tender grip on my arm increasing with every step. Her voice became softer and lower, the words more intimate and suggestive. Her breast rubbed more intently against my arm, sending shock waves through my entire body. I could feel its form. It was large and full, firm and very desirable—the type of breasts a man could feast on the entire day and be completely satisfied when finished.

Walking slowly with a woman arm-in-arm can be a very stimulating, if not downright sensual, experience. To make it work properly, you must walk together in rhythm, with total concentration on your partner and what she is doing. If done correctly, your motions will be in perfect harmony, as though you are one person rather than two. Together, you create incredible energy. It's just like having sex. The energy created in this union can take you both beyond your wildest imaginings, your mind and body to a better high than any illicit street drug provides. It takes the loneliness and sadness of your hearts and fills them with joy and love. Like a river, adrenalin fills the meandering canyons of your mind, replacing the barrenness of your thoughts with new, wonderful, and exciting dreams. When this natural wonder-drug flows, courage becomes your battle cry, opening doors to new possibilities. Fear becomes a thing of the past, replaced with the strength of confidence. Using this new confidence, you can push past your boundaries, take chances with your heart, explore new thoughts, and love as you never have before.

As we approached the corner, my mind was racing with the thought of holding and kissing this beautiful woman on my arm. I wanted to feel her breath gently caress my cheeks like a warm summer breeze, to feel her moist lips tenderly touching mine as our tongues softly search for increasing passion. Rather than only one breast, I wanted to feel the fullness of her entire stunning body pressing against mine.

Arriving at the corner, I decided to take the chance—the chance that if I reached out for a kiss she would not politely turn away, but instead accept my invitation to this intimacy. I turned my body slowly toward hers. In doing so, she released her grip on my arm and let her head drop, as though expecting me to do something. I placed the index finger of my right hand under her chin, raising her head so our eyes could meet. We gazed at each other, our eyes searching the others for a message as to what was next. In hers I saw an invitation to fulfill the desires of passion that consumed my mind—a summons for physical intimacy. I saw a request for a kiss.

Slowly raising my hands to her cheeks, I found them warm and soft—the type a man likes to caress and kiss. She dropped her eyes ever-so-slightly and then, with a slight glance back up, gave her signal. She was ready to explore the next level of intimacy. With my hands still on her cheeks and her head tilted upward, I leaned down and gently kissed her.

To my delight, there was no objection and Crystal opened her mouth the slightest bit, allowing our tongues to softly caress. Oblivious to the world, I wrapped my arms around her and pulled our bodies tightly together. Feeling her body in full contact with mine took me momentarily back to Caroline. Though totally different in size and shape, the thrill was the same. Crystal's breasts pressing against me shot waves of excitement through my deprived body. It triggered a quiver deep within that made its way to the surface, causing swelling where I did not need it just now. Crystal was very aware of my growing pulsations.

Our kiss, and my expanding interest in it, was interrupted by the catcalls from some teenage boys driving by.

With our concentration broken and attention momentarily directed to our young friends, "I see we have an audience," she remarked.

"Well, maybe they could learn something," I quipped.

We looked at each other and began to laugh. One thing was certain. We both enjoyed that kiss.

Turning back toward the restaurant, Crystal took my arm again. We silently moved together, relishing the romance in the air. With the breeze now at our backs, we were like a ship with a sail to the wind, gently moving through the water, not in any hurry to reach our destination. I pondered our kiss and whether there would be a next step.

Taking her back to her Aunt Candy's, we were like a couple of kids ending a date. We sat in the car for an hour talking and laughing, and—of course—teasing. I had one question I was burning to ask, and I waited for the right moment.

"Tell me about your Aunt Candy."

Even though we were in the shadow of a street lamp, I could see the question made her a little uncomfortable.

"She's not really my aunt," Crystal said with some hesitation. "Just ... just an old, dear friend from years past."

"And I suppose her real name isn't Candy?"

"No, it's really Catherine."

"How do you get to Candy from Catherine?" I ask curiously.

"It's a long story," she said.

Then, under her breath, with her eyes somewhere in the past, "A very long story," she added.

But the night was moving on, with aspirations of it never ending, it was time to say goodnight. Sometimes saying goodnight can be awkward. Walking her to the door, still with that high school boy feeling, I found myself at a loss for words and actions, but hoping for another kiss.

Opening the door, Crystal turned with a smile and said, "Thank you for a wonderful evening."

"I enjoyed it, too. Listen, for the next few weeks I'll be buried in work, but I would like to see you again."

Of course I meant in Seattle, since that was home for both of us.

This was met with a smile, the kind that says, "I'll play hard to get, but not too hard." Watching her tongue slightly glide along her lips, there was no doubt she liked the idea. Using one finger, she brushed down the buttons of my shirt as she considered my offer.

With a coy smile, she twinkled, "Maybe," as she gave me a quick kiss on the cheek and closed the door.

Halfway to the car, I stopped to look back at the house. The peephole on the front door was dark. Someone was watching. I smiled as I turned back and continued my stride.

"Morgan," I breathed aloud, "you still got it."

Opening the car door, I was humming that old song, "Back in the Saddle Again."

CHAPTER 21

Monday morning always comes. And this particular Monday came with an inordinately high stack of files on my desk. I didn't want to look at them, so I pivoted my chair toward the window for the comfort of watching the world go by. But from the 16th floor, that's not easy either. The tall buildings began looking like stacks of files.

Since Saturday, I'd been preoccupied with two thoughts. And unlike paperwork, they were both alluring. The first was Kathy and the second, Crystal. What could it mean that Kathy Gibson is Robert Nielsen's daughter? What was her purpose in contacting and seducing me? What are the consequences, if any, of my taking that lovely bait?

And then there's Crystal. What a refreshing diversion in the midst of this unusually complicated investigation! Not without her own complications and mystery, her secrets were buried somewhere in a bad marriage. In addition to a physical attraction any man with eyes would have, I felt such compassion for her. I wanted to see her again.

But not this morning. I had to focus even though, so far, the day was like my coffee—not that hot. But it was about to get hotter.

Sweeping into my office, Emily was wearing her "I'm not going anywhere until I get some answers" look. She began speaking as she planted herself firmly in a wingback chair.

"So, Rick, we never finished our conversation from Friday morning."

"Oh, I'm sorry," I said with some sarcasm. "I thought of it more as an interrogation."

"Rick, please! What's going on? Does it have to do with the project you had Chris working on a while back?"

"Emily," I began, "Vince and I are ..."

I stopped mid-sentence. Behind Emily, two men suddenly appeared at the threshold of my door. By their haircuts and lack of coordinated attire, I had a hunch.

"May I help you?" I asked.

"Are you Rick Morgan?" the older one asked sternly. Like he couldn't read the name on my door.

"Yes. And you are?"

"May we speak to you in private, please?" the older one continued.

"This is my confidential administrative assistant," I said, nodding to Emily. "Anything you need to say to me can be said in front of her."

Emily beamed. This is what she wanted—to be privy to whatever was going on.

"Mr. Morgan, we need to speak to you alone."

"About?"

"Certain activities you and another individual have been undertaking in Los Angeles and Las Vegas."

Emily turned to me with a raised eyebrow. My hunch about who they were was apparently correct. I asked Emily to return to her office and close the door on her way out. Without a word, she did.

As the door closed, I said graciously, "Gentleman, please sit down."

And as they were doing so, I continued, "So, what can I do for the FBI?"

Both seemed surprised with my blatant observation. The older one commented on it.

"What makes you think we're FBI?"

"Gentleman, let's not play games," I responded.

I requested their IDs. With reluctance both produced the necessary ID in identical leather wallets. The older one was a special agent.

"It's been my experience," I stated, "that special agents usually deal with, shall we say, sensitive matters."

Without comment or smile, the special agent pulled out a little black notebook and said, "Mr. Morgan, it's been brought to our attention that you and an investigator named Vince Guarino have been looking into the death of Peter Cole."

"And if we are?" I asked.

"We would like for you to stop," he said bluntly.

"Why?"

"Mr. Cole was a Congressman. At one time he sat on certain committees which handled, shall we say, certain 'sensitive' information."

"I have it on good authority that the man is dead," I returned. "How can any of the 'certain sensitive information' be jeopardized? I'm under the impression dead men don't talk."

"Look, Morgan, if you want to make this tough, we can get a court order forcing you to back off."

We locked eyes. I decided to call his bluff.

"If you could get a court order, you would have it in your hand. I'm not investigating anything about a Congressman or any of that 'sensitive information.' I am looking into a twenty million dollar insurance claim that is somehow tied to an ex-board member of this company—who just happens to be Peter Cole."

I paused and then added, "Now, if you have any information that could help me along, I would love to hear it."

"Mr. Morgan, we can …"

I held up my hand and interrupted, "Gentlemen, please. No need to bullshit. I'm going to take a stab at this and save us all a lot of time. I'll bet Cole's little black book of dirt was never recovered after his death. And someone is very afraid that my digging around may uncover it. Am I close?"

"Mr. Morgan, we can neither confirm nor deny your statement."

"Let's make a deal," I continued. "Leave me your cards and, if I find what you're so afraid of, I'll give you a call."

"Mr. Morgan," monotoned the special agent, "I don't think you quite appreciate the gravity of our request."

"On the contrary, I do. From the first day I started this investigation, someone has been one step ahead of me. That same someone sent an ex-con with a gun to scare me. And by some strange coincidence, the guy was shot dead right in front of me. Do you gentleman have any clue who our dangerous someone may be?"

Rising from their chairs, they said nothing and moved toward the door. As the younger one opened it, the special agent turned, smiled and said, "Good day, Mr. Morgan. Thank you for your time."

I stood and nodded. And as I did, that old familiar rock hit my stomach like a thrown brick.

Once they cleared the outer office, I grabbed my cell and called Vince. I told him nothing except to meet me ASAP. We agreed on the bar across the street in ten minutes. I dashed past Emily as she tried to question me, but all I could muster was, "I'll be back soon."

On my way down in the elevator I wondered if my visitors left me a shadow. Maybe I've watched too many spy movies, but I decided to test my paranoia. I slipped on my sunglasses before stepping outside. Sunglasses are great for stealth—don't let them see the whites of your eyes. I paused in the front of my building and without moving my head scanned up and down the block using the reflection of the big coffee shop window across the street. It took only a moment to find my potential shadow—a tall, thin man wearing a heavy brown jacket and sunglasses, leaning against the building just to the left of me. If he was "it," I would soon find out.

I waited on my side of the street until I saw Vince enter the bar. Then I jaywalked through traffic to get there myself. While cutting across, I focused on the large window. The tall, thin man did appear to be watching me.

Vince was already in the back at our usual table and appeared happy to see me. He had some news. I asked him to wait until we got our drinks, and I slid into a chair with my back to the door. Almost immediately, the lights reflecting on the back wall told me the front door had just opened.

"Vince, look at me."

"Is everything alright, Rick?"

"Without being conspicuous, did a tall, thin man wearing a dark brown jacket just come in?"

"Yeah. He sat down at the bar. Why?"

I explained about the man while giving Vince a thirty-second rundown on my conversation with the Feds.

Vince sat back in his chair as the wheels turned in his head.

"So," he began, "they want you to back off?"

"Pretty much," I said.

"Did they say why?"

"No, not directly. But, bottom line, I believe they're afraid we'll find Cole's little black book of secrets, and I told them so."

Shaking his head with a baffled expression, "Maybe there's some truth about Pennsylvania Avenue," Vince mumbled.

The bartender slipped our drinks onto the table and walked away.

"Thanks for buying, Vince," I said as I took a sip.

We sat drinking until I broke the silence saying, "At this point, nothing would surprise me."

"So, Rick, what do you want to do?"

"Tell me what you have first."

"I got a call from Frank this morning. He found someone at the funeral home that handled Johnson's body. And he has a secret."

I shifted in my seat and stared at a spot on the wall. Do I want to know this guy's secret and possibly use it against him to unveil a few other secrets? Or should I heed the Feds' warning and call it a day?

"What do you think, Vince?"

Tilting back his chair and rubbing his chin he replied, "You know, Rick ... I have a strange fascination for secrets."

Smiling, I nodded my head in agreement.

An hour later I was back at the office. Emily was finishing up a phone conversation. She followed me into my office.

"That was Holly in Personnel. Alicia's background check came back clean. What do you want to do?"

I plopped down in my chair saying, "Emily, you've been with me a little over two years now, right?"

"That's about right," Emily agreed.

Tilting back I continued, "Am I a fair boss?"

"When you aren't giving me the silent treatment about investigations involving my Uncle, you are."

"Besides that," I chuckled. "So ... what did you think of Alicia?"

"Seems to be fairly knowledgeable and would make a good addition to the department."

"Is there enough space in your office for a desk for her?"

Emily gave me a cross-eyed look as if to say, "What the hell are you talking about, Rick?"

"Emily, I've known for some time you're way too valuable for much of the piddly work you do—like my filing and all my other crap. I think Alicia should be your assistant. What do you think?"

"My assistant?" she exclaimed.

"Yeah, assistant," I confirmed with a smile.

Emily literally jumped from her chair and near-literally leaped onto mine, giving me an exuberant hug.

"Thank you, Rick! Thank you so very much!"

With Emily's approval, it was a done deal. Alicia became part of the team.

It was Tuesday evening when my plane touched down at McCarran. Frank had a car waiting that took me to the hotel. Vince had come down that morning to make the arrangements.

The man we would interview that night is a funeral director by the name of Bill Polanski. According to Frank, Bill is a married man who has a pet—the kind that has her own apartment and dances for a living. It usually played like this: Bill would tell his wife he needed to do a "first call"—meaning picking up a dead body and transporting it to the funeral home—but instead he'd meet his pet. Vince received word from one of his operatives that tonight Bill was meeting her at a small Italian restaurant just off The Strip. It was close by.

As we headed into the restaurant, Vince pointed to our man while Frank approached the owner to let him know there may be a brief scene, but everything was nonetheless under control. This was a small Vegas-style courtesy.

We approached the table.

"Mr. Polanski?" I began.

Looking up, "Ye-e-s ...?" he responded suspiciously.

"My name is Rick Morgan. I'd like to talk to you for a few minutes." Looking at the woman, I continued, "But I think our conversation would go better privately."

"What do you guys want?" he blurted out loudly.

I sat down in an empty chair next to him as Vince and Frank loomed over the table.

"Just information, my friend. Nothing more."

"I don't know you. Why should I tell you anything?"

"Look, let's make this easy," I returned. "You give me what I want and your secret," nodding toward the woman, "is safe. If not, I know from personal experience that divorce lawyers, even in Nevada, can be very expensive. And since you won't have a job to pay for one, you'll be screwed."

"What do you mean, no job?"

"Oh, come now. Let's not be naïve, Mr. Polanski. The funeral business is very conservative. I'm sure your employer would not be happy to hear of your supposed innocent rendezvous. Of course, you can always claim she's your sister. But somehow I don't think it will fly."

He knew I had him.

The funeral director's girlfriend looked like she may be his client soon. She was painfully skinny, with huge, hollow eyes and stringy blond hair. Probably a junkie. He told her to go powder her nose. Instead, she walked out the door in a huff, taking with her his chances at near-necrophilia that night.

"So ... what do you guys want to know?" he asked cautiously.

"About ten years ago, your firm picked up a body at the ME's office. The name was Eric Johnson. According to the DC, he was cremated. I want a copy of every record you guys have on it."

"Who are you guys? Cops?"

By the look on his face, he remembered Johnson. And the tone of his voice made it clear that the memory made him very nervous. But why? I decided to probe a little.

"Now, why would you think we were cops, Mr. Polanski?" I asked. "Could it be that something about Mr. Johnson's cremation was slightly irregular? Do I need to get a court order to look at your books? Do we need the cemetery board to come in and do a little investigation?"

"Now wait a minute guys. It's not like you think."

"Then what is it like, Mr. Polanski?"

"It's true we … er, I … picked up Johnson from the ME's office. The family approached me and asked that he be cremated ASAP. I told her we had to do the usual contract. She asked if she could make special arrangements. She said she was in a hurry to get home."

"What did she want?"

"She wanted the body cremated off the record."

"Off the record?"

"Yeah, done that day and no paperwork. I told her no. Then she offered me a $1,000 under the table and …"

"And what?"

"And sex with a high-class hooker if I could give her the remains by 3:00 the next afternoon."

Vince and I looked at each other in disbelief.

"Mr. Polanski, who offered all this to you?"

"The guy's daughter."

"Do you have a name?"

"She didn't say, and I didn't ask."

"Describe her."

"Blond, 5' 5", 120 pounds, early to mid-twenties."

Vince and I looked at each other again.

"Sounds like …" he said.

"Yeah, I know."

"So what did you do with the cremated remains?"

"I met her at a hotel on The Strip the next day about 2:30 and gave them to her."

"And?"

"She gave me an envelope with ten $100 bills and a key to a room upstairs."

"And upstairs was the hooker?" I asked.

"Yeah."

"Describe her."

"Jet black hair. About thirty. 5' 6" or maybe a little taller. She had heels on, so it was hard to tell. About 130 pounds. Very classy."

"And?"

"And what? We did it for a couple of hours then I went home."

"Did you ever see her again?"

"The daughter or the hooker?"

"Either."

He shook his head no.

"You guys won't tell my wife or boss about this, will you?"

With a slight chuckle, I replied, "Mr. Polanski, I think it's time for you to go home and see your wife. You might want to bring her some flowers."

Not knowing if my answer meant yes or no, and not asking, Mr. Polanski pulled a twenty dollar bill from his wallet, tossed it on the table, and walked out the door.

I wonder if his wife ever got roses that night.

Back at Frank's hotel, the three of us went directly to the main bar. We were weary, both from the day and from the gravity of this whole investigation. We sat quietly nursing our drinks.

Sipping on my vodka martini, I was watching the traffic through the main entrance. And you won't believe what I saw.

"Vince!" I exclaimed, grabbing his arm. "Look at the front door!"

"What?" Vince asked, not yet understanding.

"Look at the front door," I repeated. "The guy with the redhead and the blue suitcases. See him?"

"Yeah, I see."

"Isn't that …?"

"If not, it's his twin brother."

Frank was bursting with curiosity.

"What are you two talking about?"

"See the tall, thin guy walking toward the front desk? The one with the redheaded woman and blue suitcase?" Vince said.

"Yeah, what about him?"

"He was Rick's shadow after the FBI visited him yesterday."

"You're kidding! Are you sure?"

"No doubt about it," Vince said. "Followed Rick into the bar yesterday when we met."

We all went silent again as we processed this.

"Vince," Frank began, "you know what this means, don't you?"

Nodding his head, "Yeah, decoy," he declared.

"Right!"

"Decoy? What the hell are you two talking about," I blurted.

Vince began, "Rick, you notice how easy it was to spot this guy? It was like he walked through the door with a big sign that said, 'Hey, Rick, here I am—notice me!'"

"Well, yeah, I guess I did notice him."

"Chances are he knew we made him yesterday. So now his people make it easy for you to keep an eye on him. And while you're watching him … someone else is watching you."

That rock hit my stomach again.

"You mean …?"

"Yeah, Rick, somewhere in this casino right now there's someone watching us *watch him*."

The magnitude of this realization caught us all off guard. For the next few minutes we resumed our quiet drinking. I broke the silence as my eyes moved across the vibrant casino.

"There must be a few thousand people here easy."

"Yeah," Frank added softly, "and this is a slow night."

CHAPTER 22

Two weeks had passed since the FBI paid a visit, deposited a tail and Vince and I interrogated the Vegas funeral director. But most importantly, it had been too long since I'd seen Crystal. She never returned my calls, but that didn't keep her from my thoughts. Visions of her luscious body intertwined with doubts about continuing my investigation. I was gazing moodily out my window, concentrating on my misfortune, when a harsh buzzer interrupted me. It was Emily. My assessment of the day was about to move from bad to worse.

"Rick, there's a woman on line five who won't give her name, but says she *has* to talk to you."

"Did she say what it's about?" I quizzed.

"No, Rick, she didn't. But I think something's wrong," Emily worried out loud. "She sounds like she's been crying."

I hate it when a woman cries.

Pushing the button for line five, I took a deep breath and said calmly, "This is Rick Morgan. How may I help you?"

"Umm, Rick? Hi ..." came the greeting from a shaky, yet vaguely familiar voice. "This is Crystal. We met a few weeks ago on an airplane, and ..."

"Well, Crystal, yes! How are you?" I said brightly, hiding my annoyance that she'd ignored my calls and was now behaving like I wouldn't remember her.

"I'm ... I'm fine. I'm sorry for not returning your calls, but ..."

Her voice began to crack, and she couldn't finish her sentence. Emily was right. Something was definitely wrong. Her voice held an unspoken plea for help. It was a tone reminiscent of when she talked about her husband.

"Crystal, what's the matter?" I pressed gently, concerned.

"Oh, Rick, I know we really don't know each other, but would you …"

"Would I what, Crystal?"

"Would … you meet me somewhere, maybe for coffee? There's something … I need to talk to you about."

I was lost in her question for a moment. Confused by this sudden request when I thought she'd written me off.

"Well … yes, OK. Coffee would be fine," I fumbled.

We scheduled to meet the following morning. There is a coffee shop about halfway between her home and mine we were both familiar with. It was a quaint little out-of-the-way place catering mostly to locals, and by 8:00 mostly deserted. It was a perfect spot to talk discreetly. It was clear she had something delicate to discuss, but in addition to her topic, I had a question or two of my own. For example, after our dinner and kiss I was left with a warm sensation. Was I wrong? Did I misread her feelings? Was there a problem about me? … her? … the alignment of the stars? … what?

I found Crystal already sitting in an isolated booth when I arrived. She was clutching her coffee cup, looking like the weight of the world was on her shoulders. Even with all that extra weight, she was exquisite.

"Hi, gorgeous," I said softly as I sat down.

Looking up from her coffee mug, she met my greeting with a weak smile, a weaker hello and a quivery hand held out to me. It didn't take much to see that Crystal was terrified and in a state of sheer exhaustion. I took her hand with both of mine and held it across the table.

"I'm glad you had some time to meet me," she began. "I'm sorry about not calling you back. I wanted to, but …"

She never finished her thought, again.

"But what?" I asked, curious to know the reason why.

"Rick, we don't know each other well, yet I tell you things I don't tell anyone else. Not even …"

Unfinished thoughts were becoming a habit. Her volume got faint, and her head dropped as though she was ashamed. She took her hand from me and joined it with her other one, gripping her coffee for dear life. Even with both hands tightly around the cup it was obvious they were shaking.

"Crystal, tell me what's wrong," I said firmly.

"I … I don't know where to begin."

"Is someone hurting you?" I speculated. Maybe her husband was getting physical.

"No, not that. Well, yes. I don't know," she babbled.

"Crystal, look at me."

She raised her head slightly so her swollen eyes could meet mine.

"Is someone hurting you?" I quietly demanded.

Looking down, she paused before answering.

"It's Mike."

"Mike? Is that your husband?"

"No."

"Then who's Mike?" I asked, somewhat bewildered.

"He's someone who ... who knows of my past."

"And?"

"I saw him at the airport when I came back from my ... uh, my friend Candy's. I was hoping he didn't recognize me, but he did. The next day he showed up at my work and ..."

"And what? Has this Mike threatened you in some way?"

"He says if I don't do what he wants, he'll tell ..."

"Tell what?"

"Rick, you won't understand."

"Crystal, what does Mike want?" I insisted.

With her hands still shaking and her voice cracking, "He ... He wants me to work for him."

"Doing?"

Clearly humiliated, Crystal breathed almost inaudibly, "He wants me to have sex with men."

"Sex?" I exclaimed.

The answer shocked me. I wasn't expecting anything like that. But with Crystal's looks, even at forty, I suppose she could make a lot of money.

"I told him no. He told me if I didn't, he would tell about ... It was horrible. I just don't know what to do."

At this point, Crystal was on the verge of a total meltdown. Her voice was broken and completely without hope. But I was still confused, so I had to press her further.

"Crystal, he's blackmailing you, right?"

"Yes."

"What is he going to tell?"

"I ... I can't tell you. You wouldn't understand."

"Understand what? Try me," I said with frustration.

"You don't understand. I did things I'm so ashamed of."

I could see Crystal beginning to lose it, so I backed off.

"OK, we won't go there," I said.

I wondered if she had a fling at some point and was petrified Mike would tell her husband. If so, that's definitely good blackmail material.

"Oh, Rick, you were so nice in L.A. and such a gentleman. I've been so upset about Mike and could only think of you. I just need for you to tell me everything will be alright."

She began openly weeping. I moved from my seat and slid in next to her. I put my hands over hers, trying to offer some comfort. Her hands still had a death-grip on the coffee cup and were still shaking. I began gently questioning again.

"Crystal does your husband know any of this?"

"No!" she yelped. "He must never know!"

Whenever Crystal talks about her husband there's fear. The tears were now flowing down her cheeks. Her voice crackled with a quiet plea, "Rick, hold me ... hold me and never let me go."

I did what she asked, encircling her with both my arms. Instantly, she buried her head in my chest, sobbing.

For some reason, Crystal trusted me. First, on the plane when she told me personal and intimate details of her life. Then allowing herself to be vulnerable in a kiss. And now, she had revealed a secret. Though the details were sketchy, it was still a secret and one with such horrific consequences that the very thought of discovery had taken her to the verge of a breakdown.

I held her for some time as she cried. She needed to release all the emotions she had been bottling up. I gently kissed the top of her head and softly whispered that everything would be alright. As I held her, my thoughts drifted to this Mike character and the enormous secret they shared. What was it?

I'm a very curious guy, and I keep getting presented with mysteries. Why is that?!

Eventually, Crystal's crying subsided, and she pulled herself from me. With my finger under her chin, I raised her head so our eyes could meet.

"Everything will be alright," I whispered.

She had puffy eyes and black lines of mascara tracking down her face, but my words of assurance put a smile on it, too. For the first time that morning, she showed a flicker of hope.

Regaining her composure, she searched her purse for a hankie. Of course, she didn't have one! Fortunately, I did.

"Crystal, I'm going to buy you breakfast," I said while signaling our waitress. "In return, I want something from you."

She nodded her head with a frail "OK" as she dabbed at her streaky face with the hankie.

After a moment's pause, I said plainly, "Tell me about Mike. I want to know everything about him."

For the better part of an hour, we sat in our little private corner devouring our breakfast. I don't think Crystal had eaten in days. She gave me a complete dossier on Mike. He was a hustler, a low-life who had his greedy little fingers in every type of vice the streets had to offer. His specialty was marketing young girls for sex. He would find them on the street, usually runaways, and convince them there is money and glamour in prostitution. Using charisma, drugs, or intimidation, Mike capitalized on their fears and naiveté. He then added the girls to his stable, forcing them to sell themselves in seedy hotels, with the hotel management getting a piece of the action. To keep them in line, he often got them addicted to drugs, and—if that didn't work—a good beating would suffice. If a girl was above-average, she would be sold to the highest bidder in the porn industry—usually in Los Angeles—or into slavery across the border.

Another specialty of Mike's was blackmail. When a well-to-do john used the services of one of his underage girls, souvenir pictures were always made available for sale. The quality of these pictures commanded a very high selling price.

But Mike's greatest talent and pleasure was ruining lives. I could only guess what he had on Crystal, but knew I was going to help this woman. I was already percolating ideas on how to put her problem to rest.

"Crystal," I began gallantly, "let me take care of this for you."

Looking startled, she explained, "Rick, I don't want you to get involved. Mike can be a dangerous man. He hurts people."

"Don't worry. I can take care of myself."

And, honestly, this scumbag didn't worry me.

"And you'll take care of me, too," she sighed as she slipped her arm into mine.

"Do you have any sick time at work?"

"Yes, actually quite a bit," she replied, no doubt wondering where this line of questioning was going.

"Crystal, this is what's going to happen. Starting right now, you're going to be sick for a few days. Don't go to work or even answer the phone."

"I can't stay home. He knows where I live."

I pondered this briefly then asked, "Does he know about Candy?"

"He used to know her, but that was a long time ago."

"Would he have any idea she lives in Burbank?"

"No. At least I don't think so," she said and then paused. "No, it's been too many years."

"Fly down for a few days and relax in the sun. I'll call you when it's safe to come home."

"What should I tell my ... uh ... husband?"

"Tell him your Aunt Catherine is sick."

Still looking startled, it was apparent that Crystal was at a loss for words.

Taking her hand I promised, "I'll take care of it. Don't worry."

"I know. I know you'll take care of everything."

Crystal put her head on my shoulder and sighed with her whole body. I could tell she was now reasonably content. Within a few moments, she began to speak ... to confess.

"When we were on the plane, you made me feel safer than I've felt in a long time. When you kissed me, I knew you were a strong but gentle man. Thank you."

"You're welcome," I said while gently kissing her again on the top of her head. "But don't tell anyone. You'll ruin my image."

With a smile, she pulled my arm tighter, and her body sighed once more.

Before we went our separate ways, she wrote down the pertinent information on Mike—his full name, address, phone number, etc. I did in fact have a plan in mind, but it required the special touch of Vince. Being the ex-cop, he knew everyone on the force and had plenty of connections on and off the street. It's the best of both worlds that can come in very handy at times. I was sure Vince knew some people who were able to solve problems when the law couldn't. And that was what Crystal needed.

Back at my office I made a call.

"Vince, Rick. I got a problem."

"No, nothing to do with Johnson. Go figure. Could you be in my office this afternoon?"

"Great, see you soon."

Arriving mid–afternoon, Vince was escorted to my office by Alicia.

As she closed the door leaving us alone, he asked, "Is that the one from the gas station?"

"Yeah, great little worker."

"God only knows what that guy would have done to her," Vince added.

"Yeah, I know. And that leads me right to the reason I called you. We have another damsel in distress."

"You're like an addict with these women, Rick. You can't walk away," Vince chuckled.

I gave him a brief rundown on Crystal's problem, pointing out to him that she was the one in the tight Levi's at the airport. His only response was a smile and a quiet "O-o-oh."

Mentioning Mike's full name perked Vince's ears right up.

"You know this guy, Vince?" I asked.

"Yeah. Likes little girls."

Besides his obvious disgust for the guy, I could already see the wheels turning in Vince's head.

"I promised to help. Any ideas?" I continued.

The look on Vince's face was almost joyful, so he was most likely hatching an idea that would permanently stop Mike's unseemly activities. He snatched his cell phone from his pocket and dialed a number.

While it rang, he winked at me and said, "I know a way we can help your friend."

He diverted his attention back to the phone.

"Hey, it's Vince," he began. "Remember that client of yours last year—you know, the married one who had a problem with the asshole at work?"

"Yeah, that's the one. Do you think those guys would be interested in some repeat business?"

"Uh-huh. Same price as last time?"

"$100 each sounds fine. Do you want to set it up or shall I."

"Great. I'll stop by in an hour."

At this point, Vince filled me in on what he had in mind. I was amazed how simple the plan was … and for two hundred bucks? I gave the plan a green light.

About a year prior, an attorney Vince knew handled a legal matter for two rather large, unsavory gentlemen who were falsely accused of assaulting a man in downtown Seattle. Both these men were, well … let's call them "budget analysis professionals." When you borrow money on the street or obtain drugs on credit and don't live up to your end of the contract, these two would assist you with your budget and help you find the necessary capital to clear your debt ... with interest, of course.

The two were accused of helping an individual, a known drug dealer (who had some bookkeeping difficulties), figure out where in his budget he could find some cash to make good on his payment for drugs. Unfortunately, this poor soul's cash flow wasn't quite up to par with what the creditor was requiring. Consequently, our two friends were accused of assisting this borrower right into the emergency room of Harbor Medical Center.

Now, not that these two were innocent types by any means. I'm sure in their professional careers they had kept business healthy for area ERs by delivering clients—healthcare consumers, that is—with broken hands, arms, and legs to ER doctors and orthopedic surgeons. Their thriving partnership had no doubt contributed to the retirement plans of a few dentists as well.

But in this case, they were innocent.

Vince put the wheels of "Operation Mike" into motion and within twenty-four hours made contact with these two gentlemen. I appreciate this about Vince. He never procrastinates. After an explanation of the assignment and all the sensitivity and diplomacy needed for it, the two partners readily approved of the financial arrangement and the duties required. In short, a deal was struck.

They expressed additional enthusiasm when they found out who the object of their attention would be. I believe Vince said, "They smiled." It seems Mike once tried to recruit the daughter of the girlfriend of one of our new employees. Let's just say it didn't go down too well.

It was now arranged that Mike would have a come-to-Jesus meeting with these new members of our ministry team. The details of this revival were somewhat clouded, but it seems that our two new converts met up with Mike, took him for a ride up to some old logging road—the Northwest has many to choose from—and showed him the error of his ways. I never asked and never want to know what really happened up on that logging road, but I heard that Mike had an accident ... the kind that causes you to eat through a straw and use two canes to walk. I heard he slipped and fell. I guess there was a lot of ice up there.

It was safe to assume he would never bother Crystal again.

Crystal had left me Candy's phone number. It was the same number that, for some strange reason, I had kept from a few weeks back. With a quick call, Aunt Catherine was now feeling much better and Crystal could return home whenever she pleased.

When Crystal inquired curiously how I accomplished such a feat, I quipped, "It's all in the wrist, babe. It's all in the wrist."

A few days after the revival, I received an envelope in the mail—with no return address. It simply contained two photographs of a man lying on the ground. He appeared to have had an accident—nothing horrific, but enough to show the agreement had been completed.

Before I burned the pictures I looked at them one last time, focusing on Mike's facial expression. The smugness of his profession had been replaced with humility, a new respect for the gravity of life. Funny how some people change when they get religion.

CHAPTER 23

A few days after the completion of "Operation Mike" it was apparent my decoy shadow had become my constant companion. He was always by my side—indirectly, of course. Since Vince and I were at a loss as to who the real tail was, we agreed to put the investigation on hold. At least until some ruffled feathers were smoothed out—particularly Emily's and the Feds'.

Besides, we were out of leads.

So, instead of espionage on my mind, I was California dreaming … ah-h-h, to escape the office madhouse for a few days! The recipe for relaxation that I was cooking up consisted of three important ingredients: San Francisco, a steak, and a beautiful woman. Not necessarily in that order.

My reverie was interrupted by an aggravating buzz. It was Emily with a call on line one. I pushed the button and greeted the caller in my usual way.

"I understand you can work magic. Is that true?" purred the sweet voice on the other end.

It was Crystal, and judging by her teasing, her world was bright again. Good!

"Why, yes," I responded playfully, "it is. I can make things disappear. And apparently I can make *you* reappear. I also have some slight-of-hand performances that I reserve for special people …"

Giggling like a little girl, "Am I special, Magic Man?" she bubbled.

"Hmm," was my only reaction. At this point my thoughts had crossed over into a completely different bag of tricks that included secret doors to warm, soft, hidden places ... and something about a furry bunny and a top hat ... hmm ...

The sweet voice continued, "May I buy you dinner tonight? Just to say thank you. That is, if you have time for little old me?"

By her tone and choice of words, she knew damn well I'd make the time. Clear the calendar! Damn the torpedoes, full speed ahead! Like I said before, Crystal knows how to handle a man.

I enthusiastically accepted her invitation, and we set a time. But I chose the place ... because I was setting the stage for something else I had up my sleeve.

I was especially anxious to talk with Crystal about leaving her husband. She was petrified of him. It was unclear why, and she was not letting on. Mike's attempted blackmail seemed linked back to her husband somehow. But even in dire circumstances, she wouldn't spill the full story. So my gut was saying "h-u-s-b-a-n-d spells d-a-n-g-e-r," and my head was saying "maybe Operation Mike has fixed something more than I know." It could be wishful thinking. Maybe. Maybe not.

But you know me ... I had to find out. And if she was still in trouble, I had to help her.

Since Crystal was a master at guarding secrets, I couldn't just saunter through the restaurant door with questions blazing like gunfire. No, that would be futile. I needed a different approach. I had an idea.

I often meandered the backstreets of old Seattle to think or clear my head. On one of these journeys I stumbled upon a quaint family-owned Italian restaurant, an intimate place just a few blocks from the waterfront. Off the beaten path, tucked into a petite storefront on a quiet side street, the restaurant was charming. The décor was checkered tablecloths, dripping candles in wine bottles, and sawdust on the floor. Good food and romance were both on the menu. Martin and Sinatra crooned love songs in the background. It had an other-worldly feeling that suspends time, allowing a man and a woman the luxury of getting lost in each other. It was the perfect place to meet Crystal and to plant the seed of my idea. The restaurant's name was Luigi's.

Arriving a few minutes late, I found Crystal already seated in an intimate booth toward the back. As she looked up from her drink, she caught my eye and flashed the widest, most inviting smile I've ever seen. Even from across the room, I noticed a big difference in her countenance. Once at the booth, I was greeted with sustained enthusiasm.

"Sit here next to me," she bubbled as she began to slide over.

Sliding in, I felt warmth and energy radiating from her body. It was completely different from the body I held tenderly just a week earlier.

Taking my arm and pressing her head to my shoulder, "Thank you. Thank you so very much for all your help," she gushed.

"No problem," I said serenely, as though it was nothing.

Throughout dinner we both laughed and teased. I was waiting for just the right moment, the perfect opportunity, to put my idea to the test. That moment came during dessert. With Crystal's walls totally down, I made my move.

"So, Crystal," I began, "I was a little surprised by your invitation for tonight."

Looking up from her dessert plate, Crystal seemed surprised too.

"Why, Rick?"

"Oh, I thought you'd be at home having dinner with your husband tonight."

"Oh, him," she commented with a faint smile. "He's out of town for a few weeks."

"Travels a lot?" I asked.

Nodding her head she said, "Yes, he's out of the country more than he's in."

"Tell me honestly," I pressed, using her own words. "If he'd let you go, would you?"

Her eyes said, "In a heartbeat," but when a minute became two, with no verbal response, I asked again.

"Would you leave him?"

With hesitation she stammered, "I ... well, you see ..." Then, with a deep sigh, "Yes, Rick. Yes, I would. But I can't divorce him," she added.

"Why?" I pushed.

"Because we're ..."

She stopped again, in mid-sentence.

"Because if I leave him, he must never know where I go."

Settling my hand on hers, I asked, "If he knew you were leaving him, would he hurt you?"

"Rick ... I ... I know too many things."

"About?"

"His business," she replied quietly.

Her eyes were becoming swollen. A tear was dangling from an eyelash, momentarily suspended before trickling down her cheek.

"Crystal, rather than living in fear, have you ever considered running away?"

"Running away?" she returned.

A light flickered in her moist eyes. Running away was apparently something she'd never considered. The look quickly subsided, but for a brief moment her face gleamed. Good! My idea struck a chord. But she came tumbling back to reality quickly.

With a heavy sigh she breathed, "No matter where I went he would find me."

"Crystal, there's a big country out there. It would be very easy to just ... get lost."

Turning to the window with a curious look on her face, I heard her softly repeat my words "get lost?"

"Yeah, 'get lost.' It would be so easy to do."

This was my idea for her. With or without spilling the beans why she needed to get away from this man, I wanted her to seriously consider leaving him. I had taken my best shot and she seemed receptive, so I pulled out more ammunition—an old map of California. I spread it across the table.

"See," I began. "Everywhere on this map are little dots. Places to go and easily fade into the background. This is only California. There are forty-nine more states. Somewhere out there," looking toward the window, "there has to be your Camelot."

Crystal sat upright in the booth. Her face took on a glow with this epiphany.

She mumbled the word, "Camelot ..."

"Yes, Camelot," I confirmed.

I sing-songed my voice, to mimic the movie soundtrack. This delighted her, and she joined in as Guinevere.

I was pleased that she knew the lyrics too. We both beamed, put our heads together and finished in a whispered song (so as not to disturb the entire restaurant!).

Finished, she gave me a quick kiss on the cheek, "That sounds like a wonderful place," she said with a grin.

For quite awhile, Crystal intently studied the map, pointing to little towns and wondering out loud what they would be like. The idea made her sparkle. I, too, began pointing to certain towns, sharing what I knew about them or some experience I had there.

"I like San Diego," she said with gleam in her eyes.

"Have you ever been there?" I asked.

"Only once. I was ..." Crystal had become proficient at never completing a sentence.

"Was what?" I asked.

"I guess you could call it a 'business trip,'" she muttered and changed the subject to the beaches in the area.

We chattered about San Diego as our waitress came and went from the table, mostly leaving us to our private world. I gave Crystal the highlights of what I knew about the city and threw in a few fond memories I had there.

Then Crystal surprised me with an idea of her own.

"Wouldn't it be nice if we could go and have dinner there?"

"When do you want to go?" I responded impulsively.

I say it was impulsive because a trip like that, spent together, would be the next level of a relationship with Crystal, which is something I don't normally pursue with married women. Remembering what Cindy did to me automatically makes them a turn off. But Crystal was different somehow. I didn't think of her as married, even though she spoke openly about it. Maybe the difference was that hers was an obviously bad marriage.

With a somber look on her face, Crystal said, "You're serious, aren't you?"

"Yeah, why not?" I quipped. "I can take the time if you can. We could fly down for a day or two. Get a couple of rooms and see the sights. It'll be fun. Besides, it's been awhile since I've been to San Diego. It'll be good to see it again."

Suddenly Crystal stopped dead in her tracks. Dreaming is one thing, but doing is quite another.

"Rick, I don't know," she said hesitantly. "Is it something we could really do? Where would we stay?"

"Well, the Coronado's a nice place," I ventured. "I'll even pick up the cost of the rooms!"

I could see the wheels turning in her head. She was giving the suggestion her utmost attention. Her eyes were filled with a combination of doubt and excitement.

"Rick, can we really do San Diego?" she uttered again.

Kissing her on her forehead I replied, "Yes, Crystal, we can. But only if you want to."

"Let me think about it," she said.

The following day, I received a call from Crystal. After answering the phone in my usual manner, I was treated to just one word.

"Yes."

We set a date for the following weekend.

Spinning my chair to the window, I was once again California dreaming … ah-h-h, to escape the office madhouse for a few days! My relaxation recipe had cooked up nicely. Not the precise combination of ingredients I originally concocted, but close.

Smiling, I said aloud, "Two outa three ain't bad."

CHAPTER 24

Upon arriving at the Hotel del Coronado in early afternoon, I learned from the concierge that Crystal had already checked in. She left me a note.

> I have a few errands to run. Meet me in the main bar at 6:00.
>
> Love you,
>
> Crystal
> xoxo

"Love you? Huh. Something new. And it has an interesting ring to it," I thought.

But what were these errands? Did she know someone in town? Maybe she had business for the company? After all, she was a manager for a nationwide weight-loss clinic. But, whatever it was, why would it take all afternoon?

And why was everything about her shrouded in mystery?

About a quarter to six, I made my way to our rendezvous. Crystal was nowhere to be found. I described her to the bartender and asked if he had seen her. He didn't recall. If he had seen Crystal, he would have remembered. So, convinced that she hadn't yet arrived, I maneuvered a seat at the end of the bar with a view of the entrance.

The action was entertaining while I waited. There were ten men for every woman, all stumbling over themselves for a lady's favor. And some of the ladies, well … weren't. The scene reminded me of an older, married version of the mating rituals in Panama City during spring break.

A couple of barstools down was this older blond—obviously a pro—who had a few men making a to-do over her. From the instant I sat down, I caught her eye. From time to time she laughed flirtatiously at some stupid remark from one of her future clients, all the while directing her attention to me. She was 40-ish with long, stringy hair parted down the middle, slightly overweight and wearing a cocktail dress that she spilled out of. Even in a dimly-lit bar, her complexion showed the trademarks of too many years of alcohol and cigarettes. I thought of Heather in Las Vegas and silently hoped she didn't turn out like this.

The woman was sizing me up, waiting for the right moment to make her move. With a few coy smiles and tossing of the hair (like *that* was going to help) she came in for the kill. Brushing off her horny studs entirely, she eased over to the seat next to mine. She gave me the once-over with her eyes with what was intended to be a seductive smile.

With a throaty voice, she breathed, "Hi, I'm Amber."

"Hello," I returned courteously.

"Here by yourself, honey?"

"No. I'm waiting for someone."

I could see her disappointment. I wasn't going to be a paying customer.

"Well, I've been waiting for you my whole life, handsome. Maybe I'll get lucky, and she won't show."

Before Amber finished her sentence, Crystal appeared in the doorway like a bolt of lightning. Time stood still as all eyes were drawn to this vision that "Crystalized" out of nowhere. She was breathtaking in a silky black cocktail dress that plunged to reveal her ivory breasts, cinched to accent her tiny waistline, and landed well above the knees, showcasing her shapely legs. As my eyes moved down the black hose to the open-toed stiletto heels, the effect almost made my heart stop. Her hair was done in a simple yet elegant style I hadn't seen on her before, teased up slightly on top and tumbling dramatically across her buttery shoulders in waves. Slightly hidden behind these tresses were golden earrings, sparkling as they caught the light. Her face was flawless, made up to sheer perfection. Every detail dazzled. Even her toes and fingernails sparked fiery red.

Damn, she was hot.

She posed dramatically in the light and shadows of the entryway, scanning the room casually until she saw me. Her smile was radiant as she took a step in my direction. The throngs parted like the Red Sea and, one by one, conversations ceased as Crystal's seductive sway put each in a trance.

My new friend noticed the effect Crystal had on me. Maybe it was my bulging eyes, or perhaps my tongue that was bouncing cartoon-like off the floor—but she couldn't keep from commenting, hoping not to lose a trick.

"Honey, she's way out of your league," Amber croaked triumphantly.

I was unmoved by Amber as I watched Crystal move toward me. With my eyes trained only on Crystal I chuckled, "Hardly, *honey*. That *is* my date."

I think I heard Amber mutter, "You're kidding," but I'm really not sure. There was nothing else in the room other than Crystal. I was totally consumed by her presence. Her eyes were locked on mine, and I was the only man in the bar. She was in slow motion. Her dress clung to her hips and thighs, deeply stirring my imagination. Every part of her body undulated in perfect gentle rhythm—first to the right, then to the left—and the bounce of her breasts was in sync with her hips. It was mesmerizing. She made her way across the room moving silently like a sailing ship slicing through water. In her wake, she left breathless, drowning men. And Crystal knew exactly what she was doing.

She glided past poor, crusty Amber as though she didn't exist. She stopped directly in front of me and paused majestically. Crystal was eye candy of the most exquisite quality, and she was giving everyone a sweet taste. But she made it clear that the creamy center was all mine.

"Sorry I'm late, dear," she purred while gently running her tongue across her glossy lips. "I had a little shopping and fussing to do. I spent some time and money. Was it well spent?"

I dropped my eyes to her breasts then glanced back upward. My eyes were met with a seductive smile of approval. Breathless, I grinned back like the proverbial kid in the candy shop.

Trying to keep eye contact was not easy, as mine kept dropping to admire the lovely twins below. They seemed to understand my hunger for them and kept calling my name, taunting me to take them. Crystal seemed pleased by my fixation.

Somewhere during this scene, Amber returned to the boys down the bar. I didn't see her skirt around us. Next to Crystal, all other women were invisible.

When I finally caught my breath, I took both of Crystal's hands and said, "You are the most beautiful woman on earth."

Answering in a playful southern accent, Crystal drawled, "Why, thank you, suh, and may ah say you are *the* most chahmin' gentleman."

There was a small table in the corner that had just been vacated by two very intoxicated men who, I might add, had been mentally undressing Crystal ever since she entered the bar. Crystal sat down and crossed her legs, offering a peek-a-boo view of where the thigh-high hose stopped at the garter and her delicious, milky-white thighs began. I was in awe.

We ordered drinks and talked and laughed for nearly an hour. As we did, my feelings for Crystal shifted. The change was radical and swift. Still passionate, my desires were giving way to a different kind of emotion—one that made me very uncomfortable about the way Crystal was dressed. Though hot as a pistol and pleased with what I saw, I didn't like the way the other men in the bar were looking at her, particularly the one sitting on the far side of the room. With bug-eyes and wet chin, he'd been openly eyeing Crystal since she stood in the doorway. I didn't like him. I didn't like the look on his face as he looked at her. And I didn't like the lump beneath his belt.

I leaned over to whisper in her ear, "Do you know that guy at the end of the bar has his eyes glued on you?"

"Uh-huh. I want him to get an eyeful."

"You what?" I asked with some surprise.

"Yup."

Her answer left me in the wilderness without a compass. I had no idea what direction to take or what to say.

"Is there a side to you I don't know about?"

Leaning toward me, she gazed deep into my eyes—totally ignoring everyone in the bar.

In a tone that was both seductive and innocently loving, she said, "I want every man here to know what you're going to get tonight."

"Get tonight?" I repeated.

Crystal grinned impishly. But the smile was soon replaced with another look, an extremely intense look.

"In Los Angeles, you didn't try to take advantage of me. You saved me from Mike and asked for nothing. I waited to see if you would, but you never did. Catherine said you would, but she was wrong. Even with this trip, you arranged for two rooms. Rick," she said and paused, as though trying to find courage. She glanced down then returned her gaze to meet mine. "I love you," she declared openly.

In a state of shock, I needed a moment to digest her confession. This was something I wasn't expecting. I couldn't find any words. Instead, I took off my coat and placed it over her shoulders.

Looking at me strangely, Crystal said, "I'm not cold."

"I know."

"Then why the coat?" she asked, already knowing the answer.

"Because."

"Because, Rick?"

I felt like I was back in junior high, stumbling over words I wanted to say, too petrified to say them.

Taking a deep breath, I began quietly, "I just don't want anyone looking at you anymore."

"You don't? Why?"

Why do women always have to play this game to make a man say something they want to hear?

"Because, Crystal."

"'Because' is not an answer. Why does it bother you that men are staring at me?"

"Because it does."

"Rick, tell me why. Please?"

"Because I like you, Crystal. Probably more than I should. Now can we have some dinner?" I stumbled, trying to steer the conversation in a new direction.

I really didn't know what the hell to say or do.

Reaching out and taking my hand, Crystal continued, "Rick, you are the nicest, kindest man I've ever met."

"Yeah, but just don't tell anybody. You *know* I don't want my image ruined," I reminded her. "Now, can we have dinner?"

"That sounds nice," she answered. "But ... would you ... would you like me to change first?"

"Would you mind?" I asked gently.

"No. I think it's sweet. I'll go change."

Crystal was happy with my request.

"I'll wait here for you."

"No, come with me."

There was something in her voice that compelled me to go. We headed upstairs.

After opening the door to her room, Crystal turned to me and smiled. She took my hand and led me in. As I closed the door, she dropped my hand, slipped my jacket from her shoulders and laid it across the back of a chair. She walked about five feet in front of me, stopped, turned, and struck a very sexy pose.

Slyly she asked, "Are you still hungry?"

I knew what she meant. And I was.

"Very," I replied as my eyes ravished her body.

"Well then, let me feed you."

And without saying another word, but looking straight into my eyes, she pushed the straps aside, letting her dress fall to the floor.

The first time I saw Crystal in the airport I knew she had a killer body. In the bar downstairs I was treated to a preview sample of what was there. But now, standing in front of me wearing nothing but tiny black lacy panties, matching garter belt with black thigh-high nylons, and 3-inch black heels, there was no doubt she was an absolute goddess.

She glided over to me and wrapped her arms around my neck. She kissed me. It was soft and sensuous. Reciprocating, I enveloped her in my arms and held her tightly around the waist. Our kisses were exhilarating, enhanced by two firm, bare breasts pressing snugly against my chest. I wanted her so badly ...

I pushed her back gently. Still holding her, I looked directly into her eyes and asked, "Crystal, are you sure you want to do this?"

Putting her hand on my face, Crystal began, "Oh, my darling, darling Rick. You're always here to protect me, aren't you? I don't want you to have sex with me tonight. I want you to take me and hold me and love me. Tonight, just for tonight, I want to be yours. I want to feel your kisses all over my body and feel you inside of me. I want to feel the warmth of you next to me while I sleep. I want you to take me someplace I've never been before. I'm not asking for a commitment, I'm asking just for tonight."

"Crystal ..."

As I started, she moved her fingers to my lips, touched them so very gently, and said, "Shhh, don't say anything."

I took her fingers in my hand and kissed each as it gently slid across my lips. As the tip of each finger glided softly over the end of my tongue, I was consumed with its soft warmth. I could feel a deep passion building quickly in Crystal. I closed my eyes and let my imagination paint a picture of the exploding sensations I was feeling. With my eyes still shut, I moved my lips down her fingers to the palm and then the wrist, kissing emphatically as I went. I kissed hungrily up her arm to arrive finally at her most vulnerable place—the neck. Her head was tilted, awaiting my arrival, inviting me to ravage her steamy flesh. Judging by her moans, barely audible, Crystal approved.

Using just my fingers, I delicately traced up and down her arms—from her shoulders to her hands, slightly brushing back and forth. Her eyes were closed, and she had a far-away look on her face. She was enjoying my touch.

Ever so slowly, I began to move up and down her torso, feeling her warm flesh beneath the gentle touch of my fingers. With each pass, I moved closer to her breasts and sensed her desire to have me take and explore them. Barely sweeping across their fullness, I wanted desperately to claim them as mine ... they were mouth-wateringly desirable. But instead I restrained myself and willed my fingers to move lightly, tenderly. I brushed gently across a nipple and Crystal's body stiffened. This is what I was hoping for—stimulation that creates the type of reaction marking a shift to a higher plane of tension and passion.

Looking completely overwhelmed, Crystal bit her lower lip as an uncontrolled spasm shot through her quivering body. I swept her into my arms and carried her to the bed. The night was ours. And we claimed it over and over again. We feasted, we indulged, we rested, we did the bump and grind, and then we started it all over again. We rejoiced in every moment, but I discovered that Crystal enjoyed the soft touch more than anything else ... her greatest fulfillment was in the soft touch.

Sometime during the wee hours of the morning and after numerous trips to heaven, depleted of all physical and emotional strength, Crystal collapsed like a rag doll. I pulled the covers over us and encircled her naked body in my arms. I could feel her exhaustion. As our heads nestled on a shared pillow, I whispered into her ear, "Go to sleep. I will stand guard for the night." She nuzzled closer to me and stayed there until first light.

Rising early with Crystal still fast asleep, I pulled back the drapes. The night was being pushed away by the rising sun. There were already guests searching the beach as the tide was coming in. It was beautiful.

"But not as beautiful as Crystal," I thought as I turned from the window to watch her sleep. Not wanting to wake her, I quietly slipped back to my own room for a shower and shave.

I was only gone for about an hour, but when I returned, housekeeping was fixing up the room. I checked the key against the number on the door.

I was in the right room, but Crystal was gone. So were her bags. Puzzled, I asked the housekeeper if she knew where the occupant went. The woman reached into her pocket and handed me a note.

> My Dearest Rick,
>
> I pray that one day you will forgive me for what has to happen this morning. Last night was pure magic. For the first time in my life I knew what it was like to be more than just desired—I was loved and respected too. How I wish that last night could have lasted for eternity! But if we are honest, we both knew it could never really be ours. You know that map we looked at? I have found my dot on it and now must journey there alone. I need to vanish as if I never really existed in the first place. Except for my heart ... that I leave with you, the only man who has ever protected me.
>
> All my love always,
>
> Crystal

I wandered in a daze back to my room. What just happened? I opened her note and re-read it. This time I noticed little damp spots on the paper, places where the ink ran. Tear drops! I considered running after her. But to where? As she put it, she needed to "vanish as if I never really existed in the first place." Deep in my heart I knew this was right for Crystal. I guess from the first moment we met I knew it. Hell, I'm the one who suggested it! But I didn't mean run from me! And after what we shared last night? I had to know. I had to peek under her shroud of mystery.

I snatched my cell phone and pushed a button. On the third ring, there was a sleepy hello.

"Vince, Rick."

"Meet me at 9:00, Monday morning, at the coffee place. I have a job for you."

CHAPTER 25

It was early Friday afternoon, day five into his background check of Crystal, when Vince summoned me to our usual watering hole. Since I gave him the assignment, there had been nonstop rain in Seattle. My gut told me that his report, like the weather, would be dismal.

Swirling the last sip in the bottom of his glass, Vince began with small talk.

"So, Rick, your faithful companion still on the job?"

Looking back toward the front door, I replied, "I'm not sure. I haven't seen him since I left for San Diego. Think the Feds have given up?"

"Possibly," Vince said with a somber look. "But don't count on it."

Pulling out his little black notebook, Vince continued, "Crystal Rothschild."

"So, Vince, what did you find?" I asked, trying to disguise my anxiety, but not doing a very good job of it.

He looked down at a blank page, looked back up and replied, "Nothing."

"Nothing?" I repeated blankly as my heart rate climbed and fell like a roller-coaster.

"Yeah, Rick. Nothing. To start with, I went to her business, the one on her card. They've never heard of her. No one with her description has ever worked for them."

I was at a loss for words. My roller-coaster heart was spinning somewhere near the top of the Las Vegas Stratosphere.

He continued, "I then had one of my people do a credit check on her name. Again, nothing."

"You're kidding!"

"I wish I was." Vince leaned across the table. "Listen, if I hadn't seen her with my own eyes at the Burbank Airport, I would swear she didn't exist."

Oh, there was no doubt Crystal existed. Our night of passion just a week back was something even I could not have dreamt.

Vince continued, "Using the name Rothschild, we came up blank for her and her husband in the State of Washington."

"No husband either?"

Vince shook his head no.

"We did come up with a David Rothschild in Los Angeles. Could that be the same one?"

I had no idea. I shrugged and took the last sip of my vodka martini. I needed another one.

"Rick, how did you make contact with this woman?"

"Just called the number on the card or the one in Burbank."

"That's what I thought. I traced both numbers and came up empty. The first is a throw-away cell. The second has been disconnected."

Slumping into my chair, I signaled the cocktail waitress. A fresh vodka martini might help me regain my clarity. Or not. I was at a loss on how to proceed.

"So, Vince, any ideas on the next step?"

"Just one. Her old friend, Mike."

"Mike?"

"Yes, Mike. At this point, he probably knows more than we do."

"Hmm. Good idea. Think he'll talk to us?"

With a devilish smile, "If he knows what's good for him, he will," Vince said.

After Mike's recent encounter with our ministry team, I was afraid to know what Vince had in mind if he didn't.

"Do you want to go see him this afternoon? He's been discharged from Harbor, and he's in a rehab center. I have the address."

"No, let's hold off until Monday. I have a flight to catch this afternoon."

"San Francisco?"

"Yeah."

"Who is she, Rick?"

"Just a friend."

"Not according to Emily. She says one of these days you won't be coming back."

I took a healthy swig of my fresh drink, smiled wryly and declared, "Vince, that idea just gets better and better."

Refreshed from my weekend in San Francisco, I accompanied Vince on a visit to Mike. Still scraped and bruised, Mike was sitting in a wheelchair staring out a window watching the rain, probably contemplating how much his life had changed in the last few weeks. We walked into his room and Vince started the conversation.

"Hello, Mike."

Mike immediately recognized Vince. His response said it all.

"What the fuck d'ya want, cop?"

"Now, Mike, let's be civil. You have a guest here today." He moved his hand to indicate me.

"Another fuckin' cop?" he snapped, and added, "Why don't you fuckin' cops get the guys who did this to me, if ya can take the time from bangin' yer sistuhs."

Mike was such a pleasant fellow.

"Now, Mike, it sounds like we're a little bitter," Vince expressed calmly.

Giving him the once-over, I could tell our ministry team worked him over a little more than the picture revealed. He had casts on both legs, black and blue marks across the face, teeth missing, both eyes still a little swollen, and who-knows-what underneath the clothes. Mike was a mess. But considering what he did to little girls, he was lucky that was all that happened to him.

"Mike, we have some questions."

"Tough shit, cop."

Vince suddenly and violently grabbed Mike's wheelchair and spun it around to face him.

"Look, you steaming piece of crap, if you don't want the two guys that worked you over to come back and finish the job, you'll answer every question my friend here asks. Understand?"

For the first time since our arrival, Mike wasn't cocky. Speechless and afraid, he nodded his head. He understood. I pulled up a folding chair and sat next to him. Vince took out his book to take notes.

"OK, Mike," I began, "I want to know everything about Crystal Rothschild."

"Crystal who?" Mike asked.

"Rothschild," I repeated. "The one you tried to blackmail to work for you."

"You mean Crystal Bentley?"

"Is that another name for her?"

"It's the only name I know."

"What did you want from her?"

"Money."

"How much?" I asked suspiciously.

"$50,000."

Vince and I looked at each other.

"Mike, what makes you think Crystal could raise fifty grand?"

"I heard she married this rich dude. I thought she could get it outta him. If not, she could work it off."

"What do you mean 'work it off?'"

Mike got some of his cocky back. With an arrogant look he spat, "What d' ya think, asshole?"

One thing's for sure, Mike can be thankful I wasn't at his come-to-Jesus meeting. He would be talking to Jesus now instead of me.

"Mike, let's cut to the chase. You were blackmailing Crystal. What did you have on her?"

Mike's eyes pierced mine as he sat silent.

"Speak, dirtbag," Vince threatened.

Unwillingly, Mike grumbled, "'Bout ten years ago I was workin' in Vegas as a bellhop. She was a high-priced hooker workin' The Strip."

"Call girl?" I interrupted.

"Yeah. Very expensive and by appointment only. Only did high rollers."

A thought flashed through my mind. I looked at Vince. We were reading the same page. And I didn't like the content.

"Go on," I said.

"I was workin' at the ..." before Mike finished, I mentioned a hotel name. He nodded yes.

"Anyways, I take this high roller up to his suite. He always got the same one."

"So you saw him before?"

"Yeah, 'bout every Saturday night for 'bout six months."

"And?"

"An' 'bout eleven o'clock Crystal knocks on his door."

"Was he a regular for her?"

"Yeah, never seen him with anyone else."

"Go on."

"Anyways, around midnight I see her comin' out of the elevator, past the desk practically runnin' out the front door like a bat outta hell was on her tail. Besides being all mussed up, she looked scared as hell."

"And?"

"So, I go up to check on things. The housekeepin' hanger's on the door, so I knock, but there's no answer. I figure they fucked, he got a little rough, she split and he headed to the casino or somethin'."

"Did she always leave early?"

"No, that's why I even noticed. I don't care 'bout no scared whore. But she always spent the night. The next day when I come on shift, I heard this high roller died in the middle of the night. I figure Crystal was the last one to see him alive."

"So did you ever tell the cops?"

"Fuck no, man. It wasn't any of my business. Besides," he added, looking back at Vince, "I hate cops."

"So, Mike, what do you think?"

"'Bout what?"

Mike wasn't the brightest bulb in the pack.

"Do you think Crystal killed the guy, Mike?"

"Fuck no. Crystal was too soft."

"Then how do you think he died?"

He turned back to the window and mumbled, "Don't know. The fuckin' cops wouldn't say."

I paused to collect my thoughts. Mike was giving us valuable information.

"So how did you hook up with Crystal after ten years?"

"I seen her at the airport gettin' off a plane awhile back. I didn't even recognize her at first. Back then her hair was a lot darker. So I decide to follow her and caught up with her atta cab stand. She didn't recognize me at first, but when I start talkin' 'bout the dude that died in Vegas, she came unglued. I ask for her cell number and the stupid bitch gave it to me. I had no clue where she lived or nuthin'. If she woulda just walked away ..."

Mentally drifting, Mike was realizing how different things could have been.

"Anything else?"

"Huh?"

"I said, 'Anything else?'"

207

"Yeah, is Rothschild the bitch's new name?"

I didn't answer.

"Mike, tell me what you knew about the high roller who died."

"Nuthin'."

"Nothing? You carried his bag for six months and you say 'nuthin'?' What was his name?"

"Hmm, Smith?"

"Don't be a smartass, Mike," Vince interjected.

"Fuck you, cop," he blurted, then turned back to me. "That's the name he registered under … Smith."

"Do you know where he was from?"

"L.A."

"What made you think L.A.?"

"The baggage claim on his suitcase was LAX."

"Describe him, Mike."

"Early sixties, 6 foot even, kinda skinny, a lotta hair he dyed."

"What color?"

"Black. His head always looked like it just got a shine."

"Anything else?"

"I think he had a bad heart."

"What makes you think that?"

"One time comin' up in the elevator he got shorta breath and popped a little pill."

"Nitro?"

"What am I, a fuckin' doctor now?"

"And?"

"And what? That's it."

I looked over at Vince and asked, "What do you think?"

Vince only shook his head.

"I'm glad the prick died," Mike continued.

"Why's that?"

"Cheap screw never gave me a decent tip."

Leaving Mike's room, I felt as though someone kicked me in the nads. I didn't want to believe Crystal was a hooker … but … the way she handled men, her agitation about secrets from her husband, her dark sadness and mystery. It added up to Mike being on the level. And the rest of it? Now Crystal, too, was part of my fraud investigation?

It stung.

In the lobby of the rehab center there were a few couches and chairs. Vince and I picked a couch in the corner and began to talk.

"Well, Rick, at least we know now who was in that room with Johnson."

I didn't answer.

Vince continued, "It stands to reason Johnson had a bad heart."

Again, I was silent, barely taking in his words.

"Rick?" Vince asked. "Do you agree?"

I turned slowly toward him and nodded. The conclusions were evident. Since Johnson seemed to have a bad heart, the new question was, why did we insure him for twenty million? No doubt that's why the underwriting files were missing. But more of my thoughts revolved around Crystal. It was her perfume the housekeeper smelled. It was her that was riding on top of Johnson until he had a heart attack. It was her that left him to die. I don't know which sank further. My body into that old couch, or my heart into an abyss. For a few minutes, I said nothing.

It was Vince who broke the silence. "You realize, Rick, that your meeting Crystal in the airport was no accident."

"Yeah, I know, Vince," I said quietly, still at a loss for words. I was hurt and in shock. But I knew what had to be done. And at this point it didn't matter whose toes got stepped on.

Taking a deep breath, I began, "Vince, this is what I want you to do. Mike knew Crystal as Crystal Bentley. Obviously her professional name. Send someone back down to Vegas tomorrow. Since she was a hooker, there had to be some arrests. Arrests mean court records. Find them. I want to know everyone she came into contact with in an official capacity. Cops, ADAs, judges, anyone and everyone. If she was only doing high rollers, she had a pimp or madam. Someone was handling the finances and setting appointments. Find them. I want to know who they were and where they are today. Find hookers who have been around since then. Get Frank to help you. Better yet, get Heather. She should know. Talk to them. Someone was close to Crystal. I want to know who, and I want to talk with them. Crystal's husband? Let's find out about him, too."

"Where do I start for him?"

"Crystal said he was wealthy and travels out of the country a lot."

"Yeah, passports," Vince said.

"Yeah, let's see where Mr. Rothschild goes. Also, about Johnson, did you ever find a connection between him and Cole?"

Shaking his head, "Nothing," Vince answered.

"Then let's dig deeper into Johnson. Since we know what kind of woman he liked, let's find out everything else about him. And Cole. Turn his life upside down. Especially his death. I want to know every step he took, every person he talked to 24 hours before he died."

Vince had another question. His voice was low and concerned.

"Rick, why all this interest in a hooker?"

Taking a deep breath, I paused to reflect on that question. As upsetting as Mike's information was about Crystal, I just couldn't think of her as a hooker. Maybe long ago, but the Crystal I knew was a lady, an innocent victim of a dark past.

"Vince, I have three reasons," I began slowly.

Raising an eyebrow, "Three?" he repeated.

"First, Crystal isn't the brains behind this whole thing, but she knows who is. Second, though she wasn't truthful with me, she was scared. I want to know of what and who. And thirdly ..."

Picking up one of Crystal's bad habits, I didn't finish.

"Thirdly?" Vince asked.

Opening my wallet, I pulled out a note. Folded in eighths, you could see the tear stains that bleached through the paper.

"See this, Vince? It's a goodbye note from Crystal."

I handed it to him to read.

"Those spots are from her tears. She wrote it from her heart. She didn't fake that."

As he finished reading the note, Vince was quiet and, surprisingly, he was misty-eyed.

I took the note from his hand and began again, "There's someone out there with more muscle and juice than I've ever seen. Court records sealed. Cops, ADAs and judges bought off. An ex-con is dead because he was expendable. Thirdly, Vince?" I said with my voice slightly cracking, "Thirdly, I'm worried for her."

"Worried?"

"Yeah, worried that she, too, may be expendable."

Chapter 26

It was a little before lunch when Emily skirted into my office with a very concerned look. Phil Carter was hot on her heels.

"Morgan, we need to talk," he commanded.

Emily knew to shut the door. He didn't wait to be offered a seat or any other niceties.

"Morgan, I just had a visit from two FBI agents who told me a phenomenal story about an investigation you're doing. They want it stopped," he fumed. "What the hell is going on and why wasn't I informed?"

I gulped, took a deep breath, and spent the next ten minutes explaining the highlights of everything which had transpired since he sent Caroline and me to San Francisco. I emphasized the twenty million dollar claim, the fact that someone with a lot of muscle was usually one step ahead of Vince and me, and that a man was dead. As I finished, Phil was quiet, obviously troubled by what he heard.

"Morgan," he began somberly, "honestly, does your gut tell you someone hit us for twenty million?"

It's noteworthy that, having heard my story, his first concern was not for the man who died, nor for his employees who were a hair from being kidnapped (one of whom would have been raped), but rather his first concern was for twenty million dollars. Bottom line: it's always about the money.

I leaned forward over my desk and answered gravely, "*That's* what I'm trying to find out. But taking into consideration that our insured died of a heart attack a year after the policy was issued and that the underwriting files are missing, the odds are ... yes, someone hit us for twenty million."

Irritated, he huffed, "Well, why wasn't I informed?"

Taking another deep breath, I answered slowly, "Because I was told by you and Don that I report to the board and stockholders. With files missing, computer backups corrupted, learning Cole was on our board, the FBI tailing me ... I had no idea who I could trust. I'm doing my job."

Phil's demeanor changed, and he chuckled slightly as he said, "You know, Morgan, you are the cockiest, most arrogant son of a bitch we have in this company. But I can't argue with your reasoning. Take this investigation as far as you need to. I'll stay out of your way ... but ... this conversation doesn't leave this room."

Nodding, I agreed.

"And," he continued, "if we were hit, I want to know by whom."

He pointed his finger at me for emphasis and demanded, "Understand?"

Nodding again, I understood.

"What about the FBI?" I asked.

"Hmm. They could be a problem."

"Do we know anyone who could talk to them—unofficially, of course—to get them off our backs?"

"Actually, we do. We have a few friends in the Senate. Let me worry about the FBI, and you keep going. But if you find Cole's little black book, turn it over to them immediately and let me know."

After Phil left, I shut the door and spun in my chair to face the window. This was the first day in a long while the Seattle skyline was sunny and clear. As I enjoyed the view and the sunshine washed over me, my thoughts drifted from dreadful to pleasant. I toyed with the idea of a weekend in Carmel ... pizza with a certain sexy San Franciscan? Hmm ... maybe? But when I turned back to my desk, it was obvious from the files stacked ten deep where I would be this weekend.

But my noble aspiration to stay in town with my nose to the grindstone was about to be deflated. My thoughts were interrupted by the ring of my cell phone. The caller ID indicated it was Vince. Weekend plans? Consider them changed.

"Vince, what's up?"

"Really?"

"Is she willing to talk?"

"Tonight? What time?"

I glanced at my watch.

"Yeah, I can make it. I'll email you a flight number."

"Yeah, get me a room. Thanks. See you tonight."

Heather, working with Vince, had found a hooker who knew Crystal, and she agreed to talk with us.

It was 8:02 P.M. when my plane touched down at McCarran. Vince was waiting with a car. Our discussion was set in North Las Vegas—at the same dive we met up with Jack Takahashi, our degenerate retired medical examiner. Apparently, older prostitutes feel relatively comfortable at this bar, so we were meeting on Lola's turf.

It was a few hours until our appointment, which gave Vince and me time for dinner. The conversation centered on the report about Crystal's husband.

"Mr. David Rothschild, a very interesting character," Vince began. "Address unknown, but probably living in the Seattle area."

"Seattle? I thought you said you found nothing in the State of Washington."

"That's correct, but we only did a current credit check."

"Then why do you think he's in Seattle?"

"His driver's license."

Lowering my voice a tad, I said, "How the hell did you see his driver's license?"

"I didn't say I saw it, but I did manage to get an address."

"OK, but how?"

"One of my operatives has a daughter who works for the State Patrol."

"You're kidding. Vince, she could lose her job, and you could lose your license over that."

"Yeah, I know. But here's the freaky part. The address on the license is an address in Los Angeles."

"Impossible."

"Yeah, impossible. But guess what address it is?"

I had no clue.

"The same address as our friendly law firm!"

"You mean ..."

"Yeah, Greenbrier, Morris & Perry."

"Now this is where it gets better. He is a wealthy jeweler of European descent who travels frequently out of the country, mostly to South Africa, buying diamonds and other rare stones from dubious sources."

"Then sells them here in the United States?" I asked.

"If he does, I don't know to whom. However, about a year before your Mr. Johnson died, our Mr. Rothschild seemed to have vanished. But he reappeared after Johnson's death."

"Out of the country?"

"Possibly. I really don't know. But, I did manage to find an old credit report for someone who fits Rothschild's profile."

"Go on."

"This Rothschild lived in Vegas."

"Vegas?"

"Yeah, I thought that would catch your interest. For a number of years. During that time, he didn't have two nickels to rub together. Worked as a blackjack dealer."

"Connection?"

Shrugging his shoulders, Vince said, "Your guess is as good as mine."

"Do you think someone paid him off, like the funeral guy?"

"Possibly, but if they did, it was with a hell of a lot more money."

"Well, they had twenty million. But, Vince, how does a blackjack dealer—even with an onslaught of cash—end up as an international jeweler?"

"Good question, Rick. You tell me."

I found it unbelievable, but had no idea what to believe instead.

"Anything else on this guy?" I asked.

Vince smiled. He had saved the best for last.

"There is no record that I can find that Rothschild was ever married."

I gave Vince a queer look and asked, "What about Crystal?"

"Yeah, Rick," Vince replied, "what about Crystal?"

It was 11:00 P.M. when we arrived at the dive's parking lot for our appointment with Lola. We could see her standing under a dim parking lot light, hustling two gentlemen. (I use the term loosely.) She was probably 50ish but looked a lot older. About 5' 5", she had dirty blond hair (and I mean dirty) and wore an old cocktail dress that was just as filthy as her hair. When we pulled up next to them, the two men took off. Lola seemed pissed that she lost paying customers.

Drifting across the parking lot on the warm spring breeze was the nauseating scent of body odor. On the front steps, a man sat in his own vomit. The place was still a dump. As the three of us got out of the Town

Car, Lola recognized Heather immediately. Her pissed look turned to a smile.

"Lola, this is Rick," Heather began. "He wants to ask you a few questions about your old friend, Crystal."

"Hello, Lola. Yes, about Crystal Bentley."

"It'll cost ya," Lola blurted.

She seemed to like Heather more than me.

"So please tell me, Lola, what you remember about Crystal."

"Show me the money first."

I pulled out a c-note and her eyes lit up. Besides being belligerent, the track marks on her arm indicated where she would spend the money. A c-note would buy her a lot of escape from the miserable life she led.

Holding the bill I began, "Lola, information first."

"How do I know you'll pay?"

"You trust Heather?"

"Yeah."

Heather interjected, "It's alright, Lola. Answer the questions. Rick will give you the money."

She began slowly. I could tell by her glazed eyes and by the slight slur in her voice this woman had a hard life and was now at rock bottom. For the second time I was concerned for Heather, for where she could end up.

"Crystal was my friend. Even though I walked The Strip, she was always nice to me."

"You liked her a lot?"

"Yeah, when the other girls like her ..."

"You mean the high-priced escorts?" I asked.

"Yeah, them ... would make fun of me, Crystal always stuck up for me. Some nights when I wouldn't make nuthin' or got stiffed by a john, Crystal, she'd buy me breakfast then give me money so my old man wouldn't beat the shit out of me, thinkin' I was holdin' somethin' out on him."

Turning her attention to Heather, Lola said, "You remind me a lot of her, dear. You're nice."

The compliment took Heather by surprise. She smiled.

"Lola, can you tell me who Crystal worked for?" I asked.

"Worked for?"

"Yes, I'm sure she had a pimp. Do you remember who that was?"

"Met her once. She had a house somewhere here in town. Heard she treated her girls real good. If a john got out of hand she had some guys that'd teach him some manners."

"Lola, is she still in business?"

"Nah, I heard she retired 'bout ten years ago."

Vince and I looked at each other. Everything about this investigation goes back ten years.

"Do you remember where her house was?"

"Nah, I'd never been there. But I heard it had a great view of The Strip. Real nice."

"Do you remember what her name was?"

"Whose name?"

"Crystal's madam."

"Oh, gee, that was so long ago."

"Think for a minute, Lola. Her name. I know you know it. Try to remember."

Fingering her lips in a rhythmic way, Lola was really fighting to remember, but the years of drugs were fighting back hard. I motioned to Heather to help her try to remember.

Heather put her arm around Lola's shoulder and cooed softly, "Lola, it's alright. I know ten years is a long time. Just relax. It'll come to you."

Watching Heather's interaction with Lola, listening to her comforting words, witnessing her compassion … I was truly impressed.

"Candy was her name," Lola blurted happily. "Candy somebody … Why can't I remember?"

Hearing the name Candy, my ears perked and my heart raced.

"Lola, are you sure about the name Candy?"

Nodding her head, "Yeah, I remember, I met her once when I was with Crystal. She had just bought me breakfast when this car came by to pick her up. Candy was in the backseat."

"And?"

"She was real nice, like Crystal. Gave me her card and said if she could do anything for me to call her."

"Did you?"

"Did I what?"

"Did you ever call her?"

"I don't remember."

"Lola, what did Candy look like?"

"She was a blond that had a real raspy voice."

I looked at Vince excitedly and said, "I know her. Her real name is Catherine."

Vince continued taking notes.

"Lola, do you remember what happened to Crystal? What got her out of the business?"

"Heard she married some john and moved."

"Do you remember where she moved to?"

"Burbank," she said very clearly.

"Burbank, California?" I asked with some surprise.

Lola nodded her head in agreement. Seeing Lola's problem with memory, I was curious how she was so clear on where Crystal moved.

"Lola, how do you remember Burbank so clearly?"

The question caused Lola to pause. Her eyes misted up as she dropped her head and began to cry softly. Heather put her arm around Lola once more.

"Lola," I asked again, gently, "why do you remember Burbank?"

"That's ... (sniff) ... that's where my son and grandkids live."

Her answer knocked the wind out of me. And Vince was on the verge of tears himself.

Getting my breath back, I pried a little deeper.

"Lola, when's the last time you saw your family?"

Looking up with swollen eyes, she replied, "I don't remember. It's been a long time. I've ... (sniff) ... I've never met my grandkids."

Pulling out a dirty picture, she showed us two boys, about seven and nine years old. I could see the family resemblance.

I took a shot in the dark and asked, "Lola, do they know what you do for a living?"

"You mean that I'm a junky whore?"

"I wouldn't put it that way, but do they know?"

"Yes," she said shamefully.

"Do you think they would like to see you again?"

"My son wants me to get clean and come live with them. But look at me. I'll die here."

Heather's eyes were welled up with tears. I glanced at Vince. By the look on his face, he was thinking exactly what I was.

"Lola, how would you like us to help you get clean again?"

"Clean?"

"Yes, clean. Then you can go live with your son."

"You could do that?" she asked, as though we were possibly magicians.

Smiling at Vince and winking at Heather, I said, "We can do anything."

"I know a place we can take her tonight," Heather offered.

"Well, Lola, how about it? It's not going to be easy. The decision is yours."

With tears flowing down her cheeks, she said, "Yes." She wanted to try.

We loaded Lola into the Town Car, and Heather directed us to a nice home tucked deep in some suburban maze of Las Vegas. Heather called ahead and said we were coming. It was after midnight when we arrived. At the door, we were greeted by an older couple who ran the place. I explained who I was, who Lola was, and asked if they could help her. With open arms, the older woman took Lola in. Everyone was in tears. I handed the gentleman my card and told him to call me if he needed anything. Vince did the same, and he agreed to follow up with Lola and—when the time was right—help her reunite with her family.

Heading back to the hotel, we dropped Heather at her apartment. In route, she and I engaged in small talk. She was impressed with how Vince and I wanted to help Lola. The conversation was about to take a turn.

"Heather, may I ask you a personal question?"

Indicating an air of trust, "Sure, Rick, what?" she asked.

"Do you like what you do?"

"You mean do I like being a prostitute?"

"Well, yes."

"Sometimes yes, sometimes no," she replied honestly.

"How old are you?"

"Twenty three."

"Education?"

"BA in Business Administration from the University of Las Vegas," she said proudly. "And I paid for it myself."

"What do you really want in life?"

With a big smile, "Someday I want to get married and have children," she beamed.

"What's stopping you?"

"Rick," she said with a smirk, "nobody wants to marry a hooker."

"Have you ever thought about getting out of this business and applying your business degree elsewhere?"

"Just about every day," she sighed. "But I've gotten used to the money ... and ... I can't imagine myself somewhere else. I don't know where I could go or what I could do. I'm good at what I do now. But something else ... that scares me."

I looked straight into her eyes.

"Heather, maybe you should think about Seattle and the insurance business."

CHAPTER 27

Like a fighter jet, the Boeing 737 banked tightly against the mountain ridge before plummeting like a rock onto the north-south runway. Throwing the thrusters in full reverse, the pilot slammed on the brakes, and my body surged forward violently. I used my feet to brace against the force of deceleration. My seatbelt cut into my stomach. There was another sudden sharp jolt, followed by a quick left turn, that flopped me to the right and then, finally, to my original upright position. I relaxed back into my seat and began breathing again. The engines wound down. The plane arrived at the gate, but my stomach was still at 20,000 feet.

A pleasant voice came over the PA announcing, "Welcome to Burbank."

Turning to me, Vince exclaimed sarcastically, "And you do this *how* many times a month, Rick?"

"Come on, Vince. It wasn't that bad," I chuckled.

"Honestly, I'd rather pursue an armed robber into a dark alley."

"You would?" I said, still laughing.

"Yeah, there I can shoot back."

It had been twelve hours since Lola was dropped off at rehab. After delivering Heather back to her apartment (and after she agreed to consider my suggestion), Vince and I decided that a spur-of-the-moment trip to the San Fernando Valley (Burbank) was in order to pay a surprise visit to everyone's favorite madam, Candy.

But we arrived at the house a day late and a dollar short. The house stood empty. The For Sale sign in the yard announced our tardiness. Vince scanned the dilapidated house and grounds, looked down at his feet on the faded, cracked walkway and observed, "What a dump."

Although I was aware of his comment, I didn't respond because I was in the throes of a very intense déjà vu ... again!

"I've been here before," I said, trance-like.

"Well, isn't this where you picked Crystal up?" Vince replied vaguely.

"No ... well, yeah. This is where I picked her up, but I meant I've been here before that."

Turning to face me directly, Vince was confused.

"Rick, what the hell are you talking about?"

My attention was still focused on the house. I wasn't sure how to answer. A vague picture haunted me like a ghost from years past.

"I've been here before, Vince," I repeated, this time with more confidence. "But the house was different. The grass was green, the paint on the walkway looked fresh, and the roof wasn't faded. There was this little girl and ..."

"You're always with a girl," Vince interrupted with a grin.

Turning to him smiling, "You sound like Emily," I pointed out.

"Well, it's true. I saw the way you awed Heather last night, and what about the one in San Francisco? What's her name?"

I laughed, "Vince, now you *really* sound like Emily!"

"Rick, let's be serious for a minute. You were raised here in the Valley, right?"

"Yeah, out in the west end."

"This house seems to be pretty common," he continued as he looked down the street. "Hell, the one next door and across the street have the same floor plan. Isn't it possible this house reminds you of some other house you were at as a child? Maybe the little girl was your first love?"

He chuckled. It was hard to argue with Vince's observation, yet still ...

Across the street I spotted an older lady watering her flower bed in front of one of the houses with the identical floor plan. Wearing slippers and a housecoat, her hair in curlers and a cigarette dangling from her lips, she looked like your worst nightmare. You know, the kind where you would rather chew your own arm off than wake up next to it in the morning. I was betting she was the neighborhood gossip. There was only one way to find out. I walked toward her, and Vince followed.

I put on a bright and friendly smile to greet her.

"Good morning, ma'am!"

Her response was not as warm.

"I'm not buying anything," she growled.

"No, ma'am, we're not selling anything." I handed her my card. "My name is Morgan. I was wondering if you could tell me anything about the house across the street, the one that's for sale."

"Thinking of buying it?"

Still wearing my smile, I answered, "Actually, no. I'm curious about the woman who lived there. Catherine."

"You a friend of hers?"

"No, ma'am. As you can see, I work for an insurance company and …"

"Damn insurance companies," she blurted. "I was in an accident, and they …"

Interrupting, I offered, "Ma'am, we're not that kind of insurance company."

"Oh? What other kind is there?"

This is where I decided a little con might play nicely.

"I work for a life insurance company. The woman who lived there might be the beneficiary of a life insurance policy. You see, our insured died naming his nephew as the beneficiary. But the nephew died as well, poor boy, which means his mother—his only living relative—would be entitled to the money. But we can't find her. We think the woman that lived here might be her. But the only name we have is a maiden name: Nichols. Catherine Nichols. Did she live there?"

I pulled the name Nichols out of thin air. Out of the corner of my eye, I could see Vince doing his best not to laugh hysterically.

"No, it wasn't Nichols. It was Johnson. Catherine Johnson."

Hearing the name Johnson, my eyebrows raised. Vince's expression turned from whimsical to somber.

"Johnson? Are you sure?" I blathered.

"Of course I'm sure," she said, like I was stupid. "Catherine Johnson. Moved in about ten years ago. The day she moved in the yard went to hell. Next to mine, it used to be the nicest on the block."

For the moment I was drowning in a deluge of questions inside my head. Was Candy related to my deceased? I could see Vince was asking himself the same thing.

I regained my composure and continued with my questioning. "Did Ms. Johnson live there by herself?"

"Well, yes and no. A few men came in and out," she said, tossing her hair. "What they saw in her, I'll never know."

I didn't ask if she'd looked in the mirror lately. That would have been rude.

The woman continued, "She had a niece that stayed with her much of the time. I think she had problems with her husband, but I really don't know."

"Could you describe her?"

"Oh, about 40, somewhat tall, dark hair, really very beautiful. Quiet. Always kept to herself."

The description fit. I took a deep breath.

"Was her name Crystal by chance?"

"No, it was Christine. Christine Matthews. Catherine called her Chris."

Looking back across the street, I remembered the night I picked up Crystal. At the door, Candy called Crystal "Crys." I guess it was really "Chris." A shiver ran down my spine, and a rock landed in my stomach.

I turned back to the neighborhood gossip and asked, "When did Ms. Johnson move out?"

"Two weeks ago today." (That was the same day Crystal left me in San Diego.) "I came home from shopping in the morning, and a moving truck was in the driveway."

"Do you remember the name of the moving company?"

"There wasn't any. Just a big white truck. When I came out to water my flowers, it was gone."

"About what time was that?"

"Oh, I don't know. Maybe right after lunch."

A car came down the street and turned into Candy's driveway. A middle-aged brunette woman got out and headed for the front door. Since she was fiddling with the key box, I figured she was the realtor. I looked back at the picture on the For Sale sign and discovered I was right. Vince and I thanked our unknowing informer for her time, and we headed back across the street. By now the front door was open and the realtor was inside.

Walking slowly, "You caught that name?" Vince asked.

"Yeah. Do you think it's a coincidence?"

"Only if there's a tooth fairy," Vince deadpanned.

I stopped on the faded walkway and turned to Vince, "Your man doing the background on Johnson, tell him to look for a sister."

"And if Catherine is a sister, then what?"

Continuing up the walkway, I just shook my head.

"Beats the hell out of me, Vince."

When we arrived at the front door, I stood in the threshold and sounded a firm, "Hello?" My voice echoed slightly in the empty room.

Before the echo ceased, another, "Hello!" answered back. The voice was sweet but professional and was almost immediately followed by the mouth—and face and body—that it was attached to. Holding out her hand and with a big smile, the realtor said, "Hi, I'm Linda."

Watching Linda walk toward me was pure ecstasy. About 35ish, she wore a white cotton blouse, tight across the breasts (a 34C, I would guess) with the top button undone. Her black skirt clung snugly to her lower abdomen and thighs, cut just above the knee—and great knees they were. Dark nylons and 2-inch black pumps enhanced her already-gorgeous pair of legs. Numerous lustful thoughts were pulsing through my brain.

I'll bet this woman sells a lot of homes.

Taking her hand for a firm shake, I said, "Hello, Linda, my name is Rick Morgan, and this is Mr. Guarino."

As she shook Vince's hand, Linda said, "You're a little early for the open house, but I'll be glad to show it to you now."

I decided to use the same con as on the lady across the street to pump Linda for some information. Hmm, the thought of pumping Linda had a nice ring to it.

I handed her my card. "Thank you, but I came to see a Ms. Catherine Johnson. It appears I'm a little late!" I chuckled as I glanced around the bare room.

Linda was suspicious, and probably disappointed, from the realization I wasn't a prospective buyer.

"Are you friends of hers?" she asked cautiously.

"Actually, no. We've never met the woman," I said as I launched into my schtick. "There's a strong possibility Ms. Johnson may be a beneficiary to an insurance policy. It's a situation where if we—my company—can't find any heirs, the monies will become escheat and claimed by the state."

I shook my head and frowned slightly, adding, "We never want to give money to the state."

Linda grinned, touched my arm lightly and said, "I know. They just take so much!"

Touching her back, I continued, "Hey, it's California! What can we say?"

We both laughed, still touching each other. Judging by her smile, I think she was enjoying the touch as much as I was. As for Vince, he was enjoying my performance.

"Linda," I began again, "I know you want to protect your client's privacy, but would there be a way you could get a message to her to call me?"

"Gee, Rick, I would love to help, but your woman was a renter."

Another surprise! A renter? A Johnson? A renting Johnson ... for ten years?

"Renter? Darn, I was hoping we could wrap this whole thing up today. I really want to get home."

She glanced down at my card in her hand and asked, "You're from Seattle?"

Nodding my head, "Yes, the place where it rains nine months out of the year," I commented.

"Lonely for the wife?" she asked coyly.

Talk about a forward question! But a good one—it gave me a straight indication of what Linda had in mind.

With a slight laugh, "Not for a number of years," I replied.

"Oh," she countered, trying to conceal a smile. "I know what that's like."

Indeed, now I knew exactly where all this was heading.

With a slight smile back, I began again, "Linda, I need to talk to the owner to see if he can give me any forwarding information on Ms. Johnson. However, being Saturday, the assessor's office is closed. By chance, could you tell me who owns this property?"

"Sure, Rick. It's owned by a family trust."

"A trust?" I responded, surprised again. I could see Vince was surprised, too.

Linda's eyes met mine, and this time her smile was shy. I think she already knew the question I was about to ask.

"Linda, would taking you to dinner tonight get me the name of that trust?"

Pretending to ponder my invitation, Linda paused before answering. Then, with impeccable timing and a coy smile, she responded with a sly, "Maybe?"

"Hmm," I muttered, playing the game back.

I looked into her eyes again. They were full and bright, giving every indication that dinner was a go. There was no "maybe" about it.

"Shall we say about six then?"

With that same coy smile she replied, "Shall we say?"

CHAPTER 28

The ham and Swiss on rye from the food cart was a far cry from the luscious dinner I had with Linda a week earlier. After taking one bite, I threw the remainder into my trash can. If it could have, the trash would have spit it back. Yes, it was that bad.

Across the street from my office, on the corner next to the coffee place, is a burger stand. From past experience, I knew their fare wasn't much better than the food cart's, but it was fast and hot so I decided to take a chance. As I walked through the outer office, I advised Emily and Alicia that I'd be back soon. In unison, they chirped, "Have a nice lunch!"

After pushing the down button on the elevator, I pushed another button on my cell. On the first ring, there was an answer.

"Vince, Rick. Got some news for me?"

"Great. I'm on my way to lunch. Care to join me?"

"Two doors down on the corner from there."

"Yeah, the burger place."

"No, I don't need a drink now."

"I will? Well, we can go there after."

"Yeah, see you in ten."

At the front door just outside the building, I nearly bumped head-on into someone. I looked up to apologize and went into shock instead. It was the old friend I hadn't seen in awhile … my shadow.

Regaining my composure, I said sarcastically, "Hey, I've missed you! Been on vacation?"

He pretended I had him mixed up with someone else.

As he walked away, I called out, "I'm going to lunch at the burger stand on the corner. Wait here. I'll be back in 30 minutes."

He continued to walk away, never saying a word.

As I sat at the lunch counter waiting for my burger, Vince came in and sat down next to me. He was grinning ear to ear and on the verge of laughing.

"Hey, you'll never guess who I just saw?" he chuckled.

"My shadow?" I countered. We both laughed as I told him about my encounter.

Taking out his notebook, Vince began our business chat with, "So Rick, what do you want me to report on first?"

Since I was hoping for a good lunch, I whispered, "Something easy, Vince."

"Ah," he said while turning a few pages.

"The home in Burbank, as Linda the realtor told us ... ," Vince said and then interrupted himself. "Hey, you never told me about your dinner date with her."

"Nothing to tell," I replied calmly.

"Did you guys ...?"

"Actually, I have an old friend, Steve, who lives in the Valley. I stayed at his place."

"You're kidding. I thought you two would end up playing house."

Shaking my head, I replied, "Vince, Linda's a very nice lady."

"With a great body," he added enthusiastically. "Are you going to see her again?"

I didn't answer. It was my turn to change the subject.

"Who owns the house, Vince?"

"It's owned by the C & J Family Trust."

"What the hell does C & J stand for?"

"Don't know," Vince replied while rubbing his chin. His eyes said there was more. "But guess who the administrator of the trust is?"

The waitress set my burger down in front of me.

"Is the answer going to ruin my appetite?"

With a small chuckle, "Probably," he answered.

Pushing my plate slightly forward, I braced the counter with both hands.

"Alright, Vince, hit me with it."

"The law firm of Greenbrier, Morris & Perry," he said quietly.

"You're kidding!" I exclaimed.

"I wish I was, Rick. I really wish I was," he mumbled.

Shaking my head, "Damn, Vince, I should have seen that coming," I said.

Vince was right about one thing. Hearing his report killed my appetite for lunch. I sat rubbing my face with my hands.

"So, Vince, let me see if I understand this correctly. The law firm that handled the estate of Mr. Johnson who died in Vegas—and was paid twenty million dollars—is the same law firm that handled the estate of the unknown relative of the housekeeper who just happened to discover Mr. Johnson's body. *And*, in addition, this same law firm is the administrator of a family trust that owns the home in which the madam of the woman who we believe was the last person to see our insured Mr. Johnson alive—or possibly killed him—lived until a few weeks ago."

"Well, Rick, ready for that drink now?"

I didn't answer.

Sighing, Vince began again with the same solemn tone, "Rick, you haven't heard anything yet."

Two doors down, Vince and I sat in the back as the cocktail waitress took our order. Anticipating the worst from Vince's report, I ordered a double.

"Background on Johnson," Vince began, while opening his black notebook.

"Interesting guy. Seems he died ten years ago in a hotel room on the Vegas Strip."

"Gee, Vince. Tell me something I don't know."

"Actually, there's a lot about this guy you don't know, Rick."

By the look on Vince's face, I was glad I ordered a double.

"Born Los Angeles, March 22, 1936, and raised in the San Fernando Valley. Graduated Van Nuys High School, class of '54. Drafted into the U.S. Army the same year, as an interpreter."

"Really?" I interrupted. "What language?"

"Russian."

"Russian? You're kidding!"

"Not at all. His parents were Russian Jews who came to the U.S., date unknown." Vince paused for effect, then added, "Rick, it gets better. Honorably discharged two years later, he went to work for the State Department."

"Doing?"

"That's the interesting part. I don't know. His job was classified."

"Classified? You mean as in secret?"

"Yeah, one and the same. But I have a hunch."

"What?"

"That he was really with the CIA."

"CIA?" I cried with disbelief.

"Yeah, CIA."

His hunch made me nervous. For a moment I was speechless.

"Vince," I began quietly, not wanting to be overheard, "if he was fluent in Russian and was with the CIA ..."

"Right, Rick," he interjected, "you're on the right track. Now, follow me for a minute. What year was the fall of communism?"

"End of 1992," I said.

"Right. The same year he left the government and went into business with Brewster. They formed a partnership named Johnson and Brewster Imports. Johnson would travel the world buying diamonds from what looks like suspicious sources, and Brewster handled the resale of the stones here in America."

"He traveled worldwide?"

"Yes. A jeweler would be a perfect cover. He could go places and ..."

"And not be suspected as CIA," I finished.

"Right."

"Fluent in Russian, he could even travel to the Soviet Union on business."

"Yeah, Rick. Think of the implications."

I did. And that familiar shiver ran down my spine. From the look on Vince's face, he was experiencing the same cold front as I was.

"Stayed with the business until he died in 1996," Vince continued.

"Family?" I asked.

"Never married, no children. But three sisters. Names and whereabouts unknown."

"So we don't know if Catherine Johnson is or is not his sister?"

"Correct."

"Vince, if he had no children, who was the woman that claimed the body?"

"Good question. I don't know."

"If Johnson was traveling worldwide, one, how could he take on such stress with a bad heart, and two, how could he see Crystal every Saturday for the last six months of his life?"

"More good questions with no answers."

"But, Vince, all this is speculation. We're assuming our Mr. Johnson was in the spy game."

"Maybe not, Rick."

By the look on Vince's face, I could tell there was more. I took a slug of my double for fortification.

"You remember we could never find the connection between Cole and Johnson?"

"Yeah."

"I think we just did."

"I'm not following you."

"Fact: we know Johnson was with the State Department. Let's assume for a minute he was actually with the CIA."

"Right."

"Fact: he spoke Russian fluently."

"Right."

"What was going on during this time with the Russians?"

"The Cold War."

"And who's in Congress during that time?"

"Cole?"

"Right. And Cole sits on an intelligence committee."

"Ok."

"Then tell me, Rick. Tell me their paths never crossed," Vince finished dramatically with a raised eyebrow.

Vince made a good point. A damn good point.

"OK, let's say their paths crossed. What does Johnson's death in 1996 have to do with a traffic accident in 1976?"

"I asked myself that same question until two this morning. I still don't know."

"But here's another question. If Cole and Johnson did cross paths, what are the odds they happen to die the same weekend ... and both mysteriously in their own ways?"

Staring blankly at his now-empty glass, Vince quietly shook his head.

"I don't know, Rick. I just don't know."

We both sat quietly. The audacity of our speculation was overwhelming.

Fresh drinks arrived, and with them fresh conversation. Vince broke the silence.

"When Johnson died, Rothschild must have somehow taken over the business. He's basically doing exactly what Johnson did. Traveling the world buying stones."

"Do we know who he's selling them to?"

"No. But he's *not* selling them in the U.S. And there are a few more questions, Rick. If Crystal and Rothschild knew Johnson had a bad heart, did they conspire to kill him so Rothschild could take the business or take his place? But then, if Candy was Johnson's sister, what was her involvement? Did she want to kill her own brother?"

I didn't have answers … just another question.

"OK, we know Johnson had a bad heart. So why did my insurance company insure him for twenty million? Someone in my company had to be involved."

"Maybe like Cole?" Vince suggested. "He sat on the board."

"Yeah, so let's say Cole pulled a couple strings and got Johnson insured for twenty million. Got Jack to sell the policy, the doctor to turn the other way during the physical, got Kathy to expedite the claim. Why would he want Johnson insured for twenty million? No, Vince, we're missing something here. I keep going back to two questions: what's the connection to the auto accident in 1976, and why did both men die the same weekend?"

"Rick, we're forgetting another important question. If even half of what we suspect is true, what about Brewster? What was his involvement? As the partner in the business, why was the money made to the law firm rather than him?"

Another question with no answer.

Before our liquid lunch meeting came to an end, Vince shared one more thought.

"Considering everything we've experienced, everything we just discussed, whoever out there is watching us is *not* going to be happy with us still digging. Seriously, this may be a good time to walk away."

Hanging my head, I sat quietly for a moment regrouping my thoughts. My eyes fixated on the last swallow of my drink at the bottom of my glass. Vince's words rang true. Maybe we were digging a hole we couldn't get out of. Digging a grave.

"Vince," I began quietly, "dig back into Brewster's life. I'm a little curious what he did after Johnson died."

"You know, I could track down Brewster, and we could just talk with him."

I turned to Vince and said, "Maybe later. Right now I trust no one.

While you're at it, go back into the accident. Dig a little deeper into the Rose family. Maybe the Roses have a secret garden."

"What are you expecting to find?"

The last swallow of my drink burned slightly as it went down my throat. I set my glass back on the bar and turned to Vince. His eyes were expecting an answer. I didn't have one.

"Expecting? I don't know what I'm expecting. But we're in deep enough that maybe we'll strike oil instead of bedrock. It scares the hell out of me, but I've got to keep digging. Like you, I just have a hunch."

CHAPTER 29

"You've got mail," announced the disembodied voice from my computer.

The mail announcement is a male voice. It's OK, but why not flash voice and video of a gorgeous woman instead? Scantily clad, running her hands seductively up and down her hot body, commanding in her sexiest voice, "Rick, I want you ... NOW!"

This is a novel and creative idea to enrich my humdrum daily office life, so of course I presented it to the IT department and requested implementation on my computer. I even had the woman picked out. I'm not sure if it was simply their lack of imagination and skill, or if their blatant loathing for me had anything to do with it, but their answer was an emphatic, "No!"

Before I could retrieve the message, Emily was at my door. Emily was still annoyed that things were going on with Vince that were mysterious and unexplained.

In an agitated tone, she blasted, "Rick, my Uncle Vince just called. He's in the building and on his way up."

Emily quickly picked up on the fact that I was surprised Vince wanted to meet in my office. I quickly picked up on the fact that she was about to start with multiple questions. (We could read each other well.) But I was in no mood to be interrogated.

"Fine, Emily. Show him in when he arrives," I said as I swiveled my chair toward the window, cutting her off before she could start grilling me.

She stomped out of my office.

It had been a week since my last meeting with Vince. He was most likely stopping by to report on Cole or Brewster, or maybe both. I gazed out the window at my dear friend, the Space Needle, and asked aloud, "Do I *want* to hear Vince's report?" Considering the uneasiness he left me with last time, I wasn't too sure.

As always, my Space Needle listened well, but didn't answer.

I heard heavier footsteps approaching through the outer office and knew Vince had arrived. A baritone "Hi, Em" confirmed it. I didn't hear her answer. He came through my office door, closed it, then settled into a wingback chair. As I swiveled around to greet him, I could see he wasn't smiling. Was his distressed look from Emily's cold reception or from the news he had for me? Probably a little of both.

"I'm surprised you wanted to meet here," I began.

"Oh, what the hell," he said. "It's no secret anymore what we're doing."

Except maybe to poor Emily.

"True, Vince. OK. So I gather you have some information for me. Cole or Brewster?"

"Ah, dear, sweet Congressman Cole," he mocked, while taking out his book. "The champion of truth, guardian of our Constitution, and the keeper of all of Washington's dirty little secrets. Where would you like me to begin?"

I made a "whatever" motion with my hand, and Vince understood he could start wherever he wanted.

"Your insured, Mr. Johnson, died somewhere around midnight on a Saturday night. That same Saturday morning, about 6:00, Peter Cole kissed his wife goodbye in Rancho Palos Verdes and supposedly headed to Marina Del Rey where he had a boat moored. An hour's drive. According to witnesses, he arrived about noon."

"Noon?" I exclaimed. "It couldn't have taken him six hours to drive thirty miles, even in L.A. traffic!"

"That's right, Rick, it couldn't."

"So where was he?"

"Remember Harriet Miller said he was a drunk who couldn't keep it in his pants? You tell me," Vince shrugged. "As I said, arrived at Marina Del Ray about noon. Waved to a number of people, loaded his boat with fishing gear and an ice chest and cast off. When he didn't arrive home about 10:00 that night, his wife called the cops. Since he was a V.I.P. they didn't wait the customary time for a missing person. They called the Harbor Master who, at 10:23, reported that Cole's boat hadn't returned.

His car was found in the parking lot. By 11:00, the Coast Guard started a search but didn't find his boat until the following morning—about a mile off Catalina. It was adrift and abandoned. An extensive search for his body came up negative. Official conclusion: drank too much and fell overboard. That theory was supported by two facts: he was a drinker, and the boat had empty liquor bottles on it. The newspaper story of his disappearance was pretty accurate."

As captivating as Vince's report was, it really wasn't anything more than we already knew. Yet hearing it this time ... something felt wrong about it. Like Jack Webber selling two twenty million dollar policies. Something didn't fit. It took a moment to realize what.

"Vince, you said the boat had empty liquor bottles on it?"

"Yeah, a couple. Why?"

"That doesn't make sense."

Vince looked at me strangely as I continued.

"Cole was how old ... about sixty?"

"Yeah, somewhere around there."

"Then follow me, Vince. Besides his age, look at Cole's lifestyle. He drank excessively, had mistresses, didn't care whose political lives he destroyed, no remorse for killing that family in 1976 ... yet this guy's going to keep empty booze bottles on his boat? For what? To recycle? At his feet was the largest garbage dump in this world, the Pacific Ocean. No, he would have tossed those bottles overboard as soon as they were empty."

My notion struck a chord with Vince. He listened quietly as I moved on with my analysis.

"Are we sure it was Cole who got on that boat?"

"Definitely," Vince replied. "A number of witnesses saw him arrive, load the boat, and cast off."

"Then a question ..."

I stopped when I realized the implication of what I was about to suggest.

"Vince ... could there also have been someone else on that boat?"

"It's always possible. But remember the boat was found empty. Unless the other party walked on water, how did they get off that boat?"

Vince paused, but I could tell he had more to say.

"Rick, you know if there was another person or persons involved, you're suggesting something other than an accident."

I only nodded my head. The gravity of it curbed my tongue.

"Vince," I began again after a couple of minutes, "the FBI got involved in the investigation, right?"

"Correct."

"If Cole was somehow linked to the CIA, possibly through Johnson like we speculated, why did the FBI investigate? Wouldn't the CIA have done their own investigation? And conduct it very quietly?"

Vince became silent again. My question had merit.

After some contemplation, Vince said, "Following your line of thought, then why did the FBI want you to close your investigation, and for that matter, have you tailed?"

"Good question. But I have one more. We've speculated the connection between Cole and Johnson. Let's take that thought a step further. What do Cole's and Johnson's deaths have in common?"

Shaking his head, Vince replied, "I don't know. But one thing's for sure. It wasn't coincidence they both died the same day."

It was mid-afternoon before I was available to get back to my emails.

The message earlier was an advertisement from my favorite steakhouse in San Francisco, the one my friend and I have often frequented in the last five years. The idea of a quick trip south had enormous appeal. I forwarded the ad to my San Franciscan, accompanied by just three words: "Shall we indulge?"

Within two minutes I heard, "You've got mail." I was treated to a single word response: "Yes."

"Would this Sunday work for you?" I keyed back.

Again, one word: "Perfect."

"Pick you up at 5:00."

With a quick call, the dinner reservation at the restaurant was complete, and San Francisco was a go. I absolutely love this about her. No questions, no details or particulars were necessary to respond with a simple "Yes" and "Perfect."

I decided to take an extra few days and swing by Los Angeles before heading north to San Francisco. The last time I saw Steve, I had popped in about midnight. Since he was entertaining that evening—and I had to be at the airport early the next morning—there hadn't been much opportunity to talk. Actually, our only conversation was a little belligerent on his part and went something like, "What the hell are you doing here?"

Linda, my new realtor friend, had given me a standing invitation. "Whenever you're in the Valley, look me up!" As much as that thought excited me—her whole package did—after Caroline, Kathy, and Crystal, I wasn't ready for anyone new. A year back I might have jumped at the idea. But somehow, something was changing in me. Something I can't quite explain.

A quick call to Steve only got his voicemail. "This is Steve. Leave your name and number, and I'll call you back." How creative.

"Hey, it's Rick. I'm heading south and thought I would drop by this Friday night. Call me." Neither of us are big on messages.

As soon as I got back to the work on my desk, he called. I explained my agenda and asked if I could stop by ... with some warning this time.

"Sure, love to see you, but this Friday night is my company awards dinner," he noted casually. His answer took me by surprise, because Steve is a musician. I didn't know he had a job with a "company."

"You have a job?" I inquired.

"Yeah, didn't I tell you?"

"No. The last time I saw you, you were deep into another project."

He laughed. "You know, I can't remember her name."

About his new job: It seems he was jamming with some guys on the Sunset Strip when someone from a production company heard him and thought he would be a good fit in their music department, working with new bands. Taking into consideration his alcohol-saturated mind and his years of being 420 friendly, I could understand why Steve's memory wasn't where it should have been. But it might be an asset working with those new bands.

In further conversation, we agreed I should come down a day early—Thursday—and attend the dinner with him Friday night. He mentioned (again, casually) that he had moved to a condo just off Laurel Canyon south of the Boulevard. Good thing I didn't just show up at his old place! He gave me his address and the security code.

About 10:00 Thursday night, the Mustang pulled up in front of Steve's condo, with one very weary driver. I was surprised at how nice the building was. I pressed the code number and proceeded into the underground garage, parking in Steve's extra stall as directed. Even though my body felt like death warmed over, I wasn't too tired to notice a beautiful white Porsche Carrera parked next to me. Sweet.

Steve had called while I was on the road to advise he had a date. The rest I could figure out myself. Getting in was easy. The key was under the mat. I checked out his refrigerator and was glad I had eaten earlier. Bare.

Finding a clean towel was a challenge, but the shower was great, and a bed never looked so inviting—except of course, when there was a woman waiting in it.

Lying in that inviting bed, my mind whirled from the eighteen-hour drive. Though moving quickly toward incoherency, it kept replaying a haunting question from my meeting with Vince. Those empty bottles on the boat … why were they there?

But in reality it didn't take a genius to figure it out. The answer was simple yet disturbing. For those bottles to be there, someone else had to be on that boat, too. And if someone else was there, then Cole's death was no accident. It was murder.

Chapter 30

The restaurant stood atop a small, nameless mountain that was just high enough to exploit a fantastic view of the San Fernando Valley.

It had been hot and smoggy that day in Los Angeles, and the night wasn't much different. Walking from the parking lot to the front door, the breeze brushed our faces. It ran across the ridge, collecting warm air as it drifted up the side of the mountain from the valley floor. The evening lights had lost their twinkle, softly blurred instead by the lingering smog.

There were about seventy-five people at the dinner—in a private room, of course. This was a Hollywood production company event, after all. The men generally looked older, and the women looked curiously younger, some naturally and others surgically.

Making the rounds with Steve, I did the usual shaking of hands, pats on the back, "Hey, how's it going" thing until Steve left me. Dumped me with a woman I only remember as "what's-her-name." She was an accountant for the company who swore I reminded her of her ex-boyfriend. She was my age, 5' 4" in heels, 175 pounds, red hair that wasn't the same color at the roots, and a voice that cleared your ear canals with each shrill syllable spoken. From the moment we met, it was her mission to make sure I was never alone. She was like glue—sticky and annoying. After thirty seconds I understood why her boyfriend was an ex.

While "what's-her-name" was doing her best to keep me occupied, I was eyeing a beautiful brunette at the bar who seemed as bored with her suitors as I was with mine. Fawning, over-aged adolescents were hovering around her. It was entertaining to watch these idiots, each vying for her attention, each wanting to fetch her a drink and each making a big fool

243

of himself. Her body language was hilarious. They were just too stupid to figure it out.

She turned my way, and our eyes connected for a lingering moment. I smiled. She didn't.

Now, these yo-yos might have been brainless, but at least they had good taste. About 5' 5", 120 pounds, early to mid-thirties, beautiful long legs, very slim hips, nice waist, long, dark hair falling softly down her back, fantastic bust-line, and a face that could launch a thousand ships. She was dressed conservatively in a purple blouse with a black skirt—hem just above the knee—a matching blazer, black nylons, and black pumps with a 2-inch heel. This woman was gorgeous. Did I mention the legs?

But what caught my attention most was her resemblance to Caroline. Their hair was different, but their features were almost identical. She even moved the same way, handling the men with a similar hair toss and sultry look, but with a sharper edge.

My reminiscing was interrupted by the squeal of my tour guide, "what's-her-name."

"Rick, are you listening to me?"

"Uh, what? Oh, yes, of course I am. Tell me, who's the brunette at the bar?"

"Oh, that's Amanda. She's one of the company attorneys. A very cold fish."

Cold or not, Perry Mason never looked that good. Neither did Della. While my eyes were glued to those fabulous legs—again shutting out every word of sticky "what's-her-name"—an elderly gentleman took to the podium with an announcement to take our places. Dinner would soon be served.

He looked vaguely familiar.

The room was set up with individual tables, each seating between four and eight people. Since seating was assigned, everyone began scurrying around looking for their place cards.

For some reason, Steve and I ended up at different tables. He was with one of the VPs and his wife—a much younger blond—and also my newest old friend, "what's-her-name." I, on the other hand, ended up sharing a small table with a lovely couple. A man from the art department and his new wife, maybe fifteen years his junior. The fourth person at our table was … Amanda, the attorney. This couldn't have been better if I had planned it myself!

With a friendly smile, I greeted everyone at the table. The gentleman across from me introduced himself, then his wife, and we shook hands.

I turned my attention to the attorney.

"Good evening, I'm Amanda," she said.

Her handshake was soft and warm, the total opposite of the rest of her demeanor, which resembled the iceberg that sank the Titanic.

Politely she asked, "Do you work for the company?"

"No, I'm a friend of Steve's, just down for the weekend."

"Oh, how nice," she said, with an air of boredom.

"What's-her-name" hit the nail on the head. This woman *was* a cold fish, but with mermaid good looks and the allure of the deep blue sea. What's a man like me to do?

Go fishing!

As the salad was being served, I tried a little charm on Amanda, only to be met with a frosty stare. My best attempts at wit and humor were received with a polite smile. Now, don't get me wrong. She wasn't rude, just cold.

As dinner progressed, she began to melt slightly, probably from sheer boredom. But I finally found a topic that interested her.

"So, Amanda, what school did you attend?"

"UCLA," she responded coolly.

"I went to CSUN. It was easy since I lived in Canoga Park."

"You lived in Canoga Park?" she asked, with a tiny spark of interest.

"Most of my life," I responded. "Shirley Avenue Elementary, Columbus Junior High, Canoga High."

With a complete change in attitude, Amanda continued excitedly, "I went to Columbus and Canoga. Where did you live?"

"By the park."

"No way! I lived by the park," she exclaimed with more enthusiasm than I thought possible.

Come to find out, her parents bought the house just three doors down from where I lived. That was a year after my parents had moved, so our paths never crossed. But from that moment forward, the night took on a whole new meaning, and I had a new friend. I'm sorry to say we must have seemed rude to our dinner companions. Amanda and I talked and reminisced through the rest of dinner.

As dessert was being served and awards handed out, I leaned over to Amanda and whispered, "What would you think about continuing our conversation in the bar?"

Whispering back like a schoolgirl about to ditch class, she said, "I'd love to."

Excusing ourselves, we made our way out of the private room and into the main bar. We commandeered a small, intimate table in the corner. With the backdrop of a lovely view of the valley below, we talked and laughed about everything and nothing. Besides being one of the corporate attorneys, Amanda was thirty-five years old, never married, no kids, and her last boyfriend was a jerk. (Ex-boyfriends are apparently always jerks.)

But here's the coincidence that melted every last chunk of ice clinging to Amanda. It turns out she lives in the same building as Steve—in fact, just three doors down! She kidded that our meeting had to be destiny, since she lives three doors from Steve now and in a house that was three doors down from where I grew up.

Throughout the night, I told her a little about me, my history with Steve, that I am a CAE (Chief Audit Examiner), for a major insurance company, live 1136 miles away in the small town of Seattle, Washington, and that—the big news—I'm single.

After the awards, a party commenced in the other room that became more rambunctious as the night pressed forward. But Amanda and I sat quietly in the bar, lost in our own world, teasing and laughing until we cried. She tucked her arm in mine—a familiarity that surprised me— giggled like a little girl and whispered secrets about herself in my ear. As the night went deeper, so did her secrets. I wasn't sure if it was the day catching up with her, the mood, or the alcohol. But whatever it was, she was comfortable telling me things ... and I liked it.

It was a little after midnight when Steve appeared out of nowhere and pulled me aside.

"Rick, I'm beat. Let's blow this popsicle stand"

"That's fine," I said while looking back at Amanda, "but we need to offer Amanda a ride home. She's had a little too much to drink."

And, truthfully, she had. Steve agreed Amanda shouldn't drive. Back in the bar, I told Amanda my plan.

"Steve and I need to head home. It's been a long day. Now, don't get upset with me, but I'm concerned about you driving home tonight. Why don't you come with Steve and me, and we'll come back for your car tomorrow?"

"Oh, you're so sweet," she said, giggling and flashing a sultry look. "Why don't you just drive my car home? You know where I live."

I liked that look on Amanda's face, and I liked her idea! When I told

Steve the new plan, he agreed with a grin. I took Amanda on my arm, and we headed out the door.

Next to the entrance of the restaurant is a walkway that leads around the side of the building to a cozy lookout point. With her arm still tucked in mine, we slowly strolled over to see the view. The lights appeared brighter since the smog had lifted.

"Before all this was built, Amanda, Steve and I used to come here to look at the city lights. That was a lot of years ago."

Pulling me tighter to her, "What did you think about?" she asked.

Resting my hand lightly on her arm, I smiled and said, "That someday I'd be right here with you."

"Rick, you are so-o-o sweet," she cooed as she touched my cheek.

For a moment, I thought we would kiss. But for reasons I can't explain, I backed away before it could happen. From the look in Amanda's eyes, she was surprised by my action. The excitement for a kiss was not over.

We strolled back to the parking lot and Amanda gave me her claim ticket. I handed it to the valet. I was shocked and delighted when he drove up in a white Porsche Carrera—the same one I had admired the night before in Steve's parking garage. As one of the attendants helped her in, I went around and slipped the other a five spot. It felt great sliding behind the wheel. It had a six-speed stick. I was in heaven! Doors closed and seatbelts fastened, I put it in first, and away we went. It took me only a few shifts to get back into the swing of a clutch. Amanda could see the exhilaration I felt driving her car, and it gave her an idea.

"Rick, why don't you take the Golden State rather than the San Diego Freeway?"

It was a question she didn't have to ask twice. She was looking at the same gleam on my face that was there with my first car.

She giggled, "I thought you would like that."

The most direct route was the San Diego Freeway south to the Ventura Freeway, then east to Laurel Canyon, and again south below Ventura Boulevard ... but not tonight. Instead, we headed east to the Golden State Freeway and headed south through Burbank, then west on the Ventura Freeway to Laurel. This added about fifteen miles to our journey. Fifteen truly exciting miles. I loved it! But during the drive, I don't know which was more stimulating—the Porsche or those long, beautiful legs stretched out next to me. Somehow that conservative skirt kept creeping up, showing more flesh every mile of the way. And she wasn't pulling it back down.

Back at the condo, I knew where to park—right next to my Mustang.

I dearly love that car, and hoped her feelings wouldn't be hurt seeing me in the Porsche. She was probably feeling smug instead of hurt, though, when Amanda had to struggle to get out of the Carrera in her tight skirt. My Mustang's design was quite superior for such things. As I helped Amanda out, the Mustang and I were treated to a nice view of a *lot* of leg and a few other bits, too.

Amanda didn't seem to mind. She tucked her arm in mine as we took the elevator to the first floor. It was nearly 1:00 A.M., and the building was still and quiet. I noticed Steve sitting by himself in the courtyard across the way. Waiting for me, I guess.

At Amanda's door, she fished her keys from her purse and handed them to me. I unlocked the deadbolt and stepped back, holding the keys out for her to take. She paused, looking bewildered.

"Don't you want to come in?" she asked.

If ever life was cruel, it was at that moment. Here was a gorgeous woman—who I nearly kissed earlier—asking me to join her for a nightcap (or more) and I had no answer to give her. With every reason to say yes, a moment seemed like an eternity. But somehow I knew it wasn't right at *this* moment. I folded the keys into her hand.

Shaking my head, I said solemnly, "Thank you, but not tonight."

She looked puzzled, in disbelief about my answer. Then her whole countenance changed, and Amanda said something I will never forget.

"A gentleman with morals. I like that."

She headed in, paused halfway through the door, and turned back to me. Opening her purse, she pulled something out and wrote on the back. She handed it to me, kissed my cheek, giggled, went in and closed the door.

In shock, I stood wondering what had just happened. I put my hand on my cheek, leaving it there as I slowly turned and walked toward Steve's. I stopped twice to look back at Amanda's door.

Steve had witnessed our exchange. I went out to meet him in the courtyard.

"What the hell was that all about?" Steve whispered curiously.

Looking back at Amanda's door again, "I don't know," I replied quietly, still a little confused about why I'd said no and why she kissed me.

"Don't know?" Steve repeated in disbelief. "Am I missing something here? What did she give you?"

Moving under the courtyard light, I could see it was her business card. On the back she'd written her personal cell number and email address.

Steve asked, "What does that mean?"

I hesitated.

"It means, dummy ... that ... she wants me to call."

He responded with a dim-witted, "Oh."

Shaking my head, I walked to his condo door muttering, "No wonder you're still single."

For the second night in a row I laid in bed with my mind spinning. Last night, I thought of Cole and his death. Tonight two thoughts captivated me. The first was my breathtaking new friend, Amanda, and how much she reminded me of Caroline. Maybe that's why I declined Amanda's invitation at the door. Or maybe, as she suggested, I am a gentleman with morals, unwilling and unable to take advantage of a woman who's had too much to drink. Or maybe it was just the excitement of heading north to San Francisco in the morning?

But the second thought that was tormenting me was a man ... not Cole ... not Johnson ... but the old guy who announced dinner that night. There was something familiar about him, and I couldn't shake the feeling that I knew him. But ... from where?

CHAPTER 31

Tuesday morning at 10:00, I was back in the office at the monthly management meeting. By 10:30, I wished I had my gun so I could shoot a few people in the room. At 11:00, I wished they'd shoot me. When the meeting ended at 11:30, it was a lovefest of butt-kissing for the next ten minutes: "Great meeting today. Need to have more of them."

Morons.

When I arrived at my outer office, there were ladies crowded around my door. They stopped their chatter and silently parted, like the Red Sea for Moses, allowing me access to my office. Once through the crowd, they silently closed ranks again. It was weird.

Inside my office was another unusual sight. A dozen long-stem red roses in a lovely vase sat on my desk. I recognized them as top-of-the-line, and very expensive, the kind I bought for Cindy in years past. I poked around the bouquet gently, as if it was booby trapped. There was rustling behind me, followed by a voice.

"There's a card in there, Rick."

The gossip squad all had inquiring minds.

"Who are they from, Rick?" asked a second voice.

"I have no clue," I said suspiciously.

I found the card, opened it, and read silently, "Thank you for being a gentleman with morals." It was signed "1136."

"Read it, Rick. What does it say?" came a third voice.

With my back to them, I replied, "It says it's none of your business."

"Who's 1136?" someone slipped.

Surprised, I spun around immediately exclaiming, "You guys opened my card!"

Like rats abandoning a burning ship, they all scampered out ... hopefully to their own work stations and their own business. I turned back to the flowers and stared at them, thinking, "Amanda?" Honestly, I had written off my adventure with her. I figured she simply had too much to drink and was being friendly because of it. But flowers? I was still trying to digest this whole thing when Vince walked into my office.

"Hey, Rick," he chuckled, "I was nearly trampled by a herd of wild women. What's going on?"

Moving aside to give him a good view, I said, "What do you think?"

"Nice. San Francisco?"

"No. Los Angeles."

"Los Angeles? The realtor? What was her name?"

"It's Linda, but they're not from her."

"Well, who else do you know in Los Angeles?" Vince asked, grinning.

"Amanda."

"Who the hell is Amanda?"

"An attorney," I offered.

"An attorney?"

I motioned Vince to close the door, and I told him the whole story as he sat in rapt attention. He had a look of amused disbelief—the same look he had while I was conning the realtor. He shook his head slowly.

"Rick, you do have a way with women."

Smiling, but not commenting on his observation, I changed the subject.

"So, Vince, what brings you to my neck of the woods? Gonna buy me lunch?"

Ignoring my lunch question, he said, "I found someone with information on the Cole auto accident in 1976."

My ears perked up.

"Really? That's great! Who is it?"

"A retired reporter. He lives not too far from Nielsen's partner in Encino."

"When can we see him?"

"How about 9:00 this Saturday morning at his home?"

"Great, we can fly down together Friday afternoon."

"Can't. I'm flying down tomorrow, but I'll pick you up at the airport."

"Sounds good. I'll have Emily get you the flight information."

252

"Rick, there's something you need to know first."

By the look on Vince's face, I knew it was serious.

"The gentleman we're going to see had a stroke and has aphasia. Direct communication will be impossible."

"Vince, I understand what aphasia is. How is he going to tell us what he knows?"

"He won't. But according to his daughter, who's also his caregiver, he is willing to let us see his personal records of the accident."

"Personal records, huh?"

"Yeah. I understand it has names in it."

To celebrate, Vince and I headed across the street for a drink and some lunch. Somehow it all tasted better with good news than with bad.

As I came back through the outer office, I motioned to Emily and Alicia to follow me into my office. I had them close the door.

"OK. Why do women send men flowers?" I asked as we all sat down.

"Because they like you?" ventured Alicia tentatively.

"No, seriously, why do they?"

"Because, Rick, *THEY LIKE YOU*," Emily repeated in no uncertain terms.

"Really?"

"Yes, really."

For the next few minutes, I shared with them the story of Amanda. I wanted a female perspective. After hearing all the details, Emily concluded, "I think you have a new friend."

Nodding her head, "I think Emily's right," Alicia agreed.

"But, Rick," Emily continued, "What about San Francisco?"

Emily's question made me think. Indeed, what about my friend in San Francisco? I saw her the day after the encounter that scored me these gorgeous roses. Being with her that day had erased all thoughts of Amanda (which is another reason why the flowers were such a surprise). We spend time together so well, happy and comfortable. Our hours are filled with lively debate over nothing. Last time we saw each other, our verbal sparring was about farmland along the drive from San Francisco to Carmel. We deliberately took opposing points of view and argued over what type of crop was growing—both ignorant of what was planted, but laughing with every supposition. Dinner was smiles, each teasing the other unmercifully with movie and song trivia, each doing our best to trip up the other. When she snagged me with a tricky question, she flashed the broadest smile, resembling the cat that ate the canary. When I got the upper hand, she hit me on the arm, giggling like a schoolgirl in the process.

It seems like we were made for each other. Yet, neither of us ever took a next step. Even when my thoughts wandered toward it, I kept falling back to the assumption that we were just friends.

The elegant bouquet caught my eye, and it brought me back from San Francisco to thoughts of Amanda. What to do about Amanda? Pursue? Retreat? Considering Emily's words of wisdom, my analytical mind began to formulate a plan. I decided to test the waters with Amanda, not only to thank her for the flowers, but also invite her to coffee while I was in Los Angeles. Emily suggested dinner, but I didn't want to test them that much. At least for now, it would be coffee.

Dismissing Emily and Alicia, I began to type.

Dear 1136,

Thank you so very much for the flowers—a most pleasant surprise. They caused quite a stir in the office. All the women are dying to know who 1136 is. For now, I'll just keep them guessing. I will be arriving in Los Angeles Friday evening for a Saturday morning meeting in Encino. My meeting is at 9:00 and shouldn't last very long. If you have time, maybe we can have coffee before or after?

Thanks again,

Rick Morgan

About an hour later, I was in deep thought attempting to play catch-up with all my "regular" work, when my computer announced, "You've got mail." It was Amanda.

Hi Rick,

So glad you liked the flowers. It was my way of saying thank you for not trying to take advantage of me when I had a little too much to drink. Gentlemen are rare these days. Would you consider dinner Friday night? I can even pick you up at the airport, and you can use my car for your meeting. I look forward to seeing you again.

Love,

Amanda

"Love, Amanda?"

Whoa. I tried to digest what I had just read. In fact, I read it five or six more times, to make sure I read it right. Dinner Friday? You can use my car? Once again, I needed advice. I shouted to the outer office.

"Emily!"

Showing her the email, I asked, "What do you think?"

Smiling, "Again … I think you have a new friend," she concluded.

I leaned back in my chair as my face slowly assumed a smile.

"I think you're right," I agreed. "What should I do?"

One thing I like about Emily. She is always to the point. Her response?

"Go to dinner!"

That evening, Steve and I had a long conversation. He told me about the gossip pool in his office, buzzing with questions about the guy who was with Amanda at the party. As Steve continued, he described how he was bombarded with questions about me when the women of the office found out I was his friend. Each wanted to know every bit of information about my personal life—and if I have a brother (whatever that means). Amanda's response to all the chatter was, "I found him first."

As I described the flowers to Steve, a thought dawned on me that I hadn't yet considered. How did she know where to send them? I couldn't remember giving Amanda my card. I quizzed Steve a bit, asking if he gave Amanda my address. He said, "No." Curious. She must be a good lawyer since she has some detective in her.

In wrapping up our conversation, I told Steve I would be in town Friday night and needed a place to stay. As usual, it wasn't a problem.

In bed that night, my thoughts drifted back to the flowers. Mentally retracing every step and word from our evening together, I know I never gave Amanda my card. I did tell her the name of the company I worked for. I suppose from there, it wouldn't have been difficult to track me down.

But the flowers were a bold gesture where a simple phone call would have sufficed. So it made me wonder. Like Caroline, Kathy, and Crystal … is there more to Amanda than meets the eye? But how could there be? She had no ties to my company, and I met her through Steve.

Turning over and fluffing my pillow, I tried to make myself comfortable. It wasn't working. My racing thoughts continued. Maybe the investigation was getting to me, and I was growing paranoid. There is a fine line between healthy suspicion and paranoia. But considering all the surprises Vince and I had faced so far, distrust seemed like a logical choice.

Amanda reminded me so much of Caroline, I couldn't help being haunted and mixing up thoughts of the two. Caroline, Caroline … the final words from my Caroline.

"Not everything is what it appears to be."

CHAPTER 32

At the bottom of the ramp, just beyond the security check-point, stood Amanda. Still dressed for work, she was even lovelier than I remembered. Though the airport was busy, she was definitely "an attraction"—receiving smiles and glances from assorted men who passed by. I hoped the smile on her face was only for me.

"Hello, Rick," she said melodiously, giving me a wonderful hug.

The immediate physical contact surprised me, but of course I'm not complaining!

"Thanks for picking me up," I said gently while hugging her back.

She felt as good as she looked.

"Did you have a good flight?" she asked sweetly.

"Only because I knew I was seeing you," I replied with my most charming demeanor.

"Oh, you're such a darling," she said while running her hand down my tie. "Are you hungry?"

It was most certainly a suggestive question, and even though I had a thousand comebacks, I played it straight.

"Yes, I'm starving," I replied.

"Good, I have someplace special for you."

"Special?" I quizzed.

"Hmm, very," she said with her hand still on my tie.

I had a hunch dinner would be very enjoyable.

The "special" place was packed and, even with reservations, there was a wait for a table. Advised that it could be up to an hour before being seated, we opted to wait in the bar. In fact, we ended up having dinner there at a cozy table next to an exquisite rock fireplace. For romance, intimacy, and additional suggestive banter, it couldn't have been better.

The evening progressed and the wine flowed, at least for her. I stuck with only one of my usual, a vodka martini. We began to speak of personal things. She was curious about many aspects of my life. Did I like my job? My home? What happened to cause a split with Cindy? When *I* quizzed *her* as to the source of my personal data, she confessed that Steve had divulged all the precious information. She added that he gave the info quite willingly. That was Steve, alright. Never could say no to a pretty face. But there was one question in particular that aroused my curiosity. She asked it during dessert.

"Rick, has there been someone special in your life since your divorce?"

It wasn't the nature of the question that perked my ears, but rather her tone. It was as though she already knew the answer. Of course, being a woman, maybe she did already know intuitively somehow. Women move in a realm that mere mortal males will never comprehend.

"Someone special?" I muttered while pondering both Caroline and my San Franciscan.

I paused for a significant amount of time before answering her question, "No, not really. We're just friends."

Her eyebrows raised. The word "friends" sparked continued curiosity. Her eyes begged for more information. But since I wasn't offering any, it didn't take long for those beautiful eyes to show frustration.

And I had a provocative question of my own. "Amanda, why are you here with me tonight?"

Her eyes flicked from frustration to apprehension.

I continued, "You could have any guy in this room. Why me?"

Hearing the second part of my question, her eyes moved to relief. As I watched their rapid transformations, I wondered what she thought I was asking. I had caught her off guard. She wasn't prepared for an answer either way. But the question was asked. And as every attorney knows, a question must be answered. But, in addition, a good attorney would tell you, "Think before you do." And Amanda is a good attorney, so it was a long moment before she responded. With her head tilted toward the table and her eyes looking directly into mine, she spoke with a soft, sweet voice.

"You make me laugh, and ..."

She stopped in mid-sentence and hesitated.

Though not an attorney, I pressed like one for a complete answer, saying, "And?"

"And for some strange reason, I trust you."

As I began to address her comment, she stopped me with a quiet "shhh," touching my lips with a finger. Bashfully, she continued with a slight quiver in her voice.

"I'm also attracted to you."

From her body language, to the tone of her voice, to her eyes, every indication told me she was being truthful. But I felt something more ... an unspoken summons, if you will, to lean across the table into her private space, an invitation to kiss her, a request to take her lips and explore them. Intuitively, I responded to her silent directive, only to find her quietly moving to meet me. With our heads tilted and eyes closed, our lips slowly touched, tenderly pressing together for the first time.

It was a soft kiss.

Pulling back slowly, I was surprised and pleased with what we had just done, but the bigger surprise was her immediate reaction. She moved forward without a word and took another kiss. Longer and more expressive than the first, it certainly confirmed one thing: Amanda was attracted to me.

I'm not sure how long the second kiss lasted or how many there actually were, but when it was over I realized we had become the main attraction in the room—especially with the table of middle-aged men just a few feet away. By the look on their faces, it was obvious they were drooling in spirit, all craving a taste of Amanda's sweetness. But I learned years ago in the sandbox: there are some things I don't share.

Turning back to Amanda with a very contented smile, I said, "I think it's time to go."

Picking up on the vibes of the room, she agreed.

As the valet pulled up the Porsche, Amanda spoke those magic words, "You drive." Always eager to please the ladies, I slipped the guy five bones (meaning a five dollar bill, in case you're unfamiliar) and fell behind the driver's seat. With traffic, it took about thirty minutes to get to her place. And during each of those minutes, I glanced down once or twice at those beautiful, long legs.

As we pulled into the garage, I noticed Steve's car. I had forgotten to call him as promised. Sneaking another look at those long legs ... hell, I didn't care. I must have had something else on my mind.

I walked Amanda to her condo and—after I unlocked and opened her front door—she turned facing me. I knew what she wanted, and it wasn't her keys. Without saying a word I pulled her to me, completely surrounding her with my arms. I kissed her again and again. With her body tightly folded against mine, it didn't take long for both of us to realize—or feel—we were accelerating into an excited state. I felt her warm breath in my ear.

"Let's get into the hot tub," she softly whispered. I love it when a woman whispers. But her suggestion did catch me slightly off balance.

"Hot tub?"

"Yes, hot tub. I'm sure you know what that is," she scolded.

"Of course I do, but …!"

"There's a problem?"

"Ah, no, no problem at all."

For the second time that evening, Amanda took hold of my tie. This time leading me quietly into her condo. And I was happy to follow. She told me to make myself comfortable, pointed to a wet bar in the corner and disappeared into the bedroom.

The floor plan of her unit was exactly the same as Steve's, but at first glance you could see a world of difference. Steve's was a guy pad. Nothing coordinated, nothing special and it had the smell of an old gym sock forgotten under the bed. But Amanda's unit was quite the opposite. Besides a fresh smell, it was decorated with fine furnishings, probably Ethan Allen or Thomasville by the look. Everything from the walls to the couch to the carpet were color coordinated—definitely the décor of someone who enjoys and appreciates fine possessions. Another special distinction from Steve's—and other units too—was that Amanda's was on the corner of the building, offering a very private patio. The perfect place for—yes—a hot tub.

Moving over to the wet bar, I mixed us each a vodka martini. While shaking it, my eyes caught a picture on an end table on the far side of the room. Even from a distance, there was something vaguely familiar about it. I went to take a closer look. But before I could examine it closely, I heard Amanda stirring in the other room. For some reason I didn't want her to catch me looking at it. Thinking quickly, I grabbed my cell phone and took a picture. Placing the cell back in my pocket, I returned to the bar and finished our drinks as Amanda returned to the room.

She was adorable, with her hair pulled back in a bun (usually a look I don't care for) and wearing only a very short, white terrycloth robe. Even without the heels and nylons, her legs were unbelievable—long, obviously soft and smooth, and very beautiful. One look at her and I forgot about the picture.

With drinks in hand, we sat on the couch for a few minutes, at an angle with our knees touching. Conversation for me was somewhat difficult due to an intense fixation on those soft thighs disappearing under the short robe.

It wasn't long before Amanda took the drink from my hand. Setting it on a coaster, she asked provocatively, "Are you ready to get wet?"

Seeing the gleam in my eyes, she continued, "Let me show you something."

Fixing her eyes on mine—and showing no apparent modesty—she seductively undid the front tie of her tiny robe, allowing it to fall loose for a peek-a-boo look at all the treasures it covered ... most notably her breasts. Noticing my fascination with the open part of her robe, she looked down, returned her eyes to mine, and smiled, "Would you like to see more?"

I never answered her question verbally, but judging by my rapid breathing, the beads of sweat across my forehead, my wet chin, and the fixation I still had on that gap in her robe, she concluded—and rightly so—the answer was yes.

Moving up off the couch, she stood unpretentiously in front of me. Slowly and quietly, with eyes that said "just for you," Amanda pushed the robe from her shoulders. It fell in disarray behind her, exposing all the secrets and magnificence of her body from head to toe. Smooth, creamy white skin, perfect shoulders, tight breasts, firm, flat stomach, slender hips, and the most incredible thighs and legs I'd ever seen. Amanda had everything dreams were made of.

After giving me time to absorb the moment, Amanda motioned me from the couch, took me by the hand, and led me to her private sanctuary. Her patio was obviously a place she escaped to when reality became overwhelming, a personal and intimate place.

"See!" she announced, showing great pride. "Very private."

After pushing the button to start the jets, Amanda stepped gingerly into the hot tub. Gradually allowing her body to slip beneath the bubbles, she settled into what I could only describe as her "favorite spot."

With a look of increasing satisfaction, "Come join me," she coaxed.

I accepted her enticing invitation by removing my clothes and following her footsteps into the churning water of her private world. It was a world full of new possibilities and outcomes for me. A world that—for the moment—had only two occupants: Amanda and me.

Chapter 33

It was 9:00 A.M. on the dot when the Porsche pulled up to the address Vince had given. The sun was already blazing golden yellow against the blue sky. It was going to be a hot day. Vince was there, leaning against the fender of his Town Car. He looked impressed when he saw me in the Carrera. But today, the car was an easy second place behind my thoughts of test driving Amanda. I promised her I'd be back in time for lunch. The way she had smiled, she looked downright edible. I'm hoping she *is* lunch.

The retired reporter we had an appointment with worked for the Herald Examiner until its demise in 1989. His name was Ralph Monroe. According to Vince, he's a man very familiar with Peter Cole, the Rose family and what happened that horrific night of July 6, 1976.

After ringing the doorbell, it was a few minutes before someone answered. The door opened as a small, frail man in his early eighties appeared. From behind the screen, his eyes twinkled slightly as he recognized Vince. With a weak smile and shaking hand, he unlatched the screen door, motioning us to come in.

The house was dark, and it took a moment for my eyes to adjust. A woman stood silently in the shadows. Younger, maybe mid-fifties, she stepped forward and introduced herself as Jean, Mr. Monroe's daughter. She was also his caregiver and interpreter. Jean invited us to sit down at the dining room table. She turned on a light rather than pulling the curtains back from the window. She offered us coffee. (It was one of the best cups I've ever had.)

Vince started the conversation, speaking slowly and to the point as his eyes moved back and forth between the elderly man and his daughter.

"Mr. Monroe, thank you for seeing us today. We understand you are the expert on an accident that happened in 1976 involving Peter Cole."

Nodding his head, he motioned to his daughter with a finger. She got up and walked out of the room, returning instantly with a black notebook.

Handing it to Vince, she said quietly, "These are my father's notes on that story. Everything you need to know is here."

Vince and I were both delighted. We opened the book between us and began to read all of the notes, page by page. Though very detailed on how the accident happened, etc., it didn't tell us anything more than we already knew ... until we came across a newspaper clipping dated July 7, 1976. It sat loose between the pages. Yellowed from age, it was a clipping about a family that died in a traffic accident: the Rose family. It was accompanied by a picture of a young couple. The caption under the picture mentioned the name "Cohen." The name didn't ring any bells. But the picture did.

I put the picture in front of Mr. Monroe and asked who they were.

The daughter replied, "Mr. and Mrs. Cohen. She was the sister of Mrs. Rose. She also died in the accident."

"Sister?"

We knew from Harriett Miller, Cole's former aid and lover, that there had been another woman in the car. We didn't know until now that it was a family member.

"Yes, she and her husband were to accompany the Roses to a drive-in movie, but the husband had to cancel at the last minute."

Looking at Vince, I asked, "Has that name popped up anywhere in this investigation?"

Vince shook his head no.

Directing my next question to Jean, I asked, "So they were sisters? Any idea what their maiden name was?"

Taking the book back, "Ah, yes," she replied. She flipped through a number of pages before she stopped and ran her finger down the open page.

"Yes, here it is. Their maiden name was Johnson."

"Johnson?" Vince and I exclaimed in unison.

Stunned, we gaped at each other.

"Vince, didn't you say Johnson had three sisters?"

"Yes, that's right. Three."

I took the picture back and studied it. I knew the faces, but from where?

Then it dawned on me.

I turned to Vince. "Now I recognize them! This is the same picture I saw at Candy's when I picked up Crystal. At the time, I thought it was a young Candy. But now? And Vince," I added with some excitement, "look again at the photo. Tell me what you see."

Examining the picture Vince began, "A man and woman standing on a walkway in front of a house."

"Right, Vince. But take a closer look at the house."

Vince's eyes grew wide.

"Yeah, right! I see it. The house in Burbank."

"Vince, remember the name of the trust that owns it? C & J Family Trust."

"Of course, Cohen and Johnson."

I stopped for a minute before I began again, "That means ..."

Vince interrupted me. "Yeah, Rick, it does. Candy is Eric Johnson's third sister."

Vince turned back to Jean and Mr. Monroe. "My men searched high and low in every newspaper around that date. But we never found this story."

"Yes, and you wouldn't have," Jean explained. "That story was set to run the morning after the accident. But the presses were stopped in mid-run. The story was killed at the last minute."

"Do you know why?"

"Off the record, it was a request from the FBI."

Mr. Monroe stirred and said something inaudible to me, but his daughter understood.

"My father doesn't think they were the FBI, but rather CIA."

Vince and I shared a look, and then Vince directed another question at Mr. Monroe.

"Do you think Cole's death on that boat was an accident?"

The question stirred Mr. Monroe. Shaking his head violently, he blurted, "No!"

We all understood.

Jean said, "My father thinks someone else was on that boat with Cole."

Vince pressed further, asking, "Why?"

Mr. Monroe grabbed his book and fumbled with it, turning to the back pages where there were some crime scene photos. Finding the one he wanted, he pointed to it for his daughter.

Turning the picture toward us, Jean began, "In this picture you see the three bottles over in the corner by the bait tank," pointing with her finger, "then the empty beer bottles next to them."

Nodding our heads yes, we knew exactly where she was going.

"My father felt Cole would have thrown the empties into the ocean. But since they weren't, someone else staged the scene to make it look like he got drunk and fell overboard. My father thinks someone murdered him, dumped him off the boat and then placed the empty bottles around."

"Mr. Monroe, they found Cole's boat empty off Catalina. If someone did murder him, then there must have been another person and another boat. Do you have any idea who that might have been?"

Even with aphasia, he understood my question. He shook his head no.

Jean continued, "My father believes Cole was murdered, probably by the CIA, to silence him. He had become a liability, a loose cannon, maybe. Too unreliable with the combination of booze and his black book. Sitting on an intelligence committee for as long as he had, he must have known a lot of secrets. And big things. Important things. But how they did it with the boat, my father doesn't know."

Mr. Monroe was getting tired, I could tell. The last question came from me.

"What happened to the children? Why didn't Cohen take them since he was family?"

Jean said sadly, "Cohen did petition the court for custody. He was blocked by a judge, a friend of Cole's. The twins were adopted by a family locally. I'm not sure, but we think Cohen found out by whom. The older child we think was adopted by a family in the Bay Area. But we're really not sure. All the records are sealed."

Mr. Monroe again took his book and turned to the back page. Placing it in front of Vince and me, there was a list of names. Each one held a position of authority: judges, high-ranking police officials, newspaper editors, city councilmen, and one name that every person in the nation would recognize. A chill ran down my spine. All these people had apparently been in the back pocket of one United States Congressman, Peter Cole.

We spent about an hour total with Mr. Monroe and his daughter. As we left, Vince gave a word of advice to Jean, just out of hearing range of Mr. Monroe. Vince told her to burn the book. She agreed.

The connection between Cole and Johnson was now obvious. Cole was responsible for the death of two of Johnson's sisters. But there was still a major nagging question. Could it be a coincidence that Cole and Johnson died the same day? My gut said no. So what were we missing? Another piece of the jigsaw puzzle had been discovered today, but it was a border piece. There were still huge chunks missing from the middle. Were the pieces lost forever, pulverized to dust from ten to thirty years of neglect?

Or was there still someone, something, that could help me see the full picture?

CHAPTER 34

Shortly before 5:00 P.M. Emily slipped quietly into my office. I was staring out my window, oblivious to my surroundings. My thoughts were on an email I received from Amanda, inviting me to be her escort to a dinner party Saturday night. Considering what had been on the menu at last Saturday's lunch, I was fantasizing about what this dinner's dessert might include.

A hand softly touched my shoulder.

"Rick?"

Nearly jumping out of my seat, I yipped, "Damn, Emily! Will you stop that! You're always scaring the hell out of me!"

"Sorry, Rick. I won't do it again."

She's always sorry. And she'll never do it again. And she'll be sorry the next time too.

"Where are we this afternoon?" she asked slyly. "San Francisco or Las Vegas?"

"Actually, Los Angeles," I replied, turning back to the window trying to recapture my mental image of Saturday's dinner and dessert.

Emily could see my reflection in the window.

"Oh, I see. Does this have anything to do with 1136?"

I didn't answer.

"Chris is in the outer office. He'd like to see you."

Chris had been pretty quiet lately, like he had something else on his mind.

"OK, send him in. That's if you can do it without scaring the hell out of him," I added sarcastically.

Emily just smiled as she ushered Chris in.

"Chief, you have a moment?" he began.

Motioning for him to take a seat, I asked, "So Chris, what's on your mind?"

Usually calm and cool, Chris seemed nervous.

"Well, Chief, it's like this. I've been seeing, uh ... well, you see, she and I ... uh ..."

"Chris, stop for a minute," I said with my hand in the air. "Who's the 'she'?"

"Uh ... Alicia," he mumbled.

Ah, now *this* is interesting!

"And what about Alicia?" I asked with a raised eyebrow.

"Well, we've been ... that is ..."

It didn't take long to understand what he was driving at.

"Are you telling me you and Alicia have been seeing each other after hours, and you're worried about you two getting in trouble?"

He grinned and then blushed.

"Well, yeah, Chief."

Before I could respond, Emily stuck her head through the door.

"Mr. Guarino is here to see you," she announced with mock formality, since this was "Uncle Vince."

"Tell him I'll just be a minute."

Now, normally Vince would have taken precedence, but I had to see this through with Chris.

Turning my attention back to him I asked, "You like her, Chris?"

With a grin he agreed, "Yeah, Chief. A lot."

"Does she like you?"

"Uh, yeah, Chief. I think so."

I know I should have walked away at this point, but you know how curiosity gets the best of me.

"What makes you think so?"

"Well, Chief," he began bashfully, "we ... well, she ... her mother took her daughter one night, and we ..."

"Chris, I get the point," I declared mercifully, so that he could stop talking.

I got up from my chair and continued, "You and Alicia have fun together. She's a great girl. And don't worry about company policy. Just don't have sex in the file room."

With a somber look, Chris gasped, "Chief, we would never do anything like that!"

Patting him on the back as we walked to the outer office, "Chris, I was only kidding," I explained.

"Ah, thanks, Chief."

Alicia was at her desk in the corner, trying to be invisible. She had a frightened look on her face so when our eyes met, I smiled and winked. She got the message. I told Emily to hold all my calls as I motioned Vince to come into my office.

Closing my office door, I said, "So, Vince, what do you have for me today?"

Taking a seat, he began, "You asked me to get background on Brewster. You're never going to believe what I found."

Rolling my eyes, I disagreed, "At this point I will believe anything."

"Your Mr. Brewster closed down the business after Johnson died."

"Well, maybe he just took the money and ran."

"Possibly. But there's a small problem. Brewster never existed."

Bewildered, I asked, "Well, then who did we give twenty million dollars to?"

"Interesting question, Rick."

Now I was really puzzled.

"I'm not quite following you."

Vince began again, this time in plain English. Sort of.

"Brewster was only a name the guy used for the business, and then to obtain the insurance. Otherwise he didn't exist."

"Well, then who the hell is he?"

Vince sat back in his chair and folded his arms.

After a lo-o-o-ng moment, I asked again, "Who was using the name Brewster?"

"Leonard Cohen."

The name struck a chord.

"Cohen? As in the guy that was married to the Johnson sister who died in the accident?"

Vince nodded and said, "One and the same."

"That means Johnson and Brewster were brothers-in-law."

Since our meeting with Mr. Monroe, I had been working on a theory. But bits and pieces of it didn't fit together. Vince's report on Brewster, AKA Cohen, now gave me a better picture.

"Vince, I've been thinking a lot about this since our meeting with Mr. Monroe. Let's focus for a moment on what we have. We know Cole was a United States Congressman who sat on an intelligence committee. A high roller. In 1976, while drunk driving, Cole killed the Rose couple and Mrs. Cohen. Mrs. Cohen and Mrs. Rose were sisters, maiden name Johnson. Three Rose daughters survived. Cole used his position and influences to stonewall an investigation. But ultimately, Cole was forced to drop out of politics and eventually ended up on the board of directors for my company."

"Yes, Rick, that much we know as fact."

"So now let's speculate a little. Johnson works for the CIA. In 1989, he leaves the agency and he and Cohen—with CIA backing—form a business that allows Johnson to travel the world. Cohen uses the assumed name Brewster because of the covert operations."

"Go on," urged Vince.

"However, Johnson is getting older and becomes sick. He and Cohen— and, no doubt, the agency—realize Johnson's probably not going to live to a ripe old age. Remember what the medical examiner said about the bad heart?"

"Yeah, I remember."

"Over the years, Johnson and Cohen have not forgotten what Cole did and never paid for, and they kept an eye on him, probably through Nielsen. Remember, Nielsen took an early retirement from the LAPD and became an insurance investigator. No doubt just to keep tabs on Cole. For him it was personal because the asshole got away with it."

"OK. I'm following …"

"Since my company bills itself as family-friendly, the stockholders and insured customers wouldn't be happy to know Cole's background. So Johnson and Cohen—and maybe the CIA—blackmail Cole to help Johnson get insurance. Cole has no choice."

I leaned way back in my chair and swung my feet up onto the desk, feeling quite comfortable with my speculations at this point. I was on a roll.

"After careful consideration, they get Jack Webber, an idiot in San Francisco and an office away from Seattle—to write the policy knowing Johnson's in bad health. Jack doesn't care, or maybe doesn't know. He's more concerned with his big commission. In fact, it will be doubled because he'll also write Brewster."

Vince was rubbing his chin and nodding.

"Over the years, the CIA decides Cole needs to go. He likes to drink. Remember what he told Harriet Miller when he was drunk—about the visit from the FBI? No doubt Cole began talking as he got older. He became a liability. So it's decided he will be professionally taken out, and it's made to look like an accident. Everybody knew Cole was a drunk, so the falling overboard bit was believable."

"OK so far," Vince agreed. "And Johnson's death?"

"Let's say, in the meantime, Johnson's not traveling anymore because of his health. That particular day he's in Vegas, as usual, having fun with Crystal. Remember, Crystal works for Candy, and Candy is Johnson's sister. There's a direct tie. But ... during sex he has a heart attack and dies. Maybe he was celebrating the death of Cole and overdid it? Who knows? But it was an accident. Crystal panics. Remember what Mike said, how she ran out of the hotel looking scared? Crystal runs back to Candy to tell her what happened. Candy calls her brother-in-law, Cohen, who calls someone at the agency. The agency steps in and has the DA's office sweep everything under the rug, and everyone's happy. Since Johnson had no children, and Brewster was really Cohen, the blond who played the daughter and identified the body was probably one of Candy's girls. After the autopsy, she has the body cremated ASAP."

At this point, I could see Vince was captivated with my theory.

"So, Vince, what do you think?"

Vince nodded his head and muttered, "Very plausible, Rick."

I continued with my storyline.

"Jack is advised of the death. As agent, he would be. It would affect his renewals. He calls Kathy, Neilsen's daughter, who is working in the Claims Department. Maybe she was planted there, knowing someday she would have to expedite the claim paperwork? She does the rest. Since Brewster never really existed, the death benefit was paid to an L.A. law firm. Cohen now has a great retirement plan, and the agency sends in Rothschild to continue the cover."

"Yeah, I was wondering how you figured Rothschild came in here. You figure it was the CIA?" Vince interjected.

"After Johnson dies, Crystal hooks up with Rothschild. It wouldn't be hard for her. They move to Seattle. But after a number of years, she sees how he operates—remember he's CIA—and it scares her because she knows too much. And so does Candy. Cohen at first was protecting them, but our investigation changes things. She seeks me out. Why? We'll probably never know. Randomly and through sheer bad luck, Mike sees her at the airport—a side problem for her that we took care of. She told me once that she needed to disappear—like she never existed. Here's her chance. She does it, and takes Candy with her."

I paused. If I smoked cigarettes, this is where I would take a long drag off one before continuing.

"Kathy, on the other hand, was sent deliberately—probably by Cohen—to find out what I knew. But the incident with the bikers scared her. She never knew they were fakes. So she and Jack also run."

I was beginning to wish we'd started this conversation at the bar across the street. This is where I would like to be sipping a martini.

"Vince, your tail in Vegas was the same guy that died in Atascadero in the shoot-out. Probably sent by the agency just to scare us. But, he failed in his job when the bikers couldn't get Kathy and me over to his van. Suddenly he becomes a liability. He was eliminated. And the FBI agents who told me and my boss to drop the case ... they might have been doing a favor for the CIA, who probably wanted to stay in the shadows."

I swung my feet back down to the floor, and wrapped it up with, "The only thing I'm not sure about is Caroline—where or if she was involved. So, what do you think?"

Vince was silent. It was a long pause before he spoke, and when he did, it was short and to the point.

"I think I need a drink."

I laughed, "Damn, you read my mind! Let's go!"

We said goodnight to Emily and Alicia and headed to our quiet bar across the street. A bar can be a good place to help you forget about your day, but Vince and I weren't that lucky. We still had more to discuss.

"Rick, I do think your theory holds water. But realistically, legally, we're at a dead end. Even if Cole *was* murdered and somehow tied into Johnson's death—which, your own scenario was probably an accidental death-by-sex—how could we prove it? And do you want to?"

"Actually, my theory has one major flaw."

Vince raised an eyebrow.

"Which is?"

I didn't answer but continued on another path.

"I want you to track down that ADA from Vegas ten years ago. Remember Takahashi said they called her AJ? I want her full name."

"It might be tough. You know how tight-lipped they are down there, and it's been ten years."

"Yeah, I know. But if she was as good-looking as everyone said, someone will remember. Focus on the non-professional staff—someone from the mailroom or parking garage. I'm sure some guy will remember."

"I have a man down there now. I'll call him tonight. But, what are you thinking?"

"I have a hunch. There was something Jack Takahashi and Harriett Miller said. And if I'm right, I'll have the answer to that looming question why Cole and Johnson died the same day."

"Which is?"

"They had to."

CHAPTER 35

Emily stood nervously at my office door, watching as I packed my briefcase.

"Rick, will you be in Monday morning?"

"Hey, I'm like a bad penny. I always roll back."

"I know, but this time it feels different," Emily fretted.

I popped in the last item I needed for the weekend, clicked the briefcase shut, and swooped it off the desk as I walked toward Emily. When I reached her, I set it down and grabbed Emily up into a big bear hug. As she hugged me back, she started to cry.

"Emily, why the tears? I go out of town just about every weekend," I said as I released her from the hug.

I put my index finger under her chin, raising her head so our eyes could meet.

Trying to hold back the sniffles, Emily replied, "I know, Rick. It's just … one of these times you won't be coming back."

Smiling, I kissed her forehead and said, "Remember, Emily, if I don't come back,"—my eyes scanned the office—"all this is yours."

"Oh, Rick," she chirped as she gave me another quick squeeze. She wiped her eyes and scolded, "Rick Morgan, don't you ever leave me without saying goodbye."

"Goodbye?" I asked smiling. I picked up my briefcase and headed to the outer office. I turned back to Emily and repeated, "Goodbye? No, Emily! Never goodbye! You're family, dear. Wherever I go, you go."

Emily shot me a wry smile and waved me out the door.

Tucked deep in the Malibu Mountains is a private country club, the kind that demands a *minimum* mid-six-digit income. Don't have it? Don't bother applying.

The setting was similar to the awards dinner where I met Amanda two weeks before. There was a private room set up with hors d'oeuvres and cocktails, the usual BS-ing before dinner, nightclub entertainment afterward and—of course—chicken was on the menu.

The cocktail portion of the evening was a real ego-booster for me and quite amusing as well. With Amanda on my arm, we left the bar to work the room. Casually sipping our vodka martinis, we stopped to socialize. Others were not so relaxed. Many seemed intent on prying some juicy relationship details out of us. With each query from a woman (some tactful, some not so tactful) Amanda squeezed my arm tighter, looked the interrogator directly in the eye, then slowly turned her gaze to me and smiled sensuously. It was that secret womanly "hands off—he's mine" signal. When men asked the same blunt questions—and they do it so stupidly—I responded by moving my arm around Amanda's small waist. She nuzzled against me, signaling, "I'm with Rick, so take your horny thoughts and get lost."

Making a big circle around the room, I shook God-knows-how-many male hands, received a kiss on the cheek (and a gush about what a wonderful girl Amanda is and how handsome I am) from every woman in the place, and then finally arrived back at our starting place, the bar. It was exhausting.

Ordering a fresh drink for myself, I asked Amanda, "Would you like another drink, dear?"

"No," she replied. "I think I'm finished for tonight. Besides, I see someone I need to speak to for a minute. I'll be right back."

With a quick peck on the lips, Amanda headed back into no-man's land. She passed Steve as he was coming in for a landing, looking for what he didn't need: another drink.

"Hey, what's happenin'?" he asked, trying to keep his eyes focused.

"Nothing," I responded.

Leaning against the bar, looking toward Amanda with his arrogant I-got-all-the-answers look—which I hated—Steve demanded, "OK, tell me about you and Amanda."

"What's there to tell?"

"Are you really that stupid, Rick?"

And this is from a guy who's rolled one too many joints throughout the years, if you get my drift.

"What the hell are you talking about?" I countered.

"I'm talking about Amanda."

"What about Amanda?"

"In case you haven't figured it out yet, she's falling in love with you."

Although Steve's theory was flattering, he was drunk, and I'd only known Amanda two weeks. I dismissed it. Besides, something had caught my attention across the room. It was Amanda. She was speaking to an elderly gentleman who had just arrived. Though Steve's observation perhaps should have taken priority, instead my interest focused on this man. It was the same man who announced dinner at the last event. The same man who looked damn familiar. But from where?

"Rick?"

Hearing my name, I answered with a mechanical, "What?" I was preoccupied with the conversation I was observing.

"Are you in love with Amanda?"

"What's not to love?" I answered, still not really focusing on Steve.

"No, listen to me, dummy. I didn't ask if you love Amanda. Are you *in* love with her?"

I turned back to face Steve. My response consisted of a few seconds of silence.

So he answered his own question. "No, you're not."

He stared at me. His look told me his over-indulged 420-alcohol-saturated mind was processing. God only knows what, but processing! Then, with a change of countenance—as though thrilled with a new and original revelation—Steve spoke his magic words.

"Your heart's in San Francisco, isn't it?" he exclaimed, as though surprised by his own observation.

I replied sarcastically, "Yeah, and who are you? Tony Bennett?"

"No, I'm just the guy who's known you all your life. And what's more…"

He paused for a moment to turn and set his empty glass on the bar.

"What's more, I think it's been there longer than you think."

"Steve, she and I are just friends."

"By the way," he said, changing his tone to a conspiratorial whisper, "what the hell is her name, anyway?"

"Does it *really* matter?"

Picking up a fresh drink, "No, I guess it *really* doesn't," he muttered. "But you have some decisions to make."

Brushing aside Steve's comments I asked, "Who's the guy Amanda's talking to?"

Steve had difficulty focusing. Hell, she was only fifty feet away.

"That's Lenny."

"Lenny who?"

"Leonard Cohen. He's Chairman of the Board."

"Cohen?" I blurted out, nearly dropping my drink.

Steve jumped back and almost spilled as well. He was surprised by my outburst.

"Rick, are you OK?" Steve asked with some concern.

I was stunned. I immediately flashed back to the framed photo in Candy's house and the duplicate newspaper picture in Ralph Monroe's file. As I squinted at Cohen across the room, there was no doubt this was the older version of the same man. This was the man who was married to one of the women killed by Cole in 1976. The same man who, in a past life, was Richard L. Brewster, Johnson's partner and brother-in-law—the man who should have received a twenty million dollar death benefit from my company.

I took a giant gulp of my martini. My gut told me three things—unrelated to the churning from the abundance of alcohol that just hit it. First, it's no coincidence I was here tonight. Second, it was time to get a little closer look at Mr. Cohen or Brewster, or whoever the hell he was. Third, play it cool. Very, very cool.

Mumbling something incoherent to Steve, I left him standing there confused. I made my way to Amanda and was immediately greeted with a warm smile and a hug around my waist.

"Honey, I would like you to meet Leonard Cohen," she announced proudly. "He's our chairman of the board. Lenny, Rick Morgan."

Sticking out my hand, "Good evening, sir," I said evenly, trying desperately not to show my cards.

Grasping my hand in a firm shake, "Forget the 'sir' crap. My friends call me Lenny," he replied with a smile. "And I'm assuming that we will be friends."

After that bit of hogwash, I had no doubt Lenny knew exactly who I was.

"Fine, Lenny. Just call me Rick," I added.

"AJ tells me you're the CAE for an insurance company."

"That's correct," I agreed warmly, and told him the company's name. Good thing he couldn't feel my knees shaking.

Nodding his head with approval, he commented, "I did business with your company up until a few days ago."

Yeah, I'll bet you did.

"Oh, I'm sorry we don't have your business any longer. Is there something I can do to rectify that?"

Lenny never answered. With a quick glance to Amanda, he just smiled. Out of the corner of my eye, I watched Amanda, curious of what her reaction would be. She smiled back at Lenny, but with a glimmer in her eyes. A game of cat and mouse had just begun. And I was holding the cheese.

"Rick, AJ tells me you might be ready for a change."

Glancing at Amanda, I replied, "Oh, really …?"

Amanda was giving me a big ear-to-ear smile, showing her support for Lenny's implied offer of something new. The problem was we never had any such conversation. So, was Amanda doing some wishful thinking, or was there something else on the table?

I turned my attention to her and coaxed, "You did promise me a dance before dinner?"

"Amanda, I think your date wants some of your attention," Lenny mused.

"Actually, Lenny, I came over only to protect my interests. You may steal something valuable before the night's over. Then I would be left empty handed."

A little laughter ensued, but Lenny's eyes flickered. He understood that I could play the cat and mouse game as well as he could. Amanda and I excused ourselves and headed to the dance floor. About halfway through the dance, Amanda looked up and, with a coy smile, whispered into my ear, "I have a special surprise for you when we get home."

"Does it have anything to do with a job change?"

"Oh, that. We'll talk about that later. But for now I'm thinking of something a little more personal."

"Hmm, will I like it?" I asked.

With a little giggle, "You'll love it," she said, rubbing her tight body more aggressively against my special place to emphasize her point.

With the tingle of her warm breath against my ear, my arms around her waist, her abdomen slightly moving against me to the rhythm of the music, and the anticipation of her little surprise, I could feel a shot of testosterone surge through my body. Pulling Amanda tighter, she felt it too. But behind my smiles to Amanda, I had a lot of questions. Pieces of the puzzle were slowly falling in place. Yet, I couldn't be sure. I needed that call from Vince. But for now, having Amanda's body pressed up against mine was a good distraction from the bigger picture.

As the dessert was being served, I encouraged Amanda to work the room. Actually, I wanted the time to observe her and Lenny.

Graceful as a gazelle, yet as cunning as a tiger, Amanda moved from table to table playing the unofficial hostess, schmoozing with everyone from the filing room to the president's office, treating everyone equally, knowing when to be sweet and innocent and when to pounce and seize an opportunity. This was a far cry from the cold fish of two weeks ago. Why? Was she acting then ... or now? Or was my influence so powerful that her mood was permanently altered?

Lenny, on the other hand, seemed to be preoccupied with me. While watching Amanda, I would from time to time glance his way only to find our eyes meeting. More than simply sizing me up, Lenny seemed nervous. No doubt wondering how much I knew.

My question now was Amanda. Was she a pawn—someone Lenny was using to get me to show my hand—or was she a player? But I still wasn't sure.

After dessert, the DJ took to the floor and the festivities began. This was our cue to head back to Amanda's and to the surprise she had in store for me. It took about forty-five minutes to get back to her place, driving my favorite car (besides my precious Mustang, of course). During the drive, Amanda dropped the bomb regarding the job change Lenny alluded to.

"Rick," she said, placing her hand on my thigh—a little trick some women use when wanting a man to agree with something.

"What?"

"The CFO of our company has put in his resignation. I was telling Lenny about you last week, and he's very interested."

"Really? What did he say?"

"He thought you would be perfect for the position."

"Amanda, how would he know if I would or wouldn't?"

"Rick, you've already been checked out. It could be yours if you want it."

Though I didn't say anything to Amanda, I found her statement about my "being checked out" quite remarkable, considering we only met two weeks ago. But if it was a set up, what was I being set up for?

Moving my hand to her knee, "Mine if I want it?" I repeated.

"Yours!"

"So you think I should take it?"

Leaning over, Amanda slid her arm through mine and dropped her head to my shoulder. With a quiet "Uh-huh," she made herself comfortable.

It was interesting to see Amanda's face. With only the slightest glow from the dashboard lights, her face—like her actions—was childlike. She was a little girl who just asked her daddy for something special, waiting in anticipation for him to say yes. But I couldn't help wondering if behind that innocence there was something sinister.

"How much time do I have?" I continued.

"About three weeks."

"Let me think about it," I said.

With a quick kiss on my cheek and a broad smile, Amanda settled back happily on my shoulder as I drove.

Back at the condo, Amanda excused herself and slipped into the bedroom. I thought it was only to freshen up. Sitting back on the couch, I loosened my tie, kicked off my shoes, and began to relax after the hectic evening. Honestly, I was tired and looking forward to Amanda's little surprise and a good night's sleep.

A few minutes into my quiet time, the lights dimmed, some strange music began to play, and Amanda slipped out of the bedroom dressed in the sexiest lingerie I've ever seen. Her long, dark hair was teased and falling mussed across her shoulders. She wore a black see-through lacy bra, small black panties, black thigh-high hose complete with garter belt, and 4-inch black stiletto heels. I was instantly transformed into an energized, perspiring shell of a man.

"Has the jury reached a verdict, Mr. Morgan?" she asked in a dark, sexy voice.

My answer was only a nod, as I rolled my tongue up from my chest.

Moving in a full, broad circle around me, Amanda began an erotic dance, gyrating her hips seductively to the unusual music. She touched herself in all the right places, and posed her finger with a lick and a sizzle on her derrière. Hot, hot, hot! She teased me with looks and moves that took my breath away. Oh-h, she was great!

After exactly the right amount of steamy dancing, Amanda moved in closer. She struck a coy pose directly in front of me. Then in one smooth motion, she spread her gorgeous gams, bent at the waist so I was within a breath of nuzzling her cleavage, and tucked herself neatly onto my lap, straddling me like a pony. She got immediate validation that her performance had accomplished its task.

"Woo!" she cried. "I see I've been sentenced to *hard* time!"

With a big smile on her face, she proceeded to feverishly grind against me to the pounding rhythm of the music. The look in her eyes told me she was the one in control, and I was along for the ride. And what a ride it was! Breathing hard with the slightest quivering moans—and I'm talking about me—Amanda began to explore. She ran her fingers through my thick hair, all the while blowing gently in my ear, landing soft kisses, and nibbling my earlobes, lips, and eyelids.

Looking straight into my eyes, she cooed, "Would you like to continue this in the bedroom?"

After whispering back "Ye-es", Amanda requested shyly, "Carry me?"

"Carry you?" I repeated, not sure if I'd even be able to stand.

Like a little girl wanting something very badly, "Pleeease?" she begged.

There's an old saying in the confidence game: "You can't cheat an honest man." For a con to be successful, it's imperative that the mark—the sucker—believes he's receiving something he's not. Carrying Amanda into the bedroom with her arms wrapped around my neck and her face brushing against mine is a brilliant fantasy any man would want to believe.

As sayings go, I prefer "Be careful what you wish for. You might just get it."

CHAPTER 36

On a Sunday morning no one's supposed to call before 9:00 A.M. unless it's imperative or someone died. It was 7:18 A.M. when my cell rang. Amanda was sound asleep, exhausted from a night of heavy passion. I searched frantically for my phone, quickly finding it under my pillow.

I answered fairly incoherently on the third ring. It was Vince.

"No, I'm awake," I said, trying to be inconspicuous with my yawn. "What's up?"

"He did?"

"Say that again?"

Vince's operative in Vegas found someone who remembered the ADA in question. Though he couldn't remember her entire name, it was enough to indicate my hunch was right.

"You're absolutely sure?" I quizzed.

"No, I'll take it from here. Are you in your office?"

"Until when?"

"I'll call you later."

Although I was trying to be quiet, Amanda stirred at the tail end of my conversation. She opened her eyes and smiled.

"Good morning, dear."

"Good morning, love."

"Is everything alright?" she asked.

Amanda could tell by my facial expression that something had disturbed me. She grabbed my knee and grinned devilishly.

"Would a little more of last night make it all better?"

"Last night was great. But we need to talk first."

Amanda rubbed her sleepy eyes as they grew big and bold with excitement.

"You're taking the job, aren't you?" she exclaimed.

"Well, that might depend on some answers you give me in the next few minutes."

Amanda's eyes turned from excited to confused.

"Is there something special you want me to do?"

I'm not sure, but I think she was referring to some enhancement in the activities we explored a few hours earlier.

"No, dear. I wish it was that simple."

Amanda was now a little suspicious, asking, "Rick, is there something wrong?"

Looking straight into her eyes, I asked plainly, "Amanda, last night Lenny called you 'AJ.' Is that for Amanda Jane?"

"Why, yes, Rick, it is. Why do you ask? And why do you seem so concerned about it?"

I didn't know how to answer. So much in me wanted to just forget it, pretend like it never happened, to take her in my arms and continue the lovemaking of last night. But the next question needed to be asked now. I knew if I didn't ask this morning, there would be another morning or another. The question demanded an answer.

I took a deep breath.

"Amanda, where's the money?"

The audacity of my question took her completely by surprise. She turned her head away from me quickly, so I couldn't see her face. She was silent. I put my hand on her cheek and gently moved her face back toward me. Our eyes locked—hers were frightened of the question, mine of the answer.

I repeated, "Amanda, where's the twenty million dollars?"

Amanda pulled her face from my hand and turned away again. Her voice cracked as she said, "Rick, what are you talking about?"

My heart sank as Amanda tried to play innocent.

"On the contrary, my dear, you know very well what I'm talking about. That phone call I just received was from an investigator who's been working with me. I asked him earlier this week to track down the ADA in Vegas that handled the death of one of my insureds ten years ago, a man named Eric Johnson. Does the name sound familiar, Amanda?"

Still turned away from me, her answer was a curt, "No."

"My investigator found a man who worked in the Clark County

parking garage ten years ago. He happened to remember a very pretty young ADA named Amanda Jane. He couldn't remember her last name, but that everyone called her 'AJ' and by coincidence, that's what Lenny called you last night. His description of her—and the one the ME gave me—fits you perfectly. Besides, he said she had a weakness for Porsches."

Moving off the bed, I walked into the living room and grabbed that familiar photograph from the end table. I brought it back to the bedroom. Amanda hadn't moved, but a few tears were trickling down her face. I sat back down on the bed and handed it to her. She took it from me without speaking.

"Which one are you?" I asked.

"The one in my mother's arms," she said softly.

"Amanda, this might be a wild shot in the dark, but I'm guessing the one your father is holding is Caroline?"

She nodded her head yes.

"You and Caroline, and this other little girl," referring to the dark-haired one with the sultry look, "are the surviving Rose children, aren't you?"

"How did you know, Rick?"

"This same picture was in Caroline's office. When I asked who the people were, she said, 'family.' The woman in this picture is a dead ringer for Mrs. Cohen. I saw a picture of her at Candy's house in Burbank and again with a reporter. I didn't make the connection until a moment ago. I'd assumed the Johnson twins were identical."

"Caroline always said you would figure it out. Tell me, Rick, was there anything else besides this picture that made you suspicious?"

"Three things actually. After Caroline left the company, I found out she was a computer whiz. It would have been simple for her to erase or corrupt my computer files. Second, during this whole investigation someone was always one step ahead of me. It started with the old man following Vince in Vegas. Since Vince and I were the only two people who knew he would be down there, the only logical answer was someone was hacking into my email. I couldn't ask IT to investigate, because I didn't know who to trust. Though Caroline had the knowledge, I was never sure."

"It was her, Rick," Amanda said. "But we knew nothing about that old man."

Not knowing if Amanda was playing it straight, I continued. "Knowing someone was hacking my email, I set up another account on another server and only used the company one for information I wanted the hacker to know."

"Caroline said you were tricky. And what's the third reason, Rick?"

I took another deep breath for this answer.

"You and Caroline are the same woman in bed."

With a slight smile, "That's because even though we're fraternal twins, we're identical when it comes to our taste in men."

Snatching up the comforter and wrapping it around her naked body, Amanda got up and moved to the window. She gazed out. She was deep in thought … probably wondering what to do next. Or maybe what I would do. It was a couple of minutes before she began again.

"You know, Rick, Caroline was in love with you," she said softly, turning to me. "Were you in love with her?"

"It was never that simple, Amanda."

Her eyes flickered a moment, hesitating to ask the next question. "Was it because of your friend in San Francisco?"

"I see you've done your homework on me."

Shaking her head a bit, "We tried," she said weakly.

"Amanda, I'm taking another shot in the dark now … I have no proof, but I'm willing to bet Eric Johnson never died in that hotel room."

Amanda's eyes got big, and I could see she wasn't sure if she wanted to answer that question. With the comforter dragging on the floor, she walked back to the edge of the bed and sat next to me. Her eyes said yes as her head nodded silently.

"It was Peter Cole, wasn't it?"

"Yes," she said quietly.

"And Eric Johnson is today David Rothschild?"

Amanda didn't answer my question directly but rather asked, "How did you figure it out?" It was the same as a yes.

"I kept coming back to those empty liquor bottles on Cole's boat. Cole was a drunk and a self-serving bastard. He would have tossed those bottles overboard without a thought. But he didn't. I kept asking myself why. I could only come up with three possible answers. First, Cole had become an environmentalist before getting drunk and falling overboard—a long-shot at best. Second, someone was on that boat with him, killed him, dumped his body overboard and staged the scene with the empty bottles to make everyone think it was an accident. Since Cole had a lot of enemies, this was a theory I could live with. However, for Cole to allow someone on his boat, he would have to know them very well. From what I heard, Cole only got close to women. But it wasn't his style to take a woman out fishing. Also, the person who killed Cole would have to get off the boat. That meant another boat and a second party. That meant a conspiracy. And even though it was a possible scenario, my gut said it wasn't right. I kept asking myself, if someone else was on Cole's boat and staged the crime scene, then why did Cole have to be on the boat? Answer: he didn't. He could have been killed someplace else. And if he was, it would explain why the body was never found. No one was looking in the right place."

It was almost exhilarating, laying it all out for Amanda. It felt good to put it together, say it out loud, and have it confirmed or denied. Amanda listened intently while I continued.

"But ultimately I kept going back to the question of why Johnson and Cole died the same day? It drove me crazy. Then I happened to remember something the medical examiner said about Johnson. That he had a bad heart from years of drinking and smoking. If Johnson was CIA, as I suspected, he wouldn't have been a drunk. The agency would have gotten rid of him years before as a liability. So how could the ME determine that in fact Johnson had those heart problems? There could be only two possible answers. Either the ME gave us the wrong information, or Johnson wasn't the one autopsied. When I met with Takahashi, the ME in Vegas, my gut said he was playing it straight. So it couldn't have been Johnson on his table. Then who was it? The only logical answer was Cole. But I wasn't sure … until you just confirmed it."

When I finished my monologue, Amanda sat quietly for a couple minutes before speaking. She knew I had her cold. With increasing tears and a crack to her voice, she asked, "Rick, what do you plan to do?"

"I guess it all depends on what you tell me. To start with, where's the twenty million?"

"Actually, it's forty million."

"Forty?" The doubled amount caught me off guard. Was there another claim I missed? Then I realized, "Of course! You had the money invested for the last ten years. May I ask where?"

"Somewhere no one would think of looking. Your company."

"My company?" I squealed. "Ha, let me guess—a variable annuity? And I'm willing to bet it just matured."

Amanda said nothing. But her eyes told me to keep going.

"Of course," I continued, "your note to Kathy, 'Only four more months to go.' Then there's Lenny's comment about doing business with my company until a few days ago. Very smart, Amanda."

Amanda continued her silence, but now had a grin on her face. She appreciated my compliment.

"So where's the money now?" I pressed.

"Someplace very safe," she said with confidence.

"Let me guess again! An offshore bank account. Luxembourg? Switzerland?"

"Switzerland," she confessed.

"An established numbered account. And the funds were wire transferred in. Right?"

"Yes, as of a couple days ago."

"Smart again, Amanda. Completely untouchable. But I'm curious—why did you wait ten years?"

Her answer was cool and precise, but not surprising. It was one you'd expect from a good attorney.

"That's the maximum amount of time on the statute of limitations, Rick."

"But, Amanda, there's no statute of limitation on murder."

Again speaking with coolness and precision, "What murder, Rick? Where's the body?" she asked.

Nodding my head, I could only agree.

"Amanda," I began slowly, "since there's no proof of any crime, will you tell me the whole story?"

I could see her thoughts floating back to another time and place, and she spoke with an other-worldly airiness.

"Where do I begin?"

Chapter 37

Amanda had nestled herself on the bed, surrounded by pillows and wrapped tightly in her comforter. She looked very small, and her voice sounded even smaller.

"It was July 6, 1976. My biological father and mother, my aunt, me, and my two sisters were all heading home from a drive-in movie. We saw *The Bad News Bears*. The grown-ups were in the front seat and we three girls in the back. Peter Cole was heading home from a fundraiser, drunk. He was a United States Congressman, supposedly very important. His car crossed over the double line and hit our car head on. It was a horrible, messy, fiery crash, and my parents and aunt were trapped in the front seat. Some passersby got us girls out before the car exploded. Cole wasn't seriously wounded, but he was so drunk he didn't help. He should have helped. Maybe if he had helped, they could have …"

Amanda drifted off in her storyline, perhaps imagining how life might have been if her parents had been pulled from that car. But she shook it off and continued.

"After the accident, Cole used every bit of his clout to stonewall the investigation and avoid prosecution."

She looked me straight in the eye and sounded much stronger and more confident as she added, "Besides the fact my father was a lawyer, the fact that Cole was able to manipulate the system that way is what motivated me for law school."

Then her voice retreated again. I just nodded.

"An LAPD detective named Nielsen did his best to have him prosecuted, but Cole had the city attorney in his back pocket. Cole even used his friendship with a judge to make sure we girls were not adopted by the same family. My Uncle Eric—yes, he was CIA—used his own clout and intervened to make sure Caroline and I were adopted together by the Reynolds who lived in Encino at the time. Neither Cole nor anyone, except Uncle Eric and Uncle Lenny, knew the Reynolds and Roses had been friends. My mom and dad, Ben and Heidi Reynolds, were very aware of who we were and the circumstances of the adoption. Uncle Eric and Uncle Lenny always stayed in touch with the Reynolds. Unfortunately, for reasons not even Uncle Eric could uncover, our older sister was adopted by someone else. With the court records sealed, we could never figure out by whom."

"So I gather she had nothing to do with this?"

Shaking her head sadly among the pillows, Amanda whispered, "If she lived next door, I would never know."

She was silent for several minutes. I reached over and touched the one hand I could see peeking through the comforter as it clutched the fabric to her breast.

Amanda pulled herself back together and continued, "As you know, I went to UCLA, and I became friends with Kathy Nielsen there. One day, visiting her home, I met her dad, Robert Nielsen. Quite by accident I learned he was the detective who investigated my parents' deaths. I was in shock. So was he. What are the odds? After constant begging from both Kathy and me, he finally told me all about Cole, how he quit politics but was still living a grand life on the board of a large insurance company and also how Mr. Nielsen had quit the force and was working for this same company as an investigator. He never said it outright, but it was clear he couldn't let go of the case or of Cole.

"When I graduated UCLA School of Law and passed the bar, I was offered a position with the DA's office in Clark County, Nevada. Caroline in the meantime had been going to school at Georgia Tech, graduated with a BA in Computer Science, and did post-grad at Stanford.

"It was Christmas 1993 when we both came home for the holidays. I had invited Kathy for Christmas dinner, introducing her to Caroline who already knew her father was the man who investigated the death of our biological parents.

"Caroline and Kathy hit it off immediately.

"Caroline came up with the idea that she and Kathy should go to work for your company. Why, I never could understand. Maybe now, looking back, it was fate. Who knows? Since Mr. Nielsen had connections with the company, he made arrangements to have Caroline and Kathy interviewed.

They were both hired. Caroline went to work in the IT Department in Seattle and Kathy to Administration then Claims in San Francisco. Jack Webber was the office manager at the time and Kathy swept him off his feet. He got her pregnant, but she married someone else. Then got divorced. Then hooked up with him again. And you already know they both worked themselves up to different departments."

As Amanda continued, the puzzle was coming together.

"One of my first cases at the DA's office was a simple pimping case. When I first saw the defendant, I nearly fell over. I saw a family resemblance. To make a long story short, I was related to this woman. She was my Aunt Catherine, the older sister of my biological mother and Aunt Amanda. She led a colorful life as a madam in Vegas. Later, Caroline and I found out that she never wanted us to know what she did. She made Uncle Lenny and Uncle Eric pledge to secrecy. I guess she was ashamed."

"Was Crystal related in any way?" I asked curiously.

Shaking her head, "No, she was just one of Aunt Catherine's girls. But they were very close."

Amanda continued, "I recused myself from her trial, and got to know her. We stayed in touch. One day at lunch she told me about an obnoxious john she had, a man who looked familiar. It seemed he had an eerie interest in Crystal. As she was telling me about the guy, it hit her. The john was Peter Cole.

"In the meantime, Uncle Lenny and Uncle Eric were in business together. Yes, the CIA was involved, but that's all I know. Except that Uncle Eric wanted to get out of the business. Since the agency doesn't retire people, he needed to disappear. But how?

"We learned from Aunt Catherine that Cole had a bad heart. I guess Crystal always had to go easy on him. Aunt Catherine joked that he should have a heart attack during sex. She also noticed the physical similarity between Cole and my Uncle Eric. This got Uncle Eric and Uncle Lenny thinking. Uncle Eric thought he could disappear using Cole. Uncle Lenny came up with the plan."

Still digesting everything, I just nodded again as Amanda continued.

"It required Caroline and me, Kathy and Jack, Aunt Catherine and Crystal, and both my uncles. They talked to all of us, and we agreed. Jack and Kathy were a little hesitant until they learned they would be paid a million dollars ... each.

"Since my uncles were in business together, each would insure the other in a key man life insurance policy for twenty million. Jack Webber would be the agent. Jack and Kathy never knew that Cole was going to be killed. They just thought it was insurance fraud. They still don't know.

"In the meantime, Aunt Catherine arranged for Crystal to meet up with Cole every Saturday night in Vegas. That wasn't hard to do. Cole always had some excuse to get out of town. He liked telling his wife he was going on an overnight fishing trip for the weekend. We were a little shocked that she reported him missing that first night. But each Saturday night Crystal would meet him at a hotel and see how far she could push before he needed his heart meds. It didn't take long for her to know exactly how far she could take him. The plan was on a certain Saturday rendezvous she would keep him going until he had a heart attack and died."

"So she really did screw him to death," I thought.

"A day was picked. Once we knew Cole's plane touched down at McCarran, Uncle Eric dressed like Cole—even wore a false beard and a hat exactly like Cole's—picked up his car at LAX, and drove to the Marina. While loading Cole's boat, he made sure to wave to a number of people. Then he motored into the channel and staged the scene to make it look like Cole got drunk and fell overboard. At dusk, Uncle Lenny picked him up in his boat, and they went home to wait. You know what happened with the search.

"Uncle Lenny then called Aunt Catherine and told her everything was a go. Crystal went to the room at 11:00 P.M."

"I thought they normally met at 10:00?"

"For some reason she was late that night."

"Oh." Nodding my head, I beckoned her to continue.

"She had sex with Cole until he had a heart attack. But Crystal freaked out when she saw Cole lying there dead. Aunt Catherine put her into a private hospital for two weeks to calm her down. I don't think she ever recovered from it.

"Since I was an ADA, I just stepped in to make sure everything went smoothly. Caroline played the daughter and claimed the body. Since Richard Brewster never existed, the claim was paid to my father's law firm, Greenbrier, Morris & Perry. Dad never knew about the plan—still doesn't. For him, it was a routine trust case. He invested the money into a variable annuity with your company. It matured four days ago. The funds were then wired to Zurich."

"And everything was going smoothly until I started an investigation," I added.

Nodding her head, Amanda agreed, "Caroline did her best to try and steer you away from it. But you and some guy named Chris just kept going."

"I gather it was Caroline who erased the computer records?"

"Yes, but she did it years before. It was Jack who stole the physical files."

"Was he the one that put the L.A. Times into the claim file?"

Shaking her head, "I have no idea what you're talking about."

"Huh?" I said befuddled.

"Anyway, Caroline actually thought you would go to Atlanta with her. As I said earlier she was in love with you. And in case you're wondering, she still is. When you didn't go with her, it was decided to send Kathy in. You know, she liked you too. Anyway, Jack had a fit. But Kathy could always handle him. She was supposed to keep you occupied, but the incident with the group of bikers scared her. They decided to lay low until they received their money."

"Amanda, the bikers were amateurs working for the older man who was the one hired to kidnap Kathy and me. But then he was killed the next day by police. You're saying you didn't send him?"

Shaking her head adamantly, Amanda objected, "No, we didn't. We don't know who he was or who sent him!"

A familiar chill ran down my spine. There was someone else out there we both weren't sure of, and he—they?—play hardball.

"It was then we thought Crystal might deter you. You do have a reputation for taking up with beautiful women, Rick Morgan! But Crystal was running scared of my Uncle Eric. He was never happy about using someone outside of the family. Crystal knew his identity. That frightened her. She was afraid he might eliminate her at any moment. Like I said, I don't think she ever got over literally sexing Cole to death. She wasn't quite right after that, and was always afraid. But not all her fear was paranoia. Aunt Catherine and Uncle Lenny did their best to keep control of Uncle Eric, but he was always a wild card.

"When we sent in Crystal, Mike just happened to see her in the airport. I'm not sure what you did, but according to Crystal you were her hero.

"The day Crystal met you in San Diego was the day Aunt Catherine was to move. We put the Burbank house up for sale. Crystal was supposed to meet Aunt Catherine at a new location. She never showed. Do you know where she is?"

"Camelot," I said sweetly, under my breath.

Amanda looked at me strangely before she continued, "We knew from Caroline and from your emails that Steve was your friend. So we tracked him down and recruited him for the production company knowing eventually you would show up. And here you are. All we wanted was to keep you off balance until the money was transferred."

Shaking my head solemnly, I quipped, "I guess I really am that predictable when it comes to the fairer sex. You sure did keep me off balance ... off my feet ... on my back ..." Amanda managed a small smile as I continued, "All along I thought Cole was killed because of his secrets. But in reality, it was nothing more than revenge for killing your parents."

"Nothing more," she said quietly.

I couldn't help smiling as I replayed the events in my mind's eye. But murder?

"Amanda, when he died, was his little black book on him?"

"Uncle Eric asked the same question," shaking her head slightly. "No."

After pausing for a long moment she asked with an apprehensive tone, "So, what now?"

What now indeed I thought? For the second time that morning our eyes locked—except this time mine were frightened of the question, hers of the answer.

Needing space to think I got up and moved to the window. Amanda stayed on the bed, nestled in the pillows and wrapped in the comforter. Gazing out, my mind was spinning, overwhelmed from this fantastic fable. But in answer to her question, I had no clue. Amanda broke the silence.

"I'm flying out to London tomorrow, and then to meet Caroline in Zurich on Tuesday. Go with me?"

A touch of sincerity in her voice caused me to turn back. For a brief moment I believed she wanted me to go. It was tempting. But if I did, would there be a price?

I began slowly, "If I go, would it be for you, Caroline or a piece of the forty million?"

My question sparked a worried look. Her invitation had been spontaneous, caught up in the moment. Without thinking, Amanda forgot one little detail. One, by my question, she just realized. She never told Caroline about us.

Amanda sat quietly deliberating my question. I was curious to know her answer. But realistically there could be only one. And we both knew what it had to be.

"I can't." I said thoughtfully.

"I know." With a slight smile, "It would make things … complicated."

Then, with a cross examination worthy of a good attorney, "But that's not the reason. It's because of your friend in San Francisco isn't it?"

I didn't answer.

She continued, "We never figured out who she is. She's a well-kept secret."

"*You're* commenting to *me* about secrets? That's rich!" I chuckled.

But at this point, complications or secrets, it didn't matter. I knew what needed to be done.

Pulling out my cell phone, I hit the redial button. A voice answered after the first ring.

"It's me. Are you still in your office?"

"Great. I want you to take the Johnson file and shred it."

"You heard correctly. Shred every note. It never existed."

"No, I'll explain later. Just send me a final invoice, and I'll have accounting cut a check."

"What?"

"As far as anyone is concerned, the death benefit was paid in accordance with the terms of the policy."

I hung up the phone. Amanda's demeanor again changed, back to the small little girl nestled in the pillows. With the same small voice, "The job is still …" She didn't finish. We both knew enough had been said. The cards were on the table. The game was over. Though my company was the big loser, I couldn't help feeling we all lost something.

"Amanda …"

"I know." She interrupted quietly. "I'll take you to the airport."

Nothing was said on the way to the airport that morning. Sunday morning terminal traffic was light, giving the Porsche easy access to the curb. After pulling my bag from the backseat, I leaned in through the open door.

"Well, goodbye, Amanda."

With a slight quiver in her voice, "Goodbye, Rick, and thank you," she said sincerely.

As I was closing the door, I heard Amanda cry out, "Rick!"

I caught the door before it slammed and bent down, peering inside.

Amanda's face looked familiar again, like the woman I'd gotten to know.

With a sweet half-smile she said, "Rick, listen to me. After today, four women who cared for you very much will have walked out of your life. This fifth woman of yours in San Francisco must be very special. If you feel for her as I suspect you do, tell her, and don't let her go. Five may be your lucky number."

I grinned and said, "I'll consider it, Amanda. And when you see Caroline, tell her ... well, tell her she'll always be number one."

Amanda grinned back, and I continued smiling as I closed the door. I watched the Porsche move into traffic, figuring that would be the last time I ever saw the beautiful Rose sister, Amanda.

Inside the terminal was much like the outside that morning—almost empty. Walking up to the counter, I was greeted by a nice looking older lady.

"Good morning, sir," she said with that forced company smile. "How may I help you?"

Handing her my ticket, I replied, "I booked a flight for tonight back to Seattle but need to get home this morning."

Taking my ticket, "Let me see what I can do for you," she said in a cheery voice as she began to do whatever magic they do with the computer.

Looking back outside through the window, I muttered Amanda's last words, "Five may be your lucky number," loud enough that the agent heard me say something.

"I'm sorry, sir. I didn't hear what you said."

A little bewildered, I looked at her with a blank stare. Then suddenly, with more assurance, I repeated, "Five may be your lucky number."

"Well, yes sir, if you say so," she agreed, a little bewildered herself.

With my cell phone in hand, "Can you hold off for a minute?" I asked.

"Of course. Is there a problem, sir?" she asked.

Indicating no, everything's fine, I pushed a speed-dial button. Within moments, I heard a voice on the other end.

"Hey, it's me. We need to talk. Steak tonight?"

"Same time and place?"

"Great, see you there."

I redirected my attention to the reservation agent.

"When's your next flight to San Francisco?"

EPILOGUE

It was a cool and foggy evening in the City by the Bay. In the bar of my preferred upscale steakhouse I was seated toward the back, quietly nursing my vodka martini as I waited. Lost in thought, I replayed the events of the past few months, focusing especially on the turning point that morning when I closed the final chapter on this unusual investigation. After a complete and detailed confession, I was left with no case whatsoever, and my company would recover no money. A gorgeous young woman drove away in a beautiful Porsche toward forty million dollars in essentially stolen cash. And she and her cohorts got away with murder.

Why wasn't I feeling bad about this? Better yet, why was I feeling so good? Even with some very serious, unanswered questions still looming? Who sent the old white-van-guy, for example? And ordered his firing squad? And why? I may never know.

Yet, still I feel good.

As Amanda so eloquently stated, over the last six months four beautiful women had walked out of my life. They used me and deceived me, yet I wish each of them well. But I guess I was never one to play it safe—with love, cards, or business. Always willing to roll the dice and risk everything for something more, my gaming attitude has brought me battles and heartaches that could have been avoided. Yet, with each battle and with each heartache, new dimensions have been added to my life—wonders and experiences most men only read about. But I've also paid a price. I've had consequences for my actions—disturbing memories that won't fade, scars that won't heal. Yet ... could their jagged edges be smoothed by the warmth and vibrancy of the woman I was about to meet? Is this fifth woman the one I needed all along?

But, as good as I feel, that group picture of the Rose family haunts me. That little dark-haired girl in the middle with the sultry look who seems to be standing by herself... there's something about her that is familiar. It's as though we have a connection. In her I see ...

My thoughts are interrupted by a smiling presence next to me. A familiar and pleasant voice speaks, "Good evening, Mr. Morgan."

Beaming up at her, I smile back and wonder ... what are the odds?